ALMOST ADULTS

Ali Pantony is a freelance writer and editor. Her writing has appeared in *Glamour, Grazia, BBC Three, Refinery29, Vice, Red* and *Evening Standard*. Ali was born in Maidstone, Kent, and lives in North London. *Almost Adults* is her debut novel.

You can follow Ali on Twitter and Instagram @ alipantony

ALMOST ADULTS

ALI PANTONY

EBURY
PRESS

First published by Ebury Press in 2019

1 3 5 7 9 10 8 6 4 2

Ebury Press, an imprint of Ebury Publishing
20 Vauxhall Bridge Road,
London SW1V 2SA

Ebury Press is part of the Penguin Random House group of companies
whose addresses can be found at global.penguinrandomhouse.com

Penguin
Random House
UK

www.penguin.co.uk

A CIP catalogue record for this book is available from the British Library

ISBN 9781529104301

Typeset in 12.5/15.65 pt Garamond MT Std
by Integra Software Services Pvt. Ltd, Pondicherry

Printed and bound in Great Britain by Clays Ltd, Elcograf S.p.A.

MIX
Paper from
responsible sources
FSC   FSC® C018179
www.fsc.org

Penguin Random House is committed to a sustainable
future for our business, our readers and our planet.
This book is made from Forest Stewardship Council®
certified paper.

Love is like the wild rose-briar,

Friendship like the holly-tree –

The holly is dark when the rose-briar blooms

But which will bloom most constantly?

The wild rose-briar is sweeting in spring,

Its summer blossoms scent the air;

Yet wait till winter comes again

And who will call the wild-briar fair?

Then scorn the silly rose-wreath now

And deck thee with the holly's sheen,

That when December blights thy brow

He still may leave thy garland green.

Emily Brontë, *Love and Friendship*

CHAPTER ONE

Natasha

'Nat, come in, it's fucking January and you're only wearing a T-shirt,' came his voice from inside the flat.

The swearing took me back. I was the 'swearer' – Matt only swore when he was angry, or when he was watching *Question Time*. How dare he be angry right now. What gave him the right?

I was sitting on the roof, shivering in the cold and burning my throat with Johnnie Walker. The whisky was hot – hot on my lips, my mouth, my throat, and hot trickling down into my stomach – but my body was ice, the bitter seaside air whipping my hair back and biting at my skin. I remember liking the contrast. I remember everything about that night.

An hour earlier, I'd been panicking because I couldn't get hold of Matt, and that hardly ever happened, even after seven years together. He'd been at the pub with his friends and wasn't answering my WhatsApps asking when he was coming home, and if he could bring us a pizza from the Italian opposite the pub.

I didn't think much of it – probably had one too many ciders to check his phone, I thought. Besides, I wanted to binge-watch *The End of the F*cking World* on Netflix with a glass of wine and zero interruptions.

I heard his key turn in the lock – a sound I loved – and dashed to the hall. 'You didn't message me, I was worried about you!' I said with a relieved smile. Until suddenly, I clocked the look on his face, and I wasn't smiling any more.

Matt's expression, usually gentle and calm, was solemn, shell-shocked, etched with fear and panic and, for the first time in our seven years together, I felt like I didn't recognise him. He stood in the door to our home, tall, beautiful and broken, limply holding a cardbox pizza box, and said, 'Nat, we need to talk.'

I always used to laugh at those words in films – 'how clichéd, who actually says that?' I'd say – until I heard them. My chest turned tight and something thick stuck in my throat so I could hardly speak.

'What about?' I managed to mutter.

'I can't do this any more. I don't feel the same.'

You'd think the natural reaction to this would be instant tears, angrily demanding answers, maybe even throwing an IKEA plate or two. But not for me. To me, it felt so unbelievable, so unreal, that my body relaxed a little, calmed by the thought that this was just too farcical to actually be happening.

'You're just drunk, right?' I tried to reason, nearly laughing. 'But don't say things like that, we can just talk in the morning. Come to bed, it's almost one thirty.'

'No, Nat, you don't understa—'

'Of course I do! I get emotional when I'm drunk, too!'

Then suddenly his face turned stern, frown lines spreading across his forehead.

'I'm not drunk, Nat. Please, listen. I'm sorry, but I don't love you any more.'

The calm was suddenly snatched away. Then panic. Blind panic. The kind of panic that strikes your feet like a bolt of lightning and shoots up through your body, ripping through your insides as it goes, and eventually settles in your brain like a parasite. My body turned cold and I started to shake uncontrollably. I couldn't understand it – this wasn't happening. This didn't happen to people like us. This didn't happen to happy people. We were happy. Weren't we?

I ran to the bathroom to throw up. I sat with my head down the toilet for what felt like a lifetime, retching and shaking. The five most difficult words you can ever hear were rattling around my brain on loop, torturing me over and over. 'I don't love you any more'; 'I don't love you any more'; 'I don't love you any more'. He didn't love me any more. The man I loved unconditionally didn't love me any more.

Eventually – I don't know how much later – I pulled myself to my feet and walked back into the hall. Matt was through the door to my left, on the sofa in the living room, crying with his head in his hands. 'Why the hell is he the one crying?' I thought, but still, seeing him cry made something swell within me, an ocean rising up in my chest, the instinctive urge to take his pain away. He still had his black coat on; the one I'd bought him two Christmases ago. He'd worn that coat so much that the lining in one of the pockets had gone and his backpack had worn away some of the fabric at the back.

I stood, frozen. I knew I had to ask it – the question I really didn't want to ask. I turned away from him, trying to breathe deeply and restore some calm, just for a second.

'Is there someone else?' I demanded with a surprising amount of strength, desperate not to show him how much he was destroying me.

He looked up, his dark glossy eyes stained with tears and fear and guilt.

'Of course not,' he whimpered. 'We're just not the same any more. I'm different, you're different.'

'That's not fair,' I hissed instantly, anger joining the panic and shock and disbelief. 'You might feel like someone else, but I'm still right here. I never left you for one minute.'

I didn't want to hear his response. I couldn't. I walked through to the kitchen, grabbed the whisky, pulled up the window and stepped out onto the roof.

I was shaking still as my body turned to ice in the winter air. I could hear the crashing of the sea's waves on the beach as memories of my life with Matt replayed through my mind, as if fast-forwarding through some sort of torturous home video.

We'd met at university at nineteen and hit it off straight away. We were studying English and instantly bonded over our love of *Brave New World*, the smell of old books and Stephen King's short stories. We both loved terrible horror films and old-fashioned pubs. We became inseparable,

4

our friends constantly rolling their eyes when we said the same thing at the same time. We both tried to ignore our connection for a few months, not wanting to ruin our friendship. Until one evening, after watching the (very terrible) *Malibu Shark Attack* in his tiny student room, he lent across the bed to kiss me.

'I love you, Nat', he'd said softly, his hand resting on my shoulder as the outtakes of a Tara Reid lookalike being massacred by a CGI shark rolled romantically in the background. 'I can't pretend I don't any more.'

And as they say towards the end of teenage romance novels: that was that. Just as the beginning of fresh, new love should be, our relationship was easy. We soon moved into our top-floor flat in Hackton-on-Sea, where I'd grown up, and we'd been blissfully happy ever since – or so I thought.

Our home had its faults. The old lady in the flat below was a very keen smoker (she reminded us of Dot Cotton from *EastEnders*, without the religious values), so you always felt like you were walking through the smoking area of a grotty nightclub when you entered our flat. The white paint was chipping away from the edges of the large sash windows, and the farmhouse-style wooden doors were water-stained where the previous tenants had used them to hang their washing. But we didn't care. It was the very first thing that was ours, and we adored every inch of it. How could he leave all of that behind? Will he stay here while he works out where to live? Will that make him change his mind?

On the roof, frozen but for the burning whisky, my world was spinning around me. 'How did I end up here, when just over seven years ago, Matt was declaring his undying love for me?' I thought. 'How could this have happened?'

'Nat, come in, it's fucking January and you're only wearing a T-shirt.'

I pulled myself to my feet.

'Why do you care,' I spat, bending down to climb back through the window, 'if you don't love me any more?'

'Of course I care,' he said softly. 'I'm just . . . I'm just so, so sorry. I wish I didn't feel like this.'

Without thinking, I reached up and rested my hand at the nape of his neck; that instinctive urge to take his pain away too strong to suppress. It didn't register that my heart was breaking because of him. But I guess that's what love is.

'Please don't,' he said, screwing his face up in anguish and turning away from my hand. He didn't look at me, started walking towards the living room.

'Where are you going?'

'To sleep on the sofa. It's late. I don't think there's anything left to say tonight.'

There it was again. That blindsiding punch to the guts. That lightning panic.

'Will you just . . .' I trailed off, the burning subsiding, the numbness eating me whole.

Come on, Nat, the voice in my head piped up. *What do you want to say? This is important, don't screw this up. Remind him why he loves – loved – you.*

Eventually, I said. 'Will you just sleep next to me, just for tonight? Just for one last night?'

Ah, yes, desperation, said the voice inside my head. *Just what every man wants. That'll make him love you again.*

'Okay,' Matt replied. 'It is nearly three, we should try and sleep.'

Ha! Sleep! If you manage to get twenty minutes' sleep it'll be a goddamn miracle.

We walked back into the hallway and through to the door to the left of the living room into our bedroom – the place we'd spent hundreds of nights sleeping side by side.

For the love of God, try and be sexy, Nat. Maybe he'll have pity sex with you.

But I stopped in my tracks when I caught a glimpse of myself in our bedroom mirror. I was unrecognisable, the colour drained from my face, my eyes red raw and shrouded with puffy skin, my baggy T-shirt littered with holes and whisky stains.

Grim. Yeah, maybe forget the pity sex.

I tried to push down the nausea that was creeping its way back into my throat, clinging to the fast-fading feeling that this was all one huge mistake. A misunderstanding. That we'll go to sleep and everything will be okay in the morning. Everything had to be okay in the morning. It had to be.

We climbed into bed. It felt awkward, like we were two strangers who had just met on a drunken night out and now weren't sure we wanted to sleep together any more.

I lay perfectly straight, my hands resting on my stomach like a corpse in a funeral parlour being prepared for my final outing. Except my whole body was still shaking, reminding me that I was very much alive and that this was really happening.

Matt always fell asleep before me – he could sleep through anything. I could tell he was asleep because his breathing became heavier and his chest was rising and falling with a deep, steady rhythm that I knew so well. I edged over, lightly resting my head on his chest, nestling into his body, looking up at him.

'Who the fuck comes home, tells their girlfriend they don't love them any more, then just dozes off into a blissful slumber?' I thought. 'But shit, I love that face.' Hot tears stung my cold, tired eyes. 'What if this is the last time I ever lie here?'

With that, I began drinking in everything about him. His thick, sandy-blond, almost-brown hair. The smell of his skin, the slight lines at the corner of his eyes. The curves of his big ears, the hairs at the bottom of his neck that signalled the start of his chest. His broad shoulders, high tower-like cheekbones, strong arms that once had swaddled me. I wanted him to open his eyes so I could look into them and memorise everything about them – dark mahogany brown with tiny, muddy green flecks, and the kindness they held. I wanted him to melt into me, like butter into toast. I wanted our bodies to absorb each other, so that we never had to know what it was to exist apart.

That night was the longest I've ever known. It passed in waves, with ten-minute bursts of half-sleep interrupted by endless minutes of silence, with nothing but my own panic to keep me company.

The pale morning sun was creeping through the gap in the curtains when I woke up. I looked to my left. Matt wasn't there.

I put one foot after the other – slowly – onto the cold wooden floor, my mind reeling. I was jaded, felled, hazy; like the morning after a heavy night out.

In the living room, Matt was already working on packing his belongings into whatever container he could find to carry them in. The lack of planning almost made me laugh: there were Tesco 'Bags for Life' strewn over the floor, one small suitcase (the type that's slightly too big for carry-on – seriously, why do they make those?) and two cardboard boxes with WALKERS on the side.

'They were the only empty boxes the blokes at Tesco had this morning,' Matt looked up from sorting his books into piles and hesitated. 'They stink of cheese and onion. I hate cheese and onion.'

'I know you do,' I replied, the same lump from yesterday still stuck thick in my throat. 'I know everything about you.'

Suddenly, the pain crashed over me like an angry tsunami, and I clutched at the shattering in my chest which sent shockwaves through the rest of my body. I fell next to him, sobbing, pleading in shallow breaths, 'Matt, please don't do this – it's happening too fast, we can talk, we need to talk, I don't understand why you're doing this.'

'I wish I could tell you something more, but I just don't feel the same, and it isn't fair on either of us to carry on like that.'

'No, Matt. I don't understand. It's too fast; this is all too fast. How long have you even felt like this?'

'I don't know,' he muttered, looking down. 'A few months, maybe.'

'What? So you've been planning this?'

'No, not exactly. I tried to ignore how I felt. I hoped it would go away.'

I tried desperately to fight for us then – 'no one feels the same after seven years!', 'we can try counselling!', 'you've only been feeling like this for a few months, we can work on it!' – but it was futile. You can't fix something if you don't know where all the tiny shattered pieces were lost along the way. There are no steps to retrace, no trail to follow to pick them up and piece them back together. Something, somewhere along the line, had broken; I'd been too wrapped up in my love to see that his love was dying. And there was nothing that could be done to mend it now.

Matt was quick at packing up his belongings, which I guess I should be grateful for. I watched as he shoved piles of dirty underwear, socks and gym kit into old 'Bags for Life', and half-full bottles of ridiculous three-in-one shampoo into the stupidly sized suitcase. I even watched as he took the cheese plant we'd lovingly named Frank – 'you're taking Frank away from me?!' – because, as he said, he's the one who kept it alive all these years. (I mean, there was no arguing with that. I was a neglectful bitch to Frank.)

Matt made multiple trips to the car: first, the 'gross underwear in Tesco bags' trip, then the 'stupid man toiletries in stupid man suitcase' trip, followed by the 'miscellaneous cables in cheese and onion box' trip. I sat perfectly still as I watched Matt gut the very soul of our home, like a tragic version of David Attenborough observing a rare ecological phenomenon: 'Here, we can see the human male, desperately attempting to flee his nest, despite his mate's pathetic protests.' In the midst of the heartbreak and anguish, I wanted to laugh at the ridiculous scenes playing out in front of me. Sometimes choosing to laugh is the only thing you can do.

When his car was full, Matt sat down beside me on the sofa. Tears were flowing so relentlessly down my cheeks and into my lap I was worried I was going to die of dehydration.

Remember to google: 'is it possible to die of dehydration from crying?' later on, said the voice. *Your melodramatic sixteen-year-old self would be so proud.*

'I'm going to crash at Jack's for a bit, until we both figure out our living situations,' Matt said coldly, as if the disorderly man I knew were suddenly concerned with practicalities and being an actual organised adult.

I snapped out of my of my daze. '*Our* living situations?' I said. 'This is my home, Matt. I love this flat and I'm not going to leave it just because you've decided you've had enough.'

A pause. My mind both racing and unable to think straight.

Say something about Jack, that arrogant arsehole, I bet he put Matt up to this, said the voice.

'Yeah, have you spoken to Jack about this?' I hissed. 'He's one of your best mates, but he never really liked me, so he's obviously going to push you to break up with me, isn't he? Why did you listen to him, Matt? Can't you think for yourself? And how are you going to live with him? He still collects empty bottles of vodka he's drunk on his windowsill, for Christ's sake, Matt! Like a fucking teenager!'

The tears were falling faster now, my skin stinging with the sudden rush of fury.

'This isn't helping, Nat. I hate it when you cry.' Matt looked at me as he said it, that kindness in his eyes softening my temper. They always had that power over me, even now.

His words, though, struck me as odd – 'I hate it when you cry' – as if it were as unremarkable as saying 'I hate this rain' or 'I hate this traffic'. As if the crying had nothing to do with him at all; just one of those things that happened, that he had no control over.

'I'll talk to you soon. I have to go now. I'm so sorry.'

And just like that, the man I loved walked out of our home, and with him, took what felt like every fragment of me with him.

I didn't move; I couldn't move. What good would moving do? The more you move, the more alive you feel, and the more alive you feel, the greater the capacity for loneliness. So, I sat in the vastness of the silence he'd left, all but for the central heating ticking into action and Dot Cotton watching some cooking show on TV downstairs.

The house felt so empty without him, and I thought about the life we'd been building together for such a long time. I'd never realised how fragile it was, that so many years could be snatched away in a matter of hours.

I may have been physically alone, but empty houses are full of noise, loud with ghosts. The walls housed our story: the love, the fights, the laughter, the sex, the comfort, the sorrys, the mending, the promises. It was their secret to keep.

But even being surrounded by our own ghosts couldn't help me understand what had just happened. It was the absence of meaning and a clear explanation that made heartbreak so frightening; when he left, he opened a chasm in me I'd never seen before, one that had sheltered all my insecurities, fears and sadness. He was the gatekeeper of all those things. And suddenly, there was no one to keep them locked away any more.

I started to look around the flat, gawping at the graves of our memories. In the hallway hung mobiles made of Peruvian reeds and jars filled with salt from the Uyuni Salt Flats, from when we'd backpacked South America. There were wooden figures of elephants, tigers and Komodo dragons on shelves in our bedroom from our holiday to Indonesia. In the kitchen, Italian handwritten recipes for buttery broccoli orecchiette and sweet Caprese salad hung in frames from our road trips down the coast.

The £10 eBay chair, which we upholstered together in monochrome eighties fabric that we found in a vintage shop in London, sat proudly in the corner of our bedroom. The walls of the stairway leading up to the hallway were brimming with photos in mismatched frames – our graduation, my twenty-first birthday, Matt's twenty-seventh last year.

Suddenly, it was like I was suffocating, choking on my own solitude.

'I can't be alone,' I thought.

Where's your phone? You haven't looked at it since last night, said the voice helpfully.

It wasn't in the living room, on the monochrome chair or on my bedside table.

Maybe he took your phone, the voice chimed in, *you know, just to really kick a girl when she's down.*

'Don't be ridiculous,' I croakily said aloud to any ghosts that were listening.

Shit, talking to yourself now? You really are alone for the first time. And in January, of all months. Well, the promise of a New Year and making this 'a great one' has gone tits-up, hasn't it? And only twelve days into it too, so much for 'bettering yourself' this year.

My phone was on the side in the kitchen, next to the Johnnie Walker and last night's untouched pizza box. My stomach turned.

Ha, break-up pizza – that's the saddest thing I've ever seen. That's pizza off the menu for the rest of your life.

I picked up my phone and looked at the notifications. Some Instagram likes on the photo I'd uploaded of a bottle of wine in front of the Netflix home screen with the caption: 'Slumber party for one #fridaynightin'. Oh, God, that looks really bloody sad now. *Delete*. Someone's birthday alert on Facebook – I tap to see it's Jack's very attractive sister, Kimberly. Guess we know what (or who) Matt's doing tonight. Shit, don't think about that. Can't think about that.

Finally, a stream of notifications from the 'Mean Girls' WhatsApp group. Not that we actually see ourselves as 'mean', of course, or reserve the chat purely for conversations about Cady Heron and Regina George – it stands for 'Mackie, Edele, Alex and Natasha'. We've been best friends since we met in school at eleven-years-old, and we'd be lost without each other. The group WhatsApp used to be called 'Hackton Hoes n' Bitches' until Alex's step-sister saw the name flash up on Alex's phone and spent the next three weeks calling people 'hoes n' bitches'. She's seven.

EDELE: I can't believe I'm stuck at home with my bloody MOTHER on a FRIDAY NIGHT. Big Dick Nick has got zero chat tonight, Tinder's full of munters and there's no booze in the house. You're all terrible friends for letting this happen.

ALEX: Get a grip, woman. A drink- and dick-free night will do you some good.

EDELE: Piss off, Mother Theresa.

MACKIE: *sends a meme that says: 'Actually love that me and my pals are at that age when absolutely

15

fuck all is embarrassing. Pissed urself? Fell in public? £2 in ur bank? Got the clap? Hilarious'*

ALEX: E, haven't you done all of that?

MACKIE: Yeah, mate, she has, that's why it's funny.

EDELE: I resent this. I've got £31 in the bank, actually. Plus, we've all stacked it in public, as has most of Hackton after £1 drinks at Bar Chocolate on a Monday night. I've shat myself twice, but that's because I have IBS, so you're just dicks for laughing at a diagnosed medical condition. And I may have had the clap, but so's Nat before she was married off to Matt! So why don't you laugh at her?!

Some sixty ridiculous messages about chlamydia, IBS and Bar Chocolate later

EDELE: Nat, you alive? Sorry for reminding the group that you had the clap, hun.

I started typing . . .

NAT: I don't know how to say this. Matt's dumped me and taken all his stuff to Jack's. I'm a wreck.

EDELE O'CONNELL: Incoming WhatsApp Call.

Reject.

ALEX WILD: Incoming WhatsApp Call.

Reject.

EMMA MACKIE: Incoming WhatsApp Call

Reject.

I couldn't bear to have our first conversation about The Tragic End of Matt and Nat over WhatsApp audio.

MACKIE: Okay, you don't wanna talk on the phone, but we're all coming over right now. Hold tight, darling girl. We cannot believe he's done this to you, but you're not alone. We're here. We love you so, so much.

ALEX: I'm grabbing snacks, booze and fags. Mack and Ed, I'll pick you up en route and be at Nat's by 11.30 a.m. Don't care how early it is. I'm getting wine. Love you, Nat xxx

EDELE: That bastard better sleep with one eye open. Because I'm going to FUCKING KILL HIM. Bastard.

ALEX: Not helpful, babe.

Sure enough, at 11.33 a.m., I heard the sounds of chatter, bottles clinking, Edele yelling, 'All right, Ms Harris!' (Dot Cotton's real name), and Mackie's retort, 'She doesn't want to talk to you, Ed!'

I was in the kitchen – I'm not sure if I moved since sending the WhatsApp – when the girls came upstairs and into the flat. Matt must've left the door off the latch.

'We are so sorry,' Edele said as they all put down their bags and threw their arms around me. I stood still, encircled by limbs and love, until my knees buckled – perhaps from exhaustion – and I staggered over, the girls propping me up.

'Come and sit down,' Alex said, leading us into the living room.

Even though I'd watched Matt pack his things, the bareness of the living room hit me like a hammer to the chest. My books looked so lonely without his next to them on the bookshelf, the Frank-less corner ringing with emptiness.

Alex put her arm around my shoulder and Edele held on to my forearm as they placed me delicately onto the sofa, perching on either side of me, as Mackie sat on the floor, cuddling my leg and leaning her head on my knee. It was as if I were a wounded solider returning home from battle – but without any medals or heroic tales of victory.

'We can't believe it, Nat. What happened?' my best friends asked me. I tried to gather the words to try and explain what I'd lost, or the tangled mass of thoughts tying knots in my throat, stomach and head – but I couldn't find them.

'I . . . I don't know,' I said with a cracked, gritty voice. 'He just said he doesn't feel the same any more. I don't know why, or how, or when . . . it's just . . . gone. His love's gone.'

'Err, I'm sorry, gone where exactly?'

'Yeah, what does that even mean?'

Mackie poured the wine and passed me the glass. I took a deep gulp. Then another. It was sharp and tannic, not warming like the whisky. My head span.

'I don't know,' I said eventually. 'I really don't know. How do those feelings just disappear into thin air? How?' I couldn't help but feel stupid – he was my partner of seven years, how thick did I have to be to not know what he was saying, thinking, feeling?

You should've known, said the voice – and it was right. I should have known.

'Does he have someone else, the little prick?' Edele spat. She's the kind of woman who refuses to disguise what's on her mind, despite her mother's constant reminders to 'be very polite and considerate at all times' when she was growing up. I was always glad she never learnt to take that advice.

'No – well, he says he doesn't, and I think I have to believe him,' I replied. 'Because I'm not sure I can handle the alternative.'

The girls were silent as we huddled together on the sofa. They knew there was nothing they could say that would soothe the shock or dull my self-torment. But just feeling them close by eased my frailty, as if they were somehow passing their collective strength into me. That's the difference between the touch of the friends you love and the person you're in love with: one keeps you grounded, reminding you of your existence and power; the latter takes something away, making that tiny part of you theirs and not your own, ever again.

'You may feel lonely right now, but you have us, and that means you're never alone,' Alex said. 'And you're going to feel angry and sad and shitty for a long time after today, but always remember: it might get lonely, but you are not alone.'

I don't know how I would have coped without Alex, Edele and Mackie there to pick me back up the day when I fell further than I ever knew I could fall.

Because it did feel like falling. It was as if I'd fall and never stop. It felt like *The End of the F*cking World.*

CHAPTER TWO

Edele

If there's one thing I've learnt about adult life, it's that you'll never find decent people in the pub on a Wednesday afternoon. Around here, Wednesday afternoon pub people fall into one of three categories:

1. Shitty businessmen. They wear terrible suits and talk loudly about their boring jobs. They're at the pub at 3 p.m. because they've just 'smashed a meeting with a well-tough client and the boss said to celebrate'. Their boss probably just wanted them out the office so he or she could plot how to kill them all.

2. Weird tourists with cameras. The cameras were bought especially for this trip and will be sentenced to a life of solitude in a dusty drawer as soon as they return home. Home is probably Hungary, or maybe Austria. Hungarians and Austrians love taking pictures of the beach this pub looks out onto because their countries don't have beaches. I lost my virginity on that beach. Tourists keep taking photos of the place I lost my virginity. Perverts.

3. Sad loners sinking away their sadness with a glass of shitty, sad wine.

Guess which category I fall into.

'Hey, couldn't help but notice you here all on your own.'

Oh, great. One of the shitty businessmen is pulling up a chair next to me. He has a very long face, ears that stick out like they're trying to escape his head, and a thin, patchy, brown moustache. His moustache makes me feel sick. Someone needs to tell him his moustache makes him look like a paedophile.

'You have a paedophile moustache,' I blurt out, realising I'm drunker than I thought.

'A "hello" would've been fine, too,' he retorts. This is relatively funny but I don't laugh. 'Why are you here on a weekday drinking on your own? A pretty girl like you with those beautiful blue eyes shouldn't be drinking alone.'

I think Paedophile Moustache is about to put his hand on my knee, which would soon move up my thigh because Paedophile Moustache is one of those men who thinks women owe him sex. Thankfully, he doesn't put his hand on my knee, as I would've punched him in the face and potentially been barred from the pub. And I quite like this pub.

'I got fired four weeks ago, I'm still living at home with my neurotic Irish mother and annoying brother; my best friend got dumped last week and I'm trying to gather a gang of assassins to slowly torture and kill her ex, which is depressingly a better situation than I'm in because no one will ever love me; I'm destined to lead a life of solitude until I eventually die, bitter and alone, at the age of fifty-one.'

'No need to get all hysterical. Fucking weirdo,' Paedophile Moustache says as he dismounts his chat-up throne, leaving the stench of Paco Rabanne in the air and in my throat, making me feel nauseous. He skulks back to his herd of testosterone, any hopes of getting laid by the loner in the pub cruelly dashed. Men like Paedophile Moustache will happily sleep with loners. Not weirdos, though.

I don't want to sit in the cloud of throat-clogging Paco Rabanne so I go to the bar to order a pint, annoyed that Paedophile Moustache has ruined my spot. I was perfectly happy being a sad loner, drinking on my own on a weekday afternoon, before he arrived.

'Beer before wine, you'll feel fine,' I repeat in my head. 'Wine before beer, you'll feel que—' Oh, screw it.

'Pint of Peroni please, Gary'. I like bartender Gary; he has big hands, curly hair and a gentle, round face, which he's tried to disguise with facial hair. Seriously though, who is walking around in 2019 with a name like fucking Gary?

'Coming up, Ed,' says terribly named Gary. 'I hope that bloke wasn't giving you any grief. He or his mates give you any grief, you give me the nod, girl. I'll chuck 'em straight out.'

'Aww, Gary,' I say, 'my knight in beer-soaked armour.' His chubby face widens into a smile. I knew he'd like that. Sometimes it's nice to make harmless men like Gary feel like you need their protection.

Paedophile Moustache and the herd of testosterone are guffawing and pointing at me.

'Tragic loser,' says one in a pinstripe suit. 'Bet she's a virgin! Who would shag a weirdo like her? But she is pretty fit!'

Gary takes his big hands off the beer tap, plonks the pint in front of me, and goes to say something very sweet but wildly unhelpful. I stop him and order another pint. Gary looks puzzled but obliges.

Paedophile Moustache and Pinstripe Suit are still laughing when I approach the herd.

'All right, weirdo. Bought us some pints so we'll finally take your V-plates off ya?'

My heart does joyful somersaults in my chest as I throw two pints of Peroni over Paedophile Moustache and Pinstripe Suit. The herd of testosterone gasps, someone at the back of the pub cheers, and the two herd members stand speechless, mouths agape, with their awful suits covered in beer. Their suits look even cheaper and more awful now. Hoegaarden is dripping off of Paedophile Moustache's, well, paedophile moustache.

I smile, turn around triumphantly and leave the herd, then place the two empty pint glasses in front of Gary on the bar. His chubby cheeks are pressed up against his dark brown eyes in a big, beautiful grin.

'For the drinks,' I say, pulling a £10 note out of my bra and placing it on the bar.

Gary is still grinning and Paedophile Moustache and Pinstripe Suit are still stood, mouths wide open and finally silenced, watching me as I walk out of the pub and towards the beach. My life may be in a tragic state of unemployment and I might still be sleeping in my childhood bed, but at least I can feel temporarily empowered by degrading some terrible men and covering them in beer.

Outside, the street lamps are dousing the wet, cobbled pavements in a yellow glow and the sun is throbbing orange against the sky. It must have rained earlier while I was in the pub because it's not raining now. The winter wind is angry, and I don't have a hair-tie on my wrist, meaning I don't have one on me at all, so I pull my hood up to stop my long, black hair slapping me in the face. The winter air dances and drags its heels between the hairs on my arm. 'Today was the wrong day to wear a denim pinafore, old tights and a thin grey T-shirt,' I think as I shiver in the flimsy hoody. I always forget to check the weather forecast, but then again, I'm not ninety years old. Plus, going to the pub sounded far more appealing than starting on my pile of dirty laundry.

'Slow down, superwoman!' I swing around. Gary is running after me, still grinning. He's holding my handbag. 'You left this behind!'

'Oh crap, what an idiot,' I say. 'I was enjoying my dramatic exit so much that I forgot to grab it. Thanks for bringing it, I would've been lost without it.'

This isn't true. I gave Gary my last £10 so I could throw beer on some stupid men. The only items in my bag are a

25

stick of chewing gum, loose cigarette filters, a bottle of water, a condom and those tiny pots of glue you get in a box of fake eyelashes. I haven't worn fake eyelashes since 2012. Everything is covered in bag dust – you know, the particles of general crap you get in the bottom of handbags that you've owned since the dawn of time but have never cleaned. It doesn't help that this bag is enormous – a bit ridiculous considering there's nothing in it – so there's even more room for gross crap particles to grow and thrive.

'After that epic display, it's the least I can do. They're fuming, by the way! You really took those wankers down a peg or two. I've got to get back, but I'll catch you later.'

Gary's dark auburn curls bounce on top of his head as his broad frame jogs back to the pub. His pale blue shirt is slightly too tight on him and his black jeans are faded to a near-grey. But somehow, everything about him kind of suits him.

On the beach, I reach into my bag of nothingness for some water, and find my £10 note with a receipt for two pints of Hoegaarden. There's a message on the back in red biro.

'The beers are on me. I'd pay £50 to watch that again'.

I smile to myself. Gary really is a top bloke. He's sweet, kind and a little bit chubby, which probably means he's happy. He's one of the good guys. The last thing a good guy like Gary wants is a woman like me.

I tuck the money safely into my bra because I left my purse at home; there's not much point in bringing out a purse when you have no money in your account. I lay my thick yellow scarf on the sand to shield my bum from the wet ground as I sit down on the beach. I wonder if sitting on these cold, hard pebbles will give me haemorrhoids, or if I'll be finding grains of sand between my butt cheeks later. Wet sand always seems to find its way to places it shouldn't.

I glance around me. The people you find on the beach on a Wednesday afternoon fall into one of three categories:

1. Old people walking their dogs and refusing to pick up their dog's shit. I know this because I once sat in dog shit on this beach. Old people give us dog-shit-covered beaches and Brexit, but *we're* the villains for wanting recyclable keep cups and gender-neutral tissues (yes, that's right, we're looking at you with your 'man-size' boxes of Kleenex).
2. Tourists with cameras taking pictures of the place where I lost my virginity.
3. Sad loners, AKA me.

But this afternoon, I'm alone, except for two people in the distance with their dog. Ugh, a *couple* walking their dog. Even worse than old people.

I stick my hand into my bag to retrieve my phone, which is inevitably now covered in gross bag particles, and start messaging Mean Girls.

EDELE: All right, lads. Who's about tonight? I just threw beer over two men in the Fox and Whistle, so I'm on a bit of a drink-throwing high now.

NATASHA: That's my girl. God, that pub has such a stupid name. Doesn't even make sense. What use would a fox have for a whistle?! Do they still have the ridiculous painting of a fox wearing a top hat and blowing a whistle above the bar? And I should be home from work in an hour. Are you on the beach?

EDELE: Silly question. To both of those questions.

NATASHA: Well, surprisingly, I have zero plans tonight. My diary is remarkably clear these days. I'll grab some hoodies and blankets and meet you there.

ALEX: Better to have a clear diary than be wasting your time with an emotionally retarded man child, Nat. You'll get through this.

MACKIE: Yes, you've always got us and we take up a lot of time so you're never going to be lonely. I'll park at yours, Nat, and walk down with you. Should be there 5-ish. Do you need a coat, E? Just don't sit in dog shit again and get it on my coat.

EDELE: They should ban dogs on this beach. But then you wouldn't be able to come, Mack. (Also, yes please, I'm freezing.)

MACKIE: Grow up. (And okay, will do.)

EDELE: You grow up. (Thank you, love you.)

ALEX: You both need to bloody well grow up. Speaking of which, I'll see you losers in 45 to get drunk on the beach like we're 15 again. Just try not to shag Joel Hall in the sand again, Ed.

EDELE: You're just jealous he took my virginity and not yours.

ALEX: I shotgunned him. You stole my first love and my first love's beautiful cock from me.

EDELE: How do you know it was beautiful? All you and Joel ever did was snog outside the school gates and run away whenever Mr Gilbert walked past. Plus, you have Craig now. Stop being greedy. But you're not wrong Alex – he had the most beautiful cock I've ever seen.

I put my phone down and stare into the sea. The grey waves are painting the beach's mouth with swathes of snow-white foam, like rabies or toothpaste. I try not to think about toothpaste too much, which makes brushing my teeth in the morning and evening very difficult. I try not to think about toothpaste because it reminds me that I got fired from my job four weeks ago. I'd like to say I was a dentist, or a vet who regularly treated cats with gingivitis, cleaning their tiny cat teeth with a tiny cat toothbrush. But instead, after studying fashion and media relations at uni, I went into public relations, and last year, became an account executive for a well-known brand of toothpaste. It's very easy to become sick at the sight of toothpaste when you're surrounded by it all day. I got fired because I was regularly late, forgot about meetings, and never hit my targets.

Now I fucking hate toothpaste.

I stop looking at the toothpaste sea, lie back on my scarf throw, plug my headphones in, and hit play. Fleetwood Mac. 'Dream. Stevie Nicks's haunting voice sings about the rain washing her clean.

I wish the rain would wash me clean. I'd need a torrential downpour to wash me clean.

The ping of my phone's text alert momentarily drowns out Stevie.

MUM: Edele, where r u? How was the interview? U ok?

I told my mum I had a job interview with a PR firm in London this morning and that I should be home by 3 p.m. I don't know why I did that. I'd like to think it was to make her feel better, so that she'd stop worrying about me. But it was probably just to make her stop asking me when I'm going to stop moping around, get a job and sort my life out.

'Ma, please stop using text speak, it's embarrassing,' I type before going back and deleting it.

Instead, I type: 'Not sure, think it went okay. Yes, I'm grand thanks. Meeting the girls for dinner, so will be home later.' Send. Mum starts typing straight away.

MUM: Okay, pheata, I'm proud of u. Have fun, love u always xoxo

Sudden, sharp pangs of emotion hit my chest and, to my surprise, I feel like crying. Given the distinct lack of okay-ness I've been feeling lately, it would've made sense to cry more regularly. It might have been been cathartic to let a torrent of not-okay-ness gush from wherever it's trapped in my body and down my cheeks. That would've been the smart option, the sensible option. I can imagine Mackie scheduling weekly 'ten-minute outpouring of sorrow' slots in her diary. But right now, for the first time in weeks, I feel like crying because I lied to my mum. I lied to my mum about the job interview, about going for dinner, and about being okay. And she probably knows it, too. But she still called me her pheata – Irish for 'pet' – and told me she loved me. She's had to endure so much in the past two years, and I didn't even think to ask how she was.

No wonder I feel alone. The one person who will put up with my selfishness, my temper, my lack of direction – everything a twenty-seven-year-old should have already overcome – and still love me so fiercely, more than anyone else ever could, and how do I repay her? By telling her three lies in one text.

'I'll love you always, too, ma' I text my mum as Stevie tells me, one last time, about the rain.

CHAPTER THREE

Alex

The bell rang for the end of school ten minutes ago. From my classroom window, I watch the students flow out of the gates towards the bus stop, parked cars and the town centre in a sea of forest green blazers and oversized backpacks. I usually get to work between 7 and 7.30 a.m., and often don't leave before 4.30 p.m., or sometimes 7 p.m. if we have teacher training. But today, I'm leaving no later than 4 p.m. so that I can drink wine with my friends on the beach after Edele's WhatApp earlier this afternoon.

At my desk, I sort the loose papers – worksheets, marking guidelines, scanned extracts from textbooks – and organise them into different colour-coded topics folders, before making sure my lessons for tomorrow are planned. I can already hear the collective groan from my students.

'Miss, are we *still* doing Khrushchev?!'

'Yes, we are,' I'll say. 'Did you really expect to cover the Soviet economy in two lessons? Give me your concentration for the next hour, and you'll be grateful for it when you're sat in that exam.'

I grab two folders full of marking that I have to complete over the next three days and throw them into the little pink plastic trolley I use to transport heavy resources between my car and my classroom. The girls obviously find my 'toddler trolley' hilarious. Then I shut down my computer and throw on my coat before quickly glancing around my classroom.

'Update World War One display,' I write on a Post-it note using the eyeliner on my desk. Where have all my pens gone? There are some days when I really feel like I have it together, then there are others when I'm a history teacher who can't find a working pen.

I say goodbye to various faculty members and homework club students as I walk through the school hallways, out through the main doors and into the staff car park. I eagerly pick up my pace, wheeling my pink plastic trolley behind me, at the thought of seeing Edele.

Edele hates it when you call her Edele. 'Not even the good version of the name,' she always says. 'You know, with an "A" – Adele – the woman with an MBE, the British cultural icon, one of the most successful singing phenomenons of all time? Nope. Edele with an "E". You know who else is an Edele with an "E"? The chick from B*-fucking-Witched. One of the creepy twins. *That's* who people associate with my name.'

'Oi, Edele,' I shout affectionately, after leaving my car at home and dashing down to the beach. The last of the sun's rays are reaching up above the horizon and the sliver of sorbet-pink sky will soon be swallowed by the army of dark clouds. The dying light is performing its final dance of the day across the sea water as I walk up to her on the beach. She's asleep with her headphones in and her hood up.

She doesn't respond. 'Edele,' I say loudly, tugging at the dirty old Apple earphones. 'Sleeping on your own on the beach in a town like ours – do you have a death wish or something?'

Her bright, pale blue eyes shoot open. Against her hardened, pale face, sharp cheekbones and jet-black hair, she is both striking and tough-looking. 'That's those Irish genes, my girl – don't you dare think about bleaching your beautiful raven hair,' Edele's mum always used to say. Edele bleached a strip of her hair as an act of rebellion when we were fifteen. Her mum cried and said she looked like 'a fecking zebra crossing'.

'Christ, woman, my heart could've given out then! And less of the "Edele", ta. Do you hear me singing bloody "Rolling In The Deep"?'

'More like "Blame It On The Weatherman".' This is a B*Witched joke. It's a crap joke.

'Shut up. And so what if I do?'

'So what if you do what?'

'Have a death wish.'

'Don't joke like that,' I say, clutching at her hand as I perch on the edge of the yellow scarf. She smiles a weak, forced smile.

'Kidding, of course, I'm fine,' she says with the intonation of someone who is only half-fine. 'I just get a bit tired sometimes, hence the whole "falling asleep on the beach" thing.'

34

Edele squeezes my hand to try and reassure me, but I know that's not the sort of 'tired' she means. She's one of those people who's been lost for so long, she can't remember what it's like to feel settled in her own skin. She acts tough, but she's not tough – she's adrift. And I don't know what to do to help anchor her. But I need to do something, because I worry about Ed a lot. And ever since Matt broke Nat's heart last week, I worry about her, too.

'How's Craig?' asks Edele as I reach into my bag for a bottle of white wine and an old, rusty blue tobacco tin with the words 'Edgeworth Extra High Grade Sliced Pipe Tobacco' on the lid. The girls bought it for me for my twenty-seventh birthday last June. They filled a huge cardboard box – the kind you can make a fort out of if you're childish enough (we were) – with shredded paper of all different colours, so I had to search for my presents like a huge pick 'n' mix. Each present represented something I loved – a Cheryl Strayed book, tickets to a Whitney Houston tribute night, a huge frame full of photos of us, wine, a book of history-related jokes, a chai tea gift set (my mum grew up in India, so chai tea is pretty much synonymous with my childhood), and an Edgeworth tobacco tin – because I 'love a fag, and Craig's surname is Edgeworth'. They were chuffed with that one.

'Umm, yeah, he's fine,' I say.

Edele fixes her piercing blue eyes on mine and slightly arches her eyebrow. I don't know if she means to.

'Talk to me,' she says warmly. She has a way of making you want to spill your heart to her, to take a deep breath and exhale all of your gnawing thoughts and worries from your mind straight into her ears. She's used to carrying around everyone else's weights along with her own. It's one of the many things that make her so extraordinary. But I still feel hesitant. I'm used to being the settled one, the one people come to for dating and love advice. And who am I to complain about my relationship when Nat is experiencing something so much worse?

'We're fine, I mean, we're good.' Wow. That sounded painfully unconvincing.

A pause. I can feel Ed's eyes scanning my face.

'We've been together for three years, Ed. I really love him. But sometimes I don't know if love is enough. I mean, it's so awful seeing Nat go through what she's going through, but it does make you question your own relationship, you know? Maybe there are signs that I haven't noticed.'

Another pause. Edele's eyes are flitting between mine, searching to see if they hold the answers I can't find the words for. I take a swig from the wine bottle. Then another.

'Of course it's not enough, but that's okay, because it's a pretty good place to start,' she says. 'And there's no shame in starting again three years down the line, I don't think. You just need to figure out what else is missing and work on it. And I think you should work on it, because I've never seen you happier than when you've been with Craig. You know what Nat would say?'

'What?'

'That you need to work on it while you can, because something as rare as what you and Craig have is worth fighting for. That nothin' worth having comes easy. And before you realise it, it'll be too late to save. Ya know, all the clichéd shit she loves – but it's all one hundred per cent true.' She scoots over so we're sitting side by side and links her arm through mine. I pass her the bottle.

'Yeah. I know you're right. But it's hard to know exactly what's missing. I think we've just got too comfortable, you know? When we're together, I don't know if he's really *there,* or if I am, either. I think we just need to reconnect, maybe. I just feel like he's been distant with me, like his mind is somewhere else.'

'Oh, Christ.'

'What?!'

'You don't bang any more, do you? That's the problem. You're in a sexless relationship. Or, as I like to call it, hell.'

We laugh. We swig.

'We *do* have sex,' I protest. 'At least once a week! Just . . . in the exact same way. Every time. We kiss. We take our clothes off – well, pyjamas, usually. He leaves his socks on. I know he leaves his socks on because I can feel his socked feet with my naked ones. He climbs on top. He thrusts away very rhythmically for a good few minutes. He kisses my neck, a lot. My neck gets wet. My neck is now the wettest part of my body. He flips me over gently – he uses less care handling our Dartington Crystal champagne flutes – continues the thrusting for approximately two minutes, informs me that he's 'close', then lies back down, and goes to sleep. He falls *straight to sleep*, Ed. I go to the bathroom to sort myself out, if I can be bothered.'

I don't realise how quickly I've started talking until I suddenly stop.

'And you know what else?' I continue, apparently on a roll. 'It would be nice to have some romance every once in a while. I know, I know, we're not teenagers, and the honeymoon stage is well and truly over. But as much as I love a night in with Craig in front of the latest true crime documentary on Netflix, it'd be nice to do something loving and fun every now and again.'

'Well,' Edele says, 'have you tried talking to him about it?'

'Not exactly.'

'It doesn't even need to be a big deal. Why don't you suggest some date nights or something? Can't expect him to do everything. He is a bloke, after all. And we both know they're pretty useless at this kind of thing.'

'Yeah, you're right, I should. I'm just worrying about nothing; I think Nat's break-up has shaken me a bit. I just feel less secure than I did.'

'Try not to let it rock you. Of course it's awful, and no one saw it coming, but her relationship is not your relationship, okay?'

'Okay, I know.'

'And you know the good news?'

'What?' I say rolling my eyes, sensing Edele's witty jibe – her way of making me feel better – before it even leaves her mouth.

'At least we know what needs fixing now. Your middle-aged sex life.'

'Thanks.'

'Any time, pal. Don't worry, we'll sort this out. No more lying back and thinking of England for you.'

Edele uses the wine bottle to cheers an imaginary glass. I want to ask her what she means by *'we'll* sort this out' (I dread to think), but before I can, she springs to her feet.

'All right!' she shouts, using the wine bottle to salute the approaching figures of Nat and Mackie. The way she keeps using the bottle as a prop to display her enthusiasm for something reminds me of Drunk Singing Homeless Guy on Hackton High Street. He always uses a bottle of rum to point at passers-by and address them via song. Ever since I gave him a £5 note and a McDonald's coffee, he uses the bottle to point at me and sing 'My Girl' by The Temptations. I wish Craig would serenade me with 'My Girl' using a rum bottle.

Edele bounces up to Nat and throws her arms around her, planting a kiss straight on her lips. It's the kind of greeting that says, 'You got dumped last week and you're broken right now but don't worry because I'm your best mate and I've got your back.'

Mackie kisses us both on the cheek and pulls a bright pink floral picnic blanket from her backpack, laying it down so her and Nat sit facing us. She pulls a fluffy black coat around Edele's shoulders, scolding her for dressing so inappropriately for the season. Mackie has always been the most organised out of us all. She'll make a great mum.

'Guys, look, Mack made me dinner,' Nat smiles, pulling a large plastic tub from her bag.

'For the love of all that is holy, what the hell is that?' Ed says.

'It's tomato and sausage stew with kale, chickpeas and almonds,' Mackie says proudly, ignoring the look of repulsion on Ed's – and probably my – face.

'It looks someone massacred a dick and chopped it up with some tiny balls and green pubes,' Ed laughs.

'Yeah, and the almonds look like fingernails,' I say.

'Jesus, Alex, that's Nat's dinner. Have some respect!' says Ed. 'Sorry about her, Mack.'

We laugh and Mackie leans over to playfully shove Edele off the blanket. We watch the last of the sun die on the horizon, play some Nina Simone out of Mackie's portable speakers and listen to how Edele came to throw two pints of beer over two men called Paedophile Moustache and Pinstripe Suit at 3 p.m. on a Wednesday.

I wonder what Paedophile Moustache and Pinstripe Suit's actual names are. Probably Noah and Levi. Or Hugo and Matty. Or Jeffrey and Kyle. I make a mental note to myself to add those names to the list of 'shit names I can never give my children, unless I hate my children'.

Nat's laughing and smiling, but she looks fragile underneath. Her eyes are sad and dull – there's nothing more heart-breaking than a pair of big, bright eyes that have lost their life – and her complexion is sucked dry of any colour. She's looking thin, which emphasises the dark hollows under her eyes. I wonder when she last slept or ate a proper meal. No wonder Mackie is plying her with superfood stew.

'Who's in?' Nat asks as she pulls some king skins, a grinder and a baggie from her hoodie pockets and starts to roll a joint. It's a rhetorical question. 'It's Jay's finest.' Of course it is. Jay is the only guy in the whole of Hackton stupid enough to grow it in his brother's greenhouse. It'll be a sad day when Jay and Jay's weed get taken into custody. I add Jay to the list of names to never give my children.

She picks a few green buds from the small clear bag, places them between the plastic spikes, replaces the lid and begins turning. Her wrists turn back and forth as the tiny plastic mechanism grinds the sticky plant to the consistency of dried coriander leaves. She makes a roach from the paper packaging, picks some tobacco – I can smell its sweetness over the salty sea air – and carefully rolls everything together. She lights it and smokes some before passing it to me.

'Craig says weed destroys brain cells,' I say as I exhale and my body relaxes. I look around quickly to make sure none of my students or their parents are nearby to see me smoking. I don't think that would go down well at parents' evening.

'Hearing that sentence come out your mouth has destroyed my brain cells,' says Edele.

We each take three tokes before passing the joint to the next person. Nat calls it the 'three-toke pass'; Edele calls this 'lame'. Mackie will have a puff every now and again, depending on how pissed she is, but even though she doesn't mind being around us when we're smoking, she's often too sensible for weed. I admire that about her. Sometimes I'm grown-up enough to not drink or smoke on a school night; sometimes I'm not.

When the girls and I are together like this, we sometimes talk about serious subjects – like how social media is simultaneously the greatest triumph and disaster of the twenty-first century, politics, or whether it's acceptable to say Stalin was fit when he was younger. But today, we talk about local news ('Some guy got arrested in Card Factory yesterday for wearing transparent trousers; where the hell do you even buy transparent trousers?'), men we know from town ('Phil was on the news the other night for sleeping rough in the library; no, not the Phil who got drunk and threw up in psychology on the last day of school, the Phil who stamped on a pigeon in the park when we were fourteen'), and girls we went to school with ('Claire Bryant Instagrammed her spiralizer last night; I'd rather be that pigeon that Phil stood on than replace pasta with sodding vegetables; wait, do they even make spiralizers any more?').

Suddenly, I see Nat's face change. Her skin is white and her chest looks heavy, like it's battling just to take in air and push it back out again. There are deep lines across her forehead and her eyes are wet.

'Nat?' I say, turning Nina down. She's singing something about being free.

'Matt slept with Kim,' she says, her eyes streaming now, her breathing rushed and shallow.

'What?!' we all cry in disbelief, Mackie clutching at Nat's hand. I rush to her side and stroke her back in an attempt to calm her breathing. Her shoulder blade feels sharp and protuberant through her thick black jumper.

'Breathe. You're okay,' I say, trying to be as reassuring as I can, but I can't help but notice how forced and clumsy the words sound. What I meant was: 'I hope you'll be okay', because I have no way of knowing if Nat will be okay. I've never had a man destroy my life and shag his best mate's sister in practically the same breath.

'I can't believe him,' Edele says venomously, her eyes blazing with rage. 'How do you know? Are you sure?'

Nat wipes the wet clumps of old mascara from her cheeks and inhales deeply, her mouth gasping for air and her back straightening. It looks like it's taking all her strength.

'Claire Bryant's sister, Lacey, the one who's friends with Jack? She Facebook messaged me yesterday. Said it happened last Saturday at Kim's birthday party. Jack went with Matt, they got drunk, and Matt took Kim back to Jack's. The day after he dumped me. Or, technically, *the same day*. Who does that? How could he do that to me? How could he?'

Nat's breathing is shallow and fast again and her head is in her hands. She's sobbing relentlessly; the kind of crying that hurts your stomach and chest and throat and head and makes your whole body convulse. Suddenly, she starts retching, the shock and the alcohol and the weed overwhelming her body. I pull her hair back from her face as she turns away from the group heaves towards the sand, gasping for breath in-between sobs.

'Breathe, Nat,' I say, still stroking her back. 'Come on, you can do this.'

'It's all right,' Edele says, as Mackie passes me a bottle of water from her bag to give to Nat.

Nat has nothing in her body to bring up, so she spits into the sand, taking the water.

'I'm sorry, guys,' she says weakly. 'I just don't know how he could do this.'

'I don't know either, Nat,' I say. 'But you should have told us when you heard. You can't keep something like that bottled up.'

'I know,' she replies. 'I should have done. But I couldn't bring myself to say it out loud because that made it real, you know?'

'What an absolute bitch Lacey is for telling you,' Mackie adds. 'What good does that do? Why would you need to know that?'

'She said she'd been debating whether to tell me all week, but that I "had a right to know",' Nat whimpers.

'Bullshit! People like that just want to stir the pot, it's pathetic,' I say, perhaps unhelpfully, still stroking Nat's back and resting my head on her thin shoulder as she sips from the water bottle.

'Right, first off, who the fuck still uses Facebook messenger?' Edele says, passing Nat a nearly empty bottle of wine and picking up Jay's Finest to roll another joint. We all laugh, even Nat. You know you're friends for life when you can make each other laugh even when your body is shaking with sadness.

'Second, Mack's right, she's obviously some sort of sad-ist who hasn't been laid in a while so gets her kicks from hurting people. Also, how do you even know it's true? We all knew Matt for seven years too, and I can't imagine him doing it – and you know I think all men are trash, even if they're going out with one of us. Apologies, Craig,' she says mockingly, again holding up a wine bottle as some sort of signalling device, this time in the direction of my and Craig's flat. I laugh. I'm not sure Craig would.

'Lacey saw them leave together, Ed!' Nat shouts in a sudden rush of fury. 'Said they were fucking holding hands!'

There's a moment of silence now. I can feel the anger radiating from Edele.

'That pathetic little bastard,' she says quietly with pal-pable rage. 'I'm so sorry, Nat.'

'Why don't you stay at mine?' I say, turning my face towards Nat's. 'The last thing we want is for you to be alone tonight. You might feel better to have some com-pany and a change of scene,' I add, not wanting her to have to go back to the flat they shared and torture herself even more.

'It's okay,' Nat replies quickly, as if considering her answer took no time at all. 'I don't want to intrude on you and Craig! He's probably waiting for you with dinner ready or something. You guys don't want me being all sad and pathetic in your home.'

Before I can reply, Edele interrupts. 'I can stay at yours, Nat? It's not like I have anywhere else to be. Please, save me from my mother and brother for the evening!'

'That'd be nice,' she says. 'I'm sorry for shouting,' she adds, weakly.

'Don't apologise,' Edele says warmly. 'I'm sorry for pushing. I just didn't want it to be true. Here' – she passes her the joint – 'smoke this, then let's get out the freezing cold and go home. I'll stay at yours, we'll spoon, we'll smoke, we'll cry if you want to cry, we'll laugh if you can laugh, we'll watch the Holiday Armadillo episode of *Friends* because it's your favourite, we'll order takeout instead of eating Mackie's weird dick soup, and we'll be okay. Okay?' Nat smiles and nods.

'Ungrateful bitch,' Mackie laughs. 'It tastes a lot better than it looks, all right?'

'Sure it does, Nigella.' A loud laugh from Mackie, a quiet forced chuckle from Nat.

I'm so glad that Edele can be there for Nat, but I can't help but feel slightly dejected. I don't want Nat to feel like she can't rely on me right now, just because of my relationship.

Before I can dwell on it any further, my phone screen lights up in the darkness next to me. My background is a photo of Craig and me from our holiday to Dubrovnik last August. Craig chose the city because 'it looked really cool in *Game of Thrones*'. I said that wasn't a satisfactory reason to go on holiday somewhere for ten days. He said, 'It's the same as when you thought that restaurant in London looked cool on Instagram – what was it, Sexy Trout or something? – so we went there for our anniversary.' I just said, 'Okay, we'll go to Dubrovnik.' I couldn't be bothered to tell him that, actually, that's really not the same thing, it was for my birthday, not our anniversary, and the restaurant was called Sexy Fish. Why on earth would someone call a restaurant Sexy Trout?

My phone buzzes in my pocket.

CRAIG EDGEWORTH ❤: Hey, where are you? Your dinner's on the side, I made lasagne lol. Goin to bed in a bit proper knackered. Lemme know you're all right, babe x

It's very sweet that Craig made me dinner and that he cares if I'm alive or not. But what could possibly be 'lol' about making lasagne?

'Right, lads, I need to head home,' I say, concentrating on slowly climbing to my feet the way someone does when they suddenly realise they're no longer sober. 'Craig's made lasagne.'

'God, I'd murder a lasagne right now,' Mackie groans.

'Probably because you're living off that weird dick soup,' Nat says as the others girls stand up to say goodbye to me, laughing.

'You've got it so good, Al,' Mackie adds. 'He's just perfect.'

'Don't worry, he would've made it with one of those shitty Dolmio kits and ASDA Rollback mince, no veg – just Dolmio and Rollback,' I laugh. I feel a pang of guilt for being too eager to dismiss her comment and put Craig down just to prove I'm not too smugly coupled up, but I'm not sober enough to care.

'Ugh, sounds dreamy,' Edele moans in an overtly sexual way, flinging her arms around me. 'Bye, beautiful.' I hug Mackie goodbye, then turn to Nat, holding her just below her shoulders and looking into her starved eyes.

'You've got this,' I say to her determinedly.

'If I do, it's only because of you three,' she says, taking my hands in hers – they're so cold they make my arms shudder – and kissing my cheek.

The sand is still slightly damp underfoot as I walk across the beach, sticking to my trainers like tiny barnacles to coral. Maybe this is what quicksand feels like.

Nat must feel like she's living in quicksand: something pulling her down, constantly fighting to come up for air. I think how ludicrous it is – how desperately unfair, even – that just one person can have that power over your happiness. How all it takes is just one person to tear down the walls of your life, and leave you to somehow find the strength to build them back up again, and start again.

Craig could do that to me. He could come home from the pub one Friday night and tell me that our love's gone cold, so cold that he wants a new life without me in it. No more stupidly planned holidays, no more Dolmio dinners, no more birthday meals at Sexy Trout. No more evening cuddles on the sofa – the kind that make even the worst of days at work just fade away into insignificance – no more breakfast in bed on a lazy Sunday morning followed by a film he objects to, but puts on anyway because he knows it makes me happy. No more wild but quiet love, all-consuming but comfortable love, frantic and painful and maddening and set-your-chest-on-fire love, but homely and healing and euphoric love. Love that, if nothing else, is simply right.

I think I'd be broken if I lost that kind of love, too. Suddenly, I feel incredibly guilty for my and Craig's relationship in the wake of Nat's heartbreak. What gives me the right to such happiness? Although it stung a little, it's no wonder Nat didn't want to stay at mine tonight, in an environment that would constantly remind her of that happiness. And really, what's to stop Craig from breaking me, too, just like Matt has broken Nat?

The thought sends a pang of panic through my chest. I pull my phone from my pocket to reply to Craig's message.

ALEX: Hi baby. I'm sorry I didn't message earlier, I was on the beach with the girls. Ed threw beer over two guys in the Fox and Whistle 😂 😂 I'm walking home now, be 10 mins or so. Thank you for leaving me dinner, you're so good to me. Hope you had a good day at work. I love you xxx

The air is heavy with moisture. It's going to start raining again soon so I pick up my pace, shoving my headphones into my ears. The only other people on the high street are two extremely round, grey-haired men outside Ye Olde Thirsty Pig, one curly-haired blonde girl in a denim miniskirt and leather jacket waiting for the bus, and two young guys on bikes outside Ladbrokes, smoking with their hoods up. They think they look intimidating, but they can't be older than fourteen – the same age as some

49

of my students. Fourteen-year-olds can sometimes seem intimidating until you remember that being fourteen years old is strange and terrifying and lonely. I put my hood up and gaze down at my feet that are somehow pounding the pavement, just in case the smoking boys actually are my students. I really don't want to hear 'I could smell the bifta on Miss from the other side of the street!' in class tomorrow.

Drunk Singing Homeless Guy is nowhere to be seen on the high street. I open Spotify on my phone and let 'My Girl' by The Temptations fill my ears.

Eventually, I turn left onto Stonewall Road, past the bus stop where Nat once threw up, past the Tesco Express where Ed once dropped a bottle of beer, and stop in front of Nail Art – the small nail salon with a brightly lit sign and peeling leather chairs. Craig and I live above Nail Art in his old school friend, Warner's, flat-cum-studio. Tom Warner deals antiques and uses our large, open-plan living room and kitchen to display his trinkets and photograph them for Stonewall Antique's Instagram page. Warner brings home new antiques at least once a week, so it's not unusual for Craig and me to come home to the huge helm of a ship-wrecked boat, or a stone statue of a curly-haired bloke with his knob out. When he isn't dealing antiques, Warner sits in our kitchen, smokes a lot of weed and acts weird. The Chinese woman who owns Nail Art often slips notes under our door saying: 'Please stop smoking marijuana during the day. I think customers are getting high.'

Warner is sitting at the kitchen counter smoking and there is an enormous taxidermy giraffe head sitting proudly in the middle of the living room.

'Jesus Christ, Warner,' I gasp, 'it's huge – its horns are touching the ceiling!'

'Ossicones,' Warner mumbles.

'You what?'

'They're not called "horns", they're called *oss-see-cone-z*.'

'Right. Well, it and its oss-see-cone-z are very cool,' I say, walking over to grab the Dolmio lasagne.

'That lasagne tastes like shit,' Warner says dryly. I've never seen someone look so glum while smoking a joint. The lasagne must be really awful.

'Well, I'm starving and tired, so I'm going to eat in bed. Night.'

'Night, babe. Craig was worried about you, by the way. I told him you were probably just shagging that fit music teacher from your school.'

'Who, Carla Moretti? Warner, she's married, and I'm not gay.'

'Yeah, I know, but she's fit. I'd give her one.'

'Night, Warner.'

In our room, Craig is sprawled out on the bed in his navy Next boxers, snoring. His laptop is playing an old episode of *Who Wants to be a Millionaire?*, back when Chris Tarrant was blond and wore a tie.

I strip, throw on an old David Bowie T-shirt and climb into bed next to Craig. I stroke his soft blond hair and kiss his forehead lightly. He doesn't stir.

The lasagne tastes like shit. I put the plate down on the bedside table.

'Right, here's the £50,000 question, and you can still phone a friend,' Chris Tarrant says, 'what group, involved in the Russian Revolution, were led by Lenin?

A) Social Democrats
B) Anti-Bolsheviks
C) Bolsheviks
D) Mensheviks'

'The Bolsheviks,' Craig murmurs, half-asleep, as I'm closing the laptop. He lifts his arm over his head in a stretch. I didn't realise he'd stopped snoring. I must be really used to the sound of him snoring.

'Yes! I was talking to you about the Russian Revolution the other day,' I say gleefully. 'It's what I'm teaching my GCSE students.'

'I know,' Craig says mid-yawn, turning to face me with his eyes still closed, reaching his arm clumsily over my waist. 'I do listen to you, you know.' I run my fingers softly down the length of his forearm.

'Well, I geek out about history a lot, and I know it must be boring, so I don't blame you for zoning out every now and again.'

Craig opens his eyes, his gaze instantly finding mine.

'I love it when you talk to me about the stuff you're passionate about. Because it makes you happy. And I want you to be happy because I love you, Al. So, if Lenin makes you happy, you can chat to me about Lenin all night. Okay?'

This is so surprisingly touching that I almost well up.

'That's very sweet.' I shift my body so that I'm at Craig's level and kiss him. He cradles my face with his hand.

'But let's get this straight,' I say, 'Lenin doesn't make me happy. He was a problematic guy, and even though so many people see him as an idealist, he was actually really ruthless.'

He smiles, tucking my hair behind my ear and kissing my forehead.

'Can we revisit Lenin's character analysis tomorrow after work, babe?'

'Of course, I'll pencil you in for six and get my PowerPoint presentation ready. Go back to sleep.'

'Did you have some lasagne, by the way?'

'Yeah,' I reply, trying to feign satisfaction, 'thanks for leaving me some.'

'Tasted like shit, didn't it?'

I laugh loudly, nestling into the warmth of his body. I like how neatly I fit against his shape.

'Wasn't great. Sorry.'

'Let's go out for dinner tomorrow,' he says, 'somewhere nice, like Nando's or the Pizza Express near the seafront.'

'Sounds great,' I say, smiling against the familiarity of his chest. It doesn't matter that Craig's idea of a 'nice dinner' is Nando's or Pizza Express. The fact he's suggested a date night, for the first time in I can't remember how long, is enough to make me happy.

'Love you, Al.'

'I love you, too.'

CHAPTER FOUR
Mackie

From: camilla.penhaligon@ribbonmedia.com
To: emma.mackie@ribbonmedia.com
Subject: RE: Catch up today
Date: 21/01/19

Emma,

We need to find some time to catch up today RE cover (the border colours just aren't right) and the fashion spread (do you really think this layout is best? It feels very cluttered which I feel distracts the reader from the garments we're trying to showcase. Let's discuss in my office. Please have the high-res printouts ready).

I will get Sophie to liaise with you and sort a mutually convenient time for both of us, but I'm in a meeting 11–12, at a lunch 12.30–3 p.m. and need to leave promptly for an event at 4.15 p.m.

Thanks,
C x

It's just gone 10 a.m. on a Monday morning and I'm reading Camilla's email at my desk while eating a bowl of coconut yoghurt with fruit and drinking a green tea. Usually my brain is quick to engage in the morning, but today is different. Today my brain just wants to shut off and sleep. It could be something to do with the fact that I was up at 5.30 a.m. this morning for yoga class, but I thought exercise was supposed to make you *less* lethargic?

Camilla Penhaligon is the editor-in-chief of the magazine I work at. I'm the art editor, which means I'm responsible for the overall aesthetic (I wish that didn't sound so wanky) of the mag, as well as sourcing stock imagery, organising photo shoots, and creating and editing page layouts.

Sophie is Camilla's PA which means she's either desperate to work in magazines, or has a rich family member connected to the industry who Camilla is doing a favour for. I sit directly outside Camilla's glass-walled office, meaning she could've easily poked her head out of her office door and asked when I was free for a meeting. But that's not the way Camilla does things.

Now, I have three options: I could either have my 'urgent art meeting' with Camilla now, before her meeting, leaving me embarrassingly unprepared, or immediately after her meeting when she'll be stressed and snappy, or at 3.30 p.m. after her lunch. The upside of the latter is that she'll be slightly pissed off free champagne, and the downside is that she'll be slathering on lipstick for the event half-distracted while I'm trying to get her to sign off on final spreads.

'Hey, Emma,' Sophie says flatly as she approaches my desk. She is twenty years old, thin and platinum blonde, and today is wearing an enormous grey jumper and black gym leggings. She looks hungover. I don't blame her.

'Morning, Sophie. Did you have a nice weekend?'

'Fucking hell. That's one way of putting it. You?' She says the last word with a palpable lack of interest. I'm not sure this is how Sophie should be talking to a senior member of staff.

'It was fine, thanks. So, Camilla needs to see me but her diary is pretty rammed, right? I have a meeting downstairs with production at ten thirty which I really can't postpone, so how about after her lunch?' My meeting isn't until 11 a.m., but neither Sophie nor Camilla need to know that.

'Ooooo-kay,' Sophie yawns. 'How about three thirty? You won't need longer than forty-five minutes to talk colours and stuff, right?'

'You know, that's not all I d— yes, Sophie, three thirty is fine. Thanks.'

'Cool, I'll ping ya the calendar invite over email in a bit.' Sophie slopes back to her desk, sinks into her chair, pulls a green hoodie over her head and leans, face down, on her left arm. I don't think I'll be getting that calendar invite any time soon, so I go ahead and add it to my own Outlook calendar.

I was never like Sophie when I was starting out. I worked hard, wore pencil skirts and silk blouses (okay, satin-mix blouses) when my colleagues were all in maxi skirts or dresses and dirty trainers. I was always enthusiastic, even when hungover, and did everything I could to get to where I am now. I grew up reading glossy fashion magazines, tearing out the pages I liked and Blu-tacking them to my bedroom wall. I'd run my fingers over the soft-focused black-and-white photos, stare at the colourful collages that made me want to dive into the page, and use cheap disposable cameras, pencils and paints to create my own layouts.

When I landed an art internship fresh out of university with the *Hackton Times* – a lifestyle magazine for our county – I was overjoyed. Now, over six years later, I'm still at the *Hackton Times*, and I've climbed pretty much to the top of the ladder. There's no room for development, most of the team are painfully unenthusiastic, and Sandra from marketing who sits upstairs with Ribbon Media (the mag's publisher) always tells me that sales figures 'are really very poor this issue' every time I see her in the lift. Most of the time I'm too busy trying not to choke on Sandra from marketing's hairspray fumes to listen properly.

I glance around the office. Sophie is still comatose at her desk, Camilla is in her office engrossed in the week-end supplements, one of the writers has her feet up on an empty chair while texting, and the ads team are all on the phone looking very concerned. The fashion team must be on a shoot, probably in a glamorous London town house with floor-to-ceiling bookshelves and wrought-iron railings.

The desk to my left, where my junior designer Lucy should have been sitting for almost an hour, is empty.

And it's messy. Alex always calls me 'the Monica of the group' because of my obsession with cleaning, but seriously, Lucy's desk is a shit tip. There's lid-less pens, magazines, salt and paper sachets from the canteen and unidentifiable bits of paper strewn everywhere, so much so that I can't even see her keyboard, and . . . is that a half-eaten chocolate bar? I get that we're all busy, but if I can zombie my way through morning yoga, declutter my inbox, organise a meeting and shovel some yoghurt into my mouth all before 10 a.m., then Lucy can find the time to throw away her old Dairy Milk.

MACKIE: Hi Lucy, hope you had a nice weekend. Are you nearly in the office? It's almost 10.30 a.m. so just wondering where you are. Let me know if you're okay and if you're coming in. Thanks, Emma x

Lucy starts typing almost immediately.

LUCY: Hey boss! So sorry I'm late, our cat died last night and my mum was crying loads this morning so I stayed to comfort her for a bit. I'll be with you in a min, sorry again x

MACKIE: I'm so sorry about your cat! Hope you're okay, see you soon x

Before I can begin to assess whether I think Lucy is lying about her dead cat and sad mother, another WhatsApp comes through. It's the Mean Girls group.

NATASHA: Hi team, how're your Mondays? Hope you slept better than me last night. Edele stayed over again and insisted on doing that weird half-snoring, half-bleating thing she does in her sleep.

EDELE: I'm going to ignore that very rude comment and just say that my Monday is going very well, thank you, Natasha. I'm actually up and out of bed before 10am. #winning

NATASHA: By which you mean, you're out of *my* bed, and having a fag out the kitchen window in your sweatpants?

EDELE: Small victories are better than none.

ALEX: Wise, Ed. Very wise. My morning's okay. I have my Year 10s in a minute; the class with the kid who always asks if I've 'dumped my waste-man boyfriend yet?' and winks at me.

EDELE: Is he fit though?

ALEX: That's really not an okay thing to ask, Ed.

NATASHA: That's a yes.

Before I can reply, Lucy bursts through the office door and dashes to her desk. She's holding a Starbucks coffee. I wouldn't have minded her lack of urgency at turning up to work if she'd bothered to ask if I wanted a Starbucks, too.

'So sorry I'm late, Emma,' she gushes, throwing her bag to the floor and pulling off her stone-coloured trench coat and hanging it off the back of her chair. She looks like Inspector Gadget.

'Don't worry, are you all right? So sorry about your cat,' I say.

'I'm a bit cut up, I won't lie,' Lucy says, 'Beyoncé was my best friend and she's my phone background too. Look.' She holds up her phone and lights up the screen, showing a very fat but pretty white cat with ginger and black markings.

'I didn't know your cat was called Beyoncé,' I reply. 'That's . . . adorable.'

'Yeah, I know. She was the best.' Lucy picks up the half-eaten chocolate bar and takes a bite. I decide not to point out that it's been there all weekend, and that we got an email last month about mice sightings in the office. Now doesn't seem like the right time when Lucy's mourning her fat cat.

'Well, as long as you're okay to be here,' I say, trying to be comforting. 'Let me know if you need to take some time.'

'Thanks, boss. I may have to take you up on that.'

Lucy finishes the old bar of chocolate, gulps the last of her coffee and begins to tidy up the heap of shit on her desk. I wonder what time it will be when Lucy actually begins her work.

With that, a calendar invite pops up in my inbox.

Meeting: CAMILLA & EMMA ART CATCH-UP
Time: 4.30 p.m.
Location: Camilla's office
Duration: 30 minutes

'SOPHIE!' Camilla bellows from her office, 'I HAVE TO LEAVE AT FOUR FIFTEEN, SO A FOUR-THIRTY MEETING WON'T WORK, WILL IT?' She speaks articulately with letter-perfect received pronunciation. She would've made an excellent BBC news reader in the 1960s.

'Oops, I meant three thirty – sorry! Will update now!' Sophie squeals back. Camilla is shaking her head at her computer screen.

It's almost 10.45 a.m.

'Right, Lucy, I have to go to this production meeting,' I say, standing up to pull on my chequered blazer and grabbing my 'March 2019 Issue' folder.

'See you in a bit,' Lucy says, piling the salt and pepper sachets in a small tower in front of her computer screen.

I walk out of the office and down the hall, its walls filled with framed covers of the *Hackton Times*, and turn left to come out by the elevators. In the corner, there's a small marble-topped table with two blush pink chairs and a geometric hanging planter dangling from the ceiling, with golden pothos leaves trailing gracefully down by the table. Even the hallway where people wait for the bloody lift is nicer than my entire flat.

'Hold the door!' I hear as I step into the lift. I'd recognise that high-pitched estuary accent anywhere.

'Hello, Sandra,' I say, holding the lift doors.

'Fanks, love,' Sandra says, smiling and panting. She has bright red lipstick clinging to her front teeth and her dark brown curls are scraped into a bun. Her fake tan is dark and patchy on her neck. She's wearing a leopard-print coat with a plain black dress, thick tights and gold-heeled ankle boots. I'd tell Sandra that I like her outfit, but I'm trying not to die from hairspray asphyxiation.

'Good weekend, Em?' she grins. Sandra's one of those people who always seems miraculously jolly, even when she's telling me how terribly our magazine is selling.

'It was good, thanks. Glad we got a bit of sunshine. You?'

God, I hate office small talk.

'Yeah, pet, was all right, ta. You seen them sales figures the February issue?,' Sandra's shaking her head, 'Worse I've seen 'em in a long time, I couldn't believe it. Who knows what we'll do if this carries on, but I'm sure the big dogs'll think of summink, hey?' Sandra smiles.

'Either that, or we're all getting P45'ed next week,' I laugh. Sandra doesn't laugh.

'Don't joke 'bout that, pet. I have two toddlers and a labradoodle at home that I got to feed all by me-self.'

The elevator doors open. Thank God, it's my floor.

'I'm only kidding, I'm sure it'll be fine. See you later,' I say, dashing out of the lift.

'Catch ya later, pet!' Sandra calls after me, the elevator doors closing on her smiling orange face and suffocating hairspray fumes.

I've seen the February issue sales figures, so I know how bad they are. And judging by the past six months, they're not going to improve. I often wonder why I'm still in this job, but then I remember how challenging this current climate is in the media, and how rare and competitive new job openings are. But I have to keep looking. I make a mental note to spend this evening searching for roles, perfecting my CV, updating my LinkedIn profile, and drafting emails to any of my contacts who might know of upcoming opportunities. The girls would call me 'boring', but I like being productive. There's something about updating your CV that, no matter if the rest of your life is in utter tatters, just makes you feel like a proper, fully functioning adult.

'All right, Marshall,' I hear a deep London accent behind me. I spin around. It's Luke Williamson, who works in marketing with jolly, orange Sandra. He's well over six foot and half Jamaican, with short afro hair, heart-stopping dark eyes and a room-filling smile. Luke's jawline is sharp, his arms big and his facial hair short and neat. The sleeves on his white shirt are rolled up and the top two buttons undone, revealing his chest hair. He is, without a doubt, the hottest man I've ever seen. He smells like vetiver and tobacco and sex.

'Oh, hey, Luke. Still not letting that name go then?' I made the mistake of drunkenly telling Luke my nickname at the office Christmas party last year. It's what Alex, Edele and Nat sometimes call me because they think I look like Eminem. Really, I just have short, white-blond hair, blue eyes and an unintentional frown.

'No way,' he laughs sexily, shaking his sexy head and looking at me with his sexy eyes. 'But obviously it's not true, you don't look a thing like Eminem. You look great, Mackie,' Luke says, smiling. Be still my beating heart.

'Thanks, Luke, you too. I mean, obviously that you look great, too, not that you also don't look like Eminem,

63

obviously.' Shit, why do I keep saying 'obviously'? This is excruciating. Luke is smiling sweetly. Luke thinks I'm an embarrassment. My cheeks are flushing and my nipples are hard. I hold my folder up to my chest so he can't see that my nipples are hard through my tight brown turtleneck.

'Yeah, I got that, don't worry. I've gotta go, but I'll catch you later? Maybe on *8 Mile*?'

'How long have you been sitting on that Eminem joke?' I laugh.

'Just came up with it, what can I say? I'm a comic genius,' Luke beams as he starts to walk off. 'See ya, Mack,' he says, turning back to look at me.

'Yep,' I say squeakily. I suddenly realise I'm standing in the middle of the hall, my folder still clutched to my chest with one hand, while the other is waving frantically at Luke like a silly schoolgirl with a crush. Why on earth am I waving? I look at my watch – I'm five minutes late for my meeting. The last time I was late for something was in November, the day I was fifteen minutes late for work when Edele stayed over. The night before, she drunkenly thought it would be fun to hide my car keys, and couldn't remember where she'd hidden them the next morning. I eventually found them in the freezer.

My nipples are still like shards of ice. I can't walk into a meeting with nipples that could poke out my managing director's eyes.

I pull out my phone in an attempt to distract myself and my impossibly erect nipples from Luke's hotness.

MACKIE: Sorry girls, mad morning at work. You know, Al, if that student is bothering you, you could always tell your superiors. It's probably workplace harassment, or just, you know, wildly inappropriate. Also, guess who just told me I look 'great'?

NATASHA: The fat bald guy on reception? Your boss? Your mum?

ALEX: Please tell me it was Sexy Luke?

MACKIE: Shut up, Nat. Yes, Alex, it was Sexy Luke.

NATASHA: YAY! You've got his number, right? Why don't you just ask him out for a drink after work?

ALEX: Yes, Mack, do it!

EDELE: C'mon, Marshall, I believe in you. He's fit.

MACKIE: Maybe. I dunno. I'll think about it. I have to go to this meeting but I'll message you all after and you can maybe help me draft a text to Sexy Luke.

EDELE: How about: 'Hey Luke, nice bumping into you earlier, turns out I really want to suck your—'

I stop reading Edele's message and shove my phone into my pocket, clear my throat and try to get Luke out of my head. I wait a few seconds before walking into the meeting room. My nipples are still like shards of ice.

CHAPTER FIVE
Natasha

I'm lying in bed, the duvet pulled over my head, looking at my phone. Specifically, I'm scrolling through Kim's Instagram. Kim is the woman who slept with Matt after her birthday party just hours after we broke up. It was fancy dress, which makes the whole thing feel like some sort of cruel joke. Everyone had to dress up as their favourite character from a film, and to me, that feels very unoriginal. I would've made my fancy dress theme 'Steve Buscemi films and *Keeping up with the Kardashians*'. That way, you could have Kim Kardashian and Mr Pink from *Reservoir Dogs* in the same room. And that's the kind of party I want to be at.

Kim (the one who shagged my ex, not the Kardashian) dressed up as Marilyn Monroe in *Some Like It Hot*, with the triangular-tit sequin dress and platinum-blond bob. I doubt she's ever seen *Some Like It Hot* or knows who Tony Curtis was. *Basic bitch*. Matt went as the guy Tom Cruise plays in *Top Gun*, with the pilot jumpsuit and aviator glasses. I bet he never took the sunglasses off, even after the sun went down. *Prick*.

I know this because I'm looking at a photo of Matt and Kim from the party. Kim's forcefully pursing her lips together in a pout with her eyes closed, holding what looks like a gin and tonic (or maybe a vodka soda – fewer calories than a G&T; seems like the sort of thing she'd consider when consuming alcohol), and Matt has his arm around her, a wide grin spread across his face, holding a Thatchers. I wonder if Matt's thinking, 'I'm going to bone Marilyn Monroe later.' I wonder if Matt thought about me once while he was boning Marilyn Monroe.

I would say I try not to compare myself to other women, but that would be a lie. Show me a woman who doesn't automatically compare the size of her eyes, the glossiness of her hair, the largeness of her tits, the small-ness of her thighs and the gravity-defying powers of her arse with another woman, and I'll buy a long, pointy sword (like the Queen's) and make her a dame myself.

This female predisposition to scroll through another woman's social media and relentlessly compare yourself to her photos is the reason why I know the following:

- Kim has a very sharp clavicle that prominently pokes out of her chest in most of her photos. I don't think I've seen my collarbone since 2008.
- Kim has long, dark brown hair which she often tongs into a wave and seems to constantly shimmer in the light, even when it's night-time. Her hair is dyed dark because in 2014 it was mousey-brown. My hair never looks glossy and shiny. My hair looks like straw.

- Kim has very full Angelina Jolie lips. I don't think she's had them done because the skin around her mouth isn't sticking out. She has *natural Angelina Jolie lips*. My lips look like strawberry laces in comparison.
- Kim has impossibly pert tits – D, I'd say – that sit underneath her prominent clavicle like two round boulders that don't even meet in the middle. I think she may have had them done. My tits are not pert, they remind me of golf balls in a pair of socks.
- Kim has lines on her stomach from muscle definition and no cellulite around her bum, which means that Kim got 263 likes on a bikini picture from her holiday to Mykonos in 2017. My body is 90 per cent cellulite.
- Women have been conditioned to see other women as competitors to be beaten down and trampled over in order to achieve society's prescribed definition of beauty, as though Kim's sharp clavicle and boulder-like tits mean that no man will ever want to have sex with *me* again. Cheers, patriarchy.

I close Instagram and walk over to the mirror, staring at my half-naked body in the mirror. I turn around to look at the cellulite on my bum.

Cellulite's really hard to get rid of, says the voice. *And you've got enough of it to go around. I mean, Christ, there's more cellulite than arse there.*

I don't want to look at my bum any more. I face the mirror, standing upright in my plain black T-shirt bra, which I've had since I was twenty-one, and frilly-trimmed white M&S knickers, and start pinching and poking my stomach.

Wow, that's a decent handful of fat, the voice continues. *Do you think you'll ever be one of those toned, skinny girls that wear bandeau crop tops and leather miniskirts to bars? I don't think you will. Not with a flabby stomach like that. And don't even get me started on your thighs.*

I wrench my gaze from the mirror and pull on my grey sweatpants and a green jumper. But the voice is being stubborn today, and it's not finished yet.

You know, now that you're single, you're going to have to start putting in the effort to look attractive again. A baggy jumper and ill-fitting jeans won't cut it any more. Come on, seriously, what guy in a bar would look twice at you right now?

This stings. Tears prick the corners of my eyes and my fingers turn cold. I've lost weight in the past few weeks since Matt left, but not enough, I keep telling myself. This also makes my head feel heavy with guilt: I want to remember what it's like to feel good about myself, to not constantly berate my own appearance. But realistically, I know that's not going to happen any time soon. Enter 'male validation', AKA, the ultimate shortcut to better self-esteem.

This deeply knotted web of self-loathing suddenly makes me feel faint, so I go to leave the bedroom. As I place my hand on the doorknob, I pause. Matt would always hang his clean shirts on the back of our bedroom door, ready to be ironed on Sunday evenings for the week ahead. There's nothing hanging on the bedroom door now. I trace the pattern in the wood grain with my finger, pausing at the round knots that interrupt the thin lines. I realise that I can't remember the last time I properly looked at the back of this door, so often covered by Matt's work shirts. When we were viewing this flat, the estate agent told us that these round knots are seen as imperfections in woodwork, caused by branches that have died while the tree is still alive. The living grain then grows around them, which makes the ripple effect in the wood. I don't think they're imperfections, though. If something dying can leave behind something more interesting and intricate than it was when it found it, then that seems pretty perfect to me.

Matt hasn't left me more interesting or intricate than when he found me. I can't even walk around my flat without seeing him everywhere. He's on the back of the door where he used to hang his shirts. Out in the hall, he's on the empty wall hooks where he used to hang his car keys next to mine. Walking into the living room, he's in the empty spaces that used to house his board games, books, DVDs, video games, photo frames.

Flitting from room to room is too suffocating, so I pull up the kitchen window and step out onto the roof to smoke. But as soon as the winter air hits my skin, and I hear the distant sound of the waves crashing against the shoreline, I feel that all-too-familiar punch to the guts, and I'm back to the night Matt left. My head spins and I don't know where to go.

I need to get out of the flat – a change of environment, even if it's only a few metres away – so I dart back through the window, out onto the landing, down the short flight of stairs, and out of the flat door. Maybe fresh air will help.

Downstairs, I pause outside Dot Cotton's door. When I haven't seen her for a few days, I like to listen for signs of life outside her flat. Suddenly, the suffocation creeps back into my chest, thinking of how I used to pop down for a cup of tea with a few slices of homemade lemon drizzle cake or some chocolate chip cookies I'd baked. But since Matt left, I haven't done any baking. I have not done much of anything, really. The baking equipment – the muffin cases, the loaf tin, the piping bags – they were all Matt's. He must've forgotten to pack them into his miscellaneous Tesco boxes the day he walked out. We used to love baking together. One Christmas, we were baking mince pies while drinking mulled wine. We got drunk and decided to throw flour all over the kitchen floor and make 'flour angels', before we started kissing and, eventually, making love on the white-coated floor. When we'd finished we stood, naked, covered in flour, looking at the mess we'd made. Matt joked that we'd just created a piece of contemporary art. I laughed until my sides hurt.

I can't bring myself to text Matt just to say he forgot to take his muffin cases. Considering everything else he chose to leave behind that day, it seems somehow frivolous. I would like to think I'll get back into baking soon, and use the stuff he left to bake lemon drizzle cake and chocolate chip cookies for myself and Dot Cotton. But probably I won't. I'll probably buy new baking equipment and leave his in the kitchen as a reminder of happier times to emotionally torture myself.

Through Dot Cotton's door, I can hear that she's watching another cooking show on the telly. Last time I took her cookies, she told me that she records all of them, so she can watch – and stop watching– whenever she likes. 'The acidity of the plum tomatoes and the piquantness of the vinegar complements the creamy goat's cheese perfectly,' the TV says. 'And the peppery rocket adds another dimension of flavour.'

Matt used to love cooking shows. I'd watch them with him because I knew he enjoyed them, even though the verbosity of the commentary made my skin tingle with embarrassment.

'God, it's so pretentious. What ever happened to simply saying: "These foods taste nice together?"' I said once, sat next to Matt on the sofa while adding a top from Urban Outfitters to my basket on my phone.

'Come on, Nat,' Matt retaliated. 'Words like "foraged", "artisanal", "bespoke" – they make you want to *eat* the food more than if they just said, "it tastes nice"!' He always had a rebuttal ready, like a particularly vulnerable animal constantly primed for a predator's attack.

'You know, when you think about it, those words don't actually *mean* anything any more,' I said. 'When was the last time you walked past a bakery that *didn't* describe itself as "artisanal"?'

'Mmm,' Matt said, never taking his eyes off the TV screen. A signal that the conversation was finished, and I was to go back to browsing Bardot dresses from my end of the sofa.

72

The memories become too much, and my knees judder with restless anxiety. This change of environment has exhausted its usefulness, so I head down another flight of stairs and out into the bitter air. I perch on the fourth of five steps leading to our building's front door and light a cigarette. It's a bright, clear day, and as I exhale, I watch the thin plumes of grey twist perfectly into each other, before slowly dissolving against the blue of the morning sky. I wish I could follow them.

It's been twenty-eight days since Matt walked out, and apart from a few drunken 'I miss you' messages from me, we haven't spoken. I don't know if this has made the past month easier or more difficult. I'm sure Matt thinks he's doing the right thing by ignoring me – perhaps he's even feeling smug about it, as if he's actually doing me a favour. But all I know is that it's made the shock even more paralysing. It's as if Matt never left me at all, but was instead snatched away from me suddenly in some sort of tragic accident, like colliding with a cement lorry on his drive to work or being crushed by a falling piece of scaffolding while getting his morning coffee. Something quick, wretched, unanticipated. I feel bad for comparing my heartbreak to the sudden death of a loved one – I don't want to trivialise the latter – but every morning, after those few blissful seconds of sleep-dazed forgetfulness subside, that gut-wrenching, incapacitating shock sets in like a sickness, gouging at your body and your mind and really, how is that any different? Because when someone you love suddenly dies with no warning, no distress signal and no time to prepare for mourning, a piece of you withers and dies with them, too. It's your last parting gift to them, regardless of whether they know about it or even want to accept it. And that's what I've given to him. That's why when your heart gets broken it feels like grieving a wasted life. Because that's exactly what you're doing.

I stub my cigarette out on the step and light another straight away. I press the button that lights up my phone screen.

08:04. Saturday 9 February.

Before the break-up, I would never be awake before 10 a.m. on a weekend if I didn't have to. I was a good sleeper; a deep sleeper. I can't really remember what it feels like to sleep well now.

You've had, what, four hours' sleep? You look like shit. Best sort those puffy eyes and dark circles out before tonight.

The voice is right. I'm supposed to be going on a date tonight, even though, by most sensible grown-ups' standards, it's far too soon. But I'm weirdly intrigued to see what it's like. And, in all honesty, I could *really* do with that shortcut to better self-esteem via 'male validation'.

That's why, last Friday, on one of the many nights Edele has stayed over since Matt left, I told her I'd downloaded a dating app.

'Mostly out of curiosity, so don't judge me, okay? These things didn't really exist before Matt and I got together; it was terrible online dating websites with sky-high subscription charges or good old-fashioned face-to-face,' I said.

'Which one?' Edele said.

'What?'

74

'Which dating app? There are loads, Grandma.'

'Oh, umm . . . Hinge, I think? I liked the name. Sounded practical. Useful.'

'I'm not sure you should be on dating apps if you're after "practical" and "useful". Anyway, are you sure you're ready to date? Because, and prepare for the shock of the millennium, hun, but I *really* don't think you're ready to date yet. An hour ago, you cried because you found one of Matt's old socks in your underwear drawer.'

'Oh, leave off. And no, of course I'm not bloody ready, but if not now, then when? I need to throw myself in the deep end, I think. I guess it's a bit like eating your first sirloin steak after seven years of being vegan. You'll probably never feel completely ready, you know?'

'It's literally nothing like that. That was a terrible analogy.'

We laughed.

'Okay, well, I approve of Hinge,' Edele said. 'No one really looks at Tinder any more unless they're drunk and swiping through people's profiles with their mates. Let's look at your Hinge, then,' Edele said, reaching out her hand for my phone. I passed it to her. She looked thoughtfully at the screen for a minute or so, nodding every now and again, as if she were resonating with a profound piece of poetry.

'You look fit in your pictures, obviously, so that's a good start,' she said expertly. 'But get rid of this one,' she points to a photo of me on a beach in Ecuador, which I had cropped Matt out of. 'You can tell it's a bloke's arm around you, so it's obvious it's an ex, and guys will wonder why you didn't have more photos without him to choose from. Fresh out a long-term relationship will scare ninety per cent of 'em off.'

'Oh, right. Okay.'

'And Jesus, Nat, really? Your answer to: "You should *not* go out with me if . . ." is: "You don't know the difference between 'their', 'there' and 'they're'"?'

'Well, yeah. I don't want to date a dumbass.'

'No one wants to date a dumbass, dumbass. But it makes you sound boring as sin.'

'Right, okay. I'll change it.'

'And while you're at it, change your answer to "drinking" from "sometimes" to "yes", or hide it completely,' she said definitively. 'If you ever meet them, they'll soon suss you out after your fourth glass of wine. Then they'll wonder what other vices you've glossed over, and they don't need to know that yet.'

'All right. Thanks, Ed.'

'Any time,' she said, handing the phone back. 'So, you chatted to anyone yet?'

'Well, there is this one guy, Lawrence . . .'

'That's a hot name.'

'That's what I thought. So, Lawrence seems very funny – quite dry, which you know I like,' Edele nodded and smiled, slouching down on the sofa to rest her legs over mine, 'and he's a cameraman working on wildlife documentaries, so he gets to fly all over the world to film with these different animals. There are photos of him with monkeys, wolves, even diving with massive sharks! He's basically got the coolest job in the world.'

'Wow. Show me.' I found Lawrence's Hinge profile and passed Edele the phone again.

'Jesus *wept,* he's beautiful! He's like a young, sexy David Attenborough! Are you sure he's not a catfish?'

'Err, I don't think so. Yeah, pretty sure he's legit.'

'Then go on a date with him *immediately*, Nat.'

Fast forward eight days, and my date with Lawrence is less than twelve hours away and I'm tired, pasty and hairy. Very, very hairy. Winter, coupled with a break-up, means I can't actually remember the last time I shaved. Hair removal doesn't exactly fall high in your list of priorities after you get dumped.

I pull myself to my feet, unlock the front door and walk back up to my flat ready to face date prep. To my surprise, Dot Cotton is on the landing, locking her front door. She must have just smoked one of her cigarettes, too, because she's cloaked in the smell of fresh tobacco mixed with delicate floral perfume. She's wearing a black pleated skirt with black heeled boots, and her top half is wrapped in a thick, white woollen coat with a round, oversized collar. It looks incredibly soft. I feel a sudden urge to hug her and bury my head into her coat.

'Hi, Ms Harris,' I say as I reach the top of the stairs.

'For goodness' sake, child, how many times do I have to tell you? Please, call me Diane,' she smiles.

'Sorry, Diane. How are you?'

'I'm very well, but more importantly, how are *you*, sweet? I haven't seen you for a few weeks, and you don't look very well. Truth be told, you look rather terrible.'

There's a deep sympathy in Diane's eyes as she warmly touches my arm, and suddenly, I find it hard to speak.

'I, umm . . . no, I'm not, really.' I squeeze the words out of my throat before realising that they don't make much sense.

'It's that man of yours, isn't it? I did notice that his car hadn't been parked outside for a while now.'

With that, the strength required to hold normal conversation snaps, and I start sobbing relentlessly on the landing to Diane's flat.

'Come on,' she says as she places her arm firmly around my waist, ushers me up the next flight of stairs and into my flat. I must have left my front door unlocked. I don't remember.

Just like the girls did on the night Matt left, Diane guides me to the sofa like a delicate piece of china.

'He's gone,' I blurt out, sputtering between sobs. I sound like an idiot.

As if she hasn't guessed that already, genius.

'I'll put the kettle on,' Diane says, placing her shiny black handbag on the living-room table and removing her soft white coat.

I start to breathe slowly and deeply, trying to control the tears, and wipe my eyes – now even puffier than before – with tissues from the box on the coffee table. Mackie insisted on putting a fresh box of tissues in every room of the flat a few days after the break-up, 'because the last thing you'll feel like doing when you start crying is going on a flat-wide search for a tissue to wipe your snotty nose', she said. It's a very special thing when your friendship group offers different kinds of support. I have her to look after me in her own quiet, practical way, while Alex offers insight and empathy, and Edele is always there with wine to drown our sorrows and make me laugh. I think about how lucky that makes me, and realise I've stopped crying.

A few minutes later, Diane emerges from the kitchen carrying two mugs with steam swirling from their centres. As she approaches the sofa, I realise that the black pleated skirt isn't a skirt at all, but a short-sleeved dress, fitted at the waist. For an older woman, her arms are remarkably toned. I want to ask what she does to work out, but now doesn't seem like the appropriate time.

'So, sweet, you had a carton of milk in the fridge, but it was two weeks out of date, so I threw it out,' she smiles. 'I found some peppermint tea in your cupboard so I made us that instead. Nothing beats a mug of English breakfast, in my opinion, but peppermint tea is very good for you, so drink up once it's cooled down a bit.'

'Thank you,' I say, as she perches on the edge of the sofa and looks at me with a concerned but tender frown.

'My dear Natasha,' she says as if I'm her very own flesh and blood, 'I think you're simply too tired to tell me what happened, aren't you?'

'Yes, I . . . I'm exhausted, and I hope you don't think I'm rude, but I'm not sure I can go over it again.'

'Of course not. Here,' she says, pulling the grey throw on the back of the sofa over my shoulders. 'Get comfortable, and try and drift off. I'll stay here for a while, so that I'm here if you need me.'

'I can't ask you to do that, you were heading out.'

Diane looks into my eyes and smiles. 'Only to the supermarket,' she says. 'The supermarket, which will be open this afternoon, tomorrow, and the day after that.'

'Thank you,' I say again, the words catching against the familiar lump in my throat. I rub my eyes. I really am tired. Dog-tired. I've never known tiredness like this.

I don't remember falling asleep on the sofa, but when I wake up, the time on my phone says 12:47. The peppermint tea is cold. Diane's shiny bag and soft coat have gone. The coffee table has been wiped clean and the clothes that were strewn across the floor have vanished. I can hear the washing machine whirring monotonously in the kitchen.

There's a note next to the box of tissues. The handwriting is shaky but clear.

Natasha,

A broken heart cannot heal surrounded by such a mess, so I took the liberty of cleaning up a bit. You *must* start to look after yourself. Please remember that no man is worth putting yourself through the pain you currently are. It will pass, my dear. It always does.

Diane xxx

Something warm and tranquil swells in my chest and I smile. It's small, but I think it's hope. I think I might be feeling slightly hopeful.

I spend the next few hours dashing around the flat, hanging out washing, cleaning up, making toast with Marmite, trying to distract myself from the nervousness about my impending date. I even play some music from my laptop. It's the first time I've listened to music since Matt. You don't realise how many songs are about love until the last thing you want to listen to is a song about love.

I soon tire myself out, fall asleep on the sofa, and repeat the cycle.

Soon, it's 6 p.m., and I start thinking about getting ready for my date with Lawrence.

NATASHA: Lads, I'm freaking out about my date. It's in two hours.

EDELE: You'll be fine! Don't put pressure on yourself to be someone you're not. And remember, if he's a dick, you have every right to get up and walk away.

MACKIE: What she said. But you know if you really don't want to go, you don't have to, right? I'd love to come over and be there with you but I'm catching up on some work. Camilla was really cracking the whip yesterday.

EDELE: Wild Saturday night for you then, Mack.

MACKIE: Beats chauffeuring my little brother and his mates to town for a fun night out. That's your only plan tonight, right?

EDELE: Touché.

ALEX: Want me to come over, Nat? I can be there in 15.

NATASHA: YES PLEASE. You're an angel.

ALEX: On my way x

I jump in the shower quickly before Alex arrives and spend three or four minutes debating whether to shave my pubic hair.

The chances that he'll even want to go anywhere near your vagina are laughably slim. But best make it look as presentable as possible, just in case.

'What about what I want?' I think, trying to squash the voice. 'And a hairless female body is just another patriarchal standard forced on women! If he's any kind of man I'd ever want in my life, he won't care whether I have pubic hair or not!'

But seconds later, I give in and shave off all my pubic hair anyway. I feel like a terrible feminist. Maybe I should add that to my dating app profile.

Natasha, 28, Hackton-on-Sea.

Newly single.

Damaged with irreparable trust issues.

Insomniac.

Hears voices.

Wears a seven-year-old bra.

Feminist but will shave pubic hair for acceptance from opposite sex.

I can hear the flat's buzzer ring so turn off the shower, quickly wrap a towel around my now-hairless body and rush to the door, buzzing Alex in.

'Hey,' I smile as Alex climbs the last few stairs to my front door. She's wearing a huge, black turtleneck jumper, which has a thick cable knit, with green corduroy trousers and lace-up boots. Her make-up-free mahogany eyes light up against her gold hooped earrings and olive skin. The clothes hang loosely off her frame like blankets. She's the most fashionable teacher I've ever seen.

'Hello, beautiful,' she beams, lifting her arms up to embrace me, then shrinking away. 'Bloody hell, Nat, you're dripping wet! Your floor is soaked!'

'Yeah, I just got out the shower.'

'Mmm, no shit. Go and dry yourself off, I'll get the supplies out.'

'Supplies?' Alex says nothing and ushers me away with her hand.

After doing everything I can to avoid looking at my body while drying it with a towel, I walk into the lounge wearing tight black jeans and a low-cut satin blouse, which is sort of a gun-metal mauve colour, a mix of pale purple and grey. I like colours that are difficult to describe.

Alex looks up, and grins. 'You look great.'

She's laying down make-up palettes, nail polishes and hair clips on the coffee table and has filled two champagne flutes with sparkling wine. It's a pale blush pink in colour, with hundreds of minute bubbles pirouetting gracefully to its surface. It looks way more expensive than the crap we usually drink.

'I look like shit. Thanks for coming over though, this all looks great.'

'Are you looking forward to it?'

'I don't feel that great about it now, I'm so on edge.'

'It's natural to be nervous and it was always going to be daunting, your first date after—'

'And how would you know? When was the last time you went on a date?'

'I remember—'

'Look, you just don't get it. You can't relate to how I'm feeling because you've never even been dumped, Al.'

'I may not know what it feels like,' she continues, 'but that doesn't stop me being there for you whenever you need me. I promised you, the morning after Matt left, that even if you feel lonely, you are never alone. Let me keep that promise?'

The tone of her voice is soft and compassionate yet also sincere and authoritative, as if I have no choice but to accept the kindness she's offering. I wonder if this is how she speaks to her students. Maybe it's what makes her such a great teacher.

I gently move my hand so that my fingers are locked between hers and squeeze lightly. Alex is smart in almost every sense of the word. She seems to me to be one of those people who doesn't just listen to what you're telling her, but feels it, too, even if she's never experienced it. That takes an unyielding amount of insight and empathy; a type of compassion that, in my opinion, is rare to find in a person. I'm a bad friend for feeling angry at her.

'I'm sorry. You've come over to help me and I'm being a proper dick,' I say genuinely.

I want to tell her that I love and cherish and appreciate her, but that it's not that simple. That no matter how selfish it makes me – so selfish I make myself feel sick – her happiness reminds me of the happiness that I've lost. It's not quite jealousy, I don't think, but a sort of loathsome marriage between bitterness and longing. It doesn't mean that I don't want her to be happy; I want nothing else for her. It's just that I don't need another reminder that I was incapable of keeping love alive.

'I don't know what to say,' I add after a brief moment of silence. 'I love you. And thank you.'

'You don't have to say anything,' Alex says, unlinking her hand from mine to pick up her flute of posh fizz and pass me mine. 'You just need to know that you always can – say anything, talk to me, I mean – if you want to.'

I feel a sudden rush of overwhelming gratitude for Alex, and the thought of my selfishness ties a knot in the pit of my stomach.

'To people like us, people like you,' I raise my glass to hers. 'To those few friends you can always rely on; who hold your hair back while you're chucking up in the loo after a messy night out, who rush over with wine at eleven o'clock when your heart gets broken, who help you get ready before the most nerve-racking date of your life. To us.'

She clinks her glass against mine. 'You and the girls always come first, before any man. You know that.'

I take a gulp of sparkling rosé. It's sweet. I can't remember the last time I ate or drank something sweet.

'Right, Wonder Woman, please can you do something about this ugly, puffy, tired mug of mine?' I say, gesturing to the make-up on the table.

When Alex has finished covering my face and hair in miscellaneous products, I go to my bedroom to look at myself in the same mirror I used to look at my fat and cellulite earlier.

My hair is slightly wavy, its normal dry frizz tamed with sweet-smelling oil, and pulled back loosely in a half-up, half-down style. There's a nude gloss on my lips and my eyelids are a smoky grey behind thick, glossy mascara. I haven't worn make-up in the past twenty-eight days, let alone lip gloss and fifteen coats of mascara.

You look ridiculous. Your lips look thin, your hair looks dry and your tits look saggy. You're basically the opposite of Kim. What man in his right mind is going to find you attractive?

'You look so beautiful.' Alex is standing in the door to my room. I didn't hear her come in. Sometimes the voice in my head is the only thing I can hear.

'Let's finish our drinks and get your bag together,' she says, 'you need to leave in ten to get to the bar for eight. Want a lift?'

I nod. 'Thank you, Al.'

'I got you'.

The bar is dark. Really dark. It's so dark that I'm debating using the light on my phone to look around, but that doesn't seem very socially acceptable.

'Well, they should turn a fucking light on or hand out torches then,' I think.

With each millisecond that passes, the jittery nervousness builds in the pit of my stomach and I feel more and more sick. At least if I threw up right here nobody would be able to see it was me.

I'm also painfully aware that I'm standing in the bar's entrance and that I must look very awkward. If there's one thing that screams 'I'm here to meet a stranger from a dating app and I'm shitting myself about it', it's standing uncomfortably in the entrance to a bar on your own. I'm squinting very unattractively into the darkness, which is clearly intended to create a trendy ambience, but is just as practical as staring into a black hole. Actually, I'd quite like a black hole to swallow me up right now.

'Natasha?' asks a figure emerging from the dark abyss.

'Yeah? Sorry, I can't see shit.'

Great, two seconds in and I've already sworn. He must think I'm trash. He definitely thinks I'm trash.

'Yeah, I did wonder if they'd had a power cut,' the figure laughs. The figure is now standing in front of me. It's very tall – well over six foot – and has huge dark brown eyes and a wide white smile. Its face is now leaning in towards mine.

'I'm Lawrence, if you hadn't already guessed,' says Lawrence, pressing his cheek against mine and kissing the air. I've always thought the ways in which people greet each other to be really odd.

'It's nice to meet you,' I say, even though I couldn't possibly know if that's true or not yet.

'I've got us a spot over here,' he says, 'this way.' He starts to walk off and, for a terrifying moment, I think he's going to hold my hand. He doesn't, thankfully.

'To be honest, I don't really do this much,' he says as I walk next to him. 'So I asked a mate where to go, and he suggested this place. He didn't tell me it would be so, umm, dark.'

'Maybe it was tactical, so that if I was really ugly, you wouldn't have to look at me,' I say, forcing laughter so that he doesn't think I'm being serious.

'Well, you're certainly not that,' he says.

Now you look like an attention-seeking loser, says the voice.

Great. Quick, Nat, just say something.

'Thanks, neither are you.'

Nice one. What man can resist a woman who showers him with such compliments as 'you're also not ugly'?

Lawrence's voice is deep and welcoming and his accent sounds affluent; it's no wonder he works in television. His brown hair is cut close to his head and his facial hair is short and neat. His white shirt fits him perfectly, and it's easy to see that he's toned underneath. He also has a deep, olive-hued tan.

'Did you get a spray tan for tonight?' I tease jokingly as we walk past the bar and into the area with tables and sofas, which is also pitch black. I've already had three glasses of sparking rosé and feel more tipsy than I realised.

Lawrence turns, fixes his dark eyes momentarily on mine, and laughs.

'Yeah, from the tanning shop over the road. It's a good one, right?'

We both laugh. I know the real reason Lawrence is so tanned is because he travels the world for work, but he doesn't want to explain that for fear of sounding like a dick. I already like that about him.

Our table is situated between two sofas in a corner of the bar, overlooking the street outside. There's an H&M over the road, which always stocks an inordinate amount of leggings (see-through leggings are the fashion trend that never died in this town) next to a small alleyway where Edele once had sex with Joel Hall, the guy she lost her virginity to on the beach. I don't think they ever had sex inside.

Lawrence effortlessly slides onto one of the sofas, and I notice how low to the ground the table is. It's basically knee-height. What sort of monster implemented such an exposed seating arrangement in a bar?

'Great,' I think, 'I don't even have the security of hiding behind a table.' What am I supposed to do now? Do I sit next to him on one side to feel more comfortable, but that would mean we'd have to awkwardly crane our necks to look at each other, or do I brave the other sofa and attempt a super-chilled-out-yet-attractive pose?

I opt for the latter, realising Lawrence would probably think I was a freak if I chose to sit right next to him. Removing my leather jacket, my cross-body bag perched at my hip underneath, I flop down onto the sofa and shuffle over with all the elegance of a very uncoordinated hippo. I breathe an audible sigh of relief when my bum reaches the appropriate position opposite Lawrence, and thankfully I don't think he noticed the hippo-ish way in which it got there. I sit with my hands in my lap and my legs crossed, praising myself for choosing jeans over a skirt.

'I've ordered us a glass each of Condrieu, I hope that's okay,' says Lawrence.

Great. Now I have to pretend to know what that is.

'Oh, lovely,' I say with a squeakier intonation than I anticipated. I clear my throat and try to shuffle to a comfier, but still attractive, position.

As I make my hippo-ish shuffle, I notice Lawrence's eyes dart noticeably downwards towards the deep V-neck of my blouse. I follow his gaze and notice, to my horror, that the black lace of my bra covering my left boob is visible. Or is it just visible from this angle? Can he see my bra from his vantage point? Is he the kind of guy that will find that sexy or will he assume I'm a total slag?

I wouldn't worry too much. He's probably just wondering if your tits are always that saggy or if gravity is just particularly forceful today.

'So,' Lawrence says, leaning forward and clasping his hands together on the table, as if he's conducting a dimly lit job interview. 'We've talked a lot on Hinge about what I do for work. Tell me about your job.'

Honestly, there are hundreds of topics I'd rather discuss than my job, like which Domino's pizza topping is the best, how exactly did Andy Dufresne reattach the poster before escaping in *The Shawshank Redemption*, the plight of the honeybee, the existence of aliens, whatever. I often find that people who regularly talk about work are either painfully polite (boring), or genuinely enjoy what they do for a living. People who enjoy what they do for a living are, more often than not, very happy and content people. And happy people are rarely funny.

'Oh, well, you know I work in advertising,' I say. Lawrence nods supportively. 'It's pretty standard. I develop fresh strategies and ideas, write promotional copy, build client relationships. It's pretty much nine to five in an office just outside of town. But it's very boring compared to what you do. What's the coolest animal you've ever filmed with?'

The coolest animal', seriously? What are you, nine?!

'It's not boring, I'm interested in what you do,' Lawrence says earnestly as a particularly bored-looking waiter brings two glasses of what I can only assume is Condrieu to the table.

I feel myself breathing a sigh of relief and the tension in my body easing as Lawrence tells me his 'top three' favourite animals are whale sharks, orangutans and margays. I tell him mine are wolves, armadillos and raccoons. He explains that margays are small wild cats, that look a bit like mini-jaguars with huge eyes, native to the jungles of Central and South America. He talks about studying zoology at university, and I tell him about my English degree. He says he lives about half an hour away, towards London, in a studio apartment. I, for some reason, explain that my flat gets really hot in the summer and really cold in the winter. *Absolutely riveting stuff, I'm sure he's finding the insulation of your flat a totally captivating topic of conversation.* He tells me that he recently got back from Borneo, where he filmed a type of ant that self-combusts in close proximity to enemies to save the rest of its colony.

'Oh my God, exploding ants?!' I exclaim loudly after another large glass of Con-tree-ya-whatever. 'That's, like, the ultimate sacrifice to protect the ones you love. That's beautiful. I want one of those ants in my life.'

Lawrence laughs.

We smile at each other. He reaches for my hand and I give it to him without thinking. He runs his thumb gently over my knuckles. This isn't awful at all. In fact, it's going quite well. And even though it feels extremely weird and unfamiliar, getting to know someone for the first time is exhilarating. Full of newness and promise. It makes me feel hopeful for the second time today, which after the past twenty-eight days, must be some sort of record.

But I am very drunk, so when, after one more glass of wine, Lawrence leans over the table to kiss me and whisper, 'Shall we get out of here?' in my ear, I don't hesitate to agree.

'You don't live far, right?' he asks.

'No, ten minutes away,' I reply. 'Shall I order us an Uber?'

'You get the Uber, I'll grab the bill here.'

I know full well the Uber home will be no more than a tenner, and the six or seven Con-dee-yews will be at least £50. Taking into account this bar's low-hanging chandeliers, red velvet upholstery and multiple mirrors covered in paintings of birds, I'm going to assume it's more around the £70 mark. But I'm too drunk and broke to argue. Plus, I already became a terrible feminist when I shaved my pubic hair earlier.

It suddenly hits me that I'm taking Lawrence – this random thirty-two-year-old David Attenborough type who likes expensive wine and margays – home, presumably for sex. Is this really what I want to do? For a second, I consider how, after seven years of having sex with the same person and only a month since the break-up, this could potentially be a very stupid decision. But in this moment, pleasurably crushed under the weight of this stranger's power over me, I don't care. I know that it's a temporary relief from being crushed by Matt's power over me.

Soon, I find myself standing in front of Lawrence next to my bed and he's lifting his hand to my cheek and drawing his face closer to mine. I can feel his breath against my open mouth and he kisses it, slowly, moving his hands to my hips. The sensation in my body, the deep ache in my pelvic bone and the combination of too much wine with no dinner makes me feel faint.

I get onto the bed, lying against the quilt and he lies next to me, leaning over to kiss me again.

This feels different. He's not Matt.

But the voice is fainter now, drowned out by alcohol, and it's easier to fight.

The size and strength of Lawrence's upper body towering over mine makes me feel gratifyingly small and completely exposed to his power. I feel his hands on my body. My head is swimming but I like it. I am an empty space, a hollow gulf for him to make whole again.

'I don't have any condoms,' I say.

'It's okay, I do,' he says, standing up and removing his belt. I follow his lead and start taking off my clothes.

He puts on the condom and climbs on top of me. His touch is intoxicating and there's a ferocious, animal look in his eyes when he's inside me. He soon flips me over, one hand gripping my waist, the other buried in my hair but not quite pulling it. As he leans into me, harder each time, I can hear my voice crying out, high and raw, so I bury my head into the pillow to muffle the noise.

It doesn't take long before we're done and lying next to each other on our backs, the scent of his skin and our sweat washing over me. His fingertips are tracing my hip bone, gliding over my lower stomach. I don't know what time I fall asleep.

A noise outside the window – a passing car, maybe – wakes me, and I instinctively turn to my right to look at my phone on the bedside table.

07:34. Sunday 10 February.

A quiet rustle of the sheets next to me, and I can feel the warmth of someone else's body close to mine. For a moment, it feels as though the past few weeks haven't really happened, and I think Matt is there. I turn to my left, when last night suddenly comes back to me, and Lawrence is lying on his back, smiling. The sliver of morning sun creeping through the curtains diffuses light softly over his features; his eyes in a slight squint from the brightness, his brow following suit in a mild frown. He looks even better with his hair slightly messy.

'Morning,' he says.

'Hello,' I say quietly. I feel weird. I don't think I expected him to stay. Is this normal?

'Come here,' he says, lifting his arm and pulling me in to lie on his chest. His skin smells good, and I desperately want the feeling of comfort and being looked after to wash over me. But this feels unnatural, as though my body isn't supposed to fit against his, like putting the wrong type of fuel into a car. Even though we were having sex just hours ago, the act of lying on him like this, every inch of my body so close to his, feels overly intimate and tender.

As I look up at him, the daydream suddenly snaps, and I find myself back to the night Matt left, when I was lying on this exact same bed – *our* bed – looking up at him in this exact same way. The weird feeling turns to a crushing emptiness, an all-too-familiar hollow, the same one I so desperately wanted Lawrence to fill last night.

You're a fool, the voice stirs, *a damn fool to think this would fix you. You should've known this would only be temporary.*

And, just like before, the voice is right. I should have known.

'I'm sorry,' I say in a noticeably panicked tone, clutching at the sheets and pulling them close to cover my naked skin. 'But I think I'd like you to leave.'

'What?' Lawrence seems understandably taken aback. 'Have I done something wrong?'

'No, no, you haven't, sorry,' I say hurriedly, trying to stop the tears from forming. 'I just, I think I just want to be on my own. Do you mind?'

'Right,' he says, awkwardly untangling his arm. This stings, though probably more so for him. 'I'll go. But are you sure you're okay? You look really upset and I'm really sorry if I've upset you, that honestly wasn't my intention.'

I can't bring myself to look at anything except the ceiling – the thin crack creeping from the coving, the dead fly lying in the light – as he gets up and puts on last night's clothes.

'Bye, Natasha,' Lawrence says, closing the bedroom door behind him as I lie completely still in my and Matt's bed. Tears are streaming down my face and I reach for the box of tissues Mackie left on the bedside table.

CHAPTER SIX
Edele

Mum started hoovering the house ten minutes ago. She began in the hallway, but being a very small hallway, she was finished in three minutes. She then migrated to the kitchen, where she has been intermittently banging the mouth of the hoover against the loose skirting boards for approximately five minutes, and is now edging towards the living room, which is directly underneath my bedroom.

Eyes still closed, I give up on sleep and lurch my arm aimlessly towards my bedside table in search of my phone. 'Shit!' I say as my forearm catches on the table corner. There's something hard and cold pressing against my naked back. Oh, it's my phone. I must have fallen asleep with it in the bed. I open one eye.

07:58 Sunday 10 February.

Low Battery: 10% battery remaining.

I reach down in the general direction of my phone charger and leave it on the side to charge without check-ing my notifications. I know Nat had her date with Sexy Young David Attenborough last night, but there's no way she'll be awake yet, so I doubt I've heard from her. And I really don't want to see what I put on Instagram Stories after I'd dropped my brother and his mates into town, came home, got wine-drunk and watched *Notting Hill* on my own.

What kind of monster hoovers at 8 a.m. on a Sunday? I can't understand why hoovering would require any level of urgency that means it couldn't be postponed to a more humanly acceptable time – say, 10.30 a.m. or 11. But this is our mother's Sunday-morning routine when she's feeling particularly anxious or unsettled. Once she's finished hoovering downstairs, which won't take long because our house is small and didn't need hoovering in the first place, she'll start cooking breakfast. Unless my brother and his friend raided all the food in the fridge when they got in last night, breakfast will likely be bacon or sausages with Irish soda bread.

I think soda bread is dry and dense, like eating a stale scone for breakfast. This is sacrilege against my Irish heritage, according to my mother. I may as well go to Killarney and spit on the graves of my ancestors.

I rub my face and sit up in bed. My head is pounding and the flesh around my eyes feels hot and heavy. I feel so dehydrated that I wonder if my skin has shrivelled into deep, cavernous wrinkles overnight. In my mind, I look like Yoda.

Pulling back the duvet cover, I look down, and realise I slept completely naked. I wonder whether past me slept completely naked because she was too warm, or because she couldn't find any clean pyjamas to sleep in. My guess is the latter. I pull on the closest clothes I can find – jeans and a huge white jumper with a unicorn on, which I think I was wearing last night because they're on the floor next to my bed – and wander onto the landing, past my brother's room and to the bathroom.

I wee for a very long time. My wee is very dark, as though I haven't drunk a glass of water since the new millennium. I wash my hands and look at my face in the mirror. My skin is pale and puffy, but by some miracle, I don't look like Yoda yet.

I unlock the bathroom door and step back onto the landing.

'Shit!' I exclaim loudly for the second time this morning, a figure on the landing making me jump. It's my brother's best friend Eddie, waiting to use the bathroom. This is terrible because I am hungover and look like a corpse, and I think Eddie is very, very fit.

'I mean, hi,' I quickly follow up.

(Fit.)

'Hello,' Eddie says.

(Fit.)

'Did you have fun last night?'

('Did you have a sex dream about me last night?')

'Yeah, it was all right.'

('I had several dreams about your naked body and am now in love with you as a result'.)

'Good.'

('I'm going to think about you while I masturbate later'.)

'Went a bit too hard though.'

(Too easy.)

'Ah, classic.'

(Fit.)

'What did you do?'

('What would you like to do to me?')

'Not much, just watched a film.'

('Porn. I watched porn. In my head. The porn was you and me having sex.')

'Cheers for the ride, by the way.'

('I'll ride your—')

'Oh. Hi, Liam.'

Nothing like seeing your baby brother to ruin your mental fantasy of having sex with his best friend.

'What's the matter with you, Ed? Shouting "shit" at this time in the morning!' Liam says, rubbing his eyes and ignoring my greeting.

I know Liam is talking to me, and he's pissed off that I woke him up. But right now, Eddie is standing in front of me topless, wearing just a pair of grey sweatpants, and his muscle definition is the only thing that has my attention.

Liam walks past us towards the bathroom. My brother is four years younger than me, but still towers over me at six foot one and could easily pass for someone in his thirties.

'You were battered last night, Ed,' Liam says. 'Oh, and nice jumper, by the way,' he adds.

Eddie laughs. God, Eddie has a sexy laugh. I forgot I was wearing my unicorn jumper. Eddie will never have sex with me now.

'You saw me?' I say, my attention suddenly snatched away from Eddie's perfectly sculpted, god-like body.

'Yeah, when we got home, don't you remember?'

'Err, no.'

'Yeah, you were pretty gone,' Eddie remarks. I untuck my hair from behind my ear, feeling my cheeks flush. What does that mean? What did I say, or do? Jesus, what if I propositioned him?

'You loser, Ed,' Liam laughs as he shuts the bathroom door behind him.

'Piss off, dick-face. And can you please decide which one of us you're going to call "Ed", me or him?' I say, gesturing pointlessly at Eddie, who is now alone with me on the landing and, for some reason, is still not having sex with me. 'It's very confusing.'

Liam doesn't respond.

'Guess I lost my line in the bathroom queue,' Eddie says.

(So, so fit.)

'Yep.'

('While you're waiting, why don't you come into my room and, you know, just take off all your clothes?')

'That brother of yours is so annoying. I really need a piss.'

(Don't care. Still fit.)

'Yeah, he's a dick.'

('Get your dick out.')

'I may as well go and wait in Liam's room. I need to lie down.'

('I need to lie down on top of you.')

101

'Okay, see you later, Eddie.'

('See you later in my sex dream, Eddie.')

Eddie retreats back to Liam's room and closes the door. The combination of my wine hangover and the intense longing to have sex with Eddie is all too much for 8.10 a.m. and I lean against the banister, closing my eyes and holding the bridge of my nose.

The toilet flushes and, a few seconds later, Liam emerges from the bathroom.

'Too old for hangovers?' he laughs, poking me hard in the side of my stomach as he walks past. I'm too tired and sexually frustrated to think of anything remotely clever or cutting to respond with.

'You're such a knob!' I call after him, storming back to my bedroom and slamming the door. Liam and I have been playing out this sort of scene since we were children, and I don't see it stopping any time soon. Not while he's still a knob, anyway.

I shut my bedroom door and lean against it briefly, glancing around the room. This has been my bedroom for the best part of ten years, since we moved here when I was seventeen, and I've been sleeping on that bed for, well, as long as I can remember. There's a basket piled high with dirty laundry in the corner, a vibrator poking out from under one of the pillows on my bed (perhaps that explains the whole 'sleeping naked' thing) and a very old glass of gin on the windowsill. It's that 'magic' gin that changes colour from blue to pink when mixed with tonic, except now, it's a very dark bronze colour. It's definitely not supposed to be that colour.

Next to the laundry, there's a small rail of clothes and an old glass cabinet, bursting with dust-covered Harry Potter books and Disney–Pixar DVDs. *Monsters Inc* was my favourite as a ten-year-old. There's a bottle of fake tan that's so old the mousse inside has likely turned green with oxygen, and the hairbrush on the floor is so clogged with black hair that it must be time to buy a new one. How often are you supposed to replace your hairbrush; is it every six months? I've had that hairbrush for at least three years. But it still does its job of separating and flattening the strands of my hair into a socially acceptable style, so until its bristles fall out and it's no longer capable of its own basic function, I shall keep it and use it, when I remember to.

There are photos filling every corner of the room: hanging from fairy lights over my bed, in frames on my bedside table, wonkily glued over the walls with Blu-tac. I find my room claustrophobic. It is small, but that's not what I mean. It's claustrophobic because I feel like I've been trapped here for so long, this floor forming the centre stage from where my life story is playing out. If I haven't found the 'right time' to leave home by the age of twenty-seven, when will the 'right time' ever come?

The thought weighs heavy on my chest, so I walk over to the bed and sit on the mattress, picking up my phone. There are too many WhatsApp notifications for my brain to cope with right now, so I open Instagram.

Only one Story on my account. I watch it. It's a video. I'm filming the TV in the living room, which is playing *Notting Hill*. The film's about Anna (Julia Roberts), this mega-successful film star, who *really hates being a mega-suc-*

cessful film star and just wants a normal life, okay? who falls in love with Will, this lowly – but super posh – English bloke who owns a book shop in Notting Hill so, you know, can't be doing too badly for himself.

Specifically, I'm filming the bit where Anna tells Will that fame isn't real, and that he should totally be her boyfriend, even though he is but a lowly Englishman with a bookshop.

'I'm also just a girl. Standing in front of a boy. Asking him to love her.'

Then I quickly spin my phone around so that the camera is on my drunk, make-up free face, a single tear rolling down my cheek, pulling a grotesque, exaggerated crying face and making fake weeping sounds. I'm holding a full-to-the-brim glass of wine under my chin.

It's completely terrible, but it's already been seen by 211 people, so there's not much point in deleting it now. Actually, scratch that. I'm deleting it. If it saves just one more person from watching, it'll be worth it.

Before deleting, I scroll briefly through the list of people who have watched it. Mackie and Alex (not Nat). Liam and Eddie (well, that's just great). Joel Hall (the guy I lost my virginity to on the beach). Gary, the kind, chubby bartender. Some people I went to school with; some people I don't know (who are those people?); Richard, a guy who I went on a date with and slept with last month. I go onto my profile page. Richard has now unfollowed me. Screw you, Richard.

The smell of frying bacon wafts into my room so, phone in hand, I head downstairs to the kitchen, where the radio is playing quietly and the smell of food fills my nose and makes my stomach rumble. There's a full bottle of orange juice in the fridge. Hail Mary, full of grace.

'Edele Marie, what do you think you're doing?' Mum snaps from behind me.

'Shit, Ma, you made me jump. I'm drinking some orange juice,' I reply facetiously.

'Straight out of the carton that we all have to drink from, you philistine,' she barks, waving her hand at me in exasperation. 'And will you *stop* swearing, child?'

'Sorry, Ma. How are you? The floor looks . . . clean. Perfect time to do it too, at seven in the morning.'

'Yes, well, that's the magic of cleaning, girl.' I roll my eyes. 'And I'm probably feeling a darn sight better than you. You drank a whole bottle of wine last night.'

'How do you know?'

'Because you left the empty bottle and your glass in the lounge.'

'Oh, right. Sorry.' My mum still manages to make me feel like a naughty schoolgirl when she's telling me off, despite the fact that I'm twenty-seven years old.

'Yes, well.' Great. She's in one of her 'yes, well' moods.

'Is there any bacon in there for me then?' I say, gesturing towards the frying pan. The smell of sizzling bacon is making my mouth water.

'I had an inkling that the smell might lure you out of your pit,' she says, smiling. 'Yes, there's two rashers in there for you. The boys won't emerge for hours yet. Grab the bread, will you?'

I slice some of the gross, dry soda bread and spread liberally with butter. Mum takes the pan off the heat and presses some coffee, pouring it between two cups. In one cup: a heaped spoonful of brown sugar, a splash of milk, for me. The other cup: just black, no sugar, for her. She places the sugary cup on the other side of the kitchen island, where she knows I'm going to sit after I serve the bacon over the bread.

I squeeze a big dollop of ketchup onto my bread to make it less dry and sit hunched over my plate. Mum's never been very good at sitting still, so she begins tidying up the kitchen while intermittently eating her breakfast and drinking her coffee.

For the next few minutes, Bob Marley's 'Could You Be Loved?' plays on the radio and I half-listen to Mum talking about some woman she bumped into at the shop while she was purchasing the bacon.

I finish eating in no time at all, push my plate and mug aside and decide that it's time to check WhatsApp.

Twenty-eight messages in the group chat, all from Mackie and Alex, mocking my Instagram Story, talking about *Notting Hill*, and asking Nat how her date went. Nat hasn't replied.

Then, my heart does a sudden flip of fear in my chest as I see that I have three missed WhatsApp calls from Nat ten minutes ago, and a single message that says: 'Please call me. I need you, Ed.'

'Shit!' I say aloud, my body springing into action, and I leap from the chair.

'Edele? Everything okay?' Mum says.

'It's Nat,' I say, 'she needs me.'

'That poor girl,' she says as I dash to the lounge to call Nat. 'Send her my love, won't you?' Mum calls after me.

Nat's phone only rings once.

'Hello?' she says. Her voice is cracked and she sounds far away. I can't tell if that's the phone's connection or just the way her voice sounds.

'Nat, what's wrong? Are you okay?'

There's a pause now. I can hear her breathing, shallow and quick, and the movement of bed sheets. She's in bed and she's crying. The connection is fine.

'No,' she says.

'I'm coming over.'

'Okay.'

I dash back into the kitchen and up the stairs into my room, balancing the phone to my ear using my shoulder.

'Ah, shit, what jacket was I wearing when you gave me that spare key to your flat the other day?' I ask.

'Your denim one.' Again, not a suitable outerwear choice for winter. I grab the jacket from the edge of my clothes rail and search the pocket.

'Got it. I'll be there in ten minutes. I love you, Nat.'

'Love you, too. Thank you, Ed.'

My mind races as I pull the unicorn jumper over my head – doesn't seem like an appropriate choice of clothing to wear to visit your heartbroken friend – and change into something less jolly.

My feet hammer the stairs again and I grab the car keys from the hall, before running back into the kitchen.

'All right if I borrow the car, Ma?' I say quickly. I'm already making my way out of the kitchen before she responds.

'Of course, darling,' she calls after me. 'Let me know you're both okay!'

Out the front door, the sharp cold raises goosebumps on my arm and I drink the crisp air deep into my chest. It's nice to be out of the house, I think. Maybe I should take up running. Or just walking.

A curtain twitching in a window of one of the terraced houses opposite ours catches my eye. It's very difficult to be inconspicuous as a solitary person in Hackton, where everybody's business is everybody's business, even if you're just stepping foot outside your own front door.

Ten minutes later, I pull into the small space outside Nat's building, the tyres screeching slightly as I do so. The car is not straight and it's parked far too close to Nat's car. It suddenly occurs to me that I could still be over the limit. Shit. That was stupid, even by my standards. I'll make some toast upstairs, if Nat has any bread.

Up the stairs, I can smell fresh cigarette smoke from Dot Cotton's door and the muffled noise of the TV. Probably one of her terrible cooking shows again.

I unlock the front door, kick off my trainers and race up the small flight of stairs to the hallway.

'Nat?' I cry, poking my head round the kitchen door. There's an empty bottle of posh-looking sparkling wine on the counter next to two glasses, one of which must be Alex's.

'In my room,' she calls out.

She's lying down in bed, the duvet pulled up to her chin, and she doesn't look up when I open the door. It's warm in here, despite the chill occupying the rest of the flat, and there's a faint, stale smell of sweat. The bedside table on what used to be Matt's side of the bed, where I now spend so many nights, looks different to when I last slept there – the lamp has been pushed back, and a couple of the books have fallen to the floor.

I climb in bed next to Nat, her hair is messy and she still has make-up on, flakes of mascara clinging to her cheek. 'What happened?'

She moves her body to one side so that we're facing each other. I put my arm around her, my forearm resting against hers. Despite being under a thick duvet and wearing a T-shirt, her skin is ice cold and she's shivering.

'I brought him back here, Ed, back to my and Matt's flat,' she says, her voice breaking, her eyes shut. 'I don't know what I was thinking.'

I stroke her arm for a moment and try to make her laugh by saying, 'Wait, so I'm lying in your sex sheets?'

'Yep,' she giggles half-heartedly.

'You wanted to though, right?' I say, seriously now. 'I mean, he didn't guilt-trip you, or talk you into it?'

She opens her eyes now and looks at me. 'Of course not,' she says. 'I wanted to, at the time. I don't know. I think I was just drunk and wanted to try and replace Matt, just for one night. But it was different. It felt like I wasn't really me, like I was just observing someone else for the night through their eyes. Then he stayed over and when I saw him lying there . . . I just freaked out. I

109

chucked him out. I *used* him; I used him to try and fill my loneliness, and then I threw him out.'

I consider this for a moment, stroking her arm as she shivers.

'I think that's what we're all doing, isn't it?'

'What?'

'Looking for someone to fill our loneliness, in whatever way that means for us. Isn't that what this whole "dating" thing is? What I'm trying to say is that I don't think that's anything to feel guilty about. Lawrence clearly didn't mind at the time, did he?'

Nat exhales sharply through her nose in a sort of despondent half-laugh.

'I guess not.'

'I think it just means you weren't ready, and that is nothing to feel ashamed of. If anything, I'm proud of you. I think it took more strength than you realised.'

'Ed, when I woke up this morning, and I heard him move next to me, I think – for a split second – that I thought it was Matt. And that this had all just been one big nightmare.'

She shivers harder, and I edge slightly closer to her in the bed to try and give her some of my warmth. I pull the duvet higher over our bodies so that it's sitting on our shoulders, slightly covering our faces.

'Nat, you can't keep doing this—'

'What?' she asks in a panicked voice before I can finish my sentence.

'You can't keep thinking of this place as "yours and Matt's", and thinking that he might be here when you wake up in the morning. I'm not saying you have to be over it already – bloody hell, it's only been a month. But you need to start letting go of him, slowly. Otherwise you can't begin to heal. You need to let go of pieces of him, so that you can use those pieces to rebuild yourself. I don't know if that makes any sense, but do you get me?'

She starts crying then, last night's make-up running down her face in blotches of brown and black.

'I know,' she says eventually. 'But how do I do that? How can I?'

'Well, that's what I'm – we're – here for. We'll help you do it.'

'Okay, thank you,' she says.

We lie in silence for a minute or so as her crying eases. She looks at me, and sadness shoots through me when I notice the anguish in her eyes. I've never seen her look so desperately unhappy. I tuck her hair behind her ear so that it's away from her face, and wipe away some of the wet make-up from her cheek gently with my thumb, my fingers resting by her ear.

'You need to wash your face, your body and these bed sheets,' I say. 'There's a near-perfect imprint of your face on that pillow in make-up, and I'm pretty sure I know how that got there.'

Nat untangles her arm from mine and sits up to look at her pillow. 'Oh my God,' she says, clasping her hand to her mouth. We both start laughing.

Slowly, she gets out of bed and stands up, rubbing her nose and stretching. Her T-shirt is hanging limply from her frame and, in just a thong, I notice how small her body looks now. There's a gap between her thighs which I'm sure she didn't have a month ago. But now's not the right time to bring it up.

'Did you have fun though? Last night, with Lawrence?' I ask tentatively, throwing a packet of face wipes over to Nat. She removes one and starts wiping the damp mascara and eyeshadow from her face, leaning against the window.

'I did, yeah. He's smart, has a very cool job, and is obviously hot. I enjoyed his company. I just wish I hadn't brought him back. It was too soon.'

'Would you want to see him again?'

Nat stops wiping her face for a minute and stands, thinking. She's twisting the edge of the curtain fabric in her other hand, letting the white light spill further into the room.

'I think so,' she says eventually. 'But maybe not yet. I'm obviously not ready.'

'Maybe give it a few days and see how you feel. You don't owe him anything, but if you do like him, why don't you message him and just be honest about your situation? See what he says.'

'Yes, okay. I think you're right.'

'But first, go and shower,' I command, getting to my feet, 'you smell like sex and your face is a mess. I'll strip the bed.'

Nat laughs and says, 'Thanks, Ed,' before walking into the bathroom. She turns the shower on and I grab my phone, opening the list of my recent calls.

The dial tone rings three times before the call is answered.

'Ed?'

'Hey, Mack.'

'What are you doing up so early on a Sunday? Am I dreaming? Is this a dream?'

'Very funny. Are you about?'

'Yeah, I've just been for a run so was about to jump in the shower. Why? What's up? You okay?'

'God, you make me sick. Who goes for a run at the break of dawn on a Sunday?'

'Edele, it's gone nine o'clock. I've been up for hours.'

'Exactly! One day your batteries are going to run out and you'll just, like, shut down. Like a robot. And at your funeral, we'll be like: "she died doing what she loved; going for wanky morning runs and eating weird dick soup".'

'Ed, shut up. Are you okay?'

'You know me, I'm always okay. It's Nat. I'm at hers now, can you come round?'

'Where is she? What's wrong?'

'In the shower. She brought that guy back last night and she freaked out this morning.'

'What happened?'

'She just wasn't ready. She woke up earlier and thought he was Matt.'

'Oh God. How is she?'

'We need to help her, Mack. We need to somehow make this place Nat's flat, not her and Matt's flat.'

'Like some sort of heartbreak exorcism for the home?'

'Exactly. Nicely put.'

'I'm on it. I'll be there in half an hour.'

'Go shower your smelly pits.'

'They shouldn't be smelly; I used a special roll-on deodorant for athletes.'

'Of course you did, Mackie. See you soon.'

Nat spends a long time in the shower. I strip her bed and put the sheets on to wash, which makes me think that I really need to get round to doing my laundry. I start washing up the champagne flutes and folding Nat's dry laundry before I can dwell too much on the fact that I'm on the wrong side of twenty-five and my mother still does my washing for me.

'You don't need to do that, Ed.' Nat is standing in the door to the kitchen wearing black gym leggings and an oversized grey hoodie with her wet hair wrapped in a towel.

'Don't be daft,' I say. 'Mackie's coming over, if that's okay? I would've asked Alex too, but I know she's doing something with Craig's family today. I just think we need to clear some stuff out of the flat, to try and take some of the "Matt" out of it.'

She looks uneasy, her gaze drifting to the floor.

'I know you don't feel up to it,' I continue, 'but it needs to be done, Nat. And you don't have to do any of it, if you don't want to. That's what we're here for.'

'Okay,' she says. A message alert pings from the pocket of her hoody and she takes out her phone.

'It's Lawrence.'

'What does it say?'

She pauses, reading.

'He's just asking if I'm okay, that he had a nice time and didn't like the way we left things. He feels really bad that I got upset.'

'That's nice of him. He seems like a nice guy.'

'He is. I'll message him back in a bit.'

She puts her phone back in her pocket and we start cleaning the kitchen, piling anything that used to be Matt's, or that reminds Nat too much of him, onto the dining table. We fling open all the cupboard doors, rummaging through everything and creating a mess of pans, utensils and Tupperware on the floor as we do so. I rifle through the cabinets, holding items up for Nat to say 'keep' or 'chuck'. She 'chucks' two mugs – one that says 'Initech', a reference to *Office Space*, one of Matt's favourite films, and one with the initial 'M' in the shape of a Scrabble tile. She also adds two glass tumblers to the table, because they were a housewarming gift from Jack, and a) Jack is a twat, and b) Nat doesn't need any more reminders that Matt shagged Jack's sister. The dining table – and the entire kitchen – quickly descends into a total mess, as Nat adds muffin trays, piping bags and a slow cooker to the 'chuck' pile.

'I won't use it anyway,' she says as the flat buzzer goes. She presses the button to open the door for Mackie. 'And he was obsessed with this slow cooker; he cooked with it all the time.'

'Morning, you two,' Mackie grins as she walks into the kitchen, holding a thick roll of black bin liners, a wad of white labels, and a brown takeaway bag.

She puts everything down and steps cautiously a pile of baking trays on the floor. She throws her arms around Natasha, holding her close and kissing her on the cheek.

'Hey,' Nat says warmly.

'Hello, my girl,' Mackie says. 'Are you okay?'

'I'm all right,' she says.

'My priest,' I say, joining the hug, 'are you here for the home exorcism?'

'I am, my child,' Mackie laughs. 'I am at your service. And I bring baked goods!'

She reaches for the takeaway bags and pulls out an almond croissant for Nat, a chocolate muffin for me, and a cinnamon Danish for herself.

'Thanks, you know us so well,' I say.

'I also bought coffee beans for your machine, Nat,' Mackie adds, 'because I think we all need caffeine to get through this, and a few other essentials. I dread to think when you last went grocery shopping.'

'I can't actually remember, so thank you,' says Nat.

'What's with this stuff?' I ask, my mouth full of chocolate muffin, pointing to the bin bags and labels. 'Are you finally putting me in the bin?'

'I wish. They're to get rid of any Matt-related items, and we can label any bags we want to take to the charity shop.'

'That's proper smart,' Nat says, 'And makes a lot more sense than the utter chaos we've been creating. Thanks, Mack.'

The three of us go from room to room, cleaning and tidying as we go, with Nat and I creating 'Matt' piles, and Mackie sorting them into the relevant bin bags. In her bedroom, we remove three pairs of socks, an old hoody, and a jumper Nat had bought him for Christmas. In the living room, there's two cushion covers from Matt's old flat, a movie poster he'd forgotten to take with him, and eight photos of the two of them together which we peel from the walls.

'You should do the honours,' I say, passing the pile of photos to Nat.

To my surprise, she doesn't hesitate, grabbing them from me and ripping them straight down the middle, then ripping them again, and again, until they're nothing more but tiny, unidentifiable pieces of glossy paper.

'Go on, Nat,' Mackie cheers.

'Have that, prick,' I laugh.

Nat smiles, walking over to the old bar cart in the corner and picking up a bottle of amaretto.

'Matt loved this stuff,' she says, slightly grimacing. 'He bought it from the supermarket every Christmas. We must've forgotten to open it.'

'Crack it open then,' I say.

'Edele, it's still the morning,' Mackie retorts.

'I think if there's any justification to drink your ex's alcohol in the morning, it's performing an exorcism of him from your home,' Nat says, smiling.

'Plus, that stuff is so sweet it's basically not alcohol,' I shrug.

'Yep, fair enough,' Mackie laughs.

Nat opens the bottle and takes a swig before passing it around.

'It tastes like Barbie's piss,' I say, wincing as the girls laugh.

Eventually, after filling up two bin bags for the charity shop and one to throw away, we finish rearranging plant pots, books and Nat's photo frames to fill the empty spaces where Matt's stuff used to be.

'It looks different,' Nat says as we all slouch on the sofa, a quarter of the amaretto already gone.

'How do you feel?' Mackie asks.

'Weird.' She takes a sip from the bottle. 'But also quite calm, like I've definitely done the right thing. I feel a bit more in control, a bit stronger.'

'Good,' I say, 'and the flat looks great.'

'It does, doesn't it?' she replies. 'I've forgotten how much I love it here.'

'And hopefully now it can start to feel like *your* home, too.'

'Yeah,' Nat smiles, 'I hope so. It definitely feels . . . I don't know. It feels new.'

'New is good,' Mackie smiles, looping her arm over Nat's shoulders. I do the same so that Nat, sitting in the middle, is cocooned between the two of us. 'Why don't we walk these two bags to the charity shop and pick up a new plant from the garden centre to replace Frank?'

'Good shout, Marshall,' I say, 'I'll make us some of that coffee first so that we can actually walk after all this deceptively lethal Barbie piss.'

Nat pulls us both in close, so that both of our heads are resting against hers.

'Thank you, you two. I don't know how to thank you for what you've done for me today.'

'It was nothing,' I say, 'you know how much Mack loves donating to charity and I love day-drinking on a Sunday morning, so you basically did us a favour.'

'It wasn't nothing,' she replies, 'it was so much more than nothing. You're helping me to start again. So grateful that I've got you.'

'We will always be here to help you start again,' I say.

Mackie nods. 'Always. Now let's rock and roll.'

'Fucking hell, did you actually just say "let's rock and roll"? You sound like a fifty-year-old dad who's just paid the bill at TGI Friday's.'

We all laugh, our heads still leaning against Nat's.

'You're a prat, Ed,' Mackie says as we get up from the sofa.

'Wait,' Nat says. We pause. 'Can you both help me do something before we go?'

'Of course, what?'

'Can we use some of Matt's kitchen stuff to do some baking before we take them to the charity shop? I need to take some treats downstairs to Dot Cotton as a thank you for something she did yesterday.'

'Sure thing, Mary Berry,' I say. 'What do you want to bake?'

'Lemon drizzle cake and chocolate chip cookies,' she says.

CHAPTER SEVEN
Alex

He's late to meet me. The time on my phone says 5.39 p.m., and we agreed to get a drink at the pub after work at 5.30 p.m. I take a large sip of my gin and tonic, the alcohol biting at the back of my throat. I breathe in deeply, hold the air in my chest, then exhale slowly. 'You're being irrational,' I tell myself. But I can't stop.

I wouldn't normally be nervous to meet Craig for a drink – something we've probably done hundreds of times in our relationship – or be remotely concerned by his punctuality. But he's been acting differently over the last few weeks, and I find myself looking for signs of cracks in our relationship in everything he does. It's not that we've argued, though we have had cross words about whose turn it is to take the bins out, and whether we can ask Warner to get rid of the giant taxidermy giraffe head in the living room (I said: 'Yes, it scares me half to death every time I go for a wee in the night'; Craig said: 'No, it's the man's business and we shouldn't interfere'; I said: 'His business is antiques, not decapitated stuffed giraffes.') But we haven't actually spoken enough to argue properly, not about anything worthwhile. 'That's ridiculous; you live together and see each other every day,' I tell myself. But he's been too unfamiliar to hold a conversation of any substance, like something is off between us. He's distant, not himself. Lately, when we're lying next to each other in bed, I sometimes find myself looking at him – the face and body of a man I know so intimately I could draw outlines of them in my sleep – and wondering if I even know him at all.

'Stop,' I tell myself. 'He's only nine minutes late.'

Only nine minutes. This realisation douses the burning nerves in my chest with a temporary rush of relief. There are plenty of explanations that would account for being nine minutes late. He could have been caught up at work, his bus may have been stuck in traffic, or maybe he's stopped somewhere to buy us something to take home. Maybe vanilla cupcakes from the bakery he knows I love round the corner on Orchard Road, or a bottle of our favourite Malbec from the wine merchant down the street.

I scorn myself now for expecting such things after three years together. We're past the stage of showering each other with gifts in a bid to impress the other person. I think the last spontaneous 'present' I bought Craig was a big bag of his favourite flavour of Kettle Chips from the supermarket, because they were on offer for a pound. Though no one would consider a packet of crisps a 'present', I suppose. Still, it's those small, seemingly meaningless gestures that are often the most touching and hold the most significance in a relationship. Anyone can go to a department store for ten minutes with the sole purpose of choosing a gift perfectly presented in over-the-top gift wrapping, like when Alan Rickman buys that gold necklace for the office tart instead of for Emma Thompson in *Love Actually*. And if there's anything romcoms have taught us about spontaneous gifting, it's that the big, expensive presents are often a sign of guilt. But not the small, sort of rubbish presents. It seems to me that a cheap bag of crisps says a whole lot more than a gold necklace. It says, 'You occupy such a vast space in my mind, I think of you so constantly, that my day-to-day life throws up constant reminders of you.' That person is, subconsciously or not, considered in everything you do and everywhere you go. Even in somewhere as mundane as the supermarket snack aisle.

Thinking about that scene in *Love Actually* – Emma Thompson in her bedroom listening to Joni Mitchell after realising the gold necklace wasn't for her, with no breakdown or sobbing, just simply standing there with the shock and with her sadness – reignites the fiery panic across my upper body. I pull my Edgeworth tobacco tin from the pocket of my puffer jacket to roll a cigarette. This is a nice beer garden to smoke in. In the summer, lilac wisteria creeps over the wooden pergola, and today long arms of ivy are climbing up the surrounding brick walls. The sun has nearly set, but strings of festoon lights and candles on each table illuminate the small garden. It's unseasonably warm for a February evening and even though I'm sitting outside, the heat is scratchy and unsettling against my skin.

Edele and Mackie tell me that I'm just affected by Nat and Matt's break-up, even if I'm not consciously aware of it.

'You and Nat used to talk a lot about your relationships, right?' Edele said to me on the phone the other night. 'Well, it's only natural that you're feeling uneasy about the security of your relationship when another couple who you thought you were "equal" to have ended.' And Mackie said the same thing to me over WhatsApp earlier. 'You need to stop waiting for something to go wrong,' she said.

But it's not that simple. When you've existed alongside someone else for such a long time, there are intricacies about their personality and nuances of their behaviour that are almost impossible to describe to other people. And there's an uneasiness that's crept into Craig's behaviour lately. I close my eyes for a minute, trying to restore some momentary calm.

'Sleeping and having a fag? That's a fire hazard if ever I've seen one.'

Craig's smiling faintly as he pulls off his headphones and walks over to the bench. He's wearing a thick, grey sweatshirt under a bomber jacket and jeans with dirty white trainers. He looks scruffy but handsome. I always take such a distinct pleasure from the way he looks, like listening to a favourite song for the first time in months, or noticing different tiny details in a painting on the living-room wall.

'You all right?' I ask as he swings his legs over the bench and sits opposite me, shoving his hands into his jacket pockets.

'Yeah, I'm okay. Good day?'

'It was good thanks, my Year 10 kids were a nightmare though, one of them actually fell asleep and started snoring.'

'That's well bad, but I actually used to fall asleep in lessons at school all the time, especially maths. Teacher grassed me up to the headmistress about it, too. I told her I had that illness where you don't get enough iron – what's it called, bulimia? No, anaemia, that's it – but I don't think she bought it. Absolute miracle I passed that GCSE. Well, I got a D, but that's still a pass, ain't it? I know the rules are different now. Do they even call them GCSEs any more?'

Craig's speaking unusually quickly and his gaze doesn't meet mine once. He's constantly glancing at his phone, and turning it over so the screen is facing downwards into the table, before returning his hands to his pockets.

'Craig,' I say, reaching over to touch his hand, which feels colder than mine, 'are you sure you're all right?'

'Of course I am, babe,' he says, quickly meeting my eye before glancing away again. 'I'm just knackered.'

I think of how many times I've exploited the excuse of tiredness to mask anger or hurt when I haven't wanted to reveal the truth. Craig's arms are tight against his body and his shoulders are tense. I don't think I've ever seen him like this.

'Aren't you going to get a drink?'

He looks over at me through the thin grey cloud of smoke and relaxes his shoulders slightly, as if put at ease by my question. Perhaps he was expecting me to press him further. But the panic settling in my body won't let me for fear of what I might find out.

'Yeah, of course,' he says. 'Can I get you another?'

'No, thanks.'

He nods and gets up. As he's walking across the beer garden, two women about our age open the door to the pub and walk outside, one wrapping a grey scarf around her neck and carrying a bottle of red wine with two glasses; the other reaching a lighter up to the cigarette resting in her mouth. He approaches them, and the one in the grey scarf holds the door for him. Craig has his back to me, so I can't see his expression, but she smiles a wide, friendly grin, and says something I can't decipher. It looks like a familiar encounter, as if they know each other.

I rub at my chest then, feeling my sternum with my fingers, short of breath. I stub the cigarette out in the ashtray and take a long sip of my drink.

'Get it together,' I think to myself. 'You're being paranoid; this isn't you.' It's one thing to feel paranoid about Craig being late, but to start convincing yourself that he knows this random woman in the pub? That's just ridiculous. Still, despite knowing how illogical I'm being, the fearful feeling of suspicion doesn't abate.

Craig soon reappears, the door to the beer garden swinging shut behind him, carrying a pint of lager. The two women, who are sitting at a bench on the other side of the garden, look over at him, and the one in the grey scarf says something before they both start laughing. Craig doesn't seem to notice.

'No crisps?' I ask.

'Hm?'

'You usually get some crisps or nuts if we come here after work.'

'Oh, right. I'm not hungry.'

'Why not?'

'How am I supposed to know why I'm not hungry? What kind of question is that?'

'Right. Sorry.'

He's defensive now, his back straightening and the faint sheen of perspiration on his upper lip catching the warm light from the candle beneath us.

I wipe my nose with my fingers and take another large gulp of my drink, the remaining ice clinking in the glass.

'You've nearly finished that,' he says, welcoming an opportunity to change the topic, 'you should've let me get you another.'

'It's fine, I'll get one in a minute.'

We spend some time dipping in and out of idle conversation, the growing night covering us in a blanket of sharp cold.

As I light another cigarette, Craig's phone rings and vibrates against the table. He grabs it immediately and dashes to the corner of the beer garden to answer it, ensuring that I can't hear any of the conversation.

I watch him intently as he listens, shuffling his feet and looking at the ground. He barely says anything throughout the conversation before hanging up after what couldn't be longer than a minute.

'I have to go, babe, sorry,' he says, putting his phone into his pocket and pulling on his backpack.

'What? Why? Where are you going?'

'I'll explain later, it's not important.'

'It seems pretty damn important to me.'

'I promise it's nothing to worry about,' he says, leaning over to kiss me on the forehead and resting his hand on my shoulder as he does so. Why do I feel like he's trying to comfort me? What is there to feel comforted about?

'How can you expect me to not worry when you're being so secretive?'

'Al, I really have to go. Sorry. I'll see you at home later.'

I watch as Craig vanishes through the pub door and I feel the hard beat of panic inside my body.

Who was on the phone? Where is he going? Why is it so urgent? Why the secrecy? What do I do now?

I lean over and pick up Craig's pint glass, still half a pint or so remaining, and throw my head back to drink some of it. The grey-scarfed woman is looking at me, the expression on her face unreadable. Though I can imagine it's probably mild repulsion. Or maybe concern.

I replace the pint glass on the table and unlock my phone. I begin typing a message to Nat.

ALEX: Nat, what're you up to? I'm at the pub with Craig and he's being really strange. Not just now, I mean, he's been acting differently for ages. It's making me paranoid, turning me into someone I'm not. What do I do?

I reread my words before I send the message and think how uncontrolled I sound. I hesitate, a sudden guilt setting in. Why would Nat want to read this? Craig acting out of character is nothing compared to what Matt did to her. It feels too selfish, and I realise that I shouldn't be bothering her with this. I select the message and press 'delete' before searching for Mackie's name instead.

ALEX: Hey, Mack. What are you doing? I'm at the pub and Craig's being weird and I'm worrying and driving myself crazy and losing my mind. I was going to message Nat, but then I realised what a selfish cow I'd be, bothering her with my relationship worries after everything with Matt.

MACKIE: Al, are you okay? What are you talking about? Weird how? I'm still at work and I've got a mountain of proofs to work through, so I doubt I'll be out of here any time soon. Sorry, love. And you should just message the group chat, Nat won't mind.

ALEX: How can she not mind? This is nothing compared to what she's going through.

MACKIE: Come on, Al. We're adults. That isn't how this stuff works. Two people's worries are unique to them; there isn't some hierarchy of stress or grief that invalidates all instances on the lower end of the scale. She is your friend and, by definition, is there for you when you need her, just like you are for her. Stop being ridiculous. Message the group.

ALEX: All right. Yeah. I guess I also just don't want to remind her of Matt and their relationship by talking about Craig and our relationship.

MACKIE: You think she isn't already thinking about Matt and their relationship? I'm no expert, but I'm pretty sure she doesn't stop thinking about it. Don't be overprotective and end up shutting her out.

ALEX: Hmm. Okay, I'll message the group. Thanks, Mack. Let me know if you get out of work any time soon.

MACKIE: Will do. Are you all right? We can talk later or tomorrow?

ALEX: I'll be fine. Thanks.

I select Mean Girls.

ALEX: Mack's got work, but Nat and Ed, are you around? I've just had a drink with Craig and he's being shady and acting all nervous. He just got a phone call and had to leave. He basically ran out of the pub. I could do with company.

EDELE: Which pub?

ALEX: The Orchard Tavern, near that bakery I'm obsessed with.

NAT: Edele and I were just heading out to buy smokes. We can meet you at The Orchard?

ALEX: That would be great. Only if you're sure?

NAT: Yeah. Sure.

EDELE: Hope you're okay, Al.

The combination of smoking and the unrelenting building of worry makes me feel light-headed again, so I pick up my bag and head inside to wait for the girls.

I'm sitting on a deep-red-coloured armchair, ten minutes into nursing my second gin and tonic, when Edele and Natasha approach me in the pub. I'm near enough to the fireplace that my body can soak up the warmth radiating from the flames, but not so close that I'll start to sweat and look like a clammy mess.

Edele's wearing baggy blue jeans with a dark grey jumper, her hair scraped back into a messy bun, while Nat's hair is loose and wavy with a fluffy black coat thrown over black jeans and a striped sweatshirt.

Edele bounces up to me and leans over to kiss my cheek, saying, 'Hey, Al, I'm just going to grab me and Nat a drink, you want another G&T?'

I tell her I'm fine as she swaps places with Nat, walking over to the bar.

'Hello, darling,' I say, pulling Nat in close for a hug. I haven't seen her since I helped her get ready for her date with Lawrence, and she told me on the phone a couple of days later about kicking him out in the morning.

She greets me and kisses me on the cheek before sitting on one end of the sofa opposite me. We talk briefly

130

about our days at work, me telling the story of my Year 10s falling asleep, her saying how someone's expired salad in the fridge almost caused an office-wide exodus due to the smell.

'Have you heard from Lawrence?' I ask.

'Well, it's been eleven days since our date,' Nat says, 'you know he texted me the next day asking if I was okay? I was just really honest with him, and said it was nothing to do with him, and that I'm recently out a long-term relationship and thought I was ready, but clearly I wasn't.'

'What did he say about that?'

'He was really nice about it, actually,' she says, rubbing her right hand over her left and looking down. She raises her eyebrow slightly and her expression is solemn. 'He was glad I was honest and said it was a shame, because he really enjoyed our date, but that he understood.'

Edele walks over then, placing a glass of white wine on the table in front of Nat and sitting down next to her, holding a pint of lager.

'He sounds like a decent guy,' I say.

'Yeah, the one time you actually want a guy to be a prick, and he turns out to be one of the good ones,' Edele adds, shaking her head. 'What are the chances?'

'Cheers, Ed, very helpful,' Nat smiles, rolling her eyes.

'You never know,' I add, 'when you're ready, you and he might be able to pick up where you left off.'

Nat shrugs. 'I suppose. But what if I'm never ready? Realistically, I know I'm going to be happy again, but what if I just don't get over this? What if I stay in love with Matt for ever?'

'You won't,' I say. 'You need to try not to think like that, Nat.'

'Al's right,' Edele adds. 'And you know, there may be a part of you that will always love Matt, and I don't think there's anything wrong with that. Because you were together so long, you may always keep a tiny bit of your heart reserved for him; for the relationship and the happiness you two shared. But try not to be afraid of it. The things that'll go with time are the pain and the longing and how desperately you're missing him.' She reaches her arm over the sofa to stroke Nat's knee. 'And they're the worst parts, the fucking awful parts, and they will ease, eventually. I promise you.'

Nat's lip shudders and she nods her understanding so that she doesn't have to speak, wiping her eyes with the back of her hands. The skin around her eyes turns red. It's a good thing she's not wearing any make-up.

'Christ, Ed, when did you get so wise?' I say.

'I know, she should be a shrink, shouldn't she?' Nat says as Edele sips her drink. She laughs loudly at Nat's remark, a perfect line of white foam from the head of her beer perching on her upper lip.

'Seriously? I may be able to dish it out, but I've never learnt how to take my own advice,' she laughs. 'Maybe the day I start listening to my inner adult will be the day I actually grow up. Or maybe I'm destined to be Peter Pan and never grow up. Suits me fine, to be honest.'

'Don't do it,' I say, 'never grow up, I've heard it's boring.'

'Anyway, what's going on with Craig?' Nat asks. The old beat of panic rises up again at the mention of his name, the conversation about Nat providing temporary distraction.

'I don't know. There's something going on.' I pause, not quite knowing how best to explain it. The girls sit quietly, waiting for me to elaborate.

'I think he's having an affair,' I say eventually.

'What?' they both exclaim at the same time.

'Surely not,' Nat says, 'what makes you say that?'

'He's acting distant, hiding his phone from me, making secret calls, and running off from the pub.'

'Where's he gone?' Edele asks.

'I don't know, he got a phone call then had to leave straight away.'

'I'm sure you're just reading into it too much, it was probably just work.'

'But why wouldn't he tell me if it was work?'

'I don't know, but it's Craig, Al. He wouldn't hurt you like that.'

'We would've said the same about Matt though, and look what he did.'

The words leave my mouth before I have time to properly consider them. Nat's face hardens and she folds her arms across her chest, shifting her position on the sofa in discomfort.

'Shit, I'm sorry, Nat,' I say quickly. 'I didn't think.'

'Don't worry,' she shakes her head. 'You're right, of course you're going to think like that. But Craig is not Matt. He's kinder, stronger. If there was something wrong he'd have the balls to talk to you about it, rather than taking the easy route out like a coward.'

'She's right,' Edele asserts. 'Have you actually tried talking to him?'

'Every time I ask him if he's okay, he just shrugs it off by saying he's tired or that work's been stressful.'

'He's probably telling the truth. But it sounds like you need to talk to him properly.'

There's a logical part of my thoughts that knows the girls are right. I trust Craig; he's nearly thirty years old, he's loyal and honest and he loves me. But he's also never acted like this before.

'Yeah, you're probably right. How's the job hunt going, Ed?' I don't want to talk about Craig any more, and I would like to distract Nat from the comment I just made about Matt.

'It's not,' she laughs, holding the lager to her lips and drinking. 'I'm in a bit of a rut with it. I don't know. I just haven't seen anything I like the look of, I guess.'

'It's getting a job, not choosing a new sofa,' Nat says humorously, but with a serious intent. 'Have you considered settling for something you're not one hundred per cent keen on, just temporarily, while you look for something better?'

'Maybe.' Edele shrugs. 'I guess I just thought, what's the point in a job if it doesn't make you happy?'

'Money? Security? Independence?'

'Yeah, all right,' she laughs, rolling her eyes.

'Nat's right,' I say, 'but you should also make sure it's something that will make you happy, too. We should dedicate a day to it one Sunday or something. We could all take our laptops into town and help you search for jobs.'

'That'd be nice,' she replies. 'But what if we don't find anything?'

'Then you'll have to finally resort to being a Hackton hooker,' Nat says.

'Yes.' Edele slowly nods. 'My one true calling.'

Natasha, Edele and I finish our drinks and decide to go back to Nat's and order a takeaway. 'I'm basically balling right now because Mum gave me twenty quid earlier for helping her clean out the garage, like getting pocket money for doing chores when you're twelve,' Edele said.

It's dark outside now and we cross the road, turn down a small alleyway and take a left on the high street, away from the seafront. Nat's flat is only ten minutes away. As we walk, it strikes me that there's a surprising amount of people in town for a cold Wednesday evening. Before we turn right onto one of the narrow cobbled streets full of old shops, a shiny purple balloon floating overhead catches my eye. There's a crying toddler in a pram further down the street, clutching aimlessly at the air and watching the balloon make its escape into the sky.

I look down from the disappearing balloon, towards the cobbled street in front of us. Suddenly I freeze, my breath catching in my throat. I grab Nat and Edele by their clothes and pull them to the right, behind a wall, so that we can't be seen.

'Move!' I demand under my breath.

'What are you doing?' Edele shrieks.

'Ssh!' I say. 'Look there, it's Craig! What is he doing?!' My heart is thumping so hard that it feels like it might burst out my chest.

Craig is standing with his back to us and holding a bottle of wine in one hand. He's talking to someone.

'Al, why are we hiding? This is—'

'Who's he talking to?' I hiss, ignoring Nat's question.

That's when Craig hugs the person he's talking to, and I squint through the darkness to try and make out the face resting on his shoulder.

'That's Gemma, she works with Craig! I was out for dinner with them and two of Craig's other mates from work last week!'

After they finish embracing, Craig hands the bottle of wine to Gemma and rests his hand on her arm for a moment. I can just about see her smiling at him. Then they walk to the end of the street before departing in different directions.

'What the hell was that?' I say loudly, facing the girls and stepping back out onto the street.

'Don't worry, Al! I'm sure there's a reasonable explanation,' Nat says.

'But what? Why would he need to run off on me like that to meet his *colleague*? And what was with the intimate hug? And the bottle of wine?'

My heart is pounding even harder now and I can't stand still, walking a few paces and then stopping. Different thoughts are hammering at my brain at lightning speed and I can't decipher any of them. I reach into my bag and start rolling a cigarette.

'I don't know, but I agree he's being shady as fuck,' Edele says.

'Not helping,' Nat says to Ed quietly, looking at her and widening her eyes in exasperation.

'I mean, he's left her and is walking towards your place, so get that thought out of your head immediately,' Edele quickly adds.

'What thought?' I ask.

'That they're going home to have sex.'

'I swear, Edele Marie, one of these days I'm going to strangle you,' Nat growls.

'I'm only messing! Of course they're not having an affair, Al, it's Craig! She probably just did him a solid at work and he's bought her a cheap bottle of shitty wine to say thanks.'

'Coming from the woman who thinks all men are trash!' I shout, exhaling smoke. I'm suddenly ice cold and my knees are quivering. My fingers are struggling to hold my cigarette.

'I mean, I do think that most of the time,' she says, but quickly adds, 'But I don't think Craig is trash. I think Craig is one of the good ones. And yes, he's being shady, but there will be a reason why. I just think you need to talk to him.'

'Whatever.' I don't mean this to seem as cutting as it sounds, but my mind can't process anything right now.

'Come on, Al,' Nat says, starting to walk down the street. 'Let's get you out of the cold, I can see you shaking.'

We walk in silence for a few minutes as I smoke, and I can tell neither Natasha nor Edele know what to say.

'Shall I text him?'

'No, Al, don't text him,' Nat says. 'You'll look insane.'

'Why is it that women always have to worry about "looking insane"? When do you reckon a man last advised his mate not to do something for a fear of a woman thinking him "crazy" or "insane"?'

'Fair,' Nat says, 'but just don't do it. Wait until you calm down a bit, yeah?'

'Okay.'

One or two minutes pass in agonising silence as we continue walking. I've finished my cigarette, so there's nothing physical to keep my mind occupied. I pull my phone from my pocket and go to text Craig anyway.

ALEX: Hey, are you home yet? Everything okay? x

'Alex, what're you doing?'

'I'm just texting to ask if everything's okay.'

'Nat's right; I'd leave it a bit, if I were you,' Edele says.

'I know you're probably right, but I need to say something, otherwise I'm just going to keep freaking out.' When you're so racked with anxiety, sometimes even the soundest of advice can't penetrate your brain. I send the message then look at it, presented in its irrevocable permanent box, and think, 'Maybe I should've listened.'

We're soon back at Nat's and she's ordering us Thai food from an app on her phone. I said I wasn't hungry, but Nat said, 'You're eating, Al,' so I just said 'Okay' and asked for a tom yum soup. 'That's the kind of thing Mackie would order,' Edele said. We laughed.

'It looks so good in here, Nat,' I remark as we walk into the living room. 'It's so clean . . . wait, have you had a clear out? It looks really different.'

'Yeah,' she says, 'Mack and Ed helped me do it the other day.'

'When?'

'Umm, last Sunday. You were busy with Craig's family or something?'

'Oh, right.'

It may be because of the weighty anxiety that's been clinging to me all day, but this – not being with them for something so important to Nat – makes me suddenly feel distant from three of the most important people in my life, and I feel immediately angry at Craig for being the reason that I wasn't there, even though that's completely nonsensical.

'We just de-Matt-ified the place, rearranged a few bits and bought a new Frank,' Edele smiles, perhaps sensing my disappointment. She leaves the living room and I hear her walk into the kitchen.

'It looks great, Nat,' I say. 'I just wish I'd been here.'

'Don't be silly, you were busy,' Nat says, flopping down on the sofa and flicking the TV on.

'Yeah,' I say with a cracked voice, 'but if I'd known I would've changed my plans. I would've much rather been here with you, to help.'

'Al, it's really not a big deal. I wouldn't have wanted you to bail on Craig's family just to come and help me tidy my flat, okay?'

She's just trying to make me feel better, but I know it was much more significant than simply 'tidying the flat'.

'Okay,' I reply, trying to mask how slighted I feel. 'Do you feel better for it?'

'So much better. I guess it's starting to feel more like my place, rather than mine and Matt's.'

She switches to one of the movie channels, which is showing *Forrest Gump*. It's the anti-war rally scene, where Forrest and Jenny both jump into the Lincoln Memorial Reflecting Pool to greet each other. The crowd is cheering as they embrace.

'That's great,' I tell her. 'You deserve to be happy.'

'Thanks,' she says weakly, and I suddenly feel incredibly stupid for what I've just said. Of course she's not happy. I can almost hear her replying in her head – '"Happy" is a bit of a stretch, Al' – though she wouldn't say it for fear of the gravity of what she's saying.

Edele comes back into the living room then and sits in the middle of the sofa between Nat and I, placing three glasses of water on the coffee table.

'Right, let's see this Gemma bird then,' she says, opening Instagram on her phone. 'What's her surname, Al?'

I consider this for a moment, picking up the glass from the table and drinking. The water is slightly warm. As much as I want to look through Gemma's Instagram, I've also learnt that nothing good is ever gained from social-media stalking. I will likely just be left with battered self-esteem and a slightly mangled sense of identity, wondering why I'm not the kind of person who eats homemade açaí bowls and takes mirror selfies in front of the weights area at the gym.

'No, let's leave it. Can we just chill and watch a film?'

I'm conscious of how left out I've been feeling, and if I want to reconnect with my friends then this is the way to do it, not analysing Gemma's photos.

'Sure,' Edele says, locking her phone and resting it between our legs on the sofa.

With that, a message flashes up on my phone. It's Craig.

CRAIG EDGEWORTH ❤: Yeah I'm home now, sorry I had to run off like that. Where are you?

ALEX: I'm at Nat's.

CRAIG EDGEWORTH ❤: Okay. Everything all right with you?

ALEX: Yes, why wouldn't it be?

CRAIG EDGEWORTH ❤: I don't know, you just seem off. Look, I'm really sorry for dashing out of the pub earlier, but it couldn't wait. I had to pick something up.

ALEX: YEAH, A GIRL FROM WORK, YOU DIRTY CHEATING BASTARD. (*Delete before sending. Probably not smart.*) Yeah, it's cool, I'm fine. We're just getting Thai food and it's getting late, so I might just stay here the night and ask Nat to drop me off at work in the morning.

CRAIG EDGEWORTH ❤: Sure, will miss you though. Have fun. Love you x

ALEX: You too x

'Nat, is it cool if I stay the night and you drop me at work in the morning?'

'Yeah, of course. Don't you want to see Craig tonight?'

'I think it's probably best if I calm down first, then I can see him tomorrow and think about what to say. I just want a bit of space.'

'What do you want to say?'

I pause for a moment, thinking. There's a hard throbbing in my head.

'I want to ask him what's gone wrong; where we've gone wrong. What's happened to make him withdraw so much into himself, so far away from me. And what I can do to fix it. How can I get him back?'

'And you have no idea what it is that's wrong with him?' Nat asks. There's an uncomfortable pressure behind my eyes and I run my fingers over the dry cracks that have settled in my lower lip.

'No. And that's what's driving me mad and making me so irrational. If I don't know what's wrong, I can't begin to fix it. I'm always the one who fixes things. I don't have relationship drama. Craig and I are supposed to be secure, reliable, solid – I mean, I know we need to inject some excitement into our sex life, but that's natural after so many years, right? What if that's the problem? He's bored of our sex life? What if it's driven him to cheating?'

My mouth and tongue and throat are dry and my voice sounds withered. I drink two big gulps of lukewarm water.

'Well, do you trust him?' Edele asks.

'Yeah. Well, I thought I did. Maybe I don't anymore.'
Then I pause again. 'I guess I don't trust that he's immune from getting bored of me.'

Natasha and Edele instantly scold me for being 'ridiculous', and tell me that no one could ever get bored of someone as 'smart and quirky' as me; that I'm 'one of a kind'. I thank them and say it sounds as though they're describing a set of antique dining chairs for sale on eBay.

I just can't shake the thought that Craig might be losing interest in me; in us. The idea swells violently in my brain like a migraine. I think of him gradually growing tired of us, bored of our sex life and the home we've made together, of me nagging him about the bins and talking about the Russian Revolution and going to the same pub after work, of ordering the same drinks, buying the same packet of crisps, the same bottle of wine. The same flat, the same girlfriend, the same life. Who wouldn't get bored of that? And that – the irremediable, heavy, binding consequences of boredom – is something even I can't fix. The thought makes me feel sick and there's a kind of tingling in my fingers. I lean forward on the sofa and let my hands take the weight of my head.

'What's wrong?' Natasha asks.

'I don't know. I feel weird.'

'You've gone kind of white.'

'I'm fine.'

Natasha takes my hand in hers and tells me it feels damp. I can't breathe right.

'Do you feel faint?'

'A little, just . . . a little light-headed.'

Edele and Natasha instruct me to put my head between my knees and one of them strokes my back slowly. I can't tell which one it is. I close my eyes and try not to focus on the bright, sharp shapes jumping and jabbing at my vision.

'It's okay, I'm okay now,' I say after a few moments. I can hear the pathetic heaving of my own breath.

'You need to eat,' Edele says, signalling to Nat to hand over her phone. 'The takeaway guy's nearly here, according to the app. I'll go wait downstairs.'

She walks out of the living room and I hear the flat door shut behind her. It must have been her stroking my back because the stroking has stopped now.

Natasha rests the back of her hand momentarily against my forehead and, without saying anything, picks up a grey throw and wraps it around my body. She squeezes my shoulder lightly and says, 'Stay here.' I lie down and lean my head against the arm of the sofa. My eyes are getting heavy and the shapes have eased in my vision.

Only a small amount of time has passed when I wake up because the soup I ordered is on the table in front of the sofa and there's still steam whirling from the pot. There's something soft and warm pressing against my side.

'I got you a hot water bottle,' Nat says. She and Edele are eating pad thai with chopsticks. The smells of lemongrass and nut oil and sweet spices are filling the room. Forrest now has a very long beard and is, for some reason, running across the US. He looks really tired. I'm really tired.

Nat's holding my arm gently now, which makes me feel warm and peaceful. 'We'll all be fine, I know we will,' Edele says. I don't know or can't remember what they're talking about, but I feel an almost primal kind of safety surrounded by them, as though I'm a small, fragile baby bird kept warm by its siblings in the nest. I close my eyes.

CHAPTER EIGHT

Mackie

I've just finished scouring my kitchen sink and the thick smell of bleach is infiltrating my nostrils, heavy like a hangover. The window is open for ventilation, leaking pale light and a cold sea breeze into the room. Outside, a man in a suit walks out of the cafe opposite holding a reusable purple cup, and a delivery van is pulling up in front of the flats over the road. The washing machine is spinning aggressively under the countertop, just five minutes remaining before I hang my clean bed sheets on the heated dryer, and I can feel its vibrations pulsating through my feet.

I reach for a bag of peppermint tea and sit at the kitchen table, waiting for the kettle to boil. The scent of pomegranate and plum waft into the kitchen from the candle I lit in the hallway.

I'm twisting the string of the teabag around my index finger, not focusing on anything in particular, when the email alert sounds from my laptop perched on the countertop.

I wipe my hands on my apron, being careful not to get cleaning fluid on the keyboard, and open my inbox. As I read, a car horn sounds loudly and long from outside the window, making my body jolt.

From: recruitment@forwardnewspapers.co.uk
To: emma.mackie@gmail.com
Subject: RE: Art Director Role
Date: 05/03/19

Dear Emma,
Many thanks for your application for the role: ART DIRECTOR at the Forward Newspapers Group.

As you can imagine, we received a large number of applications. Unfortunately, you have not been selected to progress further for this position.

We would like to thank you for your time in attending an interview and for your interest in working for the company. We encourage you to apply for any future openings for which you qualify.

Best wishes,
FNG Recruitment

I close the lid of my laptop and lean out of the window, drinking in the air. This is the third job vacancy I've been unsuccessful for in the last few weeks – another told me they opted for someone with more experience the day after my interview, and the other never responded to my application, though I saw that they filled the position online.

The rejection makes me feel flat and dispirited, rather than tearful and upset. Even though its presence in my inbox means that I can tick one more application off my list, it feels as though it raises more questions than it answers. Those questions being, 'What did you think was lacking in my application?', 'Why have I worked so consistently hard all my life if rejection will just keep looming over me?', and the biggest of all, *'Why am I not good enough?'*

Twinges of frustration shoot through my limbs as the kettle pings off the boil and I pour the boiling water into the mug, which masks the smell of bleach with crisp peppermint. I'm disheartened but I am also embarrassed because I shouldn't be feeling like an inexperienced, inadequate work experience student who's desperate just to fill up one page of their CV. Not at my age.

The rejection doesn't exactly surprise me. I was qualified for the role and I'm good at what I do, but I completely lose myself in job interviews. I wouldn't say I'm an anxious person, but as soon as I'm in front of my potential employers trying to convince them how professionally capable and socially competent I am, all my supposed capability and competency leaves me extremely abruptly, like a Tinder date who's not over his ex. Edele calls this the 'Edele effect', because she says that I morph into her during job interviews. She's not exactly wrong.

In my interview with the Forward Newspapers Group, I got a serious case of word vomit and made some very untoward comments. I could email and ask for feedback, though it would probably read something like this:

From: emma.mackie@gmail.com
To: recruitment@forwardnewspapers.co.uk
Subject: RE: 'Your application'
Date: 05/03/19

Dear FNG Recruitment,
Thank you for your email. I would very much appreciate any feedback you can provide on my interview, so that I can use it going forward. Is it perhaps any of the following that let me down?

1. The fact that I referred to you as the 'Yard Newspapers Group', which is an entirely different word to 'Forward'. Probably not a good thing that you had to remind of the name of the company for which I was interviewing.
2. When you asked if I had proof of identity and I passed you my driving licence, saying: 'Sorry it's such a terrible photo; I look like a criminal. Which, by the way, I promise I'm not. Though it's not as bad as my friend Nat's driving licence photo – she has short black hair in hers and looks like Hitler . . . you know, if Hitler were young and female.' I'm assuming that someone you deem employable would not discuss Hitler in their interview.
3. That my answer to 'What would you describe as a successful day at work?' was: 'Meeting deadlines, instilling a happy and creative

149

work environment, and cake. Cake in the office is always a good day.' Then, when you asked, 'How do you cope with setbacks?' and I said, 'Personally or professionally? Actually, "cake" is pretty much the answer to both.' It was a joke, but I can see how jokes about cake were neither relevant nor appropriate.

I'd very much relish the opportunity to review your feedback, Hitler-related or otherwise.

Yours democratically,
Emma Mackie.

Yeah, I probably just won't respond.

The watch on my wrist says 10:12 a.m. Nat says that wearing a watch makes me an 'old soul', because 'when was the last time you saw someone under fifty wearing a wrist watch?' But I think there's something sophisticated about telling the time using an actual clock face, rather than a phone screen. Perhaps that makes me pretentious. In fact, it almost certainly does.

I have eighteen minutes until my Skype interview. I'm pleased that I booked today off work so that I wasn't distracted before the interview, but now all I can think about is that terrible interview with Forward. But at least this interview isn't in person, which means I'll hopefully be more relaxed, and they can't ask to look at my driving licence, which means I won't risk talking about Hitler.

And I've written the name of the company – Atlas Media – in red pen at the top of my notebook so that I don't forget.

'The rejection is a setback,' I tell myself, holding the mug of tea close to my face so I can feel the heat of the steam against my mouth and my nose. 'But you've got to channel it and use it to spur you on. This one will be different.'

MACKIE: Girls, I didn't get that job at Forward, and my Skype interview with the editor of Atlas Media is in 15. I'm having a minor freak-out and need to put make-up on, which you all know I'm not very good at. And I have a massive spot on my chin.

NATASHA: That sucks, Mack. 100% their loss though. Try to forget about that and focus on your Atlas interview for now. I know you can do this.

EDELE: Fuck 'em. They're fools for not taking you on. Just whack some concealer on that spot and go into that Skype remembering how amazing you are at what you do.

ALEX: So sorry to hear that, darling. As these guys said, they're the ones missing out on a talented art director, so try to forget about it and put it down to experience. You don't need make-up at all, but if you want to, I'd advise some red lippy (my go-to for a confidence boost!)

EDELE: Who invited Lisa Eldridge?

NATASHA: Just don't over-line your lips like I do. You end up looking like Pennywise.

ALEX: I could be the next Lisa Eldridge I'll have you know.

EDELE: If Lisa Eldridge smoked a pack a day and had to laser her chin hair.

ALEX: I do not smoke a pack a day and I'm half-Indian; genetically we have very persistent body hair. You're basically being racist. And just imagine the shit you'd give me if I let my beard grow.

This is why I message the girls as soon as I feel apprehensive. Even though I'm so often the one to offer counsel, the one who has the answers and has everything figured out, they know it's not permanent. They know that, no matter how many to-do lists I write, how many spin classes I attend or how many superfood stews I cook for the week, there's still an undeniable insecurity that comes with being a woman in your twenties. At work, you're told you're too inexperienced or too young for a promotion or new job, but then they appoint a young man with less experience than you. You feel fit and healthy, until you see someone else's workout routine or marathon medal online, and suddenly your fifteen-minute jog feels as though it may as well have been a pancake-eating competition. You're flooded with that raw excitement after a talk-all-night date, until the guy messages you a week later to say he's 'not feeling it right now', and then your love life feels like one big, draining waste of your time. Nothing seems concrete, and absolutely everything feels ephemeral. But these people – my closest friends – they are my constant. And I remind myself how lucky I am to have them every day.

MACKIE: Thank you, you total idiots. I'm going to put on some red lipstick, read over my pre-interview notes and company research and try and stay calm before the interview x

NATASHA: You've got this, Wonder Woman. Just remember: don't Pennywise your lips, and don't talk about Hitler this time.

EDELE: OH MY GOD I forgot about the Hitler picture.

NATASHA: Piss off, Ed

EDELE: But seriously, knock 'em dead, Marshall.

ALEX: Good luck, Mack! Will keep everything crossed for you.

I spend the next five minutes sitting still, practising a mindfulness exercise to sharpen my attention span and focus my mind. I drop my chin a little and focus on the air flowing in and out of my nose, and the rise and fall of my stomach with it. I feel calmer and more confident now that I'm not dwelling on the rejection email. I read over my notes and research before sweeping two coats of mascara over my eyelashes, pinning back my hair and applying my only red lipstick. It's a sort of bright orange-red and, looking in the mirror, I realise it's more of a 'going to a bar on a balmy summer evening' type of lipstick colour, rather than 'webcam job interview'. But it's already on, so it'll have to do.

I throw on the white satin blouse that I ironed last night and hung on my wardrobe door. For optimum comfort, I'm wearing floral pink and yellow pyjama bottoms, but my webcam cuts off just below my boobs, so there's no chance of the Atlas editor seeing my pyjamas. I look in my bathroom mirror one last time, and run my fingers over the spot on my chin. Not only is it big and bulbous, but it's starting to hurt. I wonder why I'm suffering breakouts when I've been drinking at least eight glasses of water a day and eating so many leafy greens I'm practically turning into a spinach leaf.

'I don't need this kind of distraction during the interview,' I think as I press both my index fingers against the tiny red mountain on my chin. My eyes water as the mountain erupts and shoots white liquid over my bathroom mirror.

'Gross,' I mutter under my breath, wiping my chin quickly with a cotton pad and running a wet wipe over the mirror. I glance at my watch before hurrying to my laptop on the kitchen table, straightening my blouse and tucking my hair behind my ear. The mug of peppermint tea is still on the table, so I take a sip. It's still hot.

The tone of Skype's incoming call alert makes the hairs on my arm stand to attention. I answer. First, my face pops up in a box, soon followed by the face of a middle-aged man. His cheeks are round like a pink hairless chipmunk and his light-brown hair is short and thin with a slightly receding hairline. He's smiling. There's a faint, red flush to the skin on his nose.

'Hello, Emma? Can you hear me?'

'Hi, Duncan,' I say to my laptop. 'I can hear you, can you hear me okay?'

'Yes, I can hear you fine. Nice to meet you.'

'It's nice to meet you, too. Well, over Skype, anyway.'

'Yes, quite. How are you today?'

'I'm well, thank you. Just a bit fed up of this persistent rain. How are you?' I really need to improve my small-talk skills. His chipmunk cheeks squash into a polite smile.

'Yes, I'm good, thanks. So, let's dive straight in, shall we? What made you apply for the role of art director at Atlas?'

'Well,' I say, 'I've been at the *Hackton Times* for over six years now, and while I'm really proud of everything I've achieved there, I'm ready for a fresh challenge. And I've always admired the titles you have at Atlas.'

'Which ones in particular?'

'Umm,' I absolutely cannot have another mind-blank now. Deep breath. It's natural to pause before you speak, I tell myself. 'I read the in-flight *Swan Air* magazine in October and I really loved the graphic interpretation of the travel features. I think it's an aesthetic I'd fit really well into.'

'That's great, Emma. And what are your favourite parts of your current job at the *Hackton Times*?'

'There are a lot of things I like about my job,' I start, looking at my face in the small square box on my laptop screen to make sure I still look acceptable.

Something in the small square box makes me suddenly stop mid-speech. In the middle of my perfectly ironed white satin blouse is a very noticeable red splotch. It's blood. There's a big, bright red circle on my blouse from where I squeezed my spot, and I'm only just noticing it.

'Umm,' I say, feigning contemplation as much as possible while simultaneously trying to cover the blood on my blouse with my arm.

'I really enjoy managing my junior designer, Lucy.' I'm trying to subtly shift my laptop back on the table, so that I can rest my arm on the table and have it sort of hover over my chest, so that it covers the blood.

'Mmm-hmm,' Duncan nods. It's unnerving that I can't tell exactly what he's looking at. Has he seen the blood already?

'It's just very rewarding to guide her and see her fulfil her potential,' I add, still looking at myself in the square box and trying to appropriately adjust my position. 'And with regards to the magazine itself—'

My elbow nudges something hard on the table and there's a loud clinking sound, like two solid objects striking each other. Then there's something wet and warm in my lap like urine. For a very brief moment, I think, 'Have I pissed myself? Will I have to sit in my warm piss for the remainder of this job interview?' then I realise it's the peppermint tea. By adjusting my arm to cover the blood from the spot I squeezed on my blouse, I've knocked over my mug of tea and spilt it all down myself.

I jump back in my chair, focusing all my efforts on not swearing aloud, before I glance back at the laptop and realise that my pink and yellow floral pyjamas are on display.

'I'm so sorry,' I quickly exclaim, lurching forward on the chair so that only my top half is visible. Suddenly, the bloodstain doesn't seem as damning.

'Err,' Duncan's eyebrow is raised, causing deep lines to spread across the tall expanse of his forehead, which I'm guessing isn't a good sign. 'Are you all right?'

'I'm fine, thanks. I'm really sorry about that, I just accidentally spilt some tea down myself. I don't, umm . . . I don't normally wear this.'

'It's okay, Emma,' he says after a brief pause in which he was probably trying to process what's happening. But his tone is surprisingly reassuring, which helps to ease the toe-curling embarrassment I'm currently experiencing. 'We don't care about what you wear, as long as you're a good fit for our team and can do your job well.'

'Okay.'

'Would you like to carry on the interview, or did you want to get cleaned up?'

I glance at Duncan's sincere expression, then at the drying bloodstain, and then down at the sodden, minty patch on my lap.

'I can carry on,' I say. I assume this isn't exactly going well, so the chances of me getting this job are now laughably slim. Oh well, I can just expect a polite rejection email tomorrow. I look at the damp patch and almost feel like laughing, the muscles in my shoulders loosening. It's a bit like when you touch the kerb while parallel parking during your driving test and assume you've failed, so you relax and just get the examination over with.

'Great,' says Duncan. 'So, tell me about what you think you can bring to this role.'

'My excellent taste in pyjamas, tea-throwing skills and minty-smelling vagina' are the words that instantly zoom through my head, but I decide that's probably not a wise response.

CHAPTER NINE
Natasha

I have to fill out a questionnaire. I'm sitting at the kitchen table listening to the winter wind banging aggressively at the window, like a drunk punter who's been kicked out of a pub and is demanding to be let back in.

I woke up early again this morning. I can't remember what time it was but it was still dark outside and, smoking a cigarette out of my kitchen window, there was that kind of eerie stillness before the rest of the world wakes up. The water in the shower was too hot and my skin was too cold, which made my whole body tingle. I pulled on my loose, faded grey jeans and navy blue jumper, the cheap wool on which is starting to bobble slightly, and began to tidy the flat. By the time I'd finished, the rooms smelled different – of fresh air, clean laundry and newness. I didn't have an appetite until after I'd finished, and even then it was small. Nevertheless, it was there. I ate a bowl of cereal with a cup of coffee – the coffee Mackie brought round – with a heaped spoonful of sugar. Then I took the printed out questionnaire from a plastic wallet in my bag and placed it on the kitchen table and, in doing so, felt a new sense of control, as though I were finally taking charge of some small thing.

Now, I start filling out my demographic information at the beginning of the questionnaire, but on the very first section – my title, first name, surname, date of birth and NHS number – my black biro runs out of ink, so I have to trace over the fading words with a new ballpoint pen.

Well, this is a good start. You already look like the kind of organised adult who keeps empty pens.

Turning the page, I now have to circle a number that best describes how often I have been affected by a certain problem over the last two weeks, with 0 being 'not at all', 1 being 'several days', 2 being 'more than half the days' and 3 being 'nearly every day'.

Little interest or pleasure in doing things   0   1   2   3

The inexactness of this statement strikes me as odd, or perhaps it's deliberate. I don't think most normal people derive noticeable pleasure from 'doing things', like taking a shower or going food shopping. If we did find these 'things' pleasurable, it would make it near-impossible to find any kind of worthwhile pleasure in activities that are actually designed to be pleasurable. I think back to what I did yesterday. I washed my hair, went to work, came home, ignored a council tax reminder letter, drank whisky, washed my bed sheets, tried (failed) to turn my mattress because apparently that's a thing you're sup-posed to do, spent half an hour lying completely motion-less on the roof, then fell asleep to a documentary about some serial killers in Ohio or something. It was a Friday, exactly eight weeks A.M. ('After Matt'). That's how I think of my life now: before and after 12 January. Two realities completely distinct: the Natasha of one completely unrecognisable to the other. I circle 2 and move on.

Feeling down, depressed, or hopeless   0   1   2   3

The last word triggers a prickling sensation in the tips of my fingers and my lips feel dry. Hopeless. I run my tongue over the ridges on the roof of my mouth. I do not know how to quantify the regularity of feeling hopeless – or down or depressed, for that matter. Because that feeling never fully leaves, but rather, it hangs overhead, sometimes pressing down with greater pressure on your skull than usual, while other times, you can barely feel it. But still, you know it's there. I think that means I have to circle 3.

I wouldn't, if I were you. You don't want to sound too unhinged. Or, you know, reveal how unhinged you truly are.

I circle 2 instead.

Thoughts that you would be better off dead
or of hurting yourself in some way   0   1   2   3

I rest my pen against my mouth and look up at the doorway to the kitchen. I can still see Matt standing there, then walking towards the open window. 'Nat, come in, it's fucking January and you're only wearing a T-shirt.'

The drunk wind bangs loudly at the window and I swallow hard against my brittle throat. I don't want to alarm the stranger who will receive this questionnaire by saying that I would like to kill myself. Last night, when I was lying on the roof, I let the skin on my arms go numb in the cold and thought about what it would be like to take off all my clothes and lie there until I froze to death. How long would that take? Would it even be possible? How cold does it have to be and how long does the human body need to be exposed to it for the heart to give up? Who would find me? Ms Harris? Edele? Someone in the neighbouring buildings, opening the curtains in the morning to see a half-white, half-blue naked body on a rooftop, completely motionless, eyes open but no longer there? I wouldn't care because I'd be dead.

I don't know which way I would prefer to die; freezing or burning. I've always preferred the heat. Last week, when I was drunk and alone, I extinguished a cigarette against the skin on my stomach. I don't know why I did it, but it felt just – as though I were so execrable that burning a small circle into my skin was somehow retribution. I remove the pen from my mouth and circle 1, inhaling deeply as I do so.

Feeling bad about yourself – or that you are a
failure   or   have   let   yourself   or   your   family
down.   0   1   2   3

This is the only statement that ends in a period, which makes it feel particularly weighty and final, even though

162

it's not the last on the list or by any means more weighty than: 'Thoughts that you would be better off dead'. I think most people who get dumped feel bad about themselves, because it makes you feel as if you're incapable of being loved; that you're an unlovable person, which means you've seriously screwed up the development of your personality somewhere along the line. That also makes you feel like a failure, because you've failed at your own basic human function – to be desirable for a 'mate', so that you can reproduce, or some sort of animal kingdom bullshit like that. My gaze lingers over the word 'family'. I know my parents worry about me, and my mum grows frustrated when I don't open up to her. It's not that I can't talk to her about how I'm feeling; it's that I don't want to worry her. But apparently it's having the opposite effect, and my bottling up is worrying her even more. As I draw a small circle around the number 2, I realise I'm not protecting her at all. That's failure.

You are a failure.

It was Edele's idea to refer myself for therapy. She stayed over earlier in the week, and when we were getting ready for bed, she saw the burn mark from the cigarette on my stomach. She asked me what it was and I told her. I explained that I was smoking and, when the tobacco was almost all burnt, I just decided to put it out on my skin and I almost didn't realise I was doing it. It was as though I was acting on impulse, in a daze, loathsome and desperate. I was worried all I could feel was self-loathing but this made me feel something else. It felt like relief and it felt real and it felt like retribution. It felt like what I deserved.

'You're going through a lot right now. Do you think it might be a good idea to see someone?' she'd said.

'I don't know about that, Ed,' I'd replied.

'Why not?'

'I don't know. Why am I not allowed to just try and forget about it? It seems weird to me that something bad happens to someone, and all anyone wants to do is keep banging on about it.'

'It's not like that, and you know it. They have methods, you know, strategies, to help you sort through shit in your own head. Just trying to forget about something – burying it – ain't good enough.'

'Do you honestly think it would help?' I'd asked her, 'did it help you after your dad died?'

'I suppose, yes,' she'd replied. Then she'd paused before saying, 'It doesn't, you know, cure you, or whatever, but it can help you cope. And I think that makes it worth trying.'

I'd told her that I'd feel ridiculous, saying that I need help to cope with a break-up, that I'd sound like a teenager.

'That's not fair,' she'd said. 'You're grieving, just as anyone would. In my old job – the toothpaste one – this girl at work got compassionate leave when her pet fucking rabbit died. If that's a sanctioned form of grief, then getting your heart broken out of nowhere, after seven years, most certainly is.'

I printed out the self-referral form for our local Improving Access to Psychological Therapies service the next morning.

The last page of the six-page form is mostly one big, empty box, with the heading over a blue background: 'Please let us know what you are hoping to gain from our service'. I try to think back a few weeks and months, to life before 12 January, and years, to life before Matt. I've always struggled with self-esteem, I think, just like I thought everyone else did, so maybe I should have done this sooner. Before it got too much, went too far. I listen for the voice, in case it decides to say anything remotely insightful or helpful. But it's sitting this one out.

'I want to feel worthy,' I write eventually. 'I have wonderful friends and family, and I believe that they love me, but somehow I still feel unlovable. And I feel desperately lonely, even though I'm not alone. I want to learn how to like myself'. I pause before automatically adding on the word 'again'. I decide against it, instead writing, 'Because I'm not sure I ever knew how to.'

When I've finished the questionnaire, I hold the sheets of paper limply in my hand. My head feels leaden with weariness and my arms are limp, as if I've just run a marathon without actually moving. I fold them and place them carefully in the IAPT services free-post envelope. I don't know what to expect, I think as I seal the envelope, handing over this sensitive information to a stranger. I've never shared this with anyone, not even the girls. I wonder who the stranger is who will be reading this extremely private material, and what conclusions they will draw from my form. Will it be a man or a woman? Young or old? Single, married, divorced? How will that influence what they think of me? Really, I decide, it doesn't matter.

I think about what will happen next. At the end of the form was this paragraph:

'Once we receive your referral we will send a letter confirming receipt. Your referral will be screened and we will either then place you on our waiting list or sign-post you to a more appropriate service. A member of your local team will contact you and arrange a time to meet and assess your needs.'

My 'needs' makes it sound as though I'm physically incapacitated: a paraplegic patient who needs a wheel-chair or a whiplash sufferer who needs a cervical collar. This makes me feel small and guilty and I no longer want to be in possession of this letter full of intensely personal information. I pull a zip-up hoody over my bobbly navy jumper followed by a coat, and lace-up boots over my thick socks.

Out of the front door, there's no noise coming from Diane's flat. I haven't seen or heard from her since I took some lemon drizzle cake and chocolate chip cookies round on the day Mackie and Edele helped me clear Matt from the flat. That was a month ago.

'So good to see you baking again, sweet, and with more colour in your face,' she had said, smiling her wel-coming, sunny smile as we walked into her flat.

'Hi, Ms Harris,' Edele and Mackie greeted her. Edele always tries to make herself sound posher in the company of people she doesn't know very well, enunciating her Ts and drawing out her As. It makes me feel like laughing.

'Oh, yes, the sweet, skinny blonde and the very loud Irish girl,' Diane said. We all laughed. She offered us sherry, but realising we'd already had quite a lot of amaretto and needed to go the charity shop shortly, we declined.

'Suit yourselves,' she said, as she poured some of the crimson liquid into an ornate sherry glass and disappeared into the kitchen to make us a pot of tea instead.

'Sherry!' Edele giggled in a hushed voice once Diane had left the room. 'She really is Dot Cotton!'

We arranged ourselves on her dusky-green sofa and I glanced around the room. It had been months since I had been in Diane's flat, and that time Matt was with me. I'd forgotten how warm and comfortable it made me feel. There were framed photos on every available surface: beaming faces of her with her mother and sister as young girls in black and white; of her with her late husband Ted on holiday in Spain; of her son Josh as a child, and now as a grown man. There's also a very small, square photo of a terrier puppy. His name was Max, and he died a year ago. Diane was devastated. It makes my heart hurt every time I see it.

When she eventually emerged from the kitchen, carrying a tray with four delicate, floral cups of milky tea, we cut four slices of lemon drizzle cake. We talked about the cold weather, how sad it is that the local florist is closing down, and about clearing the flat out.

'I'm so pleased,' Diane said, looking at me. 'You must start to live your life for you now.'

Outside Diane's front door, I think about knocking to make sure she's okay, but it's still relatively early on a Saturday morning so I decide against it.

The post box isn't far from my flat. The ground is wet and the sky is heavy and ashen, but it's stopped raining so I leave my hood hanging over the back of my coat. There's a brief moment of rest in the wind's aggression, so I take the opportunity to cup my hand around the lower part of my face and light a cigarette, inhaling deeply.

As I drop the envelope through the letterbox, I feel a strange mix of relief and fear. I'm pleased to no longer be holding the flimsy, seemingly trivial pieces of paper, which in fact house my darkest, most private secrets. But the thought that I can't take it back, rip open the envelope, change my words, or just put my lighter to the whole thing and forget it ever existed, makes me feel anxious.

You know what's going to happen now? says the voice. *You're going to get sectioned. Those men in white coats are going to bust down your door, strap you into one of those harnesses so you can't move your arms, and drag you away to an asylum where you'll get lobotomised, like Jack Nicholson in* One Flew Over the Cuckoo's Nest, *and turn into a vegetable, then one of the girls will have to suffocate you with a pillow. You know, like Chief does in the movie before he escapes to Canada, or wherever.*

'Stop it,' I think, 'this isn't 1963. That's not going to happen. Plus, it takes a lot of courage to ask for help. It's not a sign of weakness, it's simply admitting that you're only one person, and that sometimes, you can't manage it all.'

Manage what? Being dumped? Stop being so pathetic. People get dumped every day. Who's got the time to sit around crying about it? Time to toughen up, Nat, and get over it.

'That's not fair,' I tell the voice, 'I'm being as tough as I can, but I just can't take it any more. I've got no fight left in me. I'm tired. I'm so tired.'

Try harder.

'Shut up,' I whisper under my breath, trying hard to ignore the faint tremble running down my neck and through my chest like a fine, cold rain against naked skin.

I cannot stand next to the letterbox talking aloud to the deafening voice in my head any more. I look around. There's no one about. Which, I figure, is a good thing, otherwise the men in white coats may well turn up and take me away. I start walking on the wet pavement, towards the nearest coffee shop, which is only a couple of minutes away. I'll get a strong, black coffee, maybe buy a magazine or newspaper, text the girls and see what they're up to today, and try to forget about the whole IAPT thing.

The coffee shop is small and the white paint around the entrance is old and chipping, but the bright pink chairs and striped awning outside make it seem more spirited. I peer through the windowpane and can see that it is busy with people inside. A bearded man holding a shopping bag holds the door open for a little girl wearing a pale yellow cardigan, allowing chatter and laughter to drift into the air, joining the sound of music from passing cars and a siren in the distance.

As I'm standing outside by the bright pink chairs finishing my cigarette, my phone vibrates in my pocket. I assume it's the Mean Girls group, making last-minute Saturday plans.

The cigarette falls from my mouth and onto the wet ground when I see the name. My limbs turn to ice and panic swells violently in my body. My vision sways and I have to re-focus on my phone screen.

MATT: Nat, are you free today? I need to see you. I'm sorry to spring this on you out of the blue, but we need to talk ASAP. Let me know x

We need to talk. The same words he used when he stood in the entrance to our flat the night he broke my heart, shattering it to tiny fragments. Suddenly, I find that I can't stand. I pull over a chair from one of the outside tables and fall onto it before my knees buckle. The anxiety drives me forward, and I don't think before replying.

NAT: Yes. I'm at the coffee shop by ours now, the one we used to come to on Sunday mornings. Can you meet me here?

I quickly read the message before sending and replace 'ours' with 'mine'. Then I press 'send'. His reply is quick.

MATT: I can be there in 20 mins, if that works? Thanks, Nat.

NAT: Sure. See you then.

I'm applauding myself for my use of the word 'sure' – sounds super chilled-out, like you just don't give a damn, and your body totally didn't almost go into ana-phylactic shock when you saw his name on your phone screen – when I suddenly remember what I look like, glancing down at myself. I'm not wearing a scrap of make-up and I forgot to put a bra on under my jumper, meaning I look like a middle-aged man with saggy tits.

You need to go home, change, and try and make yourself look less ugly. If he sees you looking like this, he'll thank his lucky stars that he chucked you in.

I rush home in an anxiety-clogged daze and run up the stairs to my flat, immediately pulling off my coat, hoody and jumper and rummaging through my underwear drawer for a bra. I'm looking for my favourite – a black push-up bra with eyelash lacing – when I stop.

Why are you bothering? What exactly do you think is the purpose of this meeting? To have sex in the coffee shop loos? Get real.

Giving up on the push-up lace, I instead fasten a plain white T-shirt bra around my back and loop my arms through, tucking the overspill of boob back into the cotton casings. This bra could easily be as old as Ms Harris's china teacups.

Next, I flick frantically through the hangers in my wardrobe, cursing myself for not mentally preparing an outfit for this scenario, on the off chance it ever happened. I pull out a loose-fitting red blouse covered with small white flowers.

Yeah, great. If you're seventeen years old and heading off to your first ever Glastonbury.

Okay, fine. I hold up a silky white blouse with sort-of arty, navy blotches.

This is more: 'Desperately trying to look smart and professional for work when you're actually just a college student studying History of Art.'

I throw the Glastonbury blouse and History of Art shirt into a pile on my bed, pulling on a plain black, high-neck knitted top.

Bit tight in the stomach region. Let's hope Matt doesn't notice your fat rolls when you sit down at the table.

'I don't have time for this,' I say aloud, deciding that the grey jeans will have to do, and that doing my make-up in five minutes is now my priority. I dash to my bathroom mirror where my make-up bag is perched on the edge of a shelf, and liberally dispense a few pumps of foundation on my fingers before rubbing it madly across my face like an excitable toddler with finger paints. The next steps in this urgent, military-style operation involve: covering the vast, deep blue bags under my eyes with piles of thick concealer, contouring for that 'sculpted facial structure and defined cheekbones' look with bronzer (but in reality, just making myself look as though I've overdone it on a sun bed), and attempting to open up my eyes with an indefinite amount of mascara.

Within ten minutes, I fly back out my front door and rush back to the coffee shop. I want to be there before him, and have time to order a coffee. I want to sit for a few minutes, just breathing, trying to calm down before he arrives.

Yeah, like that's ever going to happen.

He looks thinner than before, and it is so much more agonising to see him than anyone warned me it would be.

I imagine doing anything to avoid looking at him any longer; sprinting past him, head down, out of the door he is now approaching and running until I throw up, or smacking my head so hard against the coffee table that I crack my skull and pass out. The momentary distraction from Matt's advancing figure soothes me slightly, until he's standing in front of me. His face is somewhat gaunt and colourless and he looks, it seems, almost frail.

'Matt,' I say aloud without thinking, letting go of my mug of coffee and pushing my chair back to stand up.

'Hi, Nat,' he says calmly.

I instinctively put my arms around his neck then, and he holds me tightly. The skin on his neck is cold, and I move my hand to the back of his head. His clothes don't smell of our home any more. The people in the coffee shop are watching us, I can feel it, but I don't care. I just concentrate on breathing and swallowing and not allowing my eyes to fill up. My throat is so tight it hurts. As we untangle our bodies from one another, I catch a glimpse of his eyes. There's something about them I don't recognise, and I quickly wrench away my gaze as I take my seat.

'I'm going to grab a coffee quick,' he says. 'Can I get you one?'

I gesture to the mug of coffee in front of me. 'I've got one, thank you.'

'Oh, yes. Of course.' He removes his coat – a navy blue wool coat that I haven't seen before – and hangs it on the back of his chair. He stands behind another young man in the queue and looks at his phone. I wonder what he's looking at, if he's texting anyone, or if he simply wants an excuse not to look at me.

Probably trying to avoid looking at those disgusting bags under your eyes or those deeply repulsive fat rolls.

Matt brings a large flat white over to the table and sits down opposite me. He meets my eye then, and something trembles inside me. I look down and blink into the darkness of my coffee, at the white foamy bubbles skirting the edges of the liquid. I wonder what I'm doing here and why I'm doing this to myself. I should have just said no. This is far more painful and torturous than I could ever have anticipated. And yet I love him so completely, still.

'How have you been?' Matt asks.

Oh, you know, just swell. Our elderly neighbour had to tidy the flat for me because I've been too depressed to clean. Then I shagged a stranger off a dating app, cried, and kicked him out. Oh, and I signed up for therapy today because I'm doing really fucked-up things, like lying on the roof in the freezing cold and burning myself with cigarettes. So, things are going just great for me, thanks Matt.

'I'm fine,' I say eventually. 'How are you?'

'I'm okay.'

'Good.'

'How's work?'

'Matt, why are you here?' I ask, suddenly irritated at the formality of his conversation, as if I'm now a stranger to him, and the last seven years have dissolved in his memory.

He shifts in his seat, his discomfort palpable. He takes a long sip from his coffee and replaces his mug on the table, wiping at the foamy residue on his facial hair.

'I have to tell you something,' he says. 'I really wanted you to hear it from me first, rather than through gossip.'

I inhale sharply, the irritation dying, panic and adrenalin rising up again.

'What? What is it?'

'I don't know how to say this, Nat.'

'For fuck's sake, Matt. Will you just spit it out?'

'I'm seeing someone.'

It must be adrenalin that stops the tears or the vomit, though I can feel both raging under the surface. My thoughts are speeding through my brain, too fast to hold on to any of them.

'Is it Kim?' I ask.

'Nat—'

'Is it?' I say venomously. I can feel my face hardening and my hands clenching into fists, the nails digging deep and hard into the flesh of my palms.

'Yes.'

The pain dissipates, or rather, is masked by rage. White hot, blindsiding rage; the kind that makes your eyes sting with furious tears. I blink them back hard and quickly so that he doesn't notice – blink, blink, blink like a flashing indicator on a car – and dig my nails deeper into my palms. My face is hot and my legs are trembling and everything is alight. I look at him. There's something immediately ugly about him all of a sudden, and a new feeling of disgust brews deep in my body and makes me feel ill.

'How *could* you?' I snarl, not attempting to mask the anger.

'Nat, let me—'

'Don't. Don't you dare ask me to let you explain.'

'But I need to.'

'I don't give a flying fuck about what you need.'

'I know, Nat, but just listen.' There's a desperation to his voice that temporarily extinguishes the anger, a tenderness swelling softly in the pit of my stomach like water over a fire. I try to ignore it. 'I didn't plan for this to happen,' he continues, his voice unsteady. 'I never wanted this.'

'So you didn't want to have sex with her? Not sure I believe that, Matt, considering you didn't even wait a full day before fucking her.'

He's looking down, and I can tell that my knowing about him and Kim sleeping together comes as a shock.

'I didn't plan to. But I knew I liked her, Nat. You know I wouldn't have done that if I didn't think there was something there worth pursuing. You know I'm not like that.'

'Yeah, Matt, you're a really top guy. Honestly. How could you be so fucking *heartless*?'

'Nat—'

'Did you "like" her when we were together?'

'No, of course not.'

'So, your feelings for her were just really conveniently timed? You call it quits on your relationship of seven years, then just two months later, you're official with another woman? That's some hell of a coincidence, Matt. Do you have a "romantic attachment" switch that you turned off for me and turned on for her?'

176

He shakes his head solemnly but doesn't answer, and I realise there's very little point in pressing the matter further. He'll either never be honest with me and I will agonise over how it really played out, or he will confess the truth, which will hurt like hell and I'll never be able to unknow it.

After a few seconds, he says, 'I just couldn't ignore the way I felt. I deserve to be happy, Nat.'

Hearing this suddenly makes my chest feel as though it's about to burst, like a thin sheet of glass shattering under the force of a powerful storm.

'And I am not enough to make you happy?'

He lifts his head as I say this. His expression is pained and taut.

'Yes, you are. You were.'

Were. You were enough. Not any more. You're not enough any more.

'I don't understand, Matt. I don't understand when I stopped making you happy. I don't understand when or why I stopped being enough for you.'

My breathing isn't right and I can feel my pulse in my throat. My head feels like an enormous weight on my neck and I wonder how it's holding it upright, how the bones that make up my neck haven't snapped under the pressure.

'Nat, it isn't anything to do with you—'

Rage surges up again like vomit, my pulse quickening and hard all down me.

'Don't you dare say: "It's not you, it's me", Matt. I swear to God. You owe me more than shitty, lazy clichés.'

177

'Look, I just wanted you to hear it from me first, because I care about you.'

'Liar. You are a dirty fucking liar.'

Smash that coffee mug on the table and use the shards to slit his throat and rip open his jugular. Go on, do it. He deserves it. Liar.

'What?'

'You're not telling me this because you care about me. You're telling me to try and ease your own shame, so you can forgive yourself for the damage you've caused and move on with your life. You're telling me because you are a weak, selfish, worthless man, and you need my permission to feel okay again.'

'No, Nat, listen to me, you're not listen—'

I quickly slam my hand in the middle of the table to interrupt him.

'I'm not done.'

I don't recognise the deep, furious growl of my voice as I say this, and there's a peculiar expression to Matt's face. I think it's fear.

'You expect me to allow you the opportunity to make yourself feel better? I won't do it, Matt. You can sit with your guilt, just like I've had to sit with my pain for every hour, of every day. Because you should feel guilty. After seven years of my loyalty and my love – my unconditional love – and this is how you show your respect for that love, and your respect for me? By copping off with the first girl you shag, after just eight weeks apart.'

He's crying silently now and his mouth is open as though he's been winded, but I carry on, my whole body on fire with anger. 'So, you can live with that guilt, for the way you've treated me. I hope it eats at you. I hope it fuck-ing consumes you.'

'Nat, I'm so sorry.' His voice is so quiet he almost whispers it, his shoulders shuddering slightly and his face still looking down towards his mug of coffee. Then he says it again, 'I am so sorry.'

I inhale audibly and take a final sip of my coffee. I pull on my coat.

As I push my chair back and stand up, I pause, gazing down at him. He looks up at me then. His eyes are wet.

'Me too, Matt.'

I walk out of the coffee shop and don't look back. I stand for a moment, breathing the fresh air deep into my lungs, and pull out my phone to message the girls.

CHAPTER TEN

Edele

The churchyard is always quiet on a Saturday morning. I've always thought it to be very out of place in our loud, rough town, with its creaky wooden gates and overgrown briars, thick with thorny shrubs. On this wet morning, the smell of damp soil and moss is strong and earthy. If I were in a Dickens novel, there would be marshes with bubbling streams and cattle grazing on the horizon, and a creepy old man dressed all in grey who would steal bread from my pockets.

Except the only things in my pockets are a lighter, a packet of cigarettes and a tissue. There is no creepy old man; I am completely alone, except for a white cat skulking between the tombstones. There's a solemn stillness to this place, and while there's something pleasingly melancholy about it, it's also undeniably bleaker on a morning like this. But when it's this quiet and the wind is calm, you can sometimes hear the rushing of the sea in the distance. There's something about standing above a load of dead bodies and listening to the tide that I find reassuring. Despite everything, here

I am, still breathing, and underneath me is the Earth, still rotating.

I run my fingers through my hair, pulling at a knot, feeling it give way and watching the strands of black hair snap off and fall away. I light a cigarette. I put my lighter back in my pocket. I inhale, exhale, inhale again. Is it disrespectful to smoke in a graveyard? Yeah, probably. But I've lit it now.

I don't know why I always bring a tissue when I visit my dad's grave, as I have never cried over it. Not once. Not even as he was being lowered into it. But it is a routine I've developed over the last two years since he died; one Saturday morning of the month – it doesn't matter which; I usually decide on the day, depending on the ferocity of my Friday night hangover – I gather cigarettes, a lighter and a tissue, board the number 78 bus to Mostyn Road at the edge of town, and visit my dad's grave. I'm not even sure why I do it. I don't think it's obligation, as I don't hold any obligation towards him, particularly in death. And it most certainly isn't guilt. I think that, perhaps, it's to remind myself that he is dead.

Ray was a hard man with a hard face and soft eyes, 'The kind of man it's very easy to fall in love with,' Nat always says. The girls joke about how 'hot' my dad was, I think, to alleviate the uncomfortable severity of the situation, which is exactly the sort of thing I would do. Ray's moods were violent and mercurial, like a drug addict going cold turkey. Though he used to grab our arms and put his face so close to ours that we could smell the tobacco and whisky on his breath, he was never violent with us. One time, when we were kids sitting on the stairs listening to them argue, something smashed in the kitchen, and then everything went quiet. Mum didn't speak much for a while after that, and she wore a scarf everywhere – even though it was July.

He died two years ago after crashing his car into a tree near our house. He was fifty-three. He was also drunk. Mum says he died at 2.37 a.m., even though he was pronounced dead at 3.04 a.m., because 2.37 a.m. is when she heard the crash and looked to her right – the space where her husband should've been sleeping – then at the clock, and knew instantly that he was dead. Though I've only ever admitted it to the shrink I saw for ten weeks after his death, I still have occasional nightmares about hearing my mum downstairs with the police, with a cracked and croaky voice yet not exactly crying, while I held Liam close upstairs. It later came out that Ray had been at another woman's house before getting behind the wheel.

It was quite disappointing, the way my father chose to die. I always imagined I would be at my parents' bedsides, perhaps at home or in a hospital, stroking their snow-white hair and touching their soft pink skin as they scrabbled for air or simply slipped away with one big, final exhalation. I knew Ray would go before Mum because, well, he never committed anything to living. It was almost as though he were teasing death, seeing how far he could poke and prod it until it snapped and sunk its teeth into him. Eventually, just like the rest of the people in my dad's life, death finally got sick of waiting for him to give a shit about what it takes to be alive. It almost made me angry, the fact that he got to suddenly abscond from life, with no time for reflection or regret. Another responsibility he managed to avoid.

As I stand smoking, I look down at his grave. The headstone is small – not that I know a lot about the standard sizing of headstones, but it seems small in comparison to others in the vicinity – and there are no flowers, not even dead ones, at its base. His epitaph, inscribed in a thin, scratchy font, reads:

IN MEMORY OF RAYMOND WILLIAM O'CONNELL

14 MAY 1964–3 FEBRUARY 2017

DEVOTED FATHER, HUSBAND, SON AND FRIEND

I didn't know my father had any friends. Or if he did, I never met any of them. I don't wish to meet anyone who could willingly befriend a man like Ray.

The white cat is stalking something among the graves at the side of the church porch. Its ears are pricked and it's slowly positioning its body low to the ground, preparing to pounce.

What would Ray think of me now, if we he were alive? He'd call me a rotten freeloader, and tell me to 'Get off my lazy fecking backside and get a job.' I think he'd be disappointed that I lost my job and lack the motivation to find a new one, that I'm flat broke, that I drink every day and swear and lie and sleep around. He was proud of me at one point, though. I loved studying history at school and I knew he was proud of me for that because he told me that he was. It was such a shocking thing to hear that I cried for an hour. I wanted him to be proud of me, to love me, and maybe I still do. Is that the reason I come here? It's the only promise I stick to.

I think back to the pub with Alex and Natasha the other week, when I told Nat that a part of her may always love Matt, and that that's okay. Alex said I was wise, and Nat agreed, saying I should become a shrink. I didn't want my reaction to give away how I was really feeling, so I laughed loudly and shrugged off their comments. 'Maybe the day I start listening to my inner adult will be the day I actually grow up,' I said, smiling. But really, their comments resonated with something uneasy somewhere in my mind. When will I learn to start taking my own advice? If I can help my friends start to rebuild their lives with my advice, why can't I do the same for myself?

I realise now that I'm staring at Ray's grave as I think. I look up. The white cat has gone.

My phone pings in my pocket.

NATASHA: What's everyone doing today? You won't believe what's just happened to me.

EDELE: Not much. I'm doing Grave Day right now but free later. What happened?

NATASHA: Oh, hun. Happy Grave Day. You should let us come with you one time, I don't like the thought of you there on your own. I'll tell you later, do you fancy going 'out out' tonight? We haven't been to Bar Chocolate in ages.

EDELE: Nah don't worry, you don't want to have to put up with me being a melancholy fucker. And that's because we're always the oldest people in Bar Chocolate now. Last time we went, Mackie got hammered and got off with a 19-year-old.

MACKIE: He told me he was 22 but granted, not my finest moment. But Bar Chocolate sounds fun, count me in. I haven't told you all properly about my Skype interview on Tuesday either, have I? All I'll say for now is it involves green tea and blood. Hope you're okay, Ed. x

ALEX: Sounds like a crime scene, Mack. I'm there. Craig's at some football thing tonight anyway. You didn't talk about Hitler again, did you, Mack? And thinking of you, Ed. Please come out tonight so we can give you a cuddle.

NATASHA: E, we never have to 'put up with you', stupid. It's us. You don't have to put on a front for us.

EDELE: I know. Thanks.

NATASHA: So, girls' night it is. Can't wait to hear your interview story this time, Marshall.

MACKIE: Come round to mine for pre-drinks at 7ish? I'll make us some dinner and regale you all with tales of my blood bath (quite literally) of a job interview.

ALEX: Remember when pre-drinks used to be at 10 p.m. and if someone mentioned dinner, we'd say 'eating is cheating' so we'd get drunk quicker, then all get two-for-one pizzas on the way home?

EDELE: The days of our youth. Can't wait to hear about this horror film interview. Did the Atlas guy get his throat slashed on camera or something? That would make such a good movie. Nat, make that into a movie, hun.

NATASHA: Err I work in advertising, not film, dumbass. But dinner sounds wonderful Mack, thank you. I'll bring wine.

EDELE: Yeah, you can make the ads for my horror film. And thanks, Marshall, but can I veto superfood stew?

MACKIE: Today is not the day for superfood stew.

EDELE: That's my girl. See you all later. x

I put my phone back into my pocket and drop my cigarette to the ground, stamping it into the wet grass above my dad's grave.

'See you next month, Dad.'

As I turn to leave, I notice a young woman at the other side of the churchyard, in the corner by the briars. She can't be much into her twenties, and she's holding a small bunch of flowers and I can see she's crying.

Maybe it's shame, the reason I come here every month. I'm ashamed of what my dad would think of me now. Even a dad like him.

Mackie's flat is warm and the smell of roasting vegetables and baking cheese fills every corner. It's a reassuring and comforting place to be after the bleakness of the churchyard and the solitude of my bedroom during the afternoon when I napped and watched Netflix. Hers is the sort of home that wraps you in its hospitality and makes you feel safe. I wonder if it's because Mackie has only ever lived here on her own, for the past four years. She's been able to cultivate and mould it independently, and to grow in it on her own. No hungover arguments with annoying brothers, no culling your ex's belongings after seven years with a broken heart, no taxidermy giraffe heads making you jump when you go for a wee in the middle of the night. Everything in this flat is hers, and it shows.

I'm currently arranging four mint-green plates and shiny cutlery over the kitchen table, while Nat fills up four glasses with supermarket own-brand white wine and Alex plays music from a laptop. Mackie has on a pair of bright floral oven gloves and is removing a large white dish from the oven, while she tells us about her Skype interview.

'Oh God,' Alex says, picking up a handful of Doritos from a bowl in the middle of the table. 'So, you had the gross bloody, puss-y fluid from a spot on your top, then you spilt tea on your lap so it looked like you'd pissed yourself, then you showed the man your *My Little Pony* jammies?'

'Yep, that's pretty much it. Except they were just floral pink and yellow pyjamas. No ponies.'

'Ah, good, that's far less embarrassing,' I laugh.

'Honestly, I think that's a lot better than saying you have a friend who reminds you of Hitler,' Nat says. 'When do you find out if you've got it or not?'

'Seriously? I think unless Atlas guy has some sort of acne fetish, I really don't think that's going to happen,' Mackie says, using a large silver spoon to pile four servings of food between the plates.

'Oh my God,' Alex moans. 'Mack, that smells so good.'

'It's tomato, spinach and ricotta pasta bake with parmesan and prosciutto,' she smiles. She's really pleased with herself, but trying not to show it too much for fear of seeming one of the smug adults we all take the piss out of.

'It's actually reassuring to know that someone as put together as you, who does early morning runs and makes Delia-style pasta bakes, still needs to squeeze her spots and spills tea over her vagina during job interviews,' I say, smiling.

She laughs. 'Just because I exercise and cook doesn't make me inhuman.'

'No, it makes you an adult, and adults don't get spots or spill shit.'

'Almost adults do,' she says.

'Is that what we are?' Alex says. 'Almost adults?'

'It makes us sound pre-pubescent,' Nat chuckles.

'We basically are, but with more drinking and fucking and bill-paying and drug-taking,' I say as Mackie places a bowl of salad next to the Doritos before handing us each a chalky-pink-coloured napkin.

'Seriously, Mack. Napkins as well?' Nat smiles.

'Well, yeah,' Mackie laughs. 'What else are you going to wipe your hands and mouth with?'

'The back of your hand, your sleeve, Alex's coat?' I say, jokingly reaching over to grab Alex's coat before she bats my hand away. 'I actually don't think I've ever bought napkins in my entire life. I don't even know where I'd go to buy napkins if I ever needed to.'

'These are from John Lewis, I think,' Mackie says.

'You're better at being sixty years old than most sixty-year-olds are,' I say.

I hosted a dinner party once. It was 2016 and my parents and Liam were on holiday in Killarney (because when you have family in Ireland, that place – no matter how void of anything remotely entertaining or interesting – becomes the default destination for all foreseeable holidays). I couldn't go as I was actually employed then, and work wouldn't give me the time off. At the time, that was a huge relief. So, in an attempt to behave like an adult, I threw what I termed a 'small get-together with food and drinks', because I thought 'dinner party' made me sound like an uptight twat. Alex and Craig were there, as were Matt and Nat, Mackie, Mackie's cousin Susie who is vegan (it was not my idea to invite vegan Susie), my friend Sita from university, who I normally only ever get completely trashed with, and 'semi-hot single guy from work' James. James was not hot, he was just tall. Plus, he was the only single man at work who ever spoke to me. In fact, he was rather pallid and always seemed to be permanently exhausted, even though he was never doing anything that required any form of exertion, except when he was talking about climate change or public sector cuts.

I decided to make Jamie Oliver's vegan chickpea curry, which was labelled 'not too tricky' but demanded half a teaspoon of asafoetida, which is apparently some sort of dried latex (condom jokes were made; received a mixed reaction). Everyone brought a bottle of Isla Negra or Yellow Tail wine, except for James who brought three bottles of craft beer (which he drank himself), and Mackie who brought a Tesco Finest Sauvignon, which was met with various 'posh knob' comments, largely from me and Nat. I drank half a bottle of wine before everyone arrived, which resulted in me yelling 'NO ONE CARES' when vegan Susie asked if the wine was vegan. The condom curry didn't taste like shit, or maybe people were just drunk or being polite. After dinner, we called Jay to ask for weed, and Jay ended up hanging out with us and trying to sell us cocaine. Mackie and Susie left, Craig and James argued about the welfare state, Sita was too drunk to take drugs and passed out in the bath, Matt and Nat went home at 2.30 a.m., Alex told Craig to 'shut up about the welfare state and order a fucking Uber' shortly after 3 a.m., and James left the following day at 11 a.m., after Jay left us half a gram of coke and we had sex twice. We both agreed it was a mistake and that, to avoid things being awkward at work, we probably shouldn't hang out again.

After we've finished eating and tidying away our plates, Alex and I are outside the back door, smoking. Mackie has a small garden but it's perfectly maintained, with a jasmine plant climbing up the back wall, which showers its branches and the grass underneath in delicate white flowers in the summer and fills the garden with a beautiful, heady scent. There's a set of white garden chairs surrounding a small, round table to our left, before the patio ends and the little stretch of garden begins. We often sit there in the summer after lazy days on the beach, drinking and smoking and talking well after the sun's gone down.

'How are things with Craig now?' I ask.

'They're better,' Alex says with a considered tone. 'I never asked him about Gemma or anything, because I realised I don't need to.'

'What do you mean?'

'I just calmed down and realised how much I trusted him. I don't know. I freaked out over nothing.'

'As long as you're sure. I mean, as long as you're okay.'

'I feel okay.'

'Good, but you know that, if there's ever a time when you don't feel okay again, you can talk to him? I don't like to think of you keeping things in. You should be able to talk to him, like you can talk to us.'

'I know, and I can. I just don't need to.'

'You don't need to, or you don't want to?'

'Christ, Ed. What is this, couples' counselling? And from you of all people.'

Alex looks at me then, taking a drag of her cigarette before exhaling and directing her gaze back towards the garden.

'Sorry,' she says. 'Sorry, I'm a bitch for snapping.' She shifts her position slightly closer so that she can link her arm around mine, touching my hand inside my coat pocket with hers. 'Anyway, tell me about the job hunt. What's the latest?'

'Oh, you know, fine. Just not sure how "lady of the night" is going to look on my CV.'

Alex sniggers and squeezes my hand. 'Look, you don't always need to put on a front, you know.'

I feel bare and exposed when she says this, like when Hermione removes Harry's invisibility cloak in *Harry Potter and the Prisoner of Azkaban*. I smoke and look away.

'I just worry that I've stalled, you know? Well, I don't *worry*; I know that I have. But it's not like when you stall a car and you just, like, restart the engine and get on with it. I've stalled and I can't figure out how to restart.'

She makes a 'mmm' sound and asks, 'Have you been looking for jobs?'

'Yes, and I've applied for some. Well, two. And obviously I haven't heard a word back. It's not that I haven't been looking. But when I look at these jobs – at the type of person they want – I just can't imagine myself doing it. I know it's not right, so what's the point? It'll just end up being another setback that'll make me feel like even more of a failure.'

'Well,' she says, 'I think that's the risk you've got to take, isn't it? Otherwise, the longer you're drifting for, the more of a failure you'll feel regardless. I'm not saying you are, by the way. You're one of the best people I know, and that takes a lot more than writing a stale cover letter with words like "aptitude" and "leadership" scattered everywhere and spouting all that "lean in" bollocks. What I mean is, you may be drifting right now, but you'll find the right path, Ed, and you will settle eventually. And in the meantime, us three are here to help anchor you in any way we can. You know that, right?'

'I know,' and I mean it. I do know. They're the only people I've ever relied on. Alex unlinks her arm and wraps it around my shoulders and I turn into her. My body shakes small trembles from the vulnerability of opening up as I gulp each breath.

'You've got this, my girl.'

'Thank you, Al.' My voice is muffled against Al's coat. She pulls back a little and puts her hands on either side of my face. Her eyes are soft and I can smell the smoke from her cigarette close to me. 'I mean it,' she says, 'I've never doubted you for one minute.'

I smile at her and she nods at me, taking her hands away and stepping back to take a final drag. There's a momentary silence as we both smoke, the muffled sound of the Rolling Stones' 'Gimme Shelter' echoing from inside the flat.

We walk over to the small white table and stub our cigarettes out in the damp ashtray.

'Shall we go in?' I ask.

'Yes,' Alex says, turning to look at me and smiling when I meet her gaze.

'Thanks, Al. You know I've always got your back, too, right? Any time; all the time.'

'I know,' she replies warmly.

'Good,' I say. 'Now, let's get hammered.'

In the Uber on the way to the centre of town, we talk about Nat's coffee with Matt, and him seeing Kim. A drunk and bitter bitching session about Matt erupts.

'I can't believe it,' Alex says, a visible look of concern etched over her face. 'How could he do that after seven years, when you've only been split up a couple of months?'

'Who knows,' Nat shakes her head. 'Who knows why men act like that. It's like something in their soul just snaps, like you never knew them at all, and your whole universe has to change because of it.'

I can tell Nat's also drunk because she's using words like 'soul' and 'universe'. This hasn't appeased Alex though, and I can tell she's thinking about Craig. Her eyes are enormous in her face.

'Of course you knew him,' she says. 'He just changed. People change.'

The words spill out of Nat in a messy slur. 'I don't know. I'm not sure if you ever really know someone.'

Alex looks silently anguished then as she looks out of the window, droplets of rain pattering down the glass. She takes a swig from the bottle of Evian, which we filled up with gin and tonic, despite the taxi journey into town only lasting around eleven minutes in light traffic. She winces at its strength and passes it to me.

'You know Craig,' I say quietly to Alex before taking a sip of the gin. It's strong but I don't find it overwhelming. I don't wince. 'Don't worry.'

She carries on staring out of the window, responding with a non-committal 'hmm'.

'Anyone want some more of this journey juice?' I ask to the taxi, shaking the plastic bottle so that the remaining gin and tonic splashes against its sides.

'You finish it, Ed,' Nat says. 'You're the most sober out of all of us.'

I agree by saying, 'All right,' even though I'm not sure that I am the most sober, but tap the bottle against Alex's arm to ask if she wants any more.

'No thanks, love. Get it down ya,' she says.

By the time we step out of the taxi, I can tell I'm most definitely not sober because standing upright without tripping over my own feet requires a lot more concentration than normal.

'Cheers, mate,' I call out to the driver, tapping my hand against the passenger door as I do. The Uber driver does not respond and drives off.

Mackie tries to hold her umbrella over all four of our heads as we dash, heads down, through the rain and into the Fox and Whistle for a few drinks before Bar Chocolate.

There's a sticky heat inside the pub and the noise of chatting hits you as soon as you walk in, along with the smell of stale beer and the faint trace of cigarettes. Whereas on Wednesday afternoons it's full of shitty businessmen, tourists with cameras, and unemployed loners, there are five types of people you'll find in this pub on Saturday nights:

1. Men with faces like leather, dressed in paint-spattered tracksuit bottoms or high-vis jackets that look as though they've been doing DIY, but have really been in the pub since 10 a.m. They'll nip outside to smoke and think it's an adequate reason to start a conversation with someone half their age.

2. The couple in leather jackets having a loud argument that doesn't make any sense because they're both completely battered. He's drinking lager and she's drinking rosé.

3. Eighteen-year-old girls who each have a pitcher of Purple Rain or Woo Woo and are calling each other sluts and yelling things like, 'Fuck *off*, Izzy, just neck it!' They'll soon depart in groups of two or three for a mini photo shoot in the bathroom mirrors.

4. Groups of lads who are trying to chat everyone up like they're in a club. They're trying to look tough and intimidating when they walk, but it just looks like they've shat themselves.

5. People like us, who are either way too old or way too young to be in here, depending on which of the other four categories you're observing, but are too pissed to care.

It's £1 Jägerbombs in this pub, and even though none of us particularly like Jägerbombs, we order four of them every time we come here.

'Hey, Superwoman,' Gary says from behind the bar. He's wearing a navy-blue cardigan, buttoned up over a white T-shirt with faded black jeans. His facial hair is unkempt and there's too much gel in his curls. His cardigan is hugging at his slight belly. He's smiling and looking at me as he pours a pint from the taps.

'Hello, Gary,' I say. 'How are you?'

'Good, I'm good. Still reliving that time you threw beer over those knobheads, even though I had to mop the floor afterwards.'

'Oh, shit. I'm so sorry.'

'Behave,' he grins. 'It was one of the best things I've ever seen.'

'Thanks so much for the tenner, by the way.'

He looks a bit embarrassed now, a slight pink flush creeping into his face, and passes the pint to the punter.

'It was nothing.' He takes the money and hands over the change. It's almost surreal observing a cash transaction now, when you can pay for a 70p chocolate bar by tapping your card. I half expect Gary to pull out an antique-coloured scroll and write the receipt with a quill dipped in ink.

'No, it was very kind of you.' Nat's jabbing her elbow into my side suggestively. '*Stop it,*' I whisper.

'You've bought some mates with you this time, then?'

'Yeah, I just found them on the street and convinced them to hang out with me tonight.'

'I'd make a run for it if I were you, girls. This one's a loose cannon.'

'Trust us, we know,' Nat laughs.

Gary's joking, of course he knows Nat, Alex and Mackie, because this is the sort of town where everyone knows everyone. He's picking up the bottle of Jägermeister.

'Four Jägers, yeah?'

'You know us so well,' Nat smiles, winking at me as Gary turns his back to pour the shots.

We all down the Jägers in one, except Mackie who has to pause mid-shot, and order another drink each before making our way through the pub in an attempt to find an empty, sticky table littered with half-drunk Desperados and ice buckets, which are now just buckets full of cold water.

'Thanks, Gary,' I say as we leave the bar to begin our Voyage For The Sticky Table.

'Have a good one, Ed.' His arm looks strong on the beer tap and his smile, with his adorable chubby cheeks, is earnest and warm. Looking at him stirs something unfamiliar but not unpleasant in the pit of my stomach, a feeling that's a strange mix of startling yet reassuring. I have an involuntary urge to tell Gary everything about myself, and ask him everything about him, too. But instead I follow Nat through the pub until we have eyes on The Sticky Table and make a mad dash for it, like a group of lions lurching for its prey before any other predators steal it unexpectedly.

We talk some more about Matt and Kim, and I'm surprised at the strength Nat is showing. There's something new about her; a fight in her voice that wasn't there before. I think she's found her anger, which even though it's exhausting to carry around with you, is always better than the feeling of pure, undiluted pain. I hope she holds on to that anger because it is what will help her heart to mend and to leave Matt behind, eventually. I want to ask her if she's sent off her self-referral form for therapy, but it's not the sort of question you ask in the pub before a night out.

I'm about halfway through my pint of Thatchers when a group of five boys walking past us and into the smoking area catch my eye. I'd recognise that broad, strong back anywhere.

'Shit,' I say quietly, leaning in to the girls, 'it's Liam and Eddie, and three of their toxically masculine friends who I bet all have teeny-tiny testicles.'

Does that mean my brother and his mates fall into category four: 'Groups of lads who are trying to chat everyone up like they're in a club'? Liam is walking with an unrealistically straight back and wide gait, which does make him look a bit as though he's shat himself.

'Ed, that's disgusting,' Mackie says.

'Your brother looks fit,' Nat says.

'Piss off.'

'Isn't that Eddie guy the one you're desperately in love with?'

'Yes.'

'I can see why. He looks like Richard Madden but with Jason Momoa's body.'

'I don't know who either of those people are,' Mackie says.

'Of course you don't,' I say. 'Jason Momoa was that sea bloke with the trident last year – what's his name?'

'Aquaman?'

'Yes! *Aquaman*. And Richard Madden is the main guy in *Bodyguard*, that TV show where he shags the Home Sec. They were both in *Game of Thrones*, which is basically breeding ground for hot men.'

'Not a clue what you're on about, mate,' Mackie says.

'Basically, he looks like everyone's dream man,' Alex adds.

'Jesus, I'm getting turned on just watching him walk away.'

'Tell me about it.'

'And he's got such a good face, too,'

'I would love to sit on that face.'

'You know, this is exactly the kind of degrading objectification we berate men for,' Mackie says, raising her eyebrow and sipping her vodka soda. We all roll our eyes.

'Don't give me that man-jectification crap,' I say. 'You sound like a poor privileged white dude who's pissed off with social media for not allowing him to catcall women in the street any more.'

There is a part of me that feels slightly hypocritical for ogling Eddie when I'd slap a guy if I overheard him talking about us in the same way with his mates in the pub. But male objectification doesn't carry the same consequences as it does for women. Privileged white dudes don't have to worry about being sexually harassed on their way home and have it blamed on his drunkenness or short skirt.

'Yeah, Ed's right,' Nat says. 'Long live female sexuality, *Magic Mike* and "Thirty guys who'll get you pregnant without even touching you" Buzzfeed listicles!"

'We fought hard for our right to objectify men in Buzzfeed listicles,' I say, 'and maybe one day we won't feel the need to try and make female sexuality more palatable by disguising it with humour.'

'This must be what it's like to go for a bev with Gloria Steinem,' Alex says.

'You're right, this is all getting way too boring,' I say. 'Let's down our drinks and see if we can persuade Gary to give us a free round of shots.'

As I stand up to go to the bar, I peer outside. Liam and Eddie are standing with their friends in the smoking area but they can't see me. I debate going over and saying hi, purely so Eddie can see me in a full face of make-up and a top where my tits are on display, but decide against it.

After one more drink in the Fox and Whistle, which Gary did not pay for despite my subtle drunken flirting, we walk along the road adjacent to the seafront, towards Bar Chocolate.

'Oi, Marshall, give us your umbrella?' I shout over the sound of the waves and the strong wind.

'But it's not raining any more!'

'We neeeed it to light our ciga-wets cos of tha wind!' Alex bellows with a loud, drunken slur.

'Jesus, Al, right in my fucking ear.'

'Sorry, beautiful,' she says, throwing her arm around me and planting a wet kiss on my cheek. 'I love you, Edele Marie.'

'I love you, too, you drunken twat.'

Alex attempts to hold Mackie's umbrella over me before giving up and passing it to Nat, as I light our cigarettes.

'Al, you need to act as sober as possible in the Bar Chocolate queue otherwise they won't let you in,' Nat urges.

'Acting sober when I'm hammered is one of my many talents,' Alex says.

'That's actually true,' Mackie says. 'Remember when we were at that club in London, and Al had just thrown up on the street, but managed to pull herself together in front of the bouncers, then got us chucked out when she tried to light a fag on the dance floor?'

'Precious memories,' I laugh. 'That posh club wasn't ready for our level of trashiness.'

Sure enough, after curtseying in front of the bouncers and saying, 'Good evening, gentleman', Alex and the rest of us stagger into Bar Chocolate, which is a bit like staggering into 2009. 'Hotel Room Service' by Pitbull is blaringoutandsmokemachinesarepumpingchlorine-smelling smoke onto the dance floor, making it impossible to see your own feet sticking to the drink-covered ground. My vision sways as I dance, and my drunkenness hits me like a stone on a windshield. The highs and lows that have been compacted all into one day make me feel dizzy.

'Fancy a fag?' I shout to Alex over 'Meet Me Halfway' by the Black Eyed Peas. She nods and I tap Nat on the shoulder, making a smoking gesture to my lips. She shakes her head, mouthing, 'I'll stay with Mackie', and looping her arm around Mack's shoulder.

Alex and I make our way through the chlorine smoke and perch on one of the benches in the smoking area. The crisp, chlorine-free air eases my dizziness, but I don't feel any more sober. Alex is still bopping to the sound of the music leaking from inside. There's an outside bar in the courtyard, but it's closed, its shelves empty and a couple of blokes leaning against the bar smoking.

We're only halfway through our cigarettes when they approach us.

'Evening ladies,' says the blond one in a bomber jacket. 'Mind if we sit?'

It doesn't matter what our response is, they're sitting anyway.

'Looks like we don't get a say in the matter,' Alex says forcefully and surprisingly articulately, considering how drunk she is.

'She's a bit lairy, ain't she?' Blond Bomber Jacket says to me, leaning in to nudge me on the arm.

'Not really,' I say, shuffling on the bench away from him.

'Tough crowd,' Blond Bomber Jacket says over the bench to his mate, who has parked himself next to Al. His hair is swept back away from his face, thick with gel and spray, and he has a big diamond stud in his left ear.

'We ain't your "crowd",' I say under my breath, too pissed to think of anything smarter.

'Ooh, feisty,' Blond Bomber Jacket says, pulling a packet of Richmond's out of his bomber jacket pocket and lighting one.

'Feisty's good; we like feisty,' says Hair Gel, looking Alex up and down.

'I've got a boyfriend,' she says.

'Oh yeah? Then where is he?' Hair Gel laughs, mockingly looking around us with exaggerated head movements. 'Don't look like he's here, does it?'

'Look, we clearly ain't interested, so will you leave off?' I say, anger and exasperation making the tone of my voice sound more uncontrolled than I would have liked. He didn't seem that tall when he was standing up, but now that he's sitting so close to me, he seems intimidatingly big.

'You seemed pretty interested when you were eyeing me up over there,' he says, gesturing with his cigarette to the closed bar.

'Do me a favour,' I laugh, trying to sound as unafraid as possible. 'You looked in a mirror lately?'

'No need to be rude,' Blond Bomber Jacket says in a way that unsettles me; almost too calm and calculated.

'We might like feisty, but we ain't ones to put up with rude,' Hair Gel says, smiling sideways at Alex.

There's a security guard in the corner; I clocked him on our way outside. I try to meet his eye, but he's looking the other way. Blond Bomber Jacket is edging closer to me now; he's so close I can smell the damp on his clothes.

'Edele, these guys giving you grief?'

I jerk my head past the looming shoulders to see Eddie, standing at the end of the table. His eyes are ablaze, his face in a deep frown. He looks even more enormous when I'm looking up at him from the bench.

'Nah, no grief here, mate,' says Blond Bomber Jacket, shuffling away from me.

'I weren't asking you, *mate*.'

'They were just leaving,' I say.

'Come on, we were only—'

'If you don't stand up and jog on right now, I'll make sure you never stand again,' Eddie says, his gaze darting between Blond Bomber Jacket and Hair Gel.

Blond Bomber Jacket stubs out his cigarette on the table space in front of me, blows the final puff of smoke towards my face and nods at Hair Gel. The two men stand up to leave the table. The blond one stops in front of Eddie, staring him in the face, before the two of them skulk back into the club.

'Thanks, Eddie,' Alex smiles. She looks relieved. I feel somewhat relieved, but also frustrated. I don't need a man to rescue me like a damsel in distress.

'Yeah, thanks,' I say, looking down at the black ashy mark pressed into the wood of the table by Blond Bomber Jacket's cigarette. 'But we don't need your protection, okay?'

'I know you don't,' Eddie says, fixing his eyes on mine. 'I just came outside for some air and saw you both. I was just trying to help.' He isn't sitting down next to either of us yet, so he still looks tall and strong and heroic, which is slightly sexy but still frustrating. I don't know what would've happened next though, so I try to swallow my pride.

'Yeah, I know. Thanks.'

'Where are your mates then?' Alex asks.

'Liam went home because he was too drunk.'

'Standard,' I laugh.

'The others are inside,' he says. 'Shall we get a drink?'

'Sure,' I say, gulping the dregs from my bottle of cider. 'I'm all out and need a drink after that.'

The two of us follow Eddie back inside the club. The lights are bright, jumping madly from colour to another, and the bassline is vibrating heavy in my chest. There's a vague smell of vomit as we walk past the toilets, which is soon masked by the chlorine-smelling smoke and thick odour of bleach at the bar.

'I've still got half a G&T,' Alex says over the music to Eddie and me. 'I'll see you back on the dance floor.' She walks off, and now it's just the two of us.

We lean against the bar talking and drinking, and as I look at the smoothness of his skin and trace the slight lines running from the corner of his mouth to his nose with my eyes, excitement fuses in my brain like a chemical; almost natural, as though whatever happens next was somehow anticipated subconsciously. He's speaking to me about something but I don't remember what and he's smiling at me. He's studying my face too, I can tell by the concentration in his eyes and across his brow. I look at his smile, at his mouth and teeth and at his lips. I feel a pulling sensation like a hand in my lower stomach, churning and pulsing inside. I lean in to kiss him then, propelling myself forward with my toes to reach the height of his mouth, and he kisses me back; his right hand finding the nape of my neck. He tastes like vodka and he smells of the heat of his body mixed with aftershave and everything quakes.

'Do you want to go?' I say towards his ear, my cheekbone brushing against his.

'Yes,' he says, touching the bare skin above my collarbone and locking his eyes onto mine. There is a fierceness in his expression not dissimilar to the one he had when he was threatening the men outside. 'Mine's ages away though. Yours?'

I nod and I kiss him again. He kisses me back and leans his weight against me and the proximity of his body to mine makes me ache. I do not think about my mum or Liam because right now, he is the only thing occupying my intoxicated thoughts, the only thing that matters. If I was any sort of functioning adult, I'd have stopped to think twice because:

1. He may be fit Eddie, but fit Eddie is my brother's best mate.
2. Fit Eddie and I are about to go back to mine, which is not actually mine, but the house I grew up in, and which my mum and brother are currently asleep in.
3. I'm almost certainly fucking up. Again.

But right now, I do not feel like a functioning adult; I'm a fully fledged almost adult, so he's all I think about as I leave my drink at the bar, as I text the girls to say I've gone home, and as I lock my front door behind us.

CHAPTER ELEVEN
Alex

The peace lily on my bedside table is the first thing I see when I open my eyes. Craig and I bought it from IKEA last May, when we went to buy some bits to make our room in Warner's flat more 'our own'. Craig printed out some photos of us beforehand so we could choose some frames, and he helped me choose the peace lily for my bedside table.

'What about this one?' I'd asked him.

'Yeah, I like it,' he'd replied, 'what is it?'

'It's a peace lily.'

'You should get that one. I like it; it suits you.'

'What do you mean?' I'd asked.

'I dunno. You're peaceful. I mean, not when you're going off on one about Warner or having a go at me for not taking the bins out. But you bring me peace. So it makes sense to have it next to our bed.'

Even though it made very little sense, I understood what he meant.

It's Sunday, the morning after my night at Bar Chocolate with the girls. I can feel Craig stirring on the other side of the bed but I don't want to move my head yet. I'd rather enjoy this blissful minute before I realise how debilitatingly hungover I am.

The peace lily is tall now, much taller than the table lamp next to it, and as my growing consciousness brings my vision into sharper focus, I can see a layer of dust that has gathered on its large, glossy leaves. I make a mental note to clean its leaves later, even though I know I'll forget.

There's a rustle next to me as Craig removes the duvet from his body and climbs out of bed. Soon he'll stretch his arms over his head and his back will make a loud clicking sound.

'Where are you going?' I say sleepily, rolling over slowly and rubbing my eyes.

'Morning,' he says mid-groan as he stretches and his back clicks. He stands up and pulls on his sweatpants and a hoody. 'Just going to make some coffee. Want one?'

'Yeah, please. Actually, can I have a chai tea?'

'I knew you'd say that.'

'Why?'

'You always ask for a chai when you're hungover.'

'I'm not that bad.'

'You were smashed when you got in last night.'

'Was I?'

'You don't remember?'

'Yeah, of course I do.'

'No you don't.'

'No, you're right. I don't.'

We laugh and I shift my body slightly upwards, resting against the headboard. Considering how drunk I was in the Fox and Whistle before we even got to Bar Chocolate, I don't feel like I'm about to spew up my internal organs, which is a pretty good start.

'Well, I got in pretty early after watching football at the pub. Then it must've been about two when you got home.'

'I'm sorry, did I wake you up?'

'Yeah. You were acting really weird.'

'What? How?' Shit, I try to remember what I did or said but it's too foggy. Did I say anything about us? About Gemma? That I saw them in town? That I keep panicking that he's going to leave me and also that I have dreams that he's sleeping with Gemma?

'You asked me if I still loved you and if I'd ever cheat on you.'

'Oh, God. Craig, I'm sorry. I was drunk and obviously got a bit emotional.'

'Don't worry about it. Just a chai, then?'

'What did you say?'

'Err, I asked if you wanted anything with your chai.'

'No, I meant when I asked you those questions last night.'

'Seriously?'

'What? I can't remember.'

'You've been acting so weird lately, Al. You know I love you, and of course I'd never cheat on you. Why the hell would I do that? What kind of guy do you think I am? A twenty-year-old horny rugby player with a shaved eyebrow who calls his mates "broskis"? It's like you don't trust me any more, let alone know me.'

'Of course I do. It's just . . . I don't know. Forget it, I was just drunk.'

'Okay.' He walks to the bedroom door and hesitates before opening it. 'You have nothing to worry about, okay? Just trust me.'

'Okay.'

He walks to the kitchen and I hear the click of the kettle as he turns it on to boil. His defensiveness worries me because it sounds like guilt. And it's rare of him to spring straight out of bed on a Sunday morning. Our usual routine is that he'll lift his arm up, which is an invitation for me to lie on his chest, and we'll watch an episode of the latest Netflix drama in bed with a coffee, before discussing where to go to drink more coffee. But this morning, he couldn't leave fast enough.

I reach over to get my phone from my bedside table and knock the leaves of the peace lily as I do so. A sprinkling of dust shoots off the leaves and wafts into the air. I really need to not forget to clean that plant.

It's 9.03 a.m., which is far too early for a lazy Sunday in bed.

ALEX: How's everyone doing? Ed, how come you left so early? Are you okay? Thanks for a fun night, girls x

I don't expect a reply from Edele or Natasha for at least another two hours, but of course Mackie is already typing.

MACKIE: It was a laugh. My head is banging, though. I should definitely stick to being the designated driver.

And yeah, Ed, where did you get to? Funnily enough, I didn't see Eddie for the rest of the night after you left.

ALEX: NO WAY. Edele, did you go home with fit Eddie?! What will your brother say?! We need you to confirm or deny ASAP. Wake up!!

MACKIE: Liam's not going to be happy if you did.

ALEX: Drama! Ed, if you wake up next to Eddie this morning, tell him thanks for a) gracing the human race with his wondrous physique and b) saving us from those creepy guys in the smoking area. But mostly thanks for a).

A minute or so later, Craig walks back into our bedroom carrying two mugs.

'Here you go,' he says, handing me the milky tea. I can already smell the sweet cinnamon and nutmeg. It's comforting, and I blink hard.

'Thank you.'

I hold the mug in my hand, enjoying the warmth radiating through my fingers and palms, and watch Craig as though I'm observing an animal exhibiting unusual behaviour at the zoo. He's still standing next to his side of the bed sipping his tea, and quickly picks up his phone to look at the time.

'Shall we leave in, like, an hour and a half?'

My mind is blank. Craig is tracing my face to try and gauge my expression, wondering if I've remembered whatever it is I'm supposed to have remembered.

'Hmm?'

'For brunch. On the beach? I'm packing us a picnic. I told you about it weeks ago.'

Ah, of course. The picnic beach brunch. What a terrible girlfriend I am for forgetting.

'But if you're too hungover or whatever, don't worry. We can do it another time.'

He looks dejected and my skin shivers with guilt.

'No, of course not. I want to go.'

'Okay.'

He puts his coffee down and starts looking through the wardrobe. I don't think I've ever seen him carefully curate an outfit for longer than twenty seconds, but he's been searching through his clothes in the wardrobe for about a minute and a half, which should be cause for national concern.

'Thanks for organising it,' I say as he selects a striped shirt I don't think I've ever seen him wear and looks as though it should clothe the type of man who frequents Jack Wills. 'Is there anything I can do?' I ask, suddenly feeling incredibly guilty for forgetting. Nothing kicks the nausea-churning, head-hewing brutality of a hangover into force like the emotion of guilt.

'No, don't worry. I'm going to shower.'

It's another forty minutes before I can muster the energy to get out of bed, most of which time Craig has spent 'getting the picnic ready' in the kitchen.

At around 10.30 a.m., I stagger out of our bedroom. In the living room, Warner's antiques fill every corner and make my eyes and brain hurt. The giraffe head is still occupying most of my vision, but it now has a taxidermy friend: a stag with huge antlers that could very easily be used as a weapon hanging on the wall. There are plant hangers made from tiny shells hanging from its weap-on-like antlers, and an assortment of vintage furniture arranged over a mismatch of traditional rugs. There's a set of pale-pink velvet trapezium chairs next to a huge enamel sign for a drinks company, featuring a man smil-ing maniacally and giving a thumbs up. It looks like a prop from a horror film.

Craig is in the kitchen, rummaging in his backpack. My hair is secured in an unwashed top-knot (not the #messybun type you see on social media; more the 'hair that still smells of fags and alcohol from the night before' type) and I'm wearing a huge beige jumper over my black gym leggings. Despite Craig fussing around in the kitchen for the past hour, there's nothing resembling a picnic in here.

'Where's, umm, all the picnic stuff?' I ask.

'In the car already. Are you wearing your gym leg-gings?' Craig has never shown much interest in what I wear, especially for a just-us trip to the beach ten min-utes from where we live.

'Yeah, just because they're clean, and they're comfy. Is that okay?'

'Of course, it's just . . . never mind, it's fine.'

'What?'

'Nothing, babe,' he says smiling, pulling on his back-pack. 'Shall we go?'

'Yeah, let me just grab my bag.'

Outside we get in the car, I throw my bag in the foot-well and Craig starts the engine. The radio comes on and he quickly turns it down so that the music is barely audible. As he drives, I rest my elbow against the window so that I can lean my face against my hand, while the other hand hangs limply in my lap. Craig is driving with one hand on the gear stick, which always unnerves me but I don't know why.

Fastened into the car's near-silence together, he glances at me, smiles and asks if I'm okay. I tell him that I am.

We pull into a parking space in front of the beach-front with ease because it rained last night and it's overcast today, meaning no one else wants to come to the beach.

'What can I take?' I ask, climbing out the car.

'Just grab the blanket off the backseat?' Craig calls. He's already opening the boot. He pulls out a large wicker hamper I've never seen before, and I can see a bottle of prosecco poking out under the lid.

'That looks great,' I say, feeling touched by the gesture. 'Where'd you get the hamper?'

'Warner gave it to me. Think he got it from one of his antique fairs.'

'It's nice. I feel bad for not helping with any of this.'

'It's fine. It's my treat.'

We walk down the stone steps leading from the car park and onto the beach with its wet sand and deserted seafront. Craig and I chat idly as we walk: me balancing the red and blue picnic blanket between my arm and my hip; him carrying the hamper in front of him with care.

He keeps looking behind us, as if he's expecting someone to be following us.

'You all right?' I ask.

'Yeah, of course.'

'What're you looking at?'

'Nothing, just thought I saw some other people.'

Why would Craig care if there were other people on the beach? Who's he looking for? Who doesn't he want to see us having a picnic on the beach? I decide not to question it.

'Let's go here,' he says eventually, stopping in his tracks.

I unfurl the blanket over the specific patch of sand Craig has chosen and we sit as he begins to unpack the hamper. There's the bottle of prosecco as well as a bottle of our favourite Malbec from the wine merchant's, a Thermos of chai tea and an assortment of our favourite foods. He's also packed a portable speaker to play music. The amount of thought he's put into all this moves me, and I don't know if it's because I'm tired and hungover, but I feel like crying.

'Here,' he says, wrapping a thick scarf around my shoulders. 'I have more jumpers in the car if you get too cold.'

'Thanks,' I say, trying not to act too surprised at his organisational skills. 'What kind of idiots go for a picnic on the beach in the middle of a British spring?'

'We've never been ones to do things by the book,' he smiles.

Craig plays music from the speaker and passes me a white paper plate with a napkin on top before carefully pouring some prosecco into a flute which he brought from home, balancing the glass against the hamper. He pours himself a small glass, too, saying something about driving home so only being able to have one drink. My stomach rumbles as he unpacks some crusty rolls wrapped in foil, liberally stuffed with avocado and feta and halloumi with sun-dried tomato and kale. I smile to myself. Even our sandwich fillings are terrible millennial clichés.

Over the next half hour or so, we sit on the beach eating and listening to music. We talk about Warner and his antiques, work, my upcoming Ofsted examination, and us.

'Remember our first date on this beach?'

'Um . . .'

'You probably don't. You were really drunk off boxed wine.'

'Yeah, I was also a bit high.'

'Yeah, I know.'

'You knew?'

'Yeah. You said, "I accidentally got a bit high before this date and I knew you'd ask me stuff, you know, about me, as a person and stuff, and I always seem to forget who I am when people ask me that stuff, so I wrote a list of stuff about myself."'

'Did I actually say "stuff" that much?'

'Yep.'

'That's embarrassing.'

'Do you remember the list?'

'Oh, God. Yes, I remember the list. I wrote it at Nat's after we smoked a joint to try and calm my nerves before our date.'

'Well, just in case you didn't remember it . . .' Craig pulls a crumpled, yellowing piece of lined notebook paper from his pocket.

'No way.'

'Yep.' He's grinning widely, a delicious smile.

'Is that the list? You still have it?'

'Kept it after our date. I never wanted to throw it away. It makes me laugh.'

He passes me the piece of paper and I start reading:

1. I like history. Not history like your dating history – this sounds boring, please keep that to yourself. History as in lots of white dudes killing each other and people who wear crowns.
2. I'm right-handed. Which is not very unique.
3. I'm half-Indian and no, that doesn't mean I can 'take spice'. I don't even like curry and it's kinda racist of you to assume that I do.
4. I'm more of a cat than a dog person, but I can see both sides to the argument.
5. I often get mistaken for a child because I'm small and, quite frankly, have the face of a cherub (if biblical art were ever to depict a mixed-race cherub). This means that last week I got ID'd for a lottery ticket.
6. I love *The X Factor* unashamedly. If we end up going out or whatever, I will make you watch it with me every Christmas and I will cry so hard at the final I wouldn't be surprised if you consider calling paramedics.

7. Like most women in their twenties, I partake in bi-weekly existential crises which can usually be placated with one of the following, but preferably a combination of all three: alcohol, drugs and memes.

8. I have a big family and I hope you never meet any of them because they're all either very old or very self-assured of their own opinions, which makes them very tiring and boring to be around.

9. I was one of those awful young people who still carried a glimmer of political hope and voted Lib Dem in the 2010 election. Sometimes I still see Nick Clegg's weasel face when I close my eyes at night.

10. I think 69-ing is a logistically flawed and wildly uncomfortable sex position and I honestly don't know anyone that enjoys it.

'Holy shit, this is terrible. Poor Nick Clegg. Did I give this to you as some sort of shitty keepsake?'

'No,' Craig replies, 'you read aloud from the list, then just left it on the ground. So I put in my pocket and kept it.'

He's laughing and looking at me as though my embarrassment is endearing rather than justified, but I can feel my cheeks prickling a sheepish blush.

'And it was all true,' he adds, 'I've had to sit through so many hours of *The X Factor*.'

'Well, at least I can be commended for my honesty. I warned you what you were getting into,' I smile. 'Craig, I was such an idiot on that date. Why did you even remotely like me?'

He doesn't immediately answer, shuffling his position on the blanket and tucking one leg under the other. He picks up the flute and takes a sip, draining the last of his prosecco. 'Tender' by Blur is playing at a low volume from the speakers.

'You know, our first date was exactly three years ago today.'

There's a sharpness in my tear ducts then and a tingling through my arms and down the skin on my back. He remembers the exact date of our first date.

'I didn't know that,' I say. 'I knew it was around this time, but not to the day.'

Craig turns his head to the left and then the right, scoping out the deserted beach front.

'I did,' he says then and he looks at me. 'I've always remembered the date because it was the day you changed my life for ever, Al.'

He's standing up now, picking up the picnic basket from in front of us on the blanket and moving it to the side. He's looking at me.

'Al, can you stand up?'

'Why?' I ask, panicking that he wants to do something extraordinarily lame, like dance with me or go for a romantic walk. But I oblige, getting to my feet. He turns the music down, but I stopped listening when he asked me to stand.

That's when he kneels down on the picnic blanket; one leg behind him on the wet sand, the other propped up at a right angle.

'Craig, what're you doing?'

He tilts his head towards me then, locking his gaze onto mine. My confusion ebbs and reality sets in, sending a wave of electric warmth through my cold body. My eyes sting and my legs tremble.

'I've always remembered that day because it's the day I knew you were made for me, Al. And I liked you because I knew that I'd found the missing piece to me. And as each day with you passed, it never felt like trying. I mean, obviously we work on our relationship, but what I mean is, it never felt forced. Because falling in love with you was the easiest thing I've ever done. You fitted me like a pair of comfy trainers. But not, like, in a worn-in way. Each day with you, no matter what we're doing, feels a bit like the first ever time I got drunk as a teenager. It's always exciting; we are always exciting. We – us – it never feels old or repetitive. We have so many adventures left in us, Al. Travelling to countries neither of us have ever been, building a home just the two of us – with the chesterfield armchair and claw-foot bathtub and ceiling TV we've always talked about. And starting a family, getting a dog and a cat, and you'll secretly prefer the cat and I'll prefer the dog, but we'll never tell the kids that because, you know, we shouldn't have favourites. But there's the small stuff, too – the everyday, boring life stuff – that I want us to share together. Working out our tax, cleaning the oven, doing the food shop, you going out to buy loo roll when I have the shits, me holding your hair back when you throw up. I want it all, Al. With you. And I want it every day for the rest of our lives.'

I don't know when I started crying but it's pouring out of me like a broken dam now, and I can't take my eyes from his face. I think how implausible it seems that everything about him – the plenitude of happiness he gives me like a gift; the quiet unity in our everyday lives together – can be contained in just one body. Something so inexplicable should take an army. And somehow, he manages to do it all for me, just him. It's always been just him.

But right now, I can't muster the vocabulary to articulate that, so I just stammer the words 'I love you, too' as silent tears fall down my cheeks.

He smiles back, looking back at me, clutching my hand hard in his. A few seconds pass by.

'Aren't you forgetting something?' I say, laughing quietly.

'Oh, shit! Yeah,' he says, letting go of my hand to reach into his backpack as I laugh harder. He holds the ring against my hand.

Then he says it.

'Alex, will you marry me?'

I tell him that I will and he slides the ring on to my finger and jumps to his feet. I throw my arms around his neck and he encircles his tightly around my waist, resting his head against mine and leaning down to kiss my neck.

My head is spinning from the shock, and the remnants of my hangover, so I sit back down and Craig joins me, pouring me another glass of prosecco, hanging the warm scarf around me again and tucking his arm around my shoulders.

'I can't believe you almost forgot to ask me the question,' I laugh.

'I was nervous, okay? It's not every day you ask your girlfriend to be your wife.'

'I had no idea,' I say.

'I'm glad you didn't,' he laughs, kissing my cheek. His lips are warm on my sea-breezed skin. 'I kept looking up and down the beach to see if there were people around.'

'That's what you were doing!'

'Yeah, I'm such a Brit. Couldn't stand for there to be people around when I proposed in case they cheered or clapped or some bollocks.'

'That would have been awful,' I joke. My eyes suddenly fill with tears. 'I thought you were getting bored of me.'

'What?' He pulls his arm slightly down from my shoulders but not away, looking at me with a confused expression.

'You've been so distant, and now I realise it's because you were nervous about this, right? But I just thought you were done with us; that you were just over it.'

'Are you serious?'

'Yes.'

'How could I ever get bored of us? Do you know how ridiculous that is?'

'It's not; people get bored of each other all the time. I can be quite boring, I get that. And, you know, we don't have sex as much as we used to, and it's usually . . .'

'Usually?'

'I don't know. Usually, it's quite . . . same-y.'

'Same-y?'

'Well, yeah.'

I worry that I've hurt his feelings as he looks at me blankly. Then he laughs and rests his lips against my forehead.

'Right. Well, we'll work on that, babe. But how could I ever get bored of you? You are my world.'

'Craig, you don't have to—'

'Listen, Al. You're everything. You're who I'm excited to see as soon as I wake up in the morning and the thing I look forward to every day on the bus home from work. Do you know how rare that is? Not everyone is lucky enough to have what we have. And I'm sure things will get "same-y" along the way because, well, that's life, ain't it? But as long as we talk about it and are always honest with each other, then we make sure we don't get stuck in a rut. Okay?'

'Okay,' I smile, tucking my arms around his body. He feels like home.

'Of course I was nervous,' he adds, 'I was absolutely bricking it. I wanted it all to be right for you. Do you know how much I stressed about the ring?'

I look down at it then, the thin gold band hugging comfortably at my finger, the daisy-shaped cluster of diamonds glinting in the daylight.

'How did you do it? It fits perfectly and it's so beautiful. You've always been pretty clueless with stuff like this.'

'Cheers,' he says, gently pinching the side of my stomach. 'You remember Gemma from work, the one you met at that dinner a while back?'

My skin bristles, memories of hiding behind the wall in town and witnessing Craig and Gemma's assignation seizing my mind.

'Yes. What about her?'

'It was dead sneaky. Do you remember, at the dinner, when she asked to look at that ring you were wearing, the one that changes colour in the light?'

'The moonstone one. Err, vaguely, yes.'

'She tried it on, to gauge what sort of ring size you were. It fitted her perfectly, so she came with me to give a woman's advice and try on rings, so I could make sure it fitted you.'

'What? You asked her to do that?'

'Yeah.'

'Wait, this doesn't make sense. Craig, I saw you both together in town. You were hugging and giving her a bottle of wine.'

'I was thanking her for all her help, the wine was a gift.'

'Oh.'

'Did you follow me?'

'Of course not. We were walking back to Nat's after the pub, the night you had to leave, and we saw you. It was awful, I was freaking out. I feel like a right idiot now.'

'Wait. You thought I was shagging Gemma from work? You're not serious?'

'Well, I don't know. Seeing the two of you hugging, the wine, the way you'd been acting . . . I was just scared.'

He shakes his head. 'I'm so sorry,' he says, 'to make you worry like that. I'd never do anything to hurt you.'

'I know.' I squeeze his hand, grateful for the closure he's given me on the fear that's been eating at me lately. After a while, I say, 'Today has been perfect.'

'I'm glad,' he replies. 'Can't believe I have to call you my fiancée now. Need to get out of the habit of calling you my girlfriend.'

'I know. Fiancée. It's a much nicer word than "boyfriend" or "girlfriend". More rounded.'

'Yeah. Sounds well grown-up, like we've aged ten years.'

I pick up my phone and Craig's body jolts slightly next to mine.

'What're you doing?'

'Messaging the girls to tell them, obviously.'

'Don't,' he says, quickly clutching at my wrist. 'Let's just keep this between us for a bit.'

'Why?'

'It just feels kind of nice, I guess, that it's our secret right now, shared just between the two of us. Even if it's just for half an hour or something.'

'Okay,' I smile, putting my phone down. 'What are you going to be like when we have kids? They'll be teenagers before you reveal them to our mates.'

'Depends,' he says. 'We'd have very cool kids, though.'

'What if he or she supports Spurs?'

'No kid of mine will be a Spurs fan.'

This makes me laugh and I lean over to kiss him. He kisses me softly at first, running his hand down the length of my body and towards my hip, then begins to kiss me harder, growing closer to me and touching my thigh. My legs quiver and there's a hard pulse beating through my lower body.

'Stop,' I say breathily. 'We can't have sex on the beach. We're not teenagers.'

'Okay, okay. You're right.'

'Maybe I was too harsh on our sex life earlier.'

'Yep, I think we've still got it. Are you sure we can't . . .'

'No!' I laugh. 'As much as I want to.'

'Okay. Right, we should start packing up anyway. I've booked us a table at the Black Horse for a celebratory drink and there's a cab collecting us from ours in half hour.'

'That's my favourite pub.'

'I know,' he smiles.

In the taxi on the way to the pub, after we've dropped the car at home, I can't stop looking at the ring on my finger.

'We've just got engaged!' Craig beams to the taxi driver when he asks how we are.

'Congratulations,' he says in a broad East London accent. 'How old are ya both?'

'I'm twenty-eight,' I say, 'and he's twenty-nine.'

'Good ages,' he replies. 'I got married too young. Must've been off my nut. But you two, that's just right. Good luck, yeah?'

The Black Horse is an old, period pub with chalky brick walls, worn wooden floors and hops hanging from the ceiling. It's situated just outside of town at the top of a hill with narrow, winding lanes, which lends it the creaky, cosy charm of an English countryside pub. If you walk to the end of the beer garden and peer between the bushes, you can see the sea in the distance.

It's busy inside because it's a dreary Sunday lunchtime, and the smell of beef and roast potatoes and beer wafts over as soon as you walk through the door.

'This way,' Craig says, grabbing my hand.

He leads me to a table in a quieter corner of the pub by the stone fireplace, and that's when I see Mackie, Alex and Natasha. They're looking at us and grinning. Natasha is twisting the cork on a bottle of champagne and Mackie is crying.

'Congratulations!' they shout as the bottle pops and they all fling their arms around me.

I catch Craig's eye over my friends' shoulders and he's smiling tenderly at me. Edele squeezes my stomach before they untangle their arms from me and Nat pours us all a glass of champagne. Craig steps over and kisses my cheek.

'You did this?' I ask him.

He nods. 'They had to be part of this day.'

'Damn right we did,' Edele says, hugging Craig.

'But when . . .? I don't get it,' I ask.

'He told me yesterday,' Mackie says, still crying. 'I had to keep it a secret all night.'

'Pull yourself together, Marshall,' Edele says.

'I can't believe you didn't blurt it out when you were hammered,' Nat laughs.

'So you two didn't know?'

'Craig called us this morning,' Nat says. 'Mack had already made sure we were free this afternoon, but Craig didn't trust us all knowing before a drunken night out.'

'Well,' he says, 'would you trust you lot with a secret like that before a night at Bar Chocolate?'

'Not a chance, mate,' Edele replies. 'Very wise. You definitely chose the most responsible one to tell.'

I look at Mackie and start laughing. 'Mack, why did you let me get so hammered last night if you knew Craig was going to propose? I could barely stand! I mean, I curtsied to a bouncer!'

'You would've got suspicious if I tried to stop you drinking.'

'Yeah, and we all know how agg you get when you're fucked, Al,' Edele adds. 'If Mackie tried to take a drink off you, you probably would've decked her.'

'Right, yeah,' I grin. 'That's true.'

'I'm just so happy for you both,' Mackie says, leaning across the table to grab my hand.

'To Alex and Craig,' Edele says, raising her glass. We all follow suit. 'Let's save the soppy speeches for when we've finished this bottle, shall we? But for now, let's just say we couldn't be happier for you both. It takes a lot for us to trust a fella with one of our girls, Craig, but you're all right, you know.'

We all laugh and Craig touches Edele's shoulder. 'So touching as always. Thank you, Ed.'

'To a lifetime of happiness and love,' Mackie says. Edele sticks her tongue out in a mock-vomit face. We clink glasses and drink.

'Welcome to the family, Craig,' Nat says, smiling. She looks at me and blows me a kiss across the table. This must be hard for her, but she's not letting it show. She never would.

We spend the afternoon drinking and talking and laughing, and I've never felt so surrounded by love. As the sun begins to set outside and we think about heading home, I look over at Craig, who is saying something to the girls and laughing so much that his whole upper body is shaking. I put my hand on his knee and he holds it, softly stroking my knuckles with his thumb. I think about how lucky I am, to have him woven so tightly into the intricate stitching of my future, and of all that he's taught me simply from being in my life.

He's taught me that love is a thrilling and heart-pounding thing. It's trekking up a muddy mountain on a hike in a foreign country, heavy backpacks tugging at your arms and waist, and throwing your arms around at each other at the summit, exhausted and full of adventure. It's drinking too much champagne at a friend's wedding and dancing with sore feet to music like 'All of Me' by John Legend and 'You Make My Dreams' by Daryl Hall & John Oates. It's the arm around your shoulders in bed and the warm, wet kiss on the forehead after sex when your bodies are soaked through with sweat and your cheeks are crimson. It's lying under the stars in the hot heat of summer and knowing that the only thing as heavy and heady and omnipotent as that feeling in your chest is the vast blackness stretched out above you. It's welcoming them into your family and your friendship circle, and that swelling pride when they look at you and smile, because they're simply happy that you are – finally, after everything – so happy.

But he's also taught me that love is found in the quiet and in the calm. It's in the routine, the stillness, the simply muddling along. It's lying in bed and watching the latest Netflix show you're both obsessed with. It's picking up their favourite flavour of Kettle Chips from the supermarket on your way home from work. It's strolling through the local park you've been to a thousand times before, not saying a word, just silently content in each other's company. It's leaving a bowl by their side of their bed when they're sick, and gently stroking their hair to help them drift off to sleep. It's tearing out a page of a magazine or newspaper, just because you know they'll enjoy reading it.

He's taught me that, no matter how far love pushes you to breaking point, no matter how much you may give up on it – love never gives up on you. It is there, waiting in the furthest stretches of your conscience, when you're ready to accept it again. And you know that, no matter how your story ends, knowing that kind of love is the greatest gift you will ever have; the greatest gift you will ever give. It is nothing short of a miracle.

CHAPTER TWELVE

Mackie

It's been a week since the job interview where I squeezed a spot on my top and spilt peppermint tea all over my vagina. I'm not surprised that I haven't heard back yet.

The light from my sunrise alarm woke me up at 6.30 this morning from a deep sleep – the kind where, for a second or two after you plummet into consciousness, you don't know where you are or who are you are or what the hell is going on – which is weird, because I usually stir well before my alarm goes off. Perhaps a weekend of drinking is catching up with me – gone are the days where we could go out three nights in a row, sleep for two hours, and still make it through work the next day.

Yesterday was a day of plodding through work, sluggish and slow with a sore head. It's unlike me, and I felt guilty for not particularly interacting with Lucy, but it was the Monday after the Sunday where my best friend got engaged. I think I can let myself off.

So, this morning, in an attempt to detox, I pulled on my trainers and went for a run before the sun came up. Chairs were being laid out in the cafe opposite and a fox was scuttling between the shadows of the buildings. Priory Park was dark and still, except for an elderly man walking his dog and another young woman on a run wearing big headphones. By the time I got home, the morning sun was leaking into the sombre sky and pouring puddles of soft light into my bedroom.

Now, standing in the queue to order a tea in the cafe just down the road from the office, pangs of hunger shoot through my stomach and I think about the tub of overnight oats in my bag, with a drizzle of local honey and coconut shavings and dried apricots. I prefer fresh fruit, but according to the colour-coded poster in my kitchen – which shows which fruits and vegetables are in season across different months of the year – the only seasonable produce at the moment is cabbage, cauliflower and kale. And as much as I love kale, I don't particularly want it in my oats.

'Morning, Marshall.' I spin round to see Sexy Luke standing behind me in the queue, wearing a fitted white shirt under a smart black coat.

'Oh, hey,' I say in a noticeably surprised, high-pitched voice. Why do I sound like a squeaky Disney cartoon character every time I see him? 'How are you, Luke?'

'I'm all right, thanks. How're you?'

'Yeah, I'm all good, you?'

Crap, I've already asked him how he is. This is awkward. Why, Mackie? Why are you this way?

'I've already asked you that,' I add quickly. He laughs and looks down.

'Early start, was it?' Luke asks.

'Yeah, I went for a run. Absolutely starving now though. How did you know I was up early?'

'Your Instagram Story of the sunrise. Figured you must have been doing something like going for a run.'

I forgot about the sunrise Instagram Story. He must think I'm so basic.

'Why did you assume that?'

'Well, you obviously look after yourself. You look fit. I mean, "fit" as in "healthy", obviously.' He looks embarrassed then, which strikes me as odd, given the air of confidence he normally carries around with him. I'm glad that I'm not the only one who's already embarrassed themselves during this conversation.

I lock my eyes on his and say, 'Thank you, I try to keep fit. I really like running, I want to try and do a marathon soon—' Luke doesn't say anything but interrupts me by nodding at something behind me.

'Miss? Can I help you?' I was too distracted by Luke that I didn't realise I was at the front of the queue.

'Oh, yes. Sorry.' I shuffle forward. 'Can I have a green tea to go, please?'

'And a cappuccino to go, please.' Luke comes up behind me. 'I'll get these, Mack.'

He's standing so close to me that I can smell him: clouds of cologne and Persil and warm skin breezing over from his tall frame. I had no idea the smell of Persil could turn me on.

'Thanks, that's kind. Next time it's on me,' I say as Luke pays and we move to the side of the queue to wait for our drinks.

'Any time.'

We get our drinks and walk to the office, talking about the magazine. He's grinning a lot and making regular eye contact with me. His physical proximity has a powerful effect on me, like a caffeine kick. I can't decide if there's a distinct sort of electricity between us, or if he's just one of those men that manages to convince all women that he fancies them, like a sort of sexual chemistry magician.

The lift doors open and we all pack into the enclosed space, and I find myself pushed up against Luke's sexy chest, cradling my tea so that it doesn't go on his white shirt. Although, maybe that wouldn't be such a bad thing. If this were a Hollywood romcom, I'd stumble and spill my tea all over him. He'd chuckle, tell me not to worry, then take his shirt off. I'd offer to wash it for him after work, he'd come over, we'd have wild sex and he'd fall madly in love with me and we'd be together for ever. Except this isn't a film, it's real life, and if I chuck my tea over his shirt, he'll probably think I'm a clumsy bitch, send me the dry-cleaning bill and never speak to me again.

'Well, this is my floor,' I say as the lift judders to a halt. Why did I feel the need to announce that? Luke and I work in the same building; he knows which floor I'm on. 'See you later, Luke.'

'Bye, Emma.' I turn and smile at him as the doors close. He's never called me Emma before.

To my surprise, even though I'm 15 minutes early for work, Lucy is already at her desk.

'Morning, boss,' she grins.

'Hi, Lucy. You're in early.'

'I know, I wanted to get ahead with these layouts before our ten o'clock brainstorm meeting for the next issue.'

'That's really helpful. Thanks for doing that.'

She smiles and directs her gaze back to her screen, an expression of concentration taking control of her face. I can hear the music blaring from her earphones. She's listening to 'Broken-Hearted Girl' by Beyoncé. Maybe she's thinking about her dead cat. I wonder when she suddenly decided to start taking her job more seriously. It's not that she's bad at it, but just that I've never known her to get in early. Perhaps she's somehow figured out that I'm looking for a new job, and is hoping to step into my role. I don't mind. She's welcome to it.

Various icons pop up on my desktop as the computer loads, so I take this opportunity to start eating my breakfast. The tea is still too hot to drink. I open the programme which displays all the magazine pages we're currently working on. The sub-editors are working on the interiors pages, and I think back to the day of the shoot. It was in an eighteenth-century ocean-front house an hour's drive away, which originally belonged to a sea captain and is now owned by a local artist and homeware designer, his trinkets displayed on every available surface like a grandpa's attic. It was old and big and bruised from time, and I was mesmerised by the scuffed black paint on the wooden staircase, the antique canopy bed, the layers of peeling wallpaper, tattered and messy and gritty, frayed glimpses into years and inhabitants gone by.

I remember thinking how mesmerising it was as the photographer set up and the prop stylist moved around dried pieces of coral and arranged tall tree branches in vases. In the background of the shot, big proud windows, no curtains. 'But I couldn't live somewhere like this,' I thought. I'm not a countryside girl, not at heart. I crave the rush of busy towns; somewhere that swallows you up in all of its dirty, bustling commotion. Somewhere that makes you feel part of something bigger, better. A place where I can be a tiny but fundamental cog in a big, brilliant machine. There are no cogs here. Here, we're big fish in small ponds. Too suffocated. Too seen.

I flick over to my Gmail, just to check my personal email, and my hand freezes on the computer mouse. There's an email from Duncan from this morning.

From: duncan.frampton@atlasmedia.com
To: emma.mackie@gmail.com
Subject: Art Director at Atlas
Date: 12/03/19

Dear Emma,
Hope you're well. I just tried to give you a call regarding the role. Could you give me a call back when you can, please?

Thanks,
Duncan

I push my chair back and jump to my feet.

'Everything all right?' Lucy asks, removing one earphone. She's now listening to 'Sweet Dreams'.

'Yes, of course,' I reply, rummaging in my coat pocket for my phone and minimising the Gmail window on my screen. Seven WhatsApps in Mean Girls which I'll look at later, and a missed call from an unsaved mobile number fifteen minutes ago. It must have been when I was talking to Luke in the coffee shop.

'Damn you, Luke, and your sexy distracting ways,' I think.

'I just have to make a quick call, Lucy. I'll be back in five.' She's replaced the earphone now, looking back at her screen, and cannot hear me.

Stepping out into the corridor, with its framed photos of the *Hackton Times* covers, my heart is thumping so hard that I swear I can hear it.

'Hello?', a man answers.

'Hi, Duncan. It's Emma Mackie.'

'Hello, Emma. How are you?'

'I'm very well, thanks. I'm so sorry I missed your call, I was getting a cup of tea.'

'I was getting a cup of tea', Emma? Seriously? What is wrong with you?

'Not a problem. If you're anything like me, you can't start your day without one.'

Oh, good. We're bonding over tea. How very British, next we'll talk about the weather for the full cliché.

'Exactly,' I laugh nervously.

'So, thank you for speaking to me on Skype last week.'

238

'No, thank *you*,' I say. 'I, umm. I'm really sorry about the tea incident.'

Duncan laughs. 'Honestly, it wasn't a problem. I just hope your, err, trousers were okay?'

Trousers. How sweet of him not to say 'little girl pyjamas'.

'Oh, yes. They were fine.'

'Right, so, the reason I'm calling you is obviously about the art director position with us here at Atlas.'

'Umm, obviously,' I think, but instead I say, 'Yes?'

'It's good news, Emma. We would absolutely love to have you as part of our team, if you'll still have us.'

No way. No bloody way. Is he serious? My heart is banging against my chest so hard that I think I might throw up all over the *Hackton Times* corridor.

'Are you serious?' I ask without thinking.

Duncan laughs. 'Deadly serious. Despite the unfortunate tea incident, I was very impressed with your interview, your love of design and your portfolio that you sent through. I think you'd be a perfect fit.'

'Yes,' I blurt out, 'I'd absolutely love to join the team. Thank you so much, Duncan.'

'That's great news! Do you have any questions for me, Emma?'

My head spins. How about: 'This must be a joke; is this a joke?'; 'Is this just because you have an acne fetish, Duncan?'; 'Are you not afraid I'll just walk around throwing tea on everything?'

'When would you need me to start?' I ask, composing myself.

'We'd ideally like to have you by the end of April, as we'll be very busy planning our summer issues then. You said your notice period was one month, didn't you? Anyway, I'll send over the contract so you can check over it.'

'Of course, looking forward to reading over the terms and I'll get back to you to confirm when I can start.'

'Great. I'm so pleased, Emma. We're very much looking forward to having you on board.'

'Thanks so much,' I say. 'I'll talk to you soon.'

'Speak soon. Bye.'

I hang up the phone and do an inward squeal of delight, clenching my hand into a fist and punching the air triumphantly. Finally, a new start.

Wait, a new start. A new job. A new city. The realisation hits me and I have to steady myself against the wall, like when you run for too long on an empty stomach.

Atlas Media are based just off Grays Inn Road, near Chancery Lane, in London. That would mean moving to a different city, a different flat, away from Hackton, away from the girls. I walk back to my desk where Lucy is still listening to Beyoncé and frowning in concentration at her screen. She doesn't look up.

I drum each of my fingers against the desk, my thoughts freighted with weight and worry at telling the girls. So much so, that it outweighs my own dread at starting again in an alien place, away from Natasha, Edele and Mackie, the three people who together comprise something so constant, so sound and solid in my life. Something as rare as that sort of bond surely can't be built again? And really, would I want it to?

I have to tell them soon. Will it seem like subterfuge or disloyalty if I leave it any longer than a day? 'Why didn't you tell us when you found out?' they'll chorus, and I won't have a satisfactory answer to give them.

MACKIE: Is anyone about tonight for dinner and drinks?

ALEX: I can't tonight, we're going for dinner with Craig's parents to celebrate the engagement. I'm free tomorrow?

EDELE: 'The engagement' – adorable. When did we get so grown-up? Tomorrow works for me.

MACKIE: Tomorrow's good, Nat?

NAT: I can't do tomorrow, sorry. How about Thursday?

EDELE: I said I'd hang with Mum Thursday. #cool

ALEX: This is impossible.

MACKIE: Can anyone do Friday?

NAT: I actually can.

EDELE: Yep.

ALEX: I won't be around until about 7.30 p.m., but yes, Friday works.

MACKIE: Friday at 7.30 p.m. it is. How about that little Italian place on Brewer Street, near the car park?

EDELE: Sounds good. I don't have much money and not exactly in Mum's good books at the moment so can't ask her for a loan right now. Someone share a pizza with me? Help me, I'm poor.

MACKIE: Is it because you shagged Eddie?

EDELE: It's too early to go into that. I still have PTSD.

MACKIE: And don't worry, I'll shout you a pizza, Ed. In fact, dinner's my treat. Pizzas on me. Not the wine though, I'm not balling.

EDELE: Seriously? Mack, what would I do without you? Thank you. What've you done? Is this guilt pizza?

MACKIE: No guilt pizza! I just love you three, that's all.

ALEX: We love you too xxx

I get to the Italian on Brewer Street ten minutes early. It's one of our favourite haunts – small and basic but not clinical, with bare brick walls, white tablecloths and family photos. There's a large mirror covering the back wall in an attempt to make the restaurant seem bigger than it is. It's clumsy but cosy, which seems apt somehow.

Taking my seat at the table in front of the large mirror, I order a bottle of wine with four glasses – the same one we always have when we come here – and focus on calming my breathing. In: one, two, three. Out: one, two, three. In: one, two, three. Out: one, two—

'Hey, Marshall.' An arm around my shoulder and a kiss on the cheek.

'Oh! Hi, Ed.'

'Sorry, did I make you jump? Were you asleep or something?'

'No, it's fine. You all right? Jesus, you're early for dinner by almost ten minutes. Are you some sort of impostor?'

She laughs and rolls her eyes, flinging her denim jacket over the chair opposite me.

'First date or what?' She's gesturing to the only other people in the restaurant; a boy and a girl of about fourteen years old, sharing a pizza and two Diet Cokes. I was so preoccupied I hadn't even noticed they were there.

'Hmm.'

Edele looks at me intently for a moment, and asks, 'Everything okay?'

'Of course. I was just up early for a run this morning so I'm a bit knackered, that's all.' I focus on making my smile seem as enthusiastic and believable as possible.

'You need to take it easy sometimes, you know. Ease off the Instagram-perfect life.'

'I know, I know. You're right. Any luck on the job hunt?'

She bristles. 'Let's not talk about that,' she smiles weakly, 'I could do with a relaxing evening.'

Oh, crap. Well, I'm here to tell you, Ed, that the one constant in your life – your three best friends – is about to change, just like everything else always does. Probably not the relaxing evening you had planned.

The waiter is pouring a glass of wine for Edele and me when I look up at the mirror and see Alex and Natasha approaching the glass door. They greet us both and take their seats, thanking the waiter as he pours their wine, too.

We order a pizza each – pepperoni and chillies for Edele, goat's cheese and olives for Nat, mixed veg for Alex, and a light base with rocket and ham for me. I don't even order it for health reasons, but I haven't had an appetite all day and the lighter option seems more manageable. Besides, if I order anything other than a pizza, I'm sure the girls will suspect something. Even when I'm on a health kick, I'll never turn down a pizza with these three.

'He's lovely, but bloody hell, he fancies himself some sort of Hackton mafia boss.' Alex is talking about her engagement celebration with Craig's parents on Tuesday. 'He reminds me of Fat Tony from *The Simpsons*. Kind of looks like him, too.'

'Mack? You okay?'

I'm holding a slice of pizza and staring into my wine glass. Edele, Natasha and Alex are all watching me.

'Yes, of course.'

'You kind of just, like, stopped moving,' Edele comments. 'And you look a bit pale.'

'I'm fine, I obviously just need to borrow some of your St. Moriz.' They don't look convinced.

'Okay,' I falter, putting the slice of pizza back down on my plate. 'I wanted to tell you all something.'

'Mack, you're not ill, are you?' Nat asks.

'God, no,' I exclaim quickly, 'nothing like that, don't worry.' I grip both my knees with my hands, the thick sweat on my palms sticking to the denim of my jeans.

The words spill out of my mouth like the relief of finally spitting out burning mouthwash. 'I got a new job.'

There's a chorus of elated congratulations, and Alex squeezes my shoulder next to me.

'It's about time they found you a more senior position at Ribbon Media,' Alex says. 'You've been running that art department at the *Hackton Times* for years now.'

'That's the thing,' I stumble. 'It's not at the *Hackton Times*. It's a new company – Atlas Media.'

'Oh, great!' she says quickly. 'You said new job, not promotion, that was daft of me.'

'What's Atlas Media?' Nat asks. 'Sounds very cool and worldly.'

'It is. It's very cool. They do lots of those in-flight magazines you get on planes, and they're doing well financially, so it's a much more secure company to work for.'

'Is their office far from Ribbon?' Alex asks.

I hesitate. In the mirror, I can see that Alex is looking at Nat's expression. Suddenly, the ecstasy has simmered down, replaced with the comedown of realisation.

'They're not based around here, are they?' Nat asks, her voice quavering.

'No. That's the thing, their offices are in London.'

'Please say you're going to commute?' Edele says.

'I looked into it but it would take almost ninety minutes each way on the rush-hour trains and underground, and a season ticket wouldn't cost much less than rent.'

'Wait, so you're thinking of moving?'

'To as close to London as I can afford, yeah.'

'When?'

'Well, my notice period for *Hackton Times* is a month, so I guess as soon as I can get out of my current flat and find a new place to rent.'

'Oh, that's so soon,' Nat says, leaning back in her chair and looking at me with her big, sad eyes, like a puppy who's just had its favourite toy taken away. 'I mean, of course we're happy for you, Mack. But it's always been us four. We're going to miss you.'

'This seems a bit sudden, doesn't it?' Edele says.

'You know I've been looking for a new job.'

'Yeah, yeah. I know. But what about your flat? You've got a great place here. Are you sure you want to give it up?'

'It's just a flat, Ed.'

'But it's not just a flat, is it?' Alex interjects.

'Al's right. Your whole life is here, Mack. Why would you sacrifice it all just for a job?'

'All right, Ed,' Nat says calmly. 'Laying it on a bit thick, there. Mackie knows what she's doing.'

'I'm not saying she doesn't,' she snaps. Then she turns to look at me. 'I'm not saying you don't. I just think you have made a hasty decision. You should think about it more before you decide to up and leave your home and start a completely new life.'

'I know, I get it,' I say, reaching my hand over the table to touch her forearm. She smiles at me but looks away. 'But we know we can't all stay in Hackton for ever, right? You say my whole life is here, but it isn't, Ed. I'm almost thirty, and you lot are the only thing keeping me here. It's different for you all. Al, you've got Craig and the school here; Ed, you've got your mum and brother; and Nat, you've built your home here, that you're now working so hard to reclaim as your own. That's all so important. I would only stay for you three. And I know that I don't need to do that. Because as much as I cherish being a ten-minute drive from your front doors, and knowing all our favourite local restaurants, bars and places on the beach to get drunk and watch the sunset, I also believe that nothing could ever keep us all apart. Especially not something as insignificant as a forty-mile drive.'

'Sounds like you have thought it through,' Edele says.

'I have.'

'And you're sure this will make you happy?'

'Yes.'

Edele nods her acceptance and raises her glass. 'To Mackie. We'll miss you like hell.'

We all clink our glasses. 'To Mackie.'

'To Mackie,' Nat repeats. 'And her next adventure.'

I look around the table at them all, and a newfound courage is buoyed by their warmth and assurance.

'Thank you,' I say. 'I'm going to miss seeing you all the time.'

'And we will miss you,' Nat says. 'But you have to do what's right for you. And we're never going anywhere, Mack. You've got us for good.'

CHAPTER THIRTEEN

Natasha

'I'm going to be late for therapy if I don't get a move on.'

'Yeah, that seems like the kind of thing you shouldn't be late for.'

'Doesn't really scream "getting my shit together", does it?'

'Couldn't you have asked to leave early?'

'Tried that. This place won't even let me off half an hour early to go to therapy.'

'Burn it to the ground, I say.'

'I would, if I didn't need the money to pay my overdue electricity bill.'

Kemi laughs and doesn't reply, looking into the sink as she washes her hands. The bathroom at work smells of citrus-scented disinfectant and the lights are reflecting garishly on the vinyl flooring. I position my hands under the expensive hand dryers and they whirr aggressively into action. I'm grateful that Kemi has ended the conversation because I wouldn't be able to hear what she's saying now.

I can talk to Kemi – who calls me her 'work wife' – about these things: gas bills and therapy sessions. We've sat on the same bank of desks together for almost two years, which means that she knew about my relationship with Matt, and then, inevitably, when it ended. What I like and appreciate about Kemi is that she didn't ask redundant questions – 'What did he say?', 'Are you okay?', 'Has he moved out?' – which meant that I didn't have to relive it more than I needed to. She just hugged me, told me that she was sorry, that she'd come with me to the pub after work whenever I wanted, and that she'd always cover for me if I couldn't face coming in. She removed the photo of Matt and I from the pin-board behind my computer, with my permission, and would sometimes leave breakfast and a coffee by my keyboard.

Kemi dries her hands at the other hand dryer and picks up her handbag before zipping up her black coat.

'I hope it goes well, Nat,' she says, opening the door to leave and glancing at me, a look of solidarity – not pity – on her face. 'You keep on keeping on, yeah?'

'Thanks, Kem. See you in the morning.' She nods in my direction before leaving me alone in the toilets.

I walk back over to the bank of mirrors and take a dusky-pink lipstick out of my jeans pocket. I know it seems like an odd thing to do, touch up your make-up before therapy. No, it's not because I want to shag my therapist. I think it's because I want to seem like I have one small part of my life together, papering over the cracks – some semblance of continuance or conservation of myself – even if it's just neatly applied lipstick. I pause then, staring at my face in the mirror, trying to figure out what, or who, I see.

What's the point in applying lipstick? You're still going to look the same. If anything, you should've whacked on some concealer to try and mask those big, blue bags under your eyes that make you look like a meth-head.

I shake my head and close my eyes, trying to ignore the voice.

'Keep on keeping on,' I say quietly to the mirror.

I walk back to my desk to get my bag and coat. I glance quickly at my phone. 5.46 p.m. If I leave right now, I'll only be five minutes late for my appointment, and I don't think Simon will mind.

'Natasha?'

I look up. It's my line manager, Josephine. Most Josephines are called 'Jo' by their friends or colleagues. Not this one.

'Yes, sorry, Josephine. Everything all right?'

'Yes. I know you're heading off, Natasha, but I thought I'd quickly check that the media plans for Q2 are ready for the quarterly planning meeting tomorrow?'

I tap the sheets of paper in the plastic wallet in front of my computer screen.

'Yes, all ready.'

'Great, thank you, Natasha.' God, I wish this woman would stop repeating my name. It's as if she thinks I'm so stupid I'm likely to forget what it is.

'Sorry, Natasha, I forgot, you must get off to your appointment,' she adds. 'Was it a doctor's appointment, you said?'

Nosy cow.

'Yes. I managed to get a later time slot.'

'Great. I hope everything's all right?'

Seriously, Josephine?

Tell her you have chronic vaginal dryness due to looking at her beaky face all day. That'll shut the bitch up.

'Everything's fine. Thanks, Josephine. See you in the morning.'

'Night, Natasha.' I wince. 'See you tomorrow.'

Simon doesn't get up from his chair. 'Come in, Nat,' he calls. I open the door. Before I met him, I imagined my therapist to have greying hair, thick-rimmed glasses, kind, dark eyes and an overgrown moustache. He'd wear corduroy trousers and tattered brogues. He'd make terrible jokes like an elderly uncle at Christmas, which wouldn't make me laugh but would encourage me to bare my soul to him. He'd cross his legs a lot and ask me about my feelings at every available opportunity. I'd tell him I had a cheese sandwich for lunch, and he'd respond with, 'Yes, Nat, but how did that cheese sandwich make you *feel?*'

Except, none of this is true about Simon. He is a small man with a shiny bald head like an off-white bowling ball. He does wear glasses, but they're thin and discreet, and while his eyes are dark, they give nothing away about the man beneath them. He doesn't have a moustache or make jokes or wear corduroy. He does ask about my feelings, but he prefers words like 'mindsets', 'goals', 'cycles' and 'thought patterns'. He seems to me much more scrupulous and mathematical than a shrink, who I always imagined to be outlandish with a constant expression of studious meditation, like the human version of Rodin's *The Thinker*.

This is the second time I've seen Simon, and I'm wondering what to expect. The first session was last Thursday, and I sat in the large room of the community centre as I talked about Matt. I talked about life before Matt, during Matt and after Matt. I talked about 12 January and the coffee shop conversation and about Kim. I spoke for a majority of the sixty-minute session, which was pretty exhausting. Simon asked if I had observed any negative thought patterns, an inner self-critic, a vicious cycle of self-talk. I told him about the voice. I felt lighter afterwards.

'Hi, Simon,' I say, closing the door behind me. He gestures to the low, peach-coloured armchair opposite his own and says, 'Take a seat. So, how have you been?' He asks these questions like an old school friend.

'Okay,' I say, sitting down and placing my bag next to my feet on the floor. I look up at Simon. He's smiling and saying, 'Good.' In response, I try to contort my face into a smile and then, giving up, rub at the corner of my eyes, careful not to dislodge any mascara. My eyes are itchy. I wish I hadn't worn mascara so that I could rub them freely.

Simon asks me some arbitrary questions about work and the flat, I guess to ensure that I haven't been fired or set my sofa alight. Then he says, 'And have you thought of Matt much this week?'

An acute pang of irritation hits me like a sharp needle piercing skin.

What a stupid question. How is this Phil Mitchell-looking bloke a professional shrink? If you didn't think about Matt, why would you be here? Dumb fuck.

'Well, yeah,' I say.

This sounds more aggressive, or more contemptuous, than I intended. I don't know what to say next. Simon waits. The hesitation hangs heavy in the air between us, though I think it's purposeful.

Eventually, I add, 'I guess I think about him constantly. I don't think he ever really leaves my thoughts, whether he's right at the front of my mind or, you know, somewhere at the back.'

Well, that sounded pathetic.

Simon's nodding and he isn't saying anything, which means that I'm supposed to say something.

Why do rich people pay for this shit? It's literally just an hour of you banging on about yourself. And you're so insane you could just sit at home and talk to yourself instead.

'I suppose he's been more at the front of my mind this past month,' I continue, 'because my best mate got engaged. Her boyfriend proposed to her on the beach with a picnic.'

Why the hell would Simon care about the picnic on the beach? Why don't you go ahead and tell him what sandwich fillings they had, too?

'And I know it sounds selfish – because, well, it is – but just a few months ago, I thought I'd be the first of our group to get engaged. I'm not upset with her, of course I'm not. But I guess I just see all the love she's surrounded by, and how much Craig cares for her, and I just start longing to have that love and care again. I'm not jealous of their relationship, it just makes me want my one back.'

'Does your friend know how her engagement makes you feel?'

'No. And I don't want her to. This is her time, and I don't think she'd understand. I'd rather just be happy for her.'

'It's very tiring to mask your feelings, Nat, and pretend that everything is okay when it isn't. What about the others in your friendship group? Have you discussed this with them?'

My tongue is dry. I run it over the roof of my mouth, feeling the ridges in my gums. It feels rough and I swallow hard, trying to focus on all the infinitesimal sensations in my body: the slight grumbling of my empty belly, the rise and fall of my chest with my breath. Simon told me to do this as a mindfulness exercise when my thoughts seem too overwhelming, to help bring me back to the real world.

'Not really. One of my other friends has got a new job and is moving to London, so she's pretty preoccupied, and the other is trying to find a job and get her own life together. Everyone's got their own shit to deal with.'

I think about what Mackie said when she told us she was moving: 'Nat, you've built your home here, that you're now working so hard to reclaim as your own.' Why did this have to sound so bleak and depressing? Alex is getting married, Mack is pursuing her dream job, and Edele has her tight-knit family here. What do I have? An empty house crammed full with ghosts that I am desperately trying to feel at home in again.

Simon says something about the importance of confiding in my friends but I don't really listen.

'And what about the voice you mentioned? Your self-talk that we spoke about last week? What does your inner critic make of all these changes in yours and your friends' lives?'

'It tells me off and mocks me for being pathetic, that I should be over Matt by now, says that I am selfish and a terrible friend for making my mates' lives about me, and that it's no wonder Matt left me. That I would have left me too, if I were him.'

Simon leans forward in his chair and clasps his hands together on his knee.

'How does it make you feel, when you tell yourself those things?'

'Not great.'

'How so?'

You are not good enough.

I look out of the window and rub my lips together. They feel chapped.

'It makes me feel small, inferior, worthless,' I say, 'like I'm not good enough.' I hesitate before continuing, 'But that's just the way I think, and the way I think is just part of who I am, isn't it? I don't see how I can change that. It's subconscious, right?'

'Well . . .' Simon begins with an enthusiastic intonation which is intended to give me hope. 'Would you like to change the way you think about yourself?'

'Yes, that's part of the reason I'm here.' I sound harder than I feel.

'Then my aim is to help you learn the strategies to identify these thought cycles, to challenge them, so that you can begin to change them.'

'Okay,' I say. 'So, the goal isn't to forget about Matt, but to change the way I think about him?'

'Do you think that the way you think about Matt and the way you think about yourself are linked?'

'I . . . I don't understand.'

'Okay, let me put it another way,' he says. 'Do you think the "voice", this inner critic that makes you feel bad about yourself, was created when Matt ended your relationship?'

'No,' I answer surprisingly quickly. 'I think I've always had it. But the break-up just brought it to the surface.' He nods. I find myself continuing, 'When the voice is loud, or when I listen to it more, I find I lose myself in it a little bit, to the point I don't really know if I'm me or not any more.'

I realise that this makes very little sense. What I mean to say, but can't quite find the words for, is that sometimes, I find myself dissociating from my senses, and everything feels artificial, or doesn't feel like anything at all. Things begin to look unreal, as though the whole framework through which I process the world is being dissolved. I wonder if, perhaps, it's some sort of cognitive self-sabotage, a desperation to transform into someone else because, as the voice assures me, who I am is no longer good enough.

I look at Simon. He's saying something but I don't know what.

'Sorry, Simon. Can you say that again?' I ask.

'Do you think there's any evidence to actually support the things the voice tells you?'

'I don't know.' I feel a quick rush of panic. 'I don't know. I just want to breathe out; I feel like I'm always holding my breath. And the voice . . . I want it to stop. Or, at least, to be kinder.'

'Don't worry, Natasha,' Simon urges. 'That's why you're here. This is all a step in the right direction.'

The thought that I've actively started the process of eradicating such an inhibiting impulse makes me feel relieved and a tension eases in my jaw.

Can you really do that, change the way you think? Seems pretty unrealistic. People can't change themselves.

No, I think, maybe they can't. But isn't it worth trying?

After the session with Simon, I feel tired but lighter again. I get home and the flat feels cold and empty, but I don't mind it. I'm too drained to be with anyone but myself. I perch at the kitchen window and pull my pouch of tobacco from the bottom of my bag. It's old and starting to dry out, which makes it taste stale and bitter.

My phone pings in my pocket.

ALEX: How did it go tonight Nat? Call if you need anything xx

I put my phone back in my pocket and don't reply to her. I'm conscious of not bringing Alex down at such a happy time, but I also don't have the energy to talk about it, especially to someone who probably wouldn't understand anyway.

Simon's words echo and vibrate in my ears. 'It's very tiring to mask your feelings, Nat, and pretend that everything is okay when it isn't.'

There's pretending, I think, and then there's ignoring the things you don't have the energy for. That's not inauthentic, it's just self-preservation.

Yeah. You keep telling yourself that.

For the rest of the evening, I slump on the sofa, intermittently watching the late April sun dissolve into milky red then dank navy and near-black, with my laptop perched on my lap and the TV buzzing faintly in the background, looking over my notes for the presentation at work tomorrow.

At one point, I pick up my phone, now triple-screening between the TV, my laptop and my phone. I open Alex's message and read over it, feeling guilty for ignoring her. But I still don't know what to say. I close WhatsApp and open the list of matches on my dating app. I hover over Lawrence's name, look at his photo, grinning in a grey T-shirt in front of a waterfall, and think about our date, the sex, chucking him out in the morning, his text asking if I was okay. But I don't know what to say to him either, so I put my phone down and go back to prepping for tomorrow's presentation. I carry on ignoring the TV in the background. But I like the company of the noise.

CHAPTER FOURTEEN
Edele

'If I'm going to do this whole "getting my life together" thing, I should probably order a healthy tea like Mack would – detoxifying, or something like that. Hopefully it can detoxify my soul, too.'

That's what I thought five minutes ago when I ordered a 'cleanse tea' with apple cider vinegar, milk thistle, raw honey and wheatgrass powder. Except it doesn't taste like my soul is being detoxified. It tastes like what I imagine cat piss on grass to taste like.

I'm sitting in the cafe above one of the sportswear shops in town, the kind in which you can find floral yoga leggings for £95 in sizes XXXS – L. The cafe upstairs, which is called Matcha Mornings, sells kelp smoothies, lavender lattes and quinoa and kimchi salads. There's at least seven ingredients on their breakfast menu, which is dedicated entirely to açaí bowls, which I've never heard of, including lucuma, pitaya and maca. I ordered avocado on toast from their 'main dishes' menu for £9 and asked for a poached egg on top. The man with the curly moustache behind the till said that would cost an extra £2.50. I told him that I'd just stick to the toast, thanks.

Around here, the people you'll find in a cafe during working hours fall into one of five categories:

1. Coffee shop wankers smugly typing away on their £1,000 Apple laptops. They'll be here for four or five hours and spend £30 on rose lattes and cleanse teas and açaí bowls.
2. Coffee shop wankers smugly typing away on their (miscellaneous brand) laptops. They'll be here for four or five hours and buy one bottle of water – maybe a black filter coffee in two hours' time – but will plug in their laptop charger, phone charger and portable charger charger into every available plug socket.
3. Two young, thin, blond women in workout gear with young babies in prams. The prams are ridiculously big, especially considering the people in them are the size of my forearm, and they take up 75 per cnet of the cafe. One of the blond women talks about whittling down their wedding guest list 'from 300 acquaintances, family friends and colleagues' to 'just 150 close friends and family'. The other is saying she 'needs to lose six pounds', despite the fact she's just had a baby and already looks like she might blow away if the wind picks up.
4. A small group of men and women in workwear who are having a lunch meeting. They're resting their heads on their hands and look perpetually knackered.

They all secretly wanted to order a McDonald's to the office instead, but none of them wanted to say it. Now they're all trying to figure out what half of the ingredients on the menu mean and wondering if Rob will pay the bill and put it against expenses.

5. Unemployed losers who are almost homeless after shagging their brother's best mate and are desperately trying to turn themselves into number 1 so they can feel as though they have their life together.

Guess which category I fall into.

I wince at the taste of the cat-piss tea and put the mug back on the saucer. My laptop is ancient and has a low, audible hum whenever it's switched on, as though it's on the brink of self-combustion. I stare at the dull screen which is divided into two windows: one, a website with available job listings in PR, and the other, a document displaying my CV. I've already applied for one job as a PR manager working across several restaurant chains, based in a neighbouring town to Hackton. But I've already lost what little motivation I had when I arrived and I can't stop my mind wandering to thoughts of Eddie and Liam.

Eddie and I haven't spoken since we slept together after my night out with the girls almost seven weeks ago. Outside the club, we waited for a taxi and shared a cigarette. We didn't say much to each other during the short car journey to my house, but Eddie never removed his hand from my upper leg. I remember thinking how warm his palm felt through my clothes, even though my own hands were freezing from the bitter night air. We laughed quietly to each other as we unlocked the door and crept upstairs to my room, being careful not to wake my mum or Liam. I wondered, when I shut my bedroom door slowly behind us, whether Eddie would have second thoughts then, being shut into a room he's never seen before – a room just down the corridor from where his best friend was sleeping off his drunkenness – yet in a house he's stayed at countless times. But he didn't. He walked straight up to me and kissed me hard. He started to take off my clothes so that I was just in my underwear, then his own, rushed and desperate and racked with fever. He removed a condom from his jeans pocket and sat naked on the edge of my bed and pulled me on top of him, so that my legs were bent either side of his body and I could feel how hard he was against the top of my thigh. He took off my bra and his lips walked the bareness of my chest, shoulders horizon-wide and his galloping heart beneath my hands. He slid the thin strap of my thong aside, my eyes closed, I let out one small gasp and he was inside me. I think of it now, slow then fast and faster still, rhythmic and hazy and frenetic, clutching at flesh, talking through skin, thrumming with hunger and wet sweat and electricity.

When I woke up, I was naked and resting my head on his bare, solid chest. That's when, at what must have been about 9.30 a.m., Liam's voice echoed from outside my bedroom door, calling, 'Ed?', and in our half-awake daze, both Eddie and I replied, 'Yeah?' Liam opened the door with such ferocity that it slammed against the wall with a huge bang that jolted us both awake.

'What the fuck?' Liam shouted.

'Liam, mate—' Eddie started.

'What the fuck do you think you're doing?' Liam cut him off. My head felt like a nail being hammered into a brick wall.

'It's all right, Liam, just listen—' I tried to help. My brother ignored me.

'Get the fuck out,' Liam demanded with a venom I didn't recognise, grabbing Eddie's bare arm.

'Okay, I'll go.'

Liam turned his back as Eddie pulled on his clothes in a frantic rush.

'Look, mate, it just happened, okay?' Eddie said as he pulled his coat on and picked up his phone from my bed-side table.

'What did?' Liam shouted, turning around to face Eddie. 'Fucking my sister?'

His expression was startlingly blank and his body still, as though the anger he felt was so annihilating and all-consuming that it rendered the rest of his senses powerless.

'Liam, try and cool it, yeah?' Eddie tried to reassure him, but I knew straight away that the worst thing anyone could say to my brother when he was angry was 'calm down', 'chill out' or 'cool it'. Liam's brow lowered and his lip curled into a snarl. I sprang into action then, my head spinning, clutching the duvet to my naked chest and grabbing at my dressing gown on the floor. I wrapped it around my body, still trying to cover myself, but Liam and Eddie were too focused on each other to even realise what I was doing.

'Get the fuck out of my house,' Liam spat.

'Liam, what the fuck do you think you're doing?' I said, standing up.

'Stay out of it, Edele,' he said, walking towards Eddie until Eddie was standing with his back against the wall.

'Come on, mate—'

'If you ever go anywhere near my sister again, I'll fucking ruin you,' he said. 'Okay? Do you understand?' His face was wet with perspiration.

Eddie's neck was strained but his face was hard. He looked at Liam and said, 'I'm going. Let me go.'

'Eddie,' I started.

'It's fine, Ed,' he said, still looking at Liam.

'You don't talk to her, understand?'

'Fine.'

They stood looking at each other for a moment before Liam grabbed Eddie's shoulder and pushed him through the bedroom door and into the hallway.

I followed them, not knowing what to do, feeling useless, saying, 'Liam, please.'

I couldn't understand why he was reacting like this. My brother turned around then and glared ferociously into my eyes. My vision was swimming with such severity that it felt like I was in a snow globe that someone had picked up and was shaking violently.

'You're a mess,' he said, his eyes widening, 'a fucking mess, Edele.'

I said nothing; I couldn't.

He backed away then, moving his jaw around and running his left hand through his hair, damp with sweat. 'All I've ever tried to do is protect you but you make it impossible. Eddie, of all people. He's my best mate. What is *wrong* with you? Will you fuck anything that moves?' He shook his head, then, in a sort of hushed spitting sound so as to not alert our mum, said, 'You are impossible. I can't live with you any more.' He walked back to his room. 'Grow up and move the fuck out.'

He opened his bedroom door, walked through it, and closed it behind him. I was alone on the landing. My pulse throbbed in my neck and I slumped to the floor and I thought about Liam and Eddie and Ray and I cried. I cried because I was angry with Ray for leaving something of himself behind in Liam.

I stop thinking about Liam and Eddie and Ray look out of the window to the street below the cafe. I like watching life happening in Hackton. Wispy clouds like white chalk dust hang over the rows of shops, music whines from a cracked car window. A woman in pink sweatpants holds onto a pram with one hand and searches for something in her handbag with another. There's something comforting in how unremarkable my home town is. The cracks in the concrete, the broken glass in the post office shopfront, the beer bottle shattered into tiny emerald shards by the bus stop. Its imperfections are familiar and feels like home. I wonder what it would be like to build a new sense of belonging in another place, somewhere far away. In the sort of town that smiles while handing out free magazines or newspapers, that filters men in well-fitting suits and women in belted macs onto the rush-hour trains like shuffling sardines in a metal tin. Where there are Sunday morning flower markets, cosy independent book stores and charity shops with labels that read: '£45 (vintage Valentino)'. I wonder if Mackie is looking forward to her new life in the city, or if she owns a belted mac.

My phone flashes on the table next to my laptop.

MUM: How's job applications? When u home? Am making tea. Haven't heard from ur brother x

Ever since I slept with Eddie, Liam's not been at home much. I don't know where he's been but I think he's been trying to avoid me. And honestly, I'm pleased that I haven't had to see him. He must have provided a reason to Mum as to why he's not home much because I still don't think she knows what happened. Instead, she asks if I'm all right, or if Liam and I have fallen out. I tell her that everything's fine, Liam's just on at me to get a job and sort my life out. 'Well, he has a point,' Mum says.

I text her that I'll be home for tea and that the applications are going well. I haven't heard from Liam either.

MUM: L must be at Ed's. C u later, pheata x

'Your avocado on toast.' I look up from my phone. The man with the curly moustache is smiling at me.

'Oh, yes. Thank you.' I move my laptop to make room for the plate. He puts it down in front of me. The avocado is lightly mashed over two slices of seeded toast. It's topped with a thin slice of lime and one whole pansy.

'Do I, umm, eat that?' I ask him, pointing to the white and purple flower.

'You can,' he replies, 'if you like.' He shrugs. 'It's just there to look nice, really.'

'Right, I see. Thanks.'

'Enjoy.' He walks back to the till. I remove the flower from the toast and discard it on the side of the plate.

I glance at my phone, expecting to see some messages in the group chat, but there's nothing. They're all busy, their days full. Nat's in the middle of a yoga class, Alex is viewing wedding venues with Craig and her mum, and Mack is flat-hunting in London.

I think about how rapidly time is passing and the monotonous progression of the last few weeks blurs my thoughts. I feel frightened then. I clear my throat and press my hand on my abdomen, letting my chest inflate with breath then deflate slowly.

My friends are very good at living, or doing their very best with life. In the space of just a few weeks, Mackie has a new job and will no doubt find a new flat to move into very soon. Alex is engaged to her boyfriend and they are planning their wedding for June 2020. Nat is coping and growing and rebuilding her life and I can see her heartbreak transforming her into a stronger, smarter, better person. She's going to therapy and really committing to it, and it's an astonishingly brave thing to witness. They're all moving up, moving on. It's about time I started moving up and moving on, too – and moving out.

I finish my meal and begrudgingly drink the rest of the cat piss tea, wincing as I do so. I swap the plate with my laptop on the table and start scrolling through the PR job listings in the surrounding area.

1.   Account Director – Lifestyle/ Hospitality

England, Hackton
£40,000–£50,000

Too senior.

2.   Senior Account Executive – Healthcare Marketing

England, London
£25,000–£28,000 per annum

Too boring.

3.   Media Manager – Maternity Wear Brand

England, London
£DoE

Too yummy mummy.

4.   PA/ Office Assistant – Integrated Creative Agency

England, Berks
£22,000–£27,000 per annum

Too junior.

5. PR Account Manager – Haute Dog – Fashion & Accessories Brand for Dogs

England, London
No salary specified

Too ridiculous.

6. Senior Media Officer – Children's Charity

England, Greater London
£30,000–£35,000 per annum

I stop scrolling. I click on the listing.

'We are a leading charity focused on preventing child cruelty across the UK. Our press office team is responsible for interactions with the media nationally and regionally, for example, through printed media, broadcast or digital. The team will develop a strong media platform for the charity to publicise its work to end child abuse.'

I let the thought roll around in my mind for a minute before researching the charity and reading the information on their website. There's the latest statistics and news articles, including a story on how a law loophole means that police can't act on over 650 'abuse of positions of trust' complaints. I pour over information on different types of abuse – articles on neglect, sexual abuse, cyber-bullying, emotional abuse. There's a whole section dedicated to children with alcoholic parents and I am engrossed, driven forward by purpose and a sudden demand to know more about this charity and its work.

'Can I take your plate?' The curly-moustached man is standing over me again.

'Yes. Thank you.'

'You didn't eat the flower, then.'

'No, I decided not to.'

He laughs, then asks, 'Can I get you anything else?'

I think for a moment.

'Could I have a plain black coffee please?'

'Of course. Just plain? We have some nice organic nut milks and date syrup.'

'A big teaspoon of good, old-fashioned sugar would be great, actually.'

'Okay. I'll see if we have any of that.'

'Thank you.'

I smile as he walks away and look back at my laptop screen. I click the blue button that says: 'Apply for this role'.

CHAPTER FIFTEEN

Alex

Reading about other people's weddings makes you feel one of three things: totally bereft of creativity (did Martha Stewart make those floral napkin rings especially or is everyone just better at DIY than I am?), very ignorant (I have googled it and still don't understand what 'morning dress' means) or just incredibly poor, as though you have no choice but to get hitched in your ASOS lace skater dress from 2006 in your parents' garden shed.

I'm reading a bridal magazine and there's a feature titled: 'Four *real* couples, four *really* inspirational weddings'. One was in a luxury hotel in a part of the English countryside that I've never even heard of, another was at 'her parents' farm', which looks bigger than the entire town of Hackton, one was at a fifteenth-century palace in Venice with a ten-tier cake and water taxi transportation for guests, and the last was a 'small, relaxed ceremony' on Lake Como with floral walkways and 300 fairy lights, complete with a mini-moon (which is apparently a thing) on the Amalfi Coast, followed by a six-month honeymoon around South-east Asia, New Zealand and

Fiji. Craig and I will be lucky if we get to Magaluf for our honeymoon.

I give up on reading about 'real couples' weddings' and go to the kitchen. There's a birthday cake for Nat in the cupboard, which I'll bring out later. I was planning on making it myself but time ran away from me this week, so I bought a chocolate birthday cake from my favourite bakery on Orchard Road, near the Orchard Tavern where Craig ran out on me to buy my ring. I also bought one of those elaborate sparkler candles because, I thought, Nat deserves a fuss to be made of her birthday after the last few months. Besides, I know all this wedding planning can't be easy for her so I thought we should make more of a fuss of her than we usually would on this birthday. Her present from all of us is also stashed under my bed – a huge print with dozens of photos of all of us which we had framed especially, and a bright blue ceramic plant pot to house Frank 2.0.

I'm pouring myself a glass of wine when my phone rings.

'Hello?'

'Hey, it's Nat. I'm outside.'

'Holy shit, Nat. You're here before Mackie.'

'Am I? Should we alert the police and report a missing person?'

'I told you all to get here for six thirty, and it's six twenty-seven now. Let's wait five minutes and if she isn't here, we'll launch a search party and do that "missing person" thing on Facebook.'

'Agreed. Can you let me in please? I'm freezing my tits off.'

As I run down the stairs to open the front door, I notice the glare of a passing car's headlights illuminate a fine veil of rain against the mist.

'Nat, come in. I didn't realise it was raining.'

'Don't worry,' she says, her arms in a thick black puffa jacket tucked around her torso like inflatable swimming aids. 'The sign was keeping me dry.' She gestures to the Nail Art sign, which is dousing the wet concrete below in a pool of magenta. The light in the 'A' of 'Nail' is flashing, and has been doing so for as long as we've lived here.

'Craig and Warner not in?' Nat asks, removing her puffa jacket and draping it over the back of one of the bar stools at the kitchen counter. She's wearing baggy, frayed high-waisted jeans and a striped, high-neck jumper in a bold block colours.

'No. Craig's at the pub watching some football game and Warner is . . . I don't know, actually. Getting high or selling some very strange antiques, probably.'

'Stonewall Antique's Instagram page is looking great,' she remarks, walking around to look at the furniture and trinkets on display. 'I'm not sure about this guy though.' She stands next to the enamel sign featuring the man giving a thumbs-up. 'Oh, shitting hell. He looks even worse close up. He looks like he's about to burp loudly on a late-night Southeastern train and drop an empty can of Carling on the floor.'

'Yeah, I don't think he's going to sell that one.'

'Why did he even get it in the first place?'

'I don't know. He was probably high.'

'Right, yeah. Makes sense.'

'Do you want a glass of wine?'

'Yeah, thanks. Can I still smoke in the kitchen?'

'Knock yourself out. Warner does it constantly and it's his gaff.'

Nat walks back to the bar stools and pulls a pouch of rolling tobacco from her jacket pocket. She takes a seat and pulls the thick glass ashtray closer to her. She tucks her hair behind her ear and lights her cigarette, inhaling deeply on the first drag.

'Thanks, Al,' she says as I place a glass of white wine in front of her.

'Where did you want to go later for birthday drinks?'

'Oh, I don't mind. I'm happy staying in if we'd all rather. Save some money and all that. My birthday isn't until next week anyway.'

'We have to go out and celebrate your birthday! We'll see what the other two say.'

'It's fine. We're here for wedding planning anyway, right?' She looks at me straightly and coldly, takes another drag, and continues, 'So, how's all the wedding stuff going?'

'It's . . . yeah, it's fine. Don't let me bore you with it,' I reply, replacing the wine bottle in the fridge, kicking the door shut with my foot.

My face feels suddenly hot, stinging hot, red like a cut. I'm conscious that I'm standing while Nat is sitting, which makes the interplay of conversation feel awkward and unnatural, like a flight attendant leaning over to speak to a seated passenger. I cough and sit down on one of the bar stools, putting us on the same physical level. I wonder why it is that I want to feel more at ease talking to Nat, as though she's a stranger who I've never engaged with before. Then I realise it's because we haven't spoken about the wedding just the two of us.

'You sure it's fine? You seem distracted.' She lifts her wine glass to her lips.

'Do I? I guess it's just a lot to process.'

Nat looks at me with a discomposed frown and replaces her wine glass on the counter.

'Don't think I'm telling you how you should feel or how to behave,' she begins, 'but aren't you supposed to be excited and, you know, bouncing off the walls when the love of their life asks her to marry him?'

I stare at her and she's looking back at me over the kitchen counter, two wine glasses and an ashtray between us. The thick stench of smoke hangs in the air. I can feel a shiver begin to trickle through my body, either from heat or cold, I can't tell which. Either way, it's not a nice sensation.

'Nat, I think—'

The flat buzzer cuts through my voice and I jump to my feet mechanically.

'I'll get that,' I say, happy for the interruption.

'I hope it's Mackie,' Nat replies, as though our conversation was never initiated, 'otherwise that search party needs to start assembling.'

'Hello, my sexy little bride-to-be.' Seeing Edele's smiling face and twilight-blue eyes mollifies the tension from my conversation with Nat and I sigh with relief.

'Hi, Ed. Come in, you look soaked. Do you even own an umbrella?'

'I've got a hoody, that's enough, ain't it?' She says, pulling her hood down and kissing me on the cheek. The hair around her face is wet from the rain and her skin is piercingly cold against the heat of mine, but I don't mind; I'm just pleased to see her.

'Am I still banned from that Tesco over the road for chucking up in the dog and cat food aisle?' she asks. 'I was going to buy booze.'

'Don't worry, I've got wine. And yes, you probably are, though I doubt they'd remember.'

'Excellent. I'll go later if we run out and try not to spew all over the Whiskas Ocean Fish.'

'God loves a trier,' I say, shutting the front door.

'Ooh, in the name of the Father, doesn't he just now?' Edele replies in a high-pitched, exaggerated Irish accent.

'Hey, Nat. Happy early birthday!' she calls as she walks into the flat. She stops and gasps when she sees the enamel sign. 'Fucking hell, who invited Peter Kay?'

'Thanks. I thought you were Mackie,' Nat replies. 'she isn't here yet.'

'What? You mean, Emma Mackie is late?'

'Yep. It is the harbinger of the end of days.'

I walk over to the fridge to retrieve the wine again.

'So, Al, what were you going to tell me about the wedding?' Nat asks.

'Nothing, we can talk about that later. Any luck with the job hunt, Ed?'

I pour her a glass and she perches on the bar stool next to Nat, lighting a cigarette.

'Mate, this is supposed to be a fun night; work chat is off the cards.'

'It's going that well?'

'Yeah, something like that.'

The buzzer rings again.

'Thank God,' Nat says. 'Call off the search party.'

'Hey, Mack,' I say, standing aside to let her in. 'Are you okay?'

'Yeah, I'm fine,' she says. 'Sorry I'm late. I bumped into Luke at the shop and now I definitely need a drink.'

Upstairs, she empties the contents of the tote bag onto the kitchen counter. There's three different wedding magazines, two bottles of wine, a sharing bag of chocolate and two bags of lentil crisps with a pot of low-fat hummus.

'You're golden,' I tell her. 'Thank you, Mack.'

'And,' Mackie says, as though she has a surprise, reaching into her coat pocket. She walks over to Nat and says, 'A birthday badge for the birthday girl.'

She pins a huge pink badge onto Nat's jumper which says, 'It's my birthday!'

Nat laughs. 'Thank you. Is this to try and make me feel young again, and comfort me about my advancing age?'

'Exactly, you old crone,' Mackie laughs.

'Thanks for the snacks, Marshall,' Edele adds. 'But lentil crisps? I mean, you almost make it too easy to take the piss.'

'Don't knock 'em until you've tried 'em,' Mackie smiles.

'You sound like my mum's energetic friend Sandra who brings over healthy snacks because she's constantly "doing Slimming World".'

'So, what happened with Luke?' I ask.

'What?' Edele and Nat chorus.

'She just bumped into him.'

Mackie makes a low groaning noise and slumps onto one of the bar stools. I walk past and squeeze her shoulder encouragingly, grabbing another glass from the cabinet and getting the wine out of the fridge again. I decide to just leave it out now.

'He came up behind me when I was buying the wine. We just got chatting about our plans for tonight. I said I was coming here to drink wine and talk all things "wedding"; he said he was going to Drake's Bar with some mates. I said I loved Drake's but hadn't been there in ages. Then he asked if I wanted to go with him sometime.'

We all start to make vigorous squawking noises like high-pitched vultures when Mackie interrupts us.

'But I told him it wasn't a good idea. I've wanted to spend time with him outside of work for ages, but I'm moving in a couple of weeks and it's just not the right time. It's too late.'

'You're not even going that far away!' Nat says. 'Surely it's worth giving it a shot? I think these things are pointless if you don't give it your all.' She doesn't look at me when she says this, but I can tell she wants to.

'I don't know. I've just got too much else going on,' Mackie replies. 'New job, new home, you know? That's going to take up a lot of my time, and when I'm back in Hackton to visit, you three are my priority. So it just doesn't make sense right now.'

'What did he say?' Edele asks.

'He said that he understood, and that he did think that it might not be the right time with my moving, but that he'd wanted to ask me on a date for some time and thought he'd see what I'd say.'

'So, basically, he didn't have the bottle before, but now that he knows he won't have to see you every day, he thought he'd try his luck.'

'Yes. That's pretty much it.'

'Are you okay?' I ask, looping my arm around her.

'I'm okay,' she responds, holding my forearm affectionately. 'Timing is the worst. Anyway, enough about Luke. Let's eat some food and look at these magazines, shall we?'

We remove some of Warner's antiques from the dark grey L-shaped sofa and lay them carefully on the floor, including a stack of framed paintings of forests and marshes, a heavy wooden sculpture of a tortoise and an ornate pewter cauldron. Edele opens one of the bottles of wine and Mackie pours the crisps into a large white sharing bowl, placing it on the bamboo and rattan coffee table, which has been here so long that I don't know if it's part of Warner's stock or our actual coffee table.

Soon, the second bottle of wine is nearly empty, and I walk back to the kitchen counter to light a cigarette.

'Are you going for a smoke, Al?' Nat asks.

'Yeah, want one?'

'Yeah.' Nat places the magazine she was reading on the sofa facing downwards and steps over the cauldron as she walks towards me. She asks Edele if she'd like a cigarette. Edele declines.

'What were you going to say earlier?' Nat asks me as we sit back down on the bar stools.

'When?'

'Before Edele got here.'

'Oh, that. It's not important.'

'Right. Well, it is important to me.'

She licks the adhesive strip of her cigarette papers and presses it down to secure its thin cylindrical shape. She sounds hard and her tone is abrasive. I don't yet know if this is conveying a sort of agitated concern or just irritation, likely fuelled by alcohol.

'All right.' I take one hard breath before lighting my cigarette. 'I was going to say that I am excited, okay? Of course I am. I've never been happier than that moment when Craig asked me to marry him, and when we got to the pub and he'd arranged for you all to be there. I just, I don't know. I think I feel jaded, or something.'

'Jaded? Why?'

'I don't know, Nat. I think I feel disconnected. Sometimes I feel like I need to wake up, like I might be sleepwalking through everything, through all these years. The same job, the same flat, the same man, the same *life*. What if I'm just stuck?'

'And what if you're just content? That's not the same as being stuck. You need to let yourself be happy.'

'Shouldn't I be more than content? I don't want to be one of those couples that stay at the same place, strolling idly through everything, day after day, until suddenly one of them realises that there's more; that they're worth more than their idle strolling.'

Natasha's lips purse slightly as she runs her tongue over her teeth before taking another drag of her cigarette. The pause in conversational flow looms between us, thick as tar.

'Stop it now, Al. You and Craig – you break the mould.'

'I don't know about that. We're not superhuman.'

'I just think you're fretting over nothing. Okay?'

'It's just . . . I guess it's just hard to tell where he ends and I begin.'

Nat looks at me without blinking and her expression is unsettled and, it seems after a few seconds, alarmingly stern. Anxious flutters pinch at my stomach as I wait for her to speak, gulping down some wine.

'What's the matter with you?' she asks.

'What?'

She's still looking stern. She wants me to say something else but I don't know what I should say. The nervousness pinches harder and it's uncomfortable but I wait it out.

'You've been so awkward around me, especially with wedding stuff. Whenever I bring it up you act all sheepish or just change the subject, like I'm interrogating you about a murder or something.'

My pulse starts to race and hurtles through me. Nat continues to stare at me, unflinchingly. I swallow hard, and I'm almost sure she can see my heartbeat pounding against the walls of my throat as I do so.

'I . . . I don't know to say, Nat. I suppose I'm trying to protect you.'

Her lip curls. 'What?' she says.

'I want to shield you from it. I know it can't be easy for you, to be around all this talk of engagements and weddings. I can't imagine what it's like, especially with what you're going through right now.'

She retracts her gaze and sniffs loudly, the corner of her lip curling up towards her nostril. She doesn't say anything. I can't stand the silence and press myself to say something else.

'I don't want to make you any sadder than you already are, Nat.'

'I never asked you to protect me. I don't need your protection. I'm happy for you, and it's really shit that you feel like you have to act all scared and daunted by your engagement, just to hide your happiness from me. That's not friendship, Al.'

'No,' I rush, 'I'm not acting. I *am* daunted. I mean, Jesus Christ. It's the most terrifying thing in the world; someone asking you to sign over the rest of your life to them!'

I force a laugh as I say this, trying to soothe the tension. But Nat doesn't return the laughter. She drinks the last of her wine then in a conspicuously drawn-out gulp and places the empty glass back down on the counter, hard. She extinguishes the remainder of her cigarette in the ashtray and says, 'You wouldn't know a good thing if it slapped you round the face.'

'What? That's not fair, Nat, come on. I know it's good. I think I'm just overwhelmed, that's all.'

'No, you're ungrateful. You have someone who loves you, Alex. Someone who loves you enough to ask you to spend the rest of your days with them. Someone who is promising to make you as happy as he can, for as long as he can. Do you know how rare that is? Or how many of us are looking for that exact thing? Or how many of us so nearly had that exact thing, but had it taken away? And all you can do is desperately search for the fault in it all, wondering if there could be more out there. You don't even realise how fucking unfair that is to have to hear.'

My gut stabs at her personal and sudden incursion. The superciliousness of it all – assuming that there's a set way to feel and behave after getting engaged – makes my skin sting with indignation.

'I was just trying to confide in you,' I say, outwardly enraged but biting back tears. 'I'm not ungrateful, or being unfair, or doing anything to try and upset you. This isn't about you. I was clearly asking for your opinion, or just some bloody counsel, but clearly that's too much to ask from you because you're incapable of seeing anything past your own bloody heartbreak.'

Tension leaves her face, replaced suddenly by a shocked, sad expression.

I don't know when the others realised what was happening, but Mackie and Edele are standing up now, and Edele is walking towards us.

'Come on,' she says softly. 'Let's just cool off and chat this over in a bit. We've all been drinking—'

'No, Ed,' Nat says, her eyes wide and wet. 'It's fine. I think all's been said that needed to be said.'

'Nat, look,' I say, frowning and pinching the bridge of my nose between my fingers. 'I'm sorry, okay? I didn't mean it.'

'It's okay, Al. I'm going to go.' She's pulling on her puffa jacket and looping her bag over her shoulder and I feel panic then. I'd been so blindsided by my own irrational jitteriness that I'd ignored my best friend's feelings. I feel like I might choke on my guilt.

'Please don't go,' I plead, an audible dread to my voice. 'Can we just talk it out? You know I didn't mean it, I'm really sorry.'

Edele is touching Natasha's arm but she's already starting to walk away, removing Edele's hand and holding it briefly before letting go and walking towards the stairs leading to the flat door.

'Al, it's fine,' she says, desperately trying to sound gentle and sober and unharmed. 'I'll talk to you all later.'

I stand still for a moment and then rush to the top of the stairs but Natasha is already shutting the front door behind her, disappearing into the darkness of the street outside, leaving only the hot magenta light on the cold wet concrete behind her.

CHAPTER SIXTEEN

Mackie

You don't realise how much a place like this weaves itself into the fabric of who you are until you are leaving it. It's stuck to the walls of my brain, running through my veins, it's in my bones. On the surface, what am I moving on from? Blinking street lights, honking traffic jams, car windows smashed to pieces, two-for-one pizzas and cheesy chips after a night out. The sticky nightclubs, the busy job centre, the filthy pubs, the not-so-filthy pubs, the gym, the cinema, the bowling alley, the cafe, the betting shop, the tattoo parlour, the funeral parlour, the nail parlour, the shopping centre, the off-licence, the park, the streets you could walk blindfolded, the streets you don't want to walk down on your own.

But it's also the memories and the people, the ghosts passing by on the street, the ones whose faces twist into shadows in my memory, and the ones who are still here now. The old dates, lovers, boyfriends, friends. The kids on the school bus drawing dicks in the condensation with their fingers. The tiny lady with black hair who wears hot pants all year round. The blind accordion street player who isn't actually blind. The homeless man who sings the Temptations. The landlady who lets us play on the pub quiz machine after closing. The man in the shop who said, 'Keep that chin up, girl with the sad eyes' to Nat and gave her a free bar of Dairy Milk. The chubby bartender with the terrible name who can't take his eyes off Edele. The boys built like fighting bulls with hard faces who stand in the alleyways but are actually just teenage students at Alex's school. The four of us: the walks through town to drink coffee then try on clothes and laugh at each other in the changing-room cubicles, the dancing with dog-tired legs in rain-soaked shoes on lager-stained tiles, the eating and laughing until our sides near-split, the drinking until we spill our insides into the sink and hold each other's hair back, the sobbing and shoulder-holding when one love dies, the cheering and celebration-planning when one love wins. The precious, rare relief of being so known by the three women who intuit what I am thinking and feeling before I even know it myself.

It's everything I've known, and now I'm leaving it behind. I wish I wasn't leaving it behind like this, while Alex and Nat still aren't talking to each other. It feels like bailing on a failing team for a better offer; unresolved and disloyal.

I'm arranging suitcases of clothes and storage boxes of shoes into the boot of my car and Edele and Alex are heaving plastic moving boxes into the hire van. The morning May sunshine is imprisoned by the dense, nothing-coloured clouds, lurching its warmth forward through the gaps every now and again.

'Who needs two juicers? How much juice can one woman consume?' Edele huffs, tying her long hair into a ponytail away from her face.

'It's not two juicers; it's one juicer, one food processor,' I shout to her with my head half-in my car.

'I don't think I've ever used a food processor in my life. Or a juicer. This fancy, health-conscious kitchen crap weighs a ton too,' she calls back.

'A food processor is a pretty standard piece of kitchen equipment, Ed,' Alex replies, emerging from the other side of the van.

'You're driving this thing, right?' Edele asks her.

'Yeah. Mack didn't trust you to be the named driver.'

'Fine by me,' she replies, reaching into her bag and pulling out a can of cider.

'Cruel bitch,' Alex smiles.

'Just think of the celebratory drink you'll have in London when we finish unpacking all of this.'

'You sure we can keep this van overnight and I'll drive it back and return it tomorrow, Mack?' Alex asks.

'Yeah, they said it was fine.'

'Seems dodgy to me,' Edele says, sipping.

'It's a Hackton rental van company. It's probably not even a registered company, just some guy who owns a van. The van's probably stolen.'

'Fair point,' she laughs.

'Time for a fag break,' Alex says, perching next to Edele on the edge of the open van, its doors spread wide.

I look at my watch. Natasha should have been here over an hour ago. Though we've all been busy in the last two weeks since Alex and Nat's falling out, it's still strange for us to go so long without spending time together as a group. Edele has seen Nat a couple of times, staying over at hers, but is keeping very quiet about it. Nat has spoken in the group chat though not much and not regularly.

'She's been ignoring my messages and calls but I really hope she comes,' Alex says. 'At least to say goodbye to you, Mack. I brought her birthday presents from us too, just in case.'

My arms feel clammy against the fabric of my over-sized shirt, which is covered in a leaf pattern and unbuttoned over a white T-shirt. I take it off and tie it round my waist, not knowing how to respond.

'I am sure she will,' Edele says calmly.

I smile at Edele and Alex sitting on the edge of the van, my life piled into boxes behind them, and take their photo on my phone.

'Take it again!' Edele instructs, holding her cigarette away with an outstretched arm and kissing Alex on the cheek. I tell them I'll send them the photos and that I'm going back inside the flat to bring down some more boxes.

Inside the flat, the walls are bare as shaved alabaster skin and remaining boxes loom large in the ringing emptiness. I pick up the navy holdall resting against the living-room door, heavy with photo frames, candles and cookbooks, one of which Lucy bought me as a leaving present. Though I packed this bag last week, I know exactly where the gift is that Luke bought me, wedged neatly in the zipped compartment at the back of the bag's lining.

'I got you this,' he'd said outside the pub near work on my last day, less than a week after I told him we shouldn't go on a date to Drake's Bar together.

'It's just something small,' he'd quickly said. 'I hope you like it. But it's cool if you don't, I can return it, or whatever.'

'Thank you,' I'd replied, trying to rip at the small package wrapped in blue paper with what must have been half a roll of sticky tape. 'You didn't have to get me anything.'

'I know,' Luke had smiled. 'But I wanted to.'

It was a smartphone armband.

'It's so you can take your phone with you when you go running, you know, in case your fans need to see another photo of the sunrise on Instagram.'

He was mocking me to try and mask the sentiment of the whole thing, which was dumb and childlike, but in itself a bit endearing.

'That's actually a really good present,' I'd beamed. I know I beamed because I had felt the wide spread of the smile over my face. I'd thanked him then I'd leant in to hug him, not thinking about what I was doing, just doing it, and he'd put his arms around my body. We'd stayed like that for a while without speaking or moving. I don't know how long we stood together for, swimming silently in the stillness of each other, but longer than two friends would hug before it got weird. The seconds pulsed as they passed. My torso and limbs fizzed with wanting as

Luke pulled his body slightly back, his left arm still resting at the top of my hip, his eyes glistening and narrowing towards mine, lips slightly parted and drawing closer, then I said, 'Right, we best get back to the pub, before people start wondering where we are.'

'Right,' he'd said, wiping his hand over his eye. 'I'm glad you like it, the armband.'

Now I stand still staring at the bones of my once-home, clutching at the bag with Luke's present in, the handles so tight I can feel its stitching imprinting onto my hands. With my other hand, I begin walking, following the contours of the rooms and touching them, feeling the walls cool and vacant beneath my fingers. I carry on doing this, going from room to room, until I don't want to do it any more. There's a warm kind of bursting feeling in my breastbone and I smile to myself, pick up a box of board games and books, and go back outside.

'How much is left, Mack?' Edele asks.

'Not much, only about three boxes. Will they fit in the van?'

'Should do,' she smiles.

The two of them head back into the flat. I'm rearranging some boxes in the van to create more space when I hear a voice say, 'Hello?'

I look round the open van door to see Nat. She doesn't look as though she's wearing any make-up but her face has more colour than usual, her complexion almost florid. She's wearing a huge khaki-coloured jumper, which reaches down to her thighs, and black jeans which fit as though they used to be tight. The dark rings under her eyes look less heavy now and she's smiling at me.

'Hi, Nat,' I say, putting the box down in the van. 'I'm so glad you're here.'

'Mack, I'm so sorry I'm late and haven't been here to help with all of this. Is there any left to do? Can I help?'

'Please don't worry about that, I did most of it early this morning anyway. Are you okay?'

'Yes, I'm fine. How are you feeling about all this?'

'Oh, you know. I'm okay. It's sad, you know, to leave this place. But it's what I have to do. I'm sure it'll hit me when you all leave tomorrow. Are you still staying with us all, in my new flat tonight?'

'If you'll still have me.'

'Don't be daft,' I say, hugging her then. I hold her close for a moment, let her go and say, 'You've been quiet, Nat. We've missed you.'

'I know, I'm sorry. I've missed you all, too. It just felt so weird, fighting with Alex. I know we all bicker, about mundane stuff, but I haven't fallen out with her like that in years. I just thought I'd keep my head down, wait for her to stop being mad at me for acting like a selfish bitch, and just keep busy with work and therapy.'

'She doesn't think you're a selfish bitch. She could never think that. How is therapy going?'

'Really well, actually.' I can tell she means it. 'I think I'm getting there.'

'Good. I knew you would.'

'Hey!' Edele calls, walking out of the front door, leaving the box she's carrying by the van wheel and flinging her arms around Nat. 'Where the fuck have you been, slacker?'

'Sorry,' Nat says, kissing her on the cheek. 'I just felt a bit nervous and, I guess, embarrassed, about seeing Al today so I took the morning to try and get in the right headspace.'

'Nervous and embarrassed? About seeing your best mate? Just because you had a fight when you were drunk? Give over, Nat. Alex will just be so happy to see you.'

'I hope so. I think we need to talk it out at some point, too. Maybe. I don't know.'

'Couldn't hurt, could it?' I say.

Alex walks out of the front door then, her chin almost perched atop the box she's carrying, and her expression is a mix of startled and apprehensive when she sees Natasha.

'Hi, Al.' Natasha says.

'Hi,' she says. She puts the box down next to Edele's and they hug each other.

'I don't want to fight,' Alex says. 'I hate arguing with you, with any of you.'

'Me too,' Nat says. 'I'm sorry.'

'I'm sorry, too.'

'Great!' Edele chimes in. 'Nat, there's a couple of boxes of Mack's crap left in there – probably an entire box of gym trainers or sports bras or something – and they've got your name on them, slacker.'

'On it, boss,' Nat says, walking towards the flat.

A crack in the nothingness of the sky bleaches our eyes with white sunlight as I shut the front door for the final time. I can't help but feel like I've locked myself out, as though I've forgotten my keys, when really I left them on the kitchen table as instructed by the landlord. I have a new set of keys to remember to take with me everywhere I go now.

The drive to my new flat on the outskirts of north-east London, zone four on the underground, will take around an hour and a half. As we drive, the roads get gradually narrower, the congestion heavier. Cars braking at speed bumps. Lumbering buses in hordes clogging the flow of traffic, red and tall and fat, and we all obey the arrows and lines on the tarmac, endlessly merging then separating, merging then separating. Slowing down to twenty miles per hour for speed cameras, we pass rows of terraced chicken shops, builders' merchants and hair salons, beige-brick flats and round, black satellites perched above each of them.

'I wonder if you'd a free haircut if you lived above a hair salon,' I say.

'Maybe,' Nat replies. 'You get daily rubbish collections for living above a shop, too.'

I park in the bay directly in front of the Victorian terraced houses, of which my flat is the ground floor, and Edele and Alex find a place to park on the street where the parking restrictions only apply Monday through Friday. I stand in front of the green front door, my new front door, old with chipping wood. We spend the day passing from the flat to the cars, carrying boxes and ripping them open, unloading them, finding their contents a place to live, then flattening the boxes for recycling. We all lift my sofa at an angle through the front door, shouting, 'Pivot!', like that episode of *Friends,* even though we don't have to manoeuvre a staircase. By the time we've assembled my new flat-pack bed – 'I'm never buying anything from fucking IKEA ever again,' says Edele more than once – the sun is ducking behind the row of flats opposite and the evening chill leaks in through the Victorian sash windows. We huddle on the sofa, wrapped in blankets and drinking cava and eating pizza and playing board games in lieu of WiFi, which doesn't feel strange because we often get sloppy-faced drunk and play Trivial Pursuit, complain about how hard the questions are, then just play Articulate instead. The only thing that feels strange is not being able to put a film on my laptop in the background to completely ignore.

'Anyone want water?' Alex says after the first game of Articulate.

'Please,' I say. 'The glasses are in the box on the kitchen table. They might just need a rinse.'

'I'll help you,' Nat says.

They go into the kitchen together and, after a few minutes, Edele says to me, 'They've been in there a while.' We walk quietly to the hall and stand outside the kitchen door.

'You were right,' we hear Nat saying. 'I was selfish, Al. I made it all about me, and it's your time, your time to be happy.'

'I wasn't right, I was just being a gobby cow.'

'No, I was out of line. All you need to know is that your happiness is the most important thing to me, and I love Craig for making you happy.'

'Thank you. But you never have to pretend that everything's okay, even though you're doing so well, we know when you're having a day when you're not doing so okay. We know you like the back of our hands, Nat. And you're my priority, okay? Above Craig, above the wedding, above everything.'

They're silent for a moment or two, then Nat says, 'Soppy pair, ain't we?' Edele smiles at me and we walk back into the living room. Nat and Alex soon emerge carrying two glasses of water each.

'Were you two filtering rainwater yourselves in there or something?' Edele says.

'You're welcome, shit bag,' Nat replies, picking up a slice of pizza and taking a large mouthful. It makes me very happy to see her eating again and enjoying it.

'Oh, Nat,' Alex says, 'we have something for you.' She leaves the room for a minute and soon emerges carrying two huge packages: one flat and rectangular, the other short and round, both covered in gold foil wrapping paper with pink bows.

'Your birthday presents,' I beam. Nat grins. She unwraps them in an excited rush, her hands a flurry of gold and pink.

'For Frank The Younger,' Edele explains as she hugs the plant pot to her chest.

'It's perfect,' she smiles. 'He'll love it.'

Nat spends a long time looking at the huge collage of photos after she unwraps it, wiping at her eyes, and laughing at the memories each photo holds. Alex's eighteenth birthday in London when she had sex in the toilets of a Shoreditch night club; Glastonbury Festival when we were nineteen and Edele and Nat took too much ecstasy and thought their noses were falling off; our girls holiday to Gran Canaria at twenty-one where we all got tiny, matching tattoos of the number '4' on the back of our necks; the four of us, without Matt, at Nat's graduation; Alex and I holding our medals after the Hackton Half Marathon four years ago, when Edele and Nat met us at the finish line with a hip flask of whisky; the countless nights out, nights in, weekends away, holidays, birthdays, Christmases, ceremonies, celebrations.

It's soon late and our bodies are sore and worn from a day of lifting and building. Nat is playing music softly from her phone and Edele is dozing on Alex's shoulder. I look around at the half-empty moving crates, the ill-placed furniture that doesn't quite fit yet, the empty pizza boxes and bottles, and at the three of them, and somehow, I feel okay about the parts of myself that I left behind in Hackton. The newness of it all – the flat, the city, the job – is daunting, but with them here, I can feel myself settling already. Because while my home town may be the pillars for nearly thirty years of memories, London is the vast, bustling, bountiful playground of possibilities stretched out in front of me, full of its own pillars to hold up the next two, ten, maybe thirty years of memories. And as long as this shelter belt of friends are a part of my life, there will be more tired dancing on sticky floors, more laughing in changing-room cubicles, more mending the broken hearts and celebrating the full ones. That's why this place, so new and vast and frightening, already feels a bit like home. Perhaps Hackton wasn't my home town after all. Maybe they were.

CHAPTER SEVENTEEN

Natasha

Two pigeons waddle up to me on the bench, side by side, their turquoise necks bobbing in unison, bare pink talons wrinkled as wet skin. One gobbles something from the dirt, another pecks at a discarded champagne cork on the ground. Together, they eye up their immediate surroundings: a beer cap, an orange peel, a small piece of pink paper, a cigarette filter. I reach for the bottle of water in my bag and they startle and half-scuttle, half-fly away.

Eva Cassidy flows through my headphones, her voice clean and pale as the watery morning sun illuminating the dew on the grass. I don't know why I'm here.

I look around the park, taking a long drink of water. Two women in cropped black leggings and T-shirts lie on their backs, a man standing between them with his arms outstretched like a bird about to take flight. They lift their legs up in unison, touching the man's hands with their feet, their faces red as traffic lights. To my left, at the corner of the park, two teenagers with their hoods covering their faces lean against the fence, kissing and entangled in each other's limbs. Everything is happening in pairs, perfect coequals, a symmetry. The cyclists zooming down the edge of the road, legs churning in time. The two barking dogs running free off the lead, leaping and twisting their bodies in the air. The four people playing tennis, two on each side. Everything is burning with bilateral rhythm, mechanical and equipoised, as though this is just the way the world is supposed to work: in twos, one incomplete without the other. I light a cigarette and start walking home.

There's neither noise of the TV from Ms Harris's flat nor the smell of cigarette smoke, so I assume she's gone out. Last Tuesday, it was her late husband's birthday. He would've been ninety. He passed away five years ago, and ever since Ms Harris and I have been neighbours, Matt and I have baked her a cake on Ted's birthday and taken it downstairs. This year, I did it on my own.

I baked an apple and walnut cake with a brown sugar, cream cheese and golden syrup icing. Ms Harris brought us two glasses of sherry from the kitchen and we toasted Ted. She spoke of him with a sort of tender soreness, and it was plain to see how she missed him. It wasn't raw though, more that the missing of him was just a part of who she was, wound so tightly to her like an old knot. She was used to it now, the scar it left. I saw it in her, and she saw that same knot, that same scar, in me too. She gave me a birthday present – 'For last week, I'm sorry it's late' – one of her old baking books from the sixties, its pages curly and yellow and spattered with butter and cream, and a new toaster. 'Your one is, quite frankly, old and hideous,' she'd said. 'And every woman knows that when your heart is recovering, sometimes the only thing you can manage to eat is a slice of toast or two.' I ate five slices of Marmite toast for dinner that evening.

My flat is unseasonably cold when I walk in, so cold I can feel my body hair stiffening and my nipples puckering, so I turn the heating on low. The old wooden floors need mopping, but I hoovered earlier so they look clean enough. My bed sheets hang on the clothes horse, my pillowcases over the radiators. Frank 2.0 sits proudly in his new ceramic pot, bold and blue in the corner of the living room. The enormous collage the girls gave me for my birthday hangs on my bedroom wall and I go to it now, standing in front of it, my brain catching and lingering on stills that each photo conjures up. The longer I do this, the less alone I feel.

Though I can feel myself mending most days, my thought patterns not as destructive or intrusive, it's hard not to feel alone still. 'You will feel lonely,' Alex told me, after he left. After heartbreak, loneliness. Gaping and loud. The boom of silence is the loudest thing I've ever heard. In an empty flat which was once so rich and full' brought to life by the both of us, happening in a pair, perfect coequals, a symmetry. It feels like I'm part of an exhibition at an art gallery that has been robbed of its most treasured painting – its remaining contents no less valuable or vibrant in their own right, but just lacking somehow – as though someone had stolen the Mona Lisa from the Louvre. I wonder whether it was foolish to stay living here, not only surrounded by ghosts, but by council tax reminder letters and the ever-growing numbers on the electricity meter. I wonder how much longer I can afford the rent on my own.

My phone's message alert rings twice in quick succession through the music in my headphones. It's two photos from Mackie in Mean Girls: one of her new kitchen, perfectly pristine, and the other, a selfie of her in her bedroom, grinning and arms outstretched.

MACKIE: And I'm done! That's the very last thing unpacked. I'm officially, 100%, WiFi-connected, box-free moved in. Thanks for all your help, girls.

NAT: Congratulations, Mack. I swear most people take months to properly unpack all their junk when they move.

ALEX: Yeah, and our Superwoman's done it in a week.

EDELE: Classic Marshall. That kitchen looks like something from an interior designer's Instagram grid. And your bedroom looks cleaner than mine has ever looked.

MACKIE: Couldn't have done it without your help. Looking forward to visiting you all soon.

I'm hungry, I think, putting my phone into my pocket. Really fucking hungry.

After all those weeks of starving yourself, you'll gain weight like mad if you start eating big meals now. Stretch marks, cellulite, double chins, bigger fat rolls. It's all comin' for ya.

The voice is there, echoing inside my skull, but I don't listen to it. Actually, I think, this is the first time I've heard it today, even when I was alone in the park, gawping at all the togetherness around me. A month ago, had I been in that environment, the voice would've ripped at my brain like a ravenous lion into bloody flesh. That, I think, is why people go to therapy.

I walk into the kitchen, put two slices of bread into the toaster that Ms Harris bought me, and crack two eggs into a small pan. If I'm on my own on a weekend morning, this is what I make myself to eat now. It's a routine I've developed, and routine is good, so Simon tells me. I know what he means. Routine feels safe; the opposite of lonely. I feel better now. New and safe.

I fish out a small bit of eggshell with a spoon and wipe it on a bit of kitchen roll. To the pan, I add a big square of butter, some vigorous shakes of salt and three turns of cracked black pepper, then I turn the heat on low and stir slowly.

Butter melts into the toast and I pile the scrambled eggs on top, creamy and golden. More salt and pepper on top. A big dollop of ketchup on the side.

I sit at the kitchen table, the kitchen table where I filled out my self-referral form, the kitchen table Matt stood behind when he said, 'Nat, come in, it's fucking January and you're only wearing a T-shirt.' I eat quickly, big mouthfuls of buttery, salty eggs, trying to send the thoughts back to wherever it was they came from, telling myself that this is a self-destructive thought pattern, and no good can come from it. 'Enough,' I think to myself now to interrupt these thoughts. 'That's enough.' Tension eases from between my shoulder blades and I feel good then. I stay at the table, thinking about how I'm making new memories in my flat now, forming new routines. I slow down my eating, enjoying the way the food tastes while I read an article on my phone.

When I'm finished, I put the empty plate and cutlery in the sink and lie on the sofa, turning the TV on but not concentrating on it. The voice doesn't stir, says nothing about how many calories I've just shovelled into myself. It's quiet and blissful. My stomach is satisfyingly full, my eyelids weighing down on my sockets.

A noise downstairs jolts my body awake. I quickly turn the TV off. I stay lying on the sofa, completely still, focusing my vision on nothing, concentrating on listening as sharply as I can. Nothing. Seconds echo. More nothing. Maybe it was just a door closing downstairs in Ms Harris's flat, or the front door to the building slamming shut. I sit up and that's when it catches my eye; the flashing blue lights reflecting onto the windows of the living room, sharp and surreal as an acid trip. I grab my phone. An hour and twenty minutes have passed. No frantic messages, no missed calls. I stand up. Probably a police car parked outside. Yes, must be. They're not exactly rare around here.

Sudden loud bursts of movement come from the flat below, like furniture being rearranged. I rub at my eyes and go downstairs. I open my front door and my body stops moving. Sudden, cold sharpness roars through my limbs and veins. Ms Harris's front door is wide open but she is not there. Instead, a female paramedic stands static and stony in front of a thickset man with broad shoulders and they are face to face but not looking at each other. The female paramedic is saying something but I don't know what.

'What . . . what is going on?' I say, walking over. 'Is Ms Harris . . . Diane . . . Is she okay?'

The thickset man looks at me now and I realise that I know who he is. His name is Josh and though I've never met him I've seen him in framed photos in Diane's living room. He is her son. I look deep into his face. He looks away, can't hold my gaze. There are patches of red around his eyes like fresh bruises and his brown eyes are wide and wet and why can't he look at me?

'You're Natasha. Mum talks about you a lot.'

'What's happening?' This seems abrupt but the churning void of my head won't let me say anything else.

His voice is cracked and low as though he's forgotten how to speak, like an old engine, broken and guttural. 'I'm sorry,' he says. 'Mum died this morning.'

Josh is pressing one of his hands against his closed eyelids and frowning and saying something through his shock – something about taking her for lunch and her heart and 'sudden', he says this word more than once because the letters look the same coming out of his mouth – but his words strung together are fizzy and blurred as they hit my ears like TV static. The part of my anatomy that's supposed to process sounds isn't processing them. The female paramedic is here now, looking at me. I can see her lips moving violently but I can't hear her. My jaw and neck and chest were rigid before, riddled with nervous tension, but now I can't control them and my mouth hangs down like a rusty swing. It's trying to gulp in air but the breath isn't going into my lungs. I continue looking at the scene playing out directly in front of me, unable to move my heavy head. Josh is still but crying, the paramedic bellowing something and now, as the frame of my sight gets lower as if the floor is sinking beneath me, she grabs hold of my arms and takes my weight against her body.

There's someone else next to me now but I don't know who.

'She's fainting,' the female paramedic says. I close my eyes but the nothingness in my vision makes the spinning worse, as though I'm too drunk. I quickly open them again. Josh is looking at me now.

'No, I'm fine,' I say after a few moments of being held up by these two strangers. My senses are stabilising. In my head my brain is burning, visions of times past, Matt helping her assemble a new washing machine, the girls eating lemon drizzle cake on her dusky-green sofa, drinking sherry and unwrapping gifts with her last week. The note she left me. 'This will pass, my dear. It always does.'

'I don't understand,' I say in a low voice which must be barely audible to anyone else. My breathing is fast, too fast. The air tastes like metal.

'You need to sit down,' the new paramedic says. She takes me through the open door into Ms Harris's living room and to the green sofa and I realise that my legs are shaking. I look up. The photos in frames lurch into my eyes – Josh, Ted, Max the dog. Anguish rises into my throat and through my ears, so loud and searing that it must be outwardly visible somehow, a red-hot laser shooting from my orifices.

Josh sits beside me. And here we are. Crying woman and crying man. The cold, hard beat of grief. Me, hunched into myself, blindsided by shock and sadness. Him, a different pain that will cloak him in the defensiveness of shock for much longer, composed but crying nonetheless, letting the tears flow freely.

'What happened?' I say eventually.

'They said that they think she had a heart attack. Maybe in the night or early this morning. I was supposed to take her out for lunch this afternoon and when she didn't answer I went in. She was in bed. She was cold. I felt for one but she didn't have a pulse.'

Josh stops speaking when he realises how much I'm sobbing. It's as though somebody is pressing their whole hand over the top of my windpipe. 'Sorry,' he says.

One of the paramedics brings two glasses of water and puts them on the coffee table in front of us.

'Thank you,' Josh says.

'I can't believe it,' I say. Josh doesn't say anything. 'I can't believe it,' I repeat. 'I was here just last week. I brought her a cake for Ted's birthday and she gave me a birthday present.' I correct myself. 'Two birthday presents,' as if the number of presents she gave me was any kind of mortality indicator.

'I spoke to her on the phone yesterday,' he says, staring at nothing. 'She sounded fine. I asked her how she was.

She said she was fine. It all seemed completely fine. It was sudden. That's what they said, sudden.' He pauses, then says, 'But she did smoke a lot. I always told her not to, but she's stubborn, isn't she?' He smiles and looks at me then which makes me shiver. 'Stubborn as a mule, she is.'

The clumsy stumbling over words and confusing verb tenses to describe his mum make my eyes sting with more tears, but then the paramedic – the first one, female – comes over to the sofa.

'They're leaving now, Josh,' she says.

'Right.' He taps his legs with both of his hands and gets to his feet, as though he's about to walk into an important board meeting.

'I need to go, Natasha. Will you . . . will you be okay? Can you call someone?'

'I could come with you,' I say, though I don't exactly know where it is that they are all going.

'I don't think that's wise,' Josh says. The paramedic nods to signal her agreement.

'Can you call someone?' Josh repeats.

'Oh, right. Yes, I can. Don't worry about me.'

He starts to walk away, following the paramedic, then stops to remove something from his pocket.

'Here,' he says, handing me a card. 'Take this. It has my phone number on it. I'll let you know as soon as I know the next, umm, steps.' He hesitates. 'You know, the . . . the funeral.' He's sensible and matter-of-fact, shock commanding him again like a puppet.

'Thanks,' I say, wiping my eyes hard with the bottom of my hand.

He smiles and we walk out of Ms Harris's flat together. He lets me pass, so that he can lock the door behind us. My flat door is still open. I rest my hand against it.

'She was wonderful,' I say. He looks at me. 'She really helped me. I can't believe she's gone. I'm so sorry.'

'I know,' he says, still-faced. 'I can't, either.'

'Let me know if there's anything I can do.'

'I will.'

I close my front door and lean against it. Everything is shaking as though I'm about to fall through a gap in the ground, like standing in the wobbly section of a train that separates the carriages. I take my phone out of my pocket and, without thinking, I start calling.

'Nat?'

'Hi, Matt.'

'Look, now's not a great—'

'Diane's died, Matt.'

'What?'

I hear a rustling on the end of line, like bed sheets moving hurriedly. This makes my head throb.

'I just saw him. Her son, I mean. Josh. He was downstairs, in the flat. I think they'd just taken her body away.'

The thought of her small body, cold and drained of life, zipped up in one of those black bags like an item from the dry-cleaners makes me feel sick and I cry, hard, down the phone to Matt.

'Nat, just breathe. It's okay. What happened? Do you know what happened?'

I wait before responding, catching my breath.

'They think she had a heart attack. Sudden. Maybe in her sleep or this morning. I guess they'll find out more later.'

'God, that's so sad. She was lovely.' A pause, then, 'I spent ages helping her with that new washing machine. She was funny, she made us laugh.'

I giggle through the tears remembering that day. I can tell that Matt is smiling on the other end of the phone.

'Are you okay?' he asks.

'Yes. I don't know. I think so.'

'Do you need me to come over?'

I stand against the door thinking about this, allowing the image of Matt comforting me in our home – in my home – to linger in my head. He always used to kiss my nose and run his thumb gently over my brow to comfort me when I was sad.

'No,' I say. 'No. I'm fine. I just thought you should know. Are you okay?'

'Thanks. Yes, I'll be fine. Will you keep me updated on the funeral? I'd like to be there.'

'Of course,' I say earnestly.

'Okay. Sure you'll be all right on your own?'

I pause, then say, 'Don't worry, I'm not on my own. Sorry to have sprung this on you.'

'It's fine. I'm glad you told me. Talk to you later, Nat. Let me know you're okay?'

'Yeah, all right. Bye, Matt.'

My arm drops from my ear and hangs loosely against my side. Everything feels quieter now, a shift in the way I'm interpreting my surroundings from just moments ago. Is this shock? Or did all of that not really happen? I close my eyes hard, pressing them together until I can see what looks like the outline of my own pupils. The flesh around my eyes is hot and tender. I walk to the sofa slowly, like a zombie in a post-apocalyptic film. I message Edele.

NAT: Did you say you were free today? I could do with some company, if you are. Ms Harris died this morning.

EDELE: What?! Yes, I'll be there ASAP. I just desperately need to shower then I'll come round.

EDELE: Actually, fuck that. I'll leave in 5.

The ferocity of the flat buzzer brings me to consciousness. I can't believe I fell asleep. Who falls asleep after learning that their elderly neighbour has died?

'Nat,' Edele says loudly, almost chant-like as the key turns in the lock and she walks in. 'Are you okay?'

'I'm sorry,' I say groggily. 'I fell asleep.' I sound confused as I say it. This makes sense because I feel confused, almost hungover with disbelief. I feel like I was too drunk and can't remember what just happened.

Edele makes us tea and I tell her what happened. We start talking about Diane – the note she left me when she tidied my flat as I slept, her remarkably toned arms, how immaculately she always dressed, the way she called Mackie 'the skinny one' but somehow made it sound affectionate, Edele putting on a posh accent in front of her, how much of my homemade cake she could eat for such a tiny woman, about Ted and her longing to be with him – and soon I feel a shower of gratitude for having known a woman like Diane, warm and sweet as the mug of tea in my hands, briefly palliating the pangs of grief.

'I'm quite hungry,' I say later that evening. Edele looks surprised. I feel surprised hearing myself saying it, too.

'What do you want for dinner?'

'I don't have anything in the fridge.

'I'll go to the shop for you. What do you fancy?'

'No, it's okay, I'll come with you. I've got spaghetti in the cupboard so why don't we just get some mince and veg, and have spag bol.'

'Nat, are you sure? You've just had some really shitty news.'

'Yeah, I'm sure. I know I'm probably still in shock or something but I think getting out of the flat for a bit will do me good.'

'Okay. Let's go to the shop, then. I need a fag anyway.'

We walk to the supermarket smoking, Edele's arm looped through mine, supporting me. I cook the spaghetti bolognese when we get home because Edele is a terrible cook, and we eat big bowls in front of the TV.

Edele puts on a film – 'something funny, to cheer us up' – but I don't really concentrate on it. I can't stop thinking about what Diane would've said, had I come home from the park this morning and been able to speak to her. I would have told her about the pigeons, the exercising women, the cyclists, the dogs, the people playing tennis; about everything operating in twos, and how lonely I suddenly felt. And she would've said, 'Yes, sweet, but look at what you have: you are far from alone. Look at those friends of yours. Four of you, you see? Just like those four people you saw on that tennis court. That's two pairs, and I'd say two pairs is better than one.'

And she would've been right. I look at the feisty, tough, strong, funny, foul-mouthed Irish woman who came rushing to my side – not for the first time, and not for the last – right when I needed her. Mechanical and rhythmic, as if this is just the way our two worlds are supposed to work: one incomplete without the other. Perfect coequals, a symmetry.

CHAPTER EIGHTEEN
Edele

I stayed at Nat's Saturday night, the night Ms Harris died, and the next night, too. She was shocked and fragile but she was okay. I woke up early on the Sunday morning – yesterday morning – so while she slept, I went to the supermarket and spent the last of my money for the week on food to fill her fridge. When I got back, she was awake, just showered with a towel around her head, and smoking out of the kitchen window.

'I'm okay,' she told me. 'I'm okay, honestly. I just want to keep busy today.'

We tidied the living room of our mugs and spaghetti bolognese bowls from the night before and unpacked the shopping. We cooked eggs with bacon and toasted bagels. I made us two mugs of black coffee with sugar and Nat drank hers quickly, her face hard and weary.

'You're sure you're all right?' I asked her as I washed our dishes and she hunched over the hob, spraying bleach and scrubbing the steel.

'Yeah. I promise I'll be okay if you want to head home.'

'No, I want to stay with you. Not like I'm doing anything today anyway.'

'Okay.'

7. She quickly got tired from cleaning, and we smoked roll-ups and drank more coffee and ate Marmite sandwiches. Then we watched films on the sofa in the silence and I curled myself around her as she dozed. I knew that I could leave, that she would be fine, if I wanted to. But I liked being close to her. She fell asleep a lot, and vowed to stay awake every time she woke up, but couldn't keep her eyes open for more than half an hour at a time. It was unlike her, after so many weeks of insomnia. I googled it and, under the heading: 'Why you might be tired all the time' on the NHS website, it said, 'any events that may have triggered your tiredness, such as bereavement or a relationship break-up'.

Then I told her to not try to stay awake, and to let sleep carry her whenever she felt it. 'You've got a lot of sleep to catch up on,' I said.

When her alarm went off at 7.30 a.m. for work this morning, I woke up, too.

'You don't have to get up,' she said. 'You can stay for as long as you want.'

'I know,' I replied. 'But I'm trying to get up early now. Or just not lie in until eleven on a weekday. No one's ever going to hire me if I don't apply for their jobs.'

I decided not to tell her, or Alex or Mackie, that I had a job interview last Tuesday, six days ago. I only told my mum. It was for the charity PR job that I applied for while sat in that terrible cafe. It was on the outskirts of London, not too far from Mackie's new flat but closer to Hackton, and it only took half an hour or so on the train. I don't know why I didn't tell them. I guess I didn't want them to be disappointed in me when I inevitably don't get the job. If they didn't know anything about it, then I wouldn't have to admit that I was a failure. Again.

Nat smiled at me then sat up on the edge of the bed, groaning and stretching her arms as far above her head as they'd reach. She pulled back the curtains and let the sunshine seep into the room, over the bed sheets and onto my face, warm and new.

'Coffee?' she asked. I was already taking off the T-shirt I'd slept in and pulling a jumper over my head.

'You're all right, ta. I'm going to head home. As long as you're okay?'

'You're going to walk home? Ed, it's, like, a twenty-five-minute walk to yours.'

'I could do with the exercise.'

'What've you done with my best friend? As long as you're sure, you know I can drop you off on my way to work.'

'It's fine, thanks. Nat, are you okay? If you're not, then you should call work and tell them. You've had such a shock. Maybe you should stay at home and rest.'

'I did enough of that yesterday. I should keep busy. I'm a tough old bird, Ed. Please don't worry about me.'

'Okay. As long as you're sure.'

'I'm fine, really. Thank you for always being my person.'

I smiled, held her close and tight for a few moments, kissed her on the cheek and told her to call me if she needed anything. She said she would and then I grabbed my bag and walked out of her front door. I stood in front of Ms Harris's door for a while, listening to nothing, thinking about how odd it seems that one person can be made up of such a rich tapestry of things – a late husband, a son, a dusky-green sofa, a huge white coat, a sparkling wit, a sharp but kind tongue, a neighbour who bakes cake – while, at the same time, being housed in a body so temporary and fragile. Here, then all of a sudden, not here any more. It was a simultaneously terrifying and comforting thought.

Walking home from Nat's now, I try to stop thinking about death, terrifying and comforting as it is. It makes my stomach twist to think of it too much. I stop in my tracks to light a cigarette, then carry on walking down the rain-damp pavement. I suck the smoke down into my throat and look at the sky, then down at the movement of my trainers. Scuffed and grey and worn.

The low-level roar of town rises in my ears as I draw closer to it. The rev of a car engine, the yanking up of shopfront shutters. Birds, somewhere. The blind man who isn't actually blind playing his accordion on the corner of the high street. The post office, lights on and already open. The man in the corner shop waves at me as I walk past. I want to buy a bar of chocolate and a can of Coke but I don't have any money until Mum gives me some cash to clean the car later. I really need to get a job.

Around here, the people you'll find in town this early on a Monday morning fall into one of six categories:

1. Hordes of hormonal, spotty, angry schoolchildren who are shouting loudly at each other despite the fact it's eight o'clock in the fucking morning. Just a quick glance immediately tells you which ones are smart virgins and which ones are either going to end up in prison, doing whippits on their mum's sofa at thirty-five, or working in Games Workshop.

2. The same men you see in Spoons at 10 a.m. with faces like leather, dressed in paint-spattered tracksuit bottoms or high-vis jackets, on their way to first call.

3. Middle-aged commuters. The men are bald and red-faced and will manspread on the train as if their lives depend on it. The women wear ill-fitting pencil skirts and single-buttoned blazers purchased at the outlet, with a pair of Sketchers that their mate Karen told them to buy because it 'tones your calves'. Men and women alike are half-arsed running towards the station because they're late.

4. Retail workers who are having a fag outside the shops before opening. They've likely worked all weekend and look at the rushing commuters with pure disgust, because at least they've 'had the weekend off'.

5. Young men in polo shirts with tank-like arms whose aftershave you can smell from the other side of the street. You don't know why they're up so early or

what they're doing in town, but you imagine it has everything to do with illegal substances.

6. One miscellaneous man walking his dog through town even though the shops aren't open yet and there's a park five minutes away. You imagine it has everything to do with number 5.

'Is that you, Edele?' Mum calls from the kitchen as I shut the front door behind me.

'Yes, Ma. You all right?'

I throw my bag and coat down by the kitchen counter and she pours me a coffee as I tell her about Nat and Ms Harris.

'It's so sad,' she says. 'No matter how many people you lose in life, death never becomes any less sad.' This stings. I put my coffee down on the countertop and look at my hands. 'It does get less scary, though,' she adds with a gleeful tone, as if she's talking about something as inoffensive as the weather forecast.

'Good to know, Ma.'

'Breakfast?'

'I was going to make some porridge before I get back to the applications.'

'Porridge and job applications,' Mum says with a hand on her hip and a weird look in her eye. 'It's really something,' she says with a pointed finger, turning towards the fridge. 'This change in you.'

'I don't know what you're on about.'

'Sorting yourself out. Applying for jobs, eating healthily, rosy-cheeked from getting some fresh air.'

I hadn't noticed my cheeks were 'rosy'. I don't think I've ever seen my cheeks 'rosy' from anything except alcohol.

She gets the milk out of the fridge and puts it on the countertop with a jar of honey.

'Make your old mammy some, will you, pet? I've got some emails to send.'

'Sure, Ma.'

I'm halfway through making the porridge, its consistency thick and sticky, when I hear feet shuffling down the stairs. Straight away, I recognise the footsteps as Liam's.

'Hello,' he says.

'Hi. Want some porridge?'

'You're making porridge?'

'Looks that way.'

'Wow. I'm good, thanks.' He takes two slices of bread and sticks them in the toaster to my right. I can feel his eyes on me.

'What are you doing tonight?' I ask. 'Thought maybe we could have dinner and watch a film together or something. It's been ages since we hung out. I'm starting to forget what you look like.'

'I can't. I signed up to do the pub quiz at the Fox for some reason.'

I feel like laughing. I don't hold it in. I start laughing. Relief swims through me as Liam laughs, too.

'What are you laughing at?' he says.

'Nothing, mate. Nothing. It's just, don't you have to be smart to have any hope of winning a pub quiz?'

'You're a cow,' Liam says, kicking me softly in the back of the leg.

'Leave off,' I laugh. 'You need a lift to the Fox later then?'

'Nah, Eddie's picking me up on the way.'

'Oh.' I can't mask the surprise in the tone of my voice. 'So, you and Eddie . . . you're okay now?'

'Yeah,' he says, 'I guess.' His toast springs out of the toaster and he walks past me to retrieve it. We don't speak as he butters it, scraping his knife loudly. He puts the butter back in the fridge. I can already tell there's going to be crumbs in there when I next use it.

He's standing next to me now and even though I don't look at or acknowledge him, I can tell he's looking at me and wondering what to do next. I take the pan off the heat and turn it off.

'Look, Ed,' he starts, his words dropping more softly than usual, voice wet with penitence.

'Don't, Liam,' I say, turning to face him. 'You don't have to say anything.'

'I feel like I do.'

I look at my brother. His expression is uncomfortable but doesn't hold any particular emotion, like someone's just punched him semi-hard in the stomach, as though the breath has momentarily been drained from his body.

'I'm telling you that you don't.' I reach up and hold his arm just above his elbow. 'I get it. After everything we've . . . you and I, together . . . I just get it, that you want to protect me.'

Surprise almost knocks me off my feet as Liam throws his arms around me then and squeezes me tight. He hasn't held me like this since we were teenagers. Since Ray.

'Love you,' he says quietly, in an almost-whisper.

'I love you, too, you prick,' I say, biting back tears. 'Don't think I don't have that overriding instinct to protect you, too. You're a big, dumb moron, but you're *my* little brother.'

He huffs his amusement and releases me from his grip. I look straight into his face, hard with soft eyes, just like Ray's. 'I would burn the whole fucking world to keep you safe, Liam.'

'You too,' he says with a slight nod. 'I've got your back,' he adds, punching me softly in the arm.

'I ain't one of your football "bros",' I laugh, wiping at my eyes with the back of my hand and turning back to face the hob. 'And for the record, I can shag who I damn well like.'

'I know. That's what Eddie said. I get that now. You can look after yourself.'

I want to ask him more about this: When did Eddie say that? How long have you both been talking again? Did Eddie ask after me? Is he the one who told you to apologise to me? But I decide now isn't the right time.

Liam eats his toast in what seems like two mouthfuls, pours a glass of water and starts walking towards the stairs. He's running late for work already.

'Do you want to come tonight? To the pub quiz?'

I consider what it would be like to be in the same room as Eddie; as Liam and Eddie, together.

'I can't,' I reply. 'I think I'm staying at Nat's again tonight. She needs the company.'

'Fair. Hope she's okay,' he calls, running up the stairs two steps at a time.

Mum soon comes back downstairs, thanks me for her porridge, eats it quickly. Liam leaves for work and Mum retreats back upstairs to her desk. I set myself up on the sofa with my laptop, my phone and a new mug of strong, dark coffee. I check my emails. Nothing but junk. I look at my phone screen. Nothing but a meme sent by Alex. I look at the latest job listings and start reading. I don't mean to, but soon, I start to drift off.

The blaring sound of my phone ringing cuts through the hum of sleep. I squint at the screen in an attempt to focus my vision.

Unknown number.

I clear my throat and slide to answer.

'Hello?'

'Hi, Edele?'

'Yes, speaking.'

'It's Claudia, Claudia Deon. You interviewed with me last week for the Senior Media Officer position.'

I sit bolt upright.

'Yes. Hi, Claudia.'

She asks me how I am and makes some comment about the weather and I hope that she can't hear my chewing my fingernails.

'Anyway, I won't keep you much longer. I'm calling to let you know that we were really impressed with your passion and your interest in our charity, as well as your previous experience across PR and media relations. I'm offering you the position – we'd love to have you as part of the team.'

I lean forward on the sofa and rest my head in my hand, shaking my head in disbelief. Suddenly everything in my immediate surroundings seems smaller, less gaping and obscuring. I feel bigger, as though I'm bursting with opportunity all of a sudden, like a ship setting out to sea for the very first time.

'Edele? Are you there?'

'Oh, yes. Sorry, Claudia. I just, umm. I don't know what to say, to be honest. Thank you, so much.'

'That's great. You said you can start pretty much straight away?'

'Yes, the sooner, the better,' I say. I hope she assumes this is because I'm excited, rather than in desperate need of money. Though in truth it's both.

'Brilliant. I'll email you shortly with a contract which you'll need to read, sign and send back to me and HR, then we can discuss a start date. Sound good?'

'That sounds great. Thanks so much, Claudia.'

'Talk to you soon, Edele. And well done.'

As soon as the call ends, I jump to my feet and call upstairs. 'Ma?'

'What is it, Edele?'

'Come here.'

'What have you done now?'

'No, it's a good thing.'

In the silence of the house, I hear the friction between her chair being pushed back against the wooden floor.

Walking down the stairs, she asks, 'What is it?'

'I got the job, Mam. I got the job at the children's charity.'

'You didn't?' she grins at me as she reaches the bottom of the stairs.

'Yeah, I did. I've got a job.'

'Oh, Edele Marie,' my mum says softly and pulls me into her. 'I am so proud of you.'

My arms around her, her hair smells of the same perfume it's always smelt of.

'Thanks, Ma.'

'My pheata; congratulations. I just knew you would.'

Then she lets go of me and holds me by my shoulders, looking and smiling at me, and says, 'Your dad would be so proud of you.'

This triggers some deep-lying thing in me that makes my lip quiver and pricks my skin. I go to say, 'Thank you', but I can't. I just start crying.

Mum holds me again until I stop crying – I don't know how long that takes – and asks me what Claudia said on the phone. She makes us a pot of tea and we sit in the lounge and talk about the job. After a while, she kisses me on the forehead and tells me she needs to get back to work.

'Do you mind if I go to Nat's after work?'

'Of course not,' she says. 'See your friends and we'll celebrate tomorrow.'

Nat's already changed out of her work clothes when I arrive that evening. I didn't look at Ms Harris's door this time. I've been cocooned in happiness and fizzing with excitement all afternoon. Now's not the time to be confronted with the terrifying and comforting notion of death.

'How are you feeling?' I ask her. She's sitting on the sofa with her laptop perched on her knees, wearing a grey T-shirt and big, bright blue pyjama bottoms covered in large white clouds. I flop down on the sofa next to her.

'I'm okay,' she replies, her voice raw from smoke. 'Are you okay?'

'I'm fine. What are you looking at?'

She turns the laptop to face me. It's an information page on a website. It says: 'What to do when someone dies'.

'Nat, why are you reading about this?'

'I don't know. I guess I never really knew what happened next. I want to make sure Josh is doing it all.'

'I am sure he will be.'

She doesn't take her gaze away from the screen, her eyes flicking through the words.

'It's strange, you know,' she says slowly, still reading, 'how many certificates are involved when someone dies.' She holds up her left hand to signal the motion of counting with her fingers, using her other hand to point to them. 'There's a certificate for burial or cremation – called a "green" form – which seems like an odd colour, so full of life. Though I guess something overly jolly like "the yellow form" or something too bleak like "the black form" wouldn't really work, would it? Then there's a certificate of registration of death, and a death certificate. Then there's marriage certificates, birth certificates, medical certificates. It's like a school kid mopping up prizes at sports day.'

She drops her hand, shakes her head. 'And,' she continues quickly so that there's no room for me to interject, 'did you know that you have to *pay* for a death certificate? They say you have to buy several, like a proud parent buying loads of graduation photos. Such a kick in the teeth, ain't it? "We're so sorry your loved one has popped their clogs, but if you could go ahead and fork out a load of cash just so that you can have constant, physical proof of that clog-popping, that'd be great."'

'Yeah,' I say after a short silence. 'I did know that.'

She swivels her head quickly to look at me and says, 'Shit. Ray. I'm sorry, Ed.'

'Don't be daft. Actually, that was kind of funny.'

'What?'

'I mean, you're right. It is like a school kid winning loads of sports day certificates. It's pretty twisted.'

Nat rubs her breastbone and lets out a quick laugh like a car horn.

'Yeah, I guess it is pretty funny.'

We look at each other and start laughing then, doubling up on the sofa, trying to get enough breath to laugh harder.

She wipes a tear from her left eye, says wearily, 'Fucking hell, Ed. I think we're bad people.'

'Nah,' I huff, crossing my legs underneath me on the sofa. 'We've just been through enough shit to know that sometimes you have to laugh at the bad stuff. Sometimes choosing to laugh is the only thing that you can do.'

She nods and a daydream-like expression swims over her face.

'Yeah. I remember thinking that when Matt was packing up all his stuff, the morning after.' She says the next four words slowly, drawing out the letters, 'All those stupid bags. The dirty gym kit and underwear in the Tesco bags, the cables and wires in the cheese and onion crisps box from the supermarket.' Her lips curl and she frowns and, for a moment, I think she's going to burst into tears. But then she starts laughing again. 'It was so ridiculous.'

I start laughing again too and our eyes stream, bellies aching.

'It's true, you know, that it gets a little bit better every day. I do still miss him, but I think that's okay.'

'I know,' I say softly. 'I know you do.'

'And I'm going to miss her, too.'

'She was one of a kind. She would love this, us sitting here laughing at death certificates and Matt's stupid boxes.'

'Yeah, she would.'

Nat lifts her head and looks slightly more sombre, her eyes darting around the room.

'And I'm going to miss this place, when I have to leave,' she says suddenly. 'I love it here but I can't afford the rent on my own for much longer. It's just too much to think about. I don't know how much more "missing" I can take.'

For a while I don't respond, following her gaze to the window, looking at the sky rolling inwards, sinking from deep pink to purple, through the open curtains.

'Well, actually that's what I wanted to talk to you about,' I say. 'I got the job. I got the job at the children's charity.'

'What?' she squeals, jumping to her feet.

'Yeah,' I nod. 'I didn't tell you – any of you – when I had the interview, in case I didn't get it. But they called me earlier to tell me the job was mine.'

'Oh my God, Ed,' she says, hopping up and down on the spot like a trampoliner on fast-forward. Then she hurls herself on top of me on the sofa and flings her arms around my torso, burying her head in my neck.

'I am so fucking proud of you,' she says, squeezing me until my breath feels pushed out of my lungs.

'Thanks, but it was about time I got my act together,' I manage to say.

She leaps off me then and runs out of the room.

'Where are you going, you weirdo?' I call after her.

'Where do you *think* I'm going?' she shouts back, 'to get the plonk, obviously.'

She comes back a minute or so later with a bottle of prosecco and two flutes. She pours them, lifts her glass and says, 'To you, Edele.'

We drink. She puts her glass back on the table and says, 'Tell me all about your interview, and the job. I want to know everything.'

'I will, Nat. But first, did Matt pay anything towards the deposit on this place when you guys first started renting it?'

'What?' she pauses, taken aback. 'Umm . . . no.'

'Did you pay it all?'

'No, I paid half, and because Matt couldn't afford it at the time, my mum paid the other half. She is so mad at him. I bet he forgot about that.'

'Well, if he isn't owed anything, and if your mum is okay with it, why don't I move in? I won't sleep in your bed for ever; I'm sure we can fit a bed in the loft conversion upstairs.'

Nat's limbs have stopped excitedly jittering and jolting now and she's looking directly at me, thinking. Eventually, she says, 'And money . . . you can pay rent when you start your new job?'

'That's generally how salaries work, genius.'

'Are you serious, Ed?'

'For once in my life, yeah. I'm being serious.'

A wide grin starts to spread across Nat's face, but then it begins to wither, her brow wrinkling.

'You know I'm a total shit-show to live with right?' she says. 'My hair falls out all over the bathroom, I get drunk and leave the TV on, I always forget to pay the council tax on time and I still don't know how to do so many adult things, Ed. I haven't got a clue how to bleed radiators, defrost a freezer, pump up my tyres, use a drill, test the smoke alarms. I mean, we could die in a radiator explosion or from excess smoke inhalation or from some sort of freezer-related ice age, and then you'll wish you never moved in with me. Seriously, I'm a terrible, shitty, pathetic excuse of a grown-up. I don't understand taxes or pensions, I just blindly look at the numbers on my payslip each month and hope it's fine. I know we have a smart meter for our energy usage, but I don't know what the hell that means. There's a flashing light on the washing machine that's been there for months but I'm too lazy to be even remotely concerned about it. And I can't remember the last time I scoured the sink, or cleaned the windows, or topped up the salt in the dishwasher, or bought laundry detergent, or dusted in between the railings on the st—'

'Nat, shut the fuck up for a second.'

'Okay.'

'I don't know how to do any of that stuff either. I mean, except defrost a freezer. I think that one's pretty self-explanatory.'

'Why do you have to do it though? Isn't the whole point of a freezer that it, like, stays frozen?'

'Fuck knows. The point is, it doesn't matter, because we can work out all of that stuff together. I don't care that you're a shit-show of a grown-up, because so am I. And actually, I think most people are. We're all just winging it; this whole "adulthood" thing, aren't we? Except maybe Mackie, I think she's pretty much nailing it. But all I do know is that living with my best friend would make me the happiest I've been in a really long time.'

'Me too,' she says, smiling warmly and picking up her prosecco. 'Let's do it, then.'

'Yeah?'

'Yes. Let's be flatmates.'

We clink our glasses together again and drink. I lean over on the sofa to rest my head against her shoulder.

'So, Edele Marie O'Connell. No more fun-employment for you, then.'

330

'No more mid-week pub trips at three in the afternoon.'

'No more childhood bedroom.'

'No more Mammy O'Connell's hoovering at the crack of dawn on the weekend.'

'No more Mammy O'Connell cooking you breakfast.'

'No more Liam O'Connell hogging the bathroom in the morning.'

'No more riding your baby brother's best mate in the room next door to him.'

I laugh and pretend to land a couple of punches in her belly.

'I'll miss Liam,' I say. 'Even if he is an annoying little shit.'

'Don't worry, you'll have me for that,' Nat smiles, looping her arm over my shoulder.

'I wouldn't have you any other way,' I say.

There's a pause in conversation for a moment, and I can tell that Nat is smiling. She reaches over to the coffee table to pick up the TV controls. I already feel like I'm home.

'You know,' she starts, 'I really think this is the best thing. For me and you. I think it's about time we both had the chance to start again.'

CHAPTER NINETEEN
Alex

I'm staring at the ceiling, stretching out like a cat on its favourite armchair, palms turned to the sky as though I want to reach up and feel it between my fingers. I can tell that the skin on my cheeks is aglow, tingling and shot with pink, like the magenta sign for the nail salon downstairs. I squeeze my thighs underneath the duvet. They're wet as the bed sheet pressed against my back, its corners untucked from the mattress in the frenzy. My skin hums in the warm sunlight singing through the window, heart thumping thud-thud-thud like a church bell, sweat sticky between my boobs and on my belly.

'You are really something, babe,' he pants next to me, sunk contentedly into the bed. 'I don't know what's happened, but I don't think we have to worry about our boring sex life any more.'

I know what happened. I started telling him what I want, exactly what I want and when I want it. His teeth, his tongue, gentle then slowly getting faster, circling and circling until I can't bear it any more. Pulling my hair. Needing to feel him. Waking the neighbours up. The bed, the sink, the floor, the car, his office. Most nights of the week, nonstop at the weekend. I tell him what I want now because I'm no longer scared, somewhere in the back of my mind, that he might leave or grow tired of me. And there's a confidence and assertiveness that comes with that.

Craig rolls over on to his stomach, his face towards mine, his eyes closed, his smile languid. I flip over so that I'm on my front, too, lying beside him, saying nothing, looking into his eyes with mute, lingering gratitude. The sun veils the landscape of his face in white light, turns it perfect and portrait-soft. I wing my arm across him and lean over to press my lips against his eyelids.

'I love you, girl,' he says sleepily, one eye pressed into the pillow, the other half-open in a tired squint as though blinded by sunlight.

'I love you, too.'

He lifts his left arm and places it on the small of my back, stroking with the tips of his fingers. A velvet-soft stillness cloaks us like a blanket and we sink into its silence for a little while.

'I can't fall asleep,' I moan, heaving my body upright and swinging my legs off the edge of the bed. 'I have to meet the girls in an hour.'

'Yeah, okay,' he huffs, pushing himself onto his arms.

We step into the shower together, music playing from my speakers on the bathroom floor. We wash using our different shower gels, him standing behind me and resting his lips against the slope of my neck into my shoulder, his hands sliding over and up and down me.

'Stop. I need to get ready.'

I step out of the shower quickly and wrap myself in a towel, Craig stays in the shower. I pull a pair of denim dungarees over a brown floral top and sit down at my dresser to do my hair and make-up.

The music carries on playing and he gets dressed, then starts to tidy the room and make the bed.

He's stopped and is looking at me.

'What?' he says.

It sometimes feels so obliterating of anything else that it catches my breath in its tracks, puts a stop to the ticking of my brain, my love for him. It makes it impossible to think of or do anything else but to just belong in it, for a moment.

'What?' I reply.

'You're just sitting there holding your hairbrush and staring at me, Al. Stop being creepy.'

'Sorry,' I say. 'I just like looking at you.'

'Soppy git,' he says, kissing the top of my head.

I'm ten minutes late to the restaurant where we're having bottomless brunch. It's the last Saturday in May, the bank holiday weekend, and town is bursting at the seams with people, the sort of excitement that only comes with a long weekend ringing from the streets, buzzing with chatter.

Nat stands up first and walks towards me as I walk towards her, arms out, and takes me into a tight hug, like we'd fall down if she let go.

'It's so good to see you,' she says.

'You too.'

I take a seat next to Edele and she kisses my cheek.

'You're half an espresso martini behind,' Edele says.

'I thought it was bottomless prosecco?'

'It is, but we're kicking things off with espresso martinis.'

'Obviously. How stupid of me.'

'It feels weird without Mack, doesn't it?' Nat says.

I look at the empty chair next to her.

'It does,' I say. 'But she's coming back to visit soon.'

'Yeah, that'll be nice,' Edele says.

The waitress comes over then and asks if we're all here. She's young and the dark roots of her hair fades to washed-out pink towards her shoulders. We tell her that we are and begin ordering our food.

'Can I get the one-pan eggs with chorizo, with a side of hash browns,' Edele says, the last of us to order. 'Actually, how many hash browns come with the side of hash browns?'

'Just one,' the waitress replies, 'but it's about this size.' She puts her notepad under her armpit and holds out her index fingers to gesture at the size. 'So it's, like, pretty big.' Her eyes widen in apparent excitement, or maybe sarcasm, and she looks at Edele, blowing a pink orb of bubblegum out of her mouth. It pops. She removes the notepad from her armpit and continues to chew the gum, shifting her jaw around as if she's gurning exaggeratedly.

'Great,' Edele replies. 'I'll get two of those. Oh, and some garlic mushrooms, please.'

'Is that all?'

'Yeah. Thanks.'

The waitress nods and soon reappears with a bottle of prosecco.

'Yer time starts now,' she says like a pink-haired, gurning version of John Humphrys on *Mastermind*.

'You're a gem,' I say to Edele.

'Why?'

'I just love that we're not the kind of mates who go for brunch and order a fruit bowl or raw salad or some shit. Even Mackie wouldn't.'

'It's like you've never seen me eat before,' she replies, pouring prosecco between our glasses. 'Remember that time I ate two Domino's pizzas?' I still don't know how she fit it in her tiny frame.

'Yeah, but you were actually employed then,' I say jokingly. 'Taking advantage of that overdraft?'

'Well, yes,' she shrugs. 'My gratitude for the overdraft knows no bounds. But I actually have some news.'

'Yes?' I ask. She straightens her baggy navy shirt, meets my eyes, sips her drink.

Her voice lurches with glee when she says, 'I got a job.' A bright grin spreads across and she explains that she didn't want to tell us in case nothing came of it, which makes something deep in my stomach jolt as she reminds us of her vulnerability, shrouded in the hardness of her outer shell. She describes the role – PR at a children's charity – and how she knew, when she saw the job listing, that it was exactly what she'd been looking for.

'What does this mean, then?' I ask, refilling our glasses. 'For you? Are you going to carry on living at home or look for a new place?'

'I'm moving in to Nat's, actually. We decided on Monday.'

I feel stunned for a moment and then excited and child-like, like a losing team levelling the score in the last minute of a football match.

'I'm so happy for you both. You both deserve it,' I say.

'Well, you can't keep a pair of good dogs down,' Edele says, winking at Nat.

'Damn right,' Nat says with a grin. 'And what a good pair of dogs we are. Also, this whole conversation makes it sound like me and Ed are getting married. And I'm not that desperate.'

'You should be so lucky,' Edele smirks in jest, tucking her long, messy black hair behind both of her ears.

Soon, the pink-haired gum-gurning girl brings our food to the table and when she's gone, I raise my glass to Edele and to her new job, and to Natasha, and her new flatmate, and drink-soppy smiles sink into each of our faces. We refill glasses, eat with just a fork, using our other hand to cover our mouths as we chew and laugh at the same time. We talk about Mackie's new job and how we'll FaceTime her to tell her about Edele's new job and Edele and Nat living together.

'I haven't told you,' I say to them after what must be my sixth glass of prosecco, 'Craig and I think we've found a venue.'

'Oh my God! Where?'

'Amazing. Please don't tell me it's at some posh villa that none of us can afford to fly to.'

'Seriously? How much money do you think we have?'

337

'Well, Craig's dad is that mafia boss, right?'

'He's not actually a mafia boss, Ed. It's a hotel just outside of town, about ten minutes from the Black Horse, on the hill. It's quite small but it's old and full of character, and it has views of the sea.'

'That sounds perfect,' Nat says. She seems genuinely happy for me and that feels warm and reassuring, as though I don't have to hide my engagement from her any more. 'Have you booked a date?'

'It's available on the last Saturday in June next year, so we're going to check the date with our families and hopefully book this week.'

'Shit, I'm busy then.'

'What?'

'I'm only messing, idiot,' Edele grins. 'You know I wouldn't miss a night of free booze.'

'Who said anything about a subsidised bar?' I say.

'Oh, that's fine,' she smiles. 'I'll just bring my hip flask.'

'What about bridesmaids' dresses?' Nat asks. 'You know I can't do pleats.'

'Yeah, and I can't wear yellow. And nothing too frilly, please. We're almost thirty.'

'I look shit in anything too bright, too. And sleeveless is fine, just let us know as I'll need to tone my arms.'

'How do you even do that?'

'I don't know. Weights?'

'Won't that just make you really hench and broad?'

'I don't think that's how muscles work, Ed.'

'Shut up, both of you,' I laugh. 'I haven't even looked for my dress yet, let alone yours.'

'Okay,' Edele says, slinging her arm around my shoulders. 'So we have time to make sure the dresses aren't shit.'

'You know,' Nat starts with a delicate slur, 'I've just remembered something Lawrence told me, and it's pretty obscure, but I think you will all like it.'

'Please don't tell me this about you two fucking after your date,' Edele replies, 'because I was with you in those sheets the next morning and I do not want to picture what bodily fluids I was lying in.'

'No,' Nat smiles, making a shooing gesture with her hand. 'Nothing like that.'

The waitress is back now, removing our plates and crockery and saying, 'Fifteen minutes to go.' This reminds me of Jeremy Paxman on *University Challenge* more than John Humphrys. 'Who wants something *sweet*?' Now she's Nigella, flirtatiously handing out dessert menus.

'Oh, go on then,' I say, 'we'll have a look, shall we, girls?'

Edele sniggers, looks at me and says, 'Okay, Mum.'

The waitress departs. 'What were you going to say, Nat?' I ask, eyeing up the hot apple crumble sundae.

'Oh, yes. So, Lawrence – the Hot David Attenborough – he told me about his time recently spent filming in Benidorm. No, wait. That's not right. Bangor ... Bognor. Ugh, no ... Oh, Borneo! That's the one.'

'Not quite Bognor, but okay,' Edele says.

'Shut it, Ed. Anyway, he was working in Borneo, and he told me about these ants that explode when enemies are nearby, to save the rest of its colony. They would literally self-combust to protect the people they love.'

'That's . . . sweet?' I say.

'What I mean is,' Nat continues, 'is that that's what this is like. You know, us four,' she gestures to the empty chair to include Mackie despite her absence. 'We're a colony, and you're all my exploding ants, and I'm yours, too. I'd explode the shit out of myself to protect you all.'

'Did you just refer to us as a bunch of ants?'

'Yeah,' she replies, 'but I was trying to make it cute.'

'I thought it was sweet,' I say, my throat tickled sweet with prosecco. 'Everything's changing for us – you two are moving in together like a happily married couple, Mackie's on the other side of the country—'

'She's in the neighbouring county, Al—'

'And I'm getting *fucking married.*'

A simultaneous chorus of smile-strewn cheers erupts from them then and we clink glasses for the third or fourth time, I can't remember but there's been a lot of cheering and clinking and drinking.

'So, what I mean is, everything is changing, but you three will always be my exploding ants.'

Cheering and grinning and clinking glasses to self-combusting ants, joy seeping down through my body like a warm shower that someone has switched on inside me. Pink-haired John-Jeremy-Nigella stands beside our table asking something about dessert but we leave her unanswered just for this moment. Those moments, groaning with grins and laughter, when a physical happiness begins in your shoulders and swamps the rest of your body like a deluge of dopamine. Those moments when, so thin and brief, everything in the world just seems to make sense.

CHAPTER TWENTY

Mackie

One of the first things you learn about working in London is that there is always a Pret no less than 300 yards away, and that your colleagues will each have their own favourite Pret barista, which is usually determined by the frequency at which they give out free coffee. This morning, I'm in the Pret opposite the office, which I'd estimate is approximately fifty yards away, getting a green tea for myself and a latte for my colleague Jane, when Georgia's email pings into my inbox.

From: georgia.clergeot@atlasmedia.com
To: emma.mackie@atlasmedia.com
Cc: duncan.frampton@atlasmedia.com
Subject: South Africa pages
Date: 07/06/19

Hi Emma,
How is the South Africa travel feature coming along? I'm sure you have a layout mocked up, but I've yet to see any pics from the shoot, and I'm

wary that we don't have much time. Has the photographer sent over any unedited shots, at least? Could you give me an update please?

Many thanks,
Georgia

Georgia Clergeot is Duncan's deputy at Atlas, which means that she sends all the stressed-out deadline emails on his behalf. Even though it's been just under a month since I started here, I already feel out of my depth sometimes. The imposter syndrome particularly strikes when I receive emails like this from Georgia, chasing something I should have already done. I never got emails like that at the *Hackton Times*. The team is smaller here – perhaps that's why they've managed to stay afloat – and it means that more responsibility falls on me. Not that I mind; I like responsibility. Most of the time, anyway. I just wish there was someone to show me the ropes sometimes. But I guess that's what comes with climbing the ladder.

I need to reply straight away, otherwise she might go round to my desk and see that I'm not there. I balance the tea under my arm and place the coffee on the counter. A woman behind me waiting for her coffee tuts loudly, so I step to the side and continue typing furiously on my phone.

From: emma.mackie@atlasmedia.com
To: georgia.clergeot@atlasmedia.com

Hi Georgia,
Apologies for not updating you sooner. Of course, the layouts are all mocked up and the photographer is sending over edited shots this afternoon. I'll print tit all out for you as soon as I have it.
 Just let me know if you need anything else.

Thanks,
Emma

I click send, then click on my sent box to read over the email I just sent.

 Wait. No. Please, God, no. Please tell me that doesn't say: 'print *tit* all out'. I blink and keep my eyes closed for a couple of seconds, and then look at the screen again. Oh my God. It does. It says: 'print tit all out'. Tit. I just sent the word 'tit' to a senior member of staff, with my boss copied in to the email.

From: emma.mackie@atlasmedia.com
To: georgia.clergeot@atlasmedia.com
Cc: duncan.frampton@atlasmedia.com
Subject: RE: South Africa pages
Date: 07/06/19

Hi both – just to say apologies for the typo in my previous email. I clearly meant to say 'print it all out'. Not 'tit'.

  Sorry about that.

Emma

I click 'send' before I realise that it probably would have been better just to leave it. And it definitely would've been better not to repeat the word 'tit'. Why did I say 'tit' again? Now I've said the word 'tit' to my boss and this stressed-out senior member of staff twice in the space of two minutes.

I walk back up to the office cursing myself for being such an embarrassing person, when I spy Duncan walking towards me in the hall.

'Here, let me get the door for you,' he smiles his chubby smile.

'Thanks, Duncan. Sorry about those emails, by the way.'

'Which emails? I haven't been at my desk.'

'Oh, it's nothing important. Just a typo.'

'That's fine, Emma. I'll look after lunch.'

Please, please don't.

'Another green tea?' he nods towards the drinks in my hands.

'Yep, it's becoming an addiction,' I say, propping the door open with my foot. 'Just hook the stuff to my veins.'

Hmm. That was probably a bit much.

'Careful not to spill any this time,' he says with a grin as he disappears down the stairs at the end of the hall.

'I'll try!' I call after him, feeling like I might die from cringing. First, the 'tit' email, and now, my boss reminiscing about the time I spilt tea all over my lap and general vaginal area during a job interview.

Was I this embarrassing in my old job? Has anyone ever been this embarrassing in the history of humankind? Hoping that Georgia won't see me, I dash quickly to my desk in a clumsy slow jog, which I'm sure is very conspicuous and doesn't draw attention to the fact that I'm the most embarrassing human to have existed, ever.

'Here you go,' I say, leaning over my computer to pass Jane her latte.

'Oh, Emma! You total *life saver*! I need this coffee, I am *dying* over here. Thank *God* it's Friday, right?'

I log back in to my computer as Jane continues to say something about how 'caffeine is the most important meal of the day'. I smile and nod, but really I'm smiling at the thought of how much Edele would want to punch Jane in the face.

My hand freezes over the mouse when I open Outlook. Georgia has already responded to my tit email.

From: georgia.clergeot@atlasmedia.com

To: emma.mackie@atlasmedia.com
Subject: RE: South Africa pages
Date: 07/06/19

That's great, thank you Emma. If I'm not in my office when the print-outs are ready just leave them on my desk please.

Also, no worries about the typo. I probably wouldn't have noticed if you hadn't pointed it out. Besides, it's not as bad as when I emailed my former boss telling him to 'have a *lonely* weekend'. I'm pretty sure he was recently divorced, too.

Gx

The rest of the day feels far less embarrassing after that, and as I slot myself neatly into the hordes of commuters at Chancery Lane tube at the end of the day, I think how excited I am to drive back to Hackton in the morning.

Waking up on Saturdays always feels different in London. In Hackton, I'd be able to navigate every minute of my morning with ease – if I wanted to go for a run, my route was second nature; if I wanted to make porridge, I could have located the oats, pan and spoon with my eyes closed. But this morning, everything feels unfamiliar, as though it's something I need to grow into. I'm not used to being this out of my comfort zone.

I shower and get ready quickly, grab the overnight bag, which I packed last night, and lock my front door behind me. Outside, I blink into the early summer sun, surrounded by a canvas of clear bright blue, undisturbed but for a wispy white stroke left by a plane. The 275 bus

347

shuffles past and a parked delivery van's hazard lights blink onto the concrete. Over the road, plumes of smoke pour from the flue and a topless man lifts up the window, the hum of music – Sam Cooke, I think – buzzing out onto the street. I look around me and smile, tucking my overnight bag neatly into the boot of my car. Maybe I don't mind being out of my comfort zone for once.

As my car zooms out of the tunnel, part of the London landscape looms large beyond my windscreen, the busy streets beneath hidden by its tall buildings, shard-like teeth towering above the city's bleeding gums. Over-priced, over-flowing and over-worked, its transport networks rammed, its workers queueing for Pret coffee and tutting their frustration when someone's in their way. But just the sight of it reminds me of why I wanted to move here. London may be unfamiliar to me still, but really, I think, it's thrilling, the thought that there are so many of its streets I've yet to walk down, how many bars I've yet to drink in, how many parks I've yet to run through. Though I've only lived here for a month, I already feel pleasurably swallowed whole by London. Falling hard for a place is just like falling hard for a person: you grow to adore their flaws just as much as their strengths, because they're all vital components that make them who they are. Even the underground at rush hour.

But as my car rolls over the hill and whooshes past the county border, hurtling towards my home town, I feel an immense sense of belonging. Some low-buried thing that tugs at my heart; the old drum of home.

I soon pull into Nat's driveway and see that Edele's mum's car is already here. She must be helping Edele move in, just like I am. I switch the engine off, yank up the handbrake and ring the buzzer.

I climb the stairs to Nat's flat. Ms Harris's front door triggers a wave of quiet sorrow, no sound of cooking shows coming from the TV.

'Marshall!' Edele shouts, chucking a pile of clothes onto the floor at the top of the stairs and flinging herself around me. Her long hair is tied tight and high into a ponytail and she's dressed in old, baggy sweatpants and a black vest.

'Hi, Ed,' I say. 'So good to see you.'

'And you. We can't keep seeing you at two-week intervals. It's far too long.'

She presses both her hands against my face and stands back, looking at me.

'What you so dressed up for?' she asks, eyeing up my floral chiffon dress. 'We're moving me into Nat's, not walking the Erdem runway.'

I shrug. 'Didn't think moving a few boxes around required high-performance workout gear.'

'Oh yeah. I forgot you run marathons and shit. This will literally be a walk in the park for you.'

Nat comes up behind her on the landing then, 'Meanwhile, we'll just be here sweating one out.'

She puts down the cardboard box she's holding, which looks as though it might split at any second, and hugs me.

'Hello, Mackie,' Liam says as he walks down the stairs from the loft. He's holding a hammer in one hand and an instruction leaflet in the other.

'All right, Liam.' He shuffles past us and into the kitchen.

'Fucking gash flatpack furniture,' we hear him mumble to himself. We smile.

'I've got a toolkit in the boot of my car if he needs it?' I say.

'Of course you do,' Nat laughs. 'I think we've got everything, he's just whining.'

'So, you and Liam are okay now?' I ask Edele.

'Yeah, we're grand,' she replies in a hushed voice. 'He'd never say it, but I think he's a bit gutted that I'm moving out.'

'Is your mum here?'

'Nah, she's had to go into work today. Liam drove us.'

'How's she feeling about you moving out?'

'I mean, she cried a little bit, but I'm only a ten-minute drive away. She's mostly just glad that I'm getting my shit together.'

'Yeah, about time that happened,' Liam says, re-emerging from the kitchen, grinning at his sister.

'Fuck off, Liam.'

'D'ya want this heap-of-shit bed built or not?'

'Yeah, it's the only thing brutish men like you are good for, anyway.'

'Ungrateful bitch,' he says, walking back up the stairs to where he's assembling Edele's bed.

'Love you, shit-face,' she calls after him.

'Piss off,' he yells back from upstairs.

Nat makes us all coffee and it's not long before Alex arrives. Just as we all did a month ago, we make trips

350

between the car and the landing, then from the landing to the loft, though there's much less furniture and appliances to carry this time because Edele doesn't own any of those things. Liam is making progress with the bed-building, hunched over its frame so that his muscles, thick like bison's, bulge and move beneath the skin on his back. Nat, Alex and I all notice it, schoolgirl-smiling to each other in the loft carefully out of his peripheral vision.

We take breaks during the day and Nat grabs some cans of beer from the fridge. I talk about my new job, how Duncan and I have laughed about my Skype interview and how I'll likely get to travel to different destinations around the world for work now to help with shoots. Edele tells us about the first two weeks at her new job – 'The fit guy from fundraising showed me how to use the printer this week . . . I don't remember how to use the printer, but I do know he's about six foot two and smells of pine needles – and Nat talks about Ms Harris's funeral last week.

'Matt didn't come.'

'Why? Don't know why we're surprised really, heartless prick.'

'Said he couldn't get the time off work during the day in the middle of the week.'

'What kind of company doesn't give you a morning off for a funeral?'

'That's what I thought.'

'Sounds like he just couldn't face it, especially just the two of you.'

'Honestly, I'm glad he wasn't there. My mum came with me, even though I told her she didn't need to and it was, I don't know. I never know how to describe funerals. They're just some sort of weird, sad ceremony so you can say goodbye and go home afterwards wishing you didn't have to say goodbye. People always talk about "closure", but I don't really know what that is. It's such an abstract thing. I think you have to be a certain type of person – one of those people who doesn't really question anything, you know? – to experience closure or understand what it is. The rest of us just carry on and let whatever it was become a part of us. That's not "closure". It's just acceptance.'

'Nat,' Edele says, popping another can of beer, 'I love you dearly, but all those therapy sessions have turned you into some sort of wise old crow, dishing out profound monologues on life. You're like the chick from *Eat Pray Love*.'

Nat laughs, a scoffing laugh, puts down her beer on the table and leans over to Edele until she's close to her face, holding it rigidly between her palms. Edele is still holding her beer and looks as though she's prepared for a severe telling off, like a petulant child.

'You really don't make it easy to like you, Edele Marie,' Nat says with a wide smile, taking her right hand away and landing it gently against Edele's cheek in a soft slap. 'And you live with me now, so you will listen to my pretentious monologuing until your ears fall off and your brain turns to shit and you're sick of the sound of my voice. Got it?' She sits back down and picks up her drink, sipping.

'You just have to love me, you don't have to like me. Like a mum with her bratty daughter.'

'Except you've got three mums to keep you in check,' I grin.

Dusk is slowly settling over the houses and the shoreline when we walk into the Fox and Whistle. It's a Saturday evening, which means there is already a thick cluster of punters queueing around the bar. We join the cluster and wait our turn. I'm chatting to Alex when I feel someone looking at me, eyes scorching themselves onto my back. I turn around. Luke is standing there, a few paces behind me, a grey-haired man standing between us. Something lurches forward from the pit of my stomach and into my chest, sending it spinning.

'Hey,' I wave over the grey-haired man who looks at me with a confused expression before realising I'm not speaking to him.

'Hi, Mack. What are you doing here? Thought you were a city girl now.'

'I'm just visiting for the weekend. What do you want? I owe you a drink.'

'That'd be great. Pint of Estrella, please. I'll meet you outside? It's rammed in here, we can have a quick catch-up.'

'Okay. See you in a sec.'

I order our drinks and say I'll be back in a minute. Outside the front of the pub, Luke is leaning against the brick wall and staring into the brightness of his phone.

'Here,' I say. He thanks me and puts his phone into his jeans pocket. He takes his pint and asks me about 'life in the Big Smoke', about the new job and what I'm doing for the weekend in Hackton. I tell him, drink my wine, ask him about work, laugh about orange Sandra.

Luke is taking a sip of beer during the pause in conversation when he seems to suddenly stop, as if holding the pint glass to his lips but not moving, maybe just thinking. Then he continues the natural motion of drinking, like someone's just pressed 'resume' on his body's reactions.

'It's not the same without you,' he says then, turning his face to look towards the sea. 'It's like the high point of my day has gone, seeing you.'

He turns back and looks straight into my eyes. Something about the way he's doing this cuts me right through the middle and a strange dissociative feeling washes over me, as though I might drown in it. Everything around him darkens and fades into unimportance, the edges of him smudging. It's as if this is my first time locking eyes with anyone.

He recognises the delay in my response – to him, I don't know what to say; to me, my brain paralysed and failing to kick back into action like a stalled engine – so he quickly continues speaking and delving his eyes into me.

'It made me think . . . it's a shame that nothing ever happened with us.' His words are sweet and slow, they leave his mouth steeped in hesitancy and honey.

I continue not saying anything and Luke seems taken aback by his own words. He sniffs loudly, his lip curling slightly, and takes a big gulp of beer. The silence weighs heavily on us, compact and intrusive.

'I wanted it to,' I say eventually. 'I really did. I like you, Luke. But I'm old enough and smart enough to know that liking someone isn't enough, not any more. And . . . look, this is going to sound like the cliché "it's not you, it's me" bullshit, but it just hasn't been the right time for me to date anyone. My career was always my focus, and everything I've done these past few years has been about bettering myself, for me. And, you know, I have the girls – I'm basically already in three relationships. I guess that seemed like enough to be getting on with. I never saw how a man could fit into it. And I was fine with that.'

'Fair enough,' he says airily, drinking. 'But you'll never know if you never try.'

'No, it was different with you. You weren't just some bloke off a dating app; you weren't mine to just pick up and drop when I was done "trying". I always knew I would leave Hackton eventually, something was always pulling me away. And it wouldn't have been fair on you – or on me – to try anything when I knew I wasn't going to be sticking around.'

He smiles a warm but sharp smile and puts his pint glass on the pub windowsill.

'That's exactly what makes you one of a kind,' he says, 'that kindness; always thinking about other people,' and it's like someone's lit a bonfire in my chest; not unpleasant but not particularly pleasant either. 'I get it, Mack,' he says. 'I mean, I kind of do.'

Luke stands with his feet planted to the ground, holds his arms out and takes me into a hug. I feel so small against the breadth of his torso, can feel his black chest hair above the opening of his shirt, the scent of his after-shave clinging to them. I inhale deeply then pull myself away from him, making sure to avoid his gaze.

'Thanks, Luke, for understanding.' I pick up my glass of wine. I want to say, 'If it was going to be anyone, it would have been you.' But I do not think that would be particularly helpful or kind.

Instead, I say, 'I'll see you inside?'

'Yeah. I'll be there in a bit.'

For a brief moment, I feel angry, as though this is a game to him and he just wanted to see what I'd say. He's so cocksure, I say to myself, self-assurance flowing through him like blood through his veins. I wonder how many women he's told are the 'high point' of his day. But then I put my hand on the door to the pub and, before I open it, I look back at him. He is facing out to sea again but not focusing on anything, huge darting eyes, a quiet-ness in his expression that I haven't seen before. I don't know what it means but I do not think it's self-assurance.

Inside the pub, Edele, Alex and Nat are sitting at The Sticky Table, the same one where they likened Eddie to a sort of sexual hybrid between Richard Madden and Jason Momoa, whoever they are. They must be reasonably attrac-tive though because Edele had sex with Eddie that night.

'Mack! You'll never guess what just happened,' Alex says with a mischievous giggle.

'What?'

'Gary asked her out,' Nat says sitting next to Edele, biting her lip and beaming, digging Edele in the side with her elbow.

'He didn't *ask me out*,' she objects, rolling her eyes. 'We just exchanged numbers and he said he'd message about getting dinner sometime.'

'Well, that's great, isn't it?'

'Yeah. He's chubby and wonderful. I don't know what he'd see in a woman like me.'

'Enough,' I say. 'You are one of the best people I know and any man would be lucky to have you. Even chubby and wonderful Gary. It's about time you started believing it now.'

She looks at me inquisitively, her eyes like polished larimar in her alabaster face.

'You're an angel, Marshall,' she says with a sideways smile. 'What would I do without you?'

As much as it ignites some terrible burning thing in me to leave Luke with no more than a flicker of what might – what could – be, I know that I did the right thing. It's the wrong love, the wrong man, the wrong time. And besides, focusing on myself and 'doing me' – getting a new job, moving to a new city – is a pretty full-time gig. I still don't see how a man, not even Sexy Luke, could fit into that; not for the time being, anyway. And the best thing about it? I'm still fine with that. Until I'm not, these four relationships – Alex, Natasha, Edele, and me – will do just fine.

'Ed's right,' Alex says, swinging her arm around me. 'You are our guardian angel, Emma Mackie.'

CHAPTER TWENTY-ONE

Natasha

The warm air of late June wraps itself around me as I walk down Wheeler Street. I'm falling in step behind a tall, broad woman, watching the muscles in her back moving together as she walks, fluid and defined. A thin trickle of perspiration runs down between the divisions of her shoulder blades. At the end of the street, she turns left, towards the children's centre and tool hire shop, and I turn right and then left, past The Swan and the small car park.

I'm wearing a black spaghetti-strapped top tucked into loose jeans and too much make-up. I can feel the mascara clumping and sticking my eyelashes together, and the concealer under my eyes cementing into the creases in my skin. I wish I could run home and wash all of it off, pressure-hosing myself down like a crime-scene cleaner. I want to climb into Edele's bed with her and eat cereal straight from the box and watch some ridiculous documentary about a Midwestern cult, or some blokes who grow skunk in their mum's garage, and we'll squint at the screen and see if any of the blurred-out faces resemble Jay.

But I can't do any of those things. I just have to continue walking, past the train station now, then the Sue Ryder's that used to be a Blockbuster. I think about when Al and I used to rent a film from there on a Friday night with a litre of Fanta and a tub of ice-cream. Blockbuster used to be the only place in town where you could buy Häagen-Dazs Chocolate Midnight Cookies Ice Cream. I'm too nervous to think about ice cream, my pulse picking up pace and sprinting through my body as I cross the road and walk onto Hatherall Road.

The restaurant is small and French and as I walk up to it my mind is whirring deafeningly, a motherboard of misfiring synapses. This place is too small to be a restaurant. Is it a cafe? No, a bistro, I think it's called. It's a new addition to the glittering fine-dining scene in Hackton, only opening last month. Five years ago, the community would have laughed at such a fancy thing as a bistro opening and demanded it be replaced by a new KFC because the one on the high street is full of rats the size of small dogs. Last week, Edele saw a rat holding and nibbling a chip in that KFC, like a monkey eating a banana. Anyway, isn't a bistro just a glorified cafe? Does this mean we're being gentrified?

'Hello. May I take your jacket?'

'No, I'm fine. Thank you.' This top is thin and exposes the skin on my arms and chest, plus my fags are in my jacket pocket and I want them as close to me as possible.

I glance around the glorified cafe. The tables are covered in plastic red and white gingham and each one has an old wine bottle with a candlestick poking out of it, the glass neck covered in lava-like dried paraffin.

He sees me then and he stands up: deep eyes, olive-skinned, watching me, in a slim-fit shirt – pale blue, slightly creased, rolled up to the elbows.

I walk towards him, desperately trying to keep a polite smile pinned to my face.

'Hi, Nat.'

That deep voice, that posh 'not from around here' accent.

'Hello, Lawrence.'

He leans forward, a hand placed on my arm just below my shoulder, and tells me it's good to see me. He presses his cheek against mine and kisses the air again. I still think the ways in which people greet each other to be really odd.

'And you,' I say. 'Thank you for coming all the way to Hackton.'

'No problem. It's really not far and I finished work an hour before you, so it makes sense.'

I messaged Lawrence last week after Edele and I made risotto and drank a bottle and a half of wine.

'Hey, did you ever hear from Lawrence again?' she asked me, her legs swung over mine on the sofa.

'No. You remember he messaged me after that dreadful morning to see if I was okay? Then I explained about Matt and the break-up, and he said he understood? Well, that was pretty much it. We chatted for a bit after that, just a couple of messages, then it just sort of stopped. It's a shame, really.'

'What do you mean? You want to see him again?'

'I don't know. Maybe. I mean, it's not his fault I slept with him too soon after Matt. He wasn't to know. And he was a great guy.'

'Is,' Edele corrected me, 'he *is* a great guy. He didn't die just because you pied him off, Nat. Text the man.'

'What? But it's been months? He's probably got a girl-friend by now.'

'That's not how it works. You'll never know if you don't at least—'

'All right, all right.'

I thought then of Matt, all those weeks before, sat opposite me in the coffee shop near my flat, saying, 'I deserve to be happy, Nat.' It felt like dying, hearing those words. Sitting with Edele in our home then, talking about Lawrence, all I could think was, 'I deserve to be happy, too.' And I did. I do.

'Let's drink the rest of this shitty wine,' I said to her, 'and I'll message Lawrence.'

'I'm really glad you messaged,' he says now, glancing up from the menu in his hand. 'Even if we weren't going to go on another date or anything, I wasn't happy with how we left it.'

'I know. I'm sorry about that whole thing, the morning after. I know I explained it to you briefly over text, but I just wasn't ready. I really enjoyed our date, and I wanted to see you again, but while I felt that way it wouldn't have been fair on you.'

'Or you,' he says, still looking at me, his lips spread warmly into the slightest of smiles and a studious expression on his face. It's not a knowing or smug look. I recognise it as the look of someone who cares.

'Yeah.' I look back at the menu and try to figure out what *'en écailles'* means.

'I know you probably didn't expect this to happen again – us seeing each other – but I enjoy spending time with you.'

We order our food and a bottle of wine – Lawrence lets me order this time, which is good because I automatically order the second-cheapest which is a Cabernet Sauvignon and I know how to pronounce that – and we talk about both of our lives since we last saw each other in February.

I tell him about Mackie wearing pyjamas during her job interview, about Craig proposing to Alex, about Edele moving in, about helping Mackie move into her flat in London, and about Diane dying. He tells me that he filmed a documentary in April about protecting our oceans on the Mediterranean Sea, about how it's the most over-fished sea in the world with more than 90 per cent of fish stocks affected. He describes the discarded fishing lines they removed from the water's surface, the hooks on the snagged lines which cause internal bleeding to wildlife. When I talk about Diane, and Josh and the paramedics, he leans over and clutches at my hand and he doesn't stop running his thumb over my knuckles until I've stopped talking. He tells me that his mum died six years ago of breast cancer, and how his dad behaved like Josh when he told him, straight and scrupulous, directed by the desensitisation of shock like a puppet on strings.

We laughed about all the certificates involved in death, just like Edele and I did, and say how we're glad we're both the sort of people that can laugh at things like that.

We pay for our food, retrieve our jackets and stand outside the restaurant while I smoke and Lawrence tells me that he likes Hackton. I don't know whether I believe him but his voice is still as low and gentle as I remember. It's a sound I take pleasure from, like the light patter of rain on a tent.

I glance past him, at the amber-drenched street and the howling main road. I look back, vision skewered, at his lips, and everything surrounding us begins to evaporate and shrink into him. The charge of proximity as he leans forward until he's just centimetres from my face, and I can feel the brush of his nose against my skin. He kisses me and some hurtling thing pulls at my stomach. It feels different to last time. Safer.

I pull my face back slightly.

'Let's take it slow this time, yeah?' I say to him.

'Yeah,' he nods, backing off sensitively with a small step. He smiles. 'Of course.'

He leaves a pause, lets it linger between us. I feel the gentle breeze ripple through my hair, longer now since he last saw it and less brittle, and I can see him watching it. I tuck it behind my ear, take a drag.

'I've had a really nice evening,' I say, focusing on the depth and width of his eyes like two neat geometrical shapes.

'Same. And the food in there was great.'

'Yeah, it was. That's got to be the best food in Hackton.'

'I'll have to think of a way to top it for our next date, then.'

'I'd like that,' I say. 'Another date, I mean. Not you "topping" this one. You don't have to take me to some fancy bar or anything like that. You know I'd be happy with a bag of chips on the seafront or a takeaway Chinese.'

'Let's do it all,' he grins a grin so wide I might fall into it, 'a fancy bar, then a bag of chips on the seafront, then a takeaway with a film.'

'Sounds good,' I smile back; an unforced, big, happy smile.

'Well, I'll be seeing you, Nat.'

'I hope so. Do you want me to walk you to the train station?'

'No, you're all right. I remember where it is. Just up there and round the corner?'

'Yep.'

He kisses me again, a soft quick kiss, tells me goodbye, and then walks away. I stand still finishing my cigarette for a moment or so, then I turn around to see that he's gone. I watch the last space he would have occupied, at the corner of Hatherall Road before turning towards the Sue Ryder, formerly Blockbuster, and then the station.

I start walking home, the opposite way, so that I don't have to awkwardly follow Lawrence towards the station. It took courage, I think as I walk, for him to meet me again after I threw him out of my flat last time. Because, ultimately, aren't we all looking for an easy life; a secure life? For that person who brings us that glorified balance of peace and thrill, of safety and surprise? To him, surely,

364

I would seem to be too much surprise, not enough safety. In business, I suppose they'd say, 'Too much risk, not enough reward.' Yet here he was, talking about fancy bars and chips on the beach. It seemed to me that he was either naive and hopeful, or someone who was willing to take a risk when he recognised something worth putting himself on the line for.

I guess that's what I'm doing, too – putting myself on the line. But it'll be different this time. It has to be. Because I gave everything I had to give to Matt; I put so many pieces of myself into him over the years that I didn't even realise I was doing it. Thousands of tiny parts of two people mixed together until you could hardly tell which was which. We made a home out of each other because we knew no other way. I knew him so intimately – from the exact rhythm of his twitching muscles to the sound of his footsteps on the stairs – that we were, to me, two halves of the same brain. We housed ourselves so tightly inside one another that, eventually, there were no tiny pieces of me left to give any more. He carried all of me with him, and that meant that when he walked away, he took all of me, too. The only thing he left behind was some small, unrecognisable thing, a withered shell of myself, like a snapped off piece of seaweed, dried and discarded on the shoreline. That is why I refuse, not to love any less, but to give it all again. This time – whether it be Lawrence, the man after him or the man after that – I will save some of the pieces for me. It's what we all, battle-hardened and bruised, sore and weary, learn to keep locked away. We lock them away deep and secret and secure, where no one else can reach down and snatch them away. Those parts of us are our most cherished stock because they are what make us resilient and reparable. They are ours, and ours alone.

I walk up the stairs to mine and Edele's home and fumble for the flat key, jangling loud in the quiet corridor. I turn the lock in the door and stop for a moment. No smell of smoke any more. I turn my head to look at Diane's door, no longer Diane's door, but just an entrance to a life once lived, a rich, full life that I was lucky enough to be a part of. I feel the old silent thrum of sadness and pleasure inside my body; sorrow for a life lost, joy for a life lived. And I smile to myself.

'Edele?'

'In here,' she calls from the living room.

I throw my jacket across the top of the banister, dump my bag in the hallway and walk into the living room.

'We have company,' she says.

On the sofa, either side of her, sit Alex and Mackie, beaming at me as I walk into the living room.

'What are you both doing here?'

'You haven't checked Mean Girls, have you?'

I shake my head.

'I asked if everyone was free,' Al says.

'And I have tomorrow off work, so thought I'd drive down,' Mackie adds.

'Great,' I say, plonking myself down on top of Mackie and Edele until they shift to make room on the sofa.

They ask how my date was and I tell them. I say how much I like talking to Lawrence, the way I can tell that he's really, properly listening to me when I speak, and hearing his stories that he tells with such vibrancy.

'That's one of the most important things in life, I reckon,' Edele says. 'Having good stories to tell.'

'And don't we have hundreds of them?' Mackie laughs.

'So, you like him, Nat? Are you going to see him again?'

'Yeah. I know I'm not ready for anything too serious yet, but I can see it, you know? I can see that he's the type of man I could open up to. I could let him in, I think.'

Mackie squeezes my knee. 'That's our girl.'

'You amaze me,' Alex says. 'I don't mean to sound like a patronising dick in "teacher mode", but I am so very proud of you.'

'We all are,' Edele adds. 'She's tough as old boots, our Natasha.'

She stands up and goes to the kitchen, soon emerging with four glasses and a bottle of wine, with a sharing bag of popcorn tucked under her arm.

'You never told us,' Mackie says, 'how did your last therapy session go?'

'Yeah, good. I don't need to see Simon any more.'

I think back to that appointment at the start of the month, when Simon asked me if I saw an improvement in myself.

'Yes, kind of,' I told him.

'How so?'

I stopped to think, frowning and crossing my arms across my body. It's funny, I thought, how I never used to know or understand what I felt; different emotions like contrasting colours surging and ebbing, changing with the tide, too fast to catch any of them. Now, they have names, labels, tangible things which make them identifiable to me, like a meteorologist forecasting storms on a supercomputer.

'I suppose I'm kinder to myself. The way I talk to myself isn't as cruel as it used to be.'

'You mean "the voice"?'

'Yeah.'

'It's interesting,' he considered as he leant back in the peach-coloured armchair and pushed his frameless glasses further up the bridge of his nose. 'You don't refer to your self-talk as "the voice" any more. Why do you think that is?'

'What do you mean?'

'Before, you thought of it as some sort of separate entity, controlling your happiness. You gave it that autonomy to do whatever it wanted. But now, it's as though you recognise it as part of yourself, and that means it's something you can work on.'

'Right, yeah. So it's like I've realised that I'm in control of it, not the other way around?'

'Is that how you feel? In control of the way you talk to yourself?'

'Yeah, I think so. Most of the time, anyway.'

Simon smiled at me, then we talked about Matt one last time.

'I don't think of him any less,' I started.

'How do you feel, when you think of him now?'

'It hurts less, I suppose, like an old sting. I don't know if I'm "moving on",' I said and then I paused for what seemed like a very long time, but Simon waited in watchful silence, which made me feel as though I had no choice but to carry on speaking.

'I guess,' I continued, and then it poured out of me like confession, heavy like concrete leaving my mouth. 'It's just like constantly hitting refresh on an old laptop, or learning to swim for the first time and practising when to come up for air, or leaving a busy city for a cleaner environment; not constantly breathing in the fumes of our old life together. You just kind of adjust.'

I couldn't articulate what I wanted to say, looking back on it. 'Getting over it' and 'moving on' sounded so uncomplicated and final, as though I've started to uncheck the myriad boxes of things that I loved about him, and really, I'm not sure I'll ever be able to do that. Adjusting to my new life isn't about forgetting. It's finding the strength to say goodbye. It's figuring out how to feel at home in the world without him. It's learning how to, finally, be enough for myself, on my own.

At the end of the session, Simon said that he didn't think I needed to see him any more. It seemed fitting that he told me that exactly six months after Matt left. It made my final therapy appointment feel like some sort of messed up party – the occasion, my break-up anniversary; the refreshments, a single glass of room-temperature tap water; the entertainment, Simon desperately trying to bat away a fly that kept zooming past his nose; the unwitting host, my mental health.

'It did help,' I tell the girls then, tucking my legs underneath myself on the sofa. 'I feel a bit like a part of my brain has been rewired. It doesn't mean I'm constantly happy or anything; I don't spring out of bed every morning with a zest for life, like enthusiastic Parker in *Friends*. But I guess I'm not in self-sabotage mode any more.'

'That's the most important thing,' Mackie says reassuringly.

Edele pours the dark red wine between our glasses and Alex opens the bag of popcorn.

'I'm disappointed you never shagged your shrink though,' Edele says, passing me a glass. 'That would've been the ultimate cliché.'

'I think that only really happens in films, Ed.'

'No way,' she retorts. 'I'm sure my therapist was a sex addict.'

'How the hell would you know that?'

'He liked to talk about my sex life, a lot.'

'That's just part of his job, you tit. Especially with a sex life as self-destructive as yours.'

'Yeah, fair point.'

We pass the popcorn between us and I turn on the TV, choosing a film to watch on Netflix.

After a while, Edele says, 'We're out of wine. Shall I go and get us another bottle?'

'No, wait,' Alex says quickly. 'Wait a minute, Ed. Sit down. I need to tell you all something.' She leans forward to put her wine glass on the table.

'What?'

'It's me and Craig—'

'What?' Edele asks quickly, interlocking her fingers and cracking her knuckles like bubble-wrap.

'Don't worry, Ed, it's nothing like that. You ain't gotta get a hit out on anyone.'

'Good.'

'It's about our future, after the wedding.'

'Al, are you knocked up?' I ask, 'because if you are, you know we can deal with it together.'

'Nah, screw that, you're on your own there, Al.'

'I think you and Craig would make wonderful parents.'

'I'm not pregnant! Can you all just pipe down a minute?'

'Okay.'

'Craig's been offered a job – a big promotion – up north.'

'What? Where?'

'A place in Cumbria near the Lake District, not far from Cockermouth.'

'Sorry, not far from where?'

'Cock-er-mouth.'

'What?'

'Cock-er-mouth.'

'Cock-in-her-mouth? As in, "it was so big, she couldn't fit the whole cock in her mouth"?'

'No, cock–*uh*–mouth.'

'Cock–inna–mouth?'

'No, for fuck's sake, Edele. Cockermouth.'

'What fucking perv sat down and named a town "cock-in-her-mouth"?'

'Wait, did you say Cumbria?'

'Yeah.'

'That . . . that's really far away.'

Alex pauses then. 'Yeah,' she says, exhaling slowly and loudly.

'Where exactly are we talking?' Mackie says.

'I think it's about a five-hour drive away.'

A pause, and then, with a declining tone, Edele says, 'Wow. That's far.'

All of us fall into the uneasiness of silence, as if we all hoped our quietness would make this new information disappear or morph it into something less ugly.

'So you're moving up there?' I ask.

'I don't know yet,' she says shaking her head, her eyes like big sad balloons. Edele snakes her arm over Alex's shoulders. 'There are a lot of decisions to make.'

'Do you want to?'

'I don't know. I suppose so, if it's an opportunity Craig needs to take. He's going to be my husband. That means we go where the other goes.'

I nod. 'I know.' She's telling the truth.

'When would you need to move, if you do?' Mackie asks.

'Craig only found out about the job at the start of the week. He doesn't start the new job for three months yet.'

'So, we have plenty of time to change your mind?' Edele says with a smile.

'You can try,' she laughs.

'If you do move up there, will you drive down and visit all the time?'

'Just try and stop me.'

Inside of me, sadness and pleasure again; sorrow at the thought of a friend far away, joy for the adventure stretched out before her and everything it offers. Inevitably though, in this moment, the sorrow is greater than the joy. That will change, I know. The pain of distance will be nothing compared to the pain I used to carry with me through the first half of this year.

I didn't lose a boyfriend in January, I lost a life together; the life I gave to him, all those thousands of tiny pieces I can never get back. It was hollow and hopeless and utterly annihilating and it felt like fucking dying. It was sometimes a sad and silent thing, others it was so heart-shatteringly loud it felt like it might burst out of me like lightning. But it was lonely all of the time.

Yet I did not feel alone. 'It may feel lonely, but you are never alone,' they said, and there they were, just as they said they would be, just as I knew they would. The moments of joy they offered up despite everything. They felt like holding new life, like scoring a winning goal, like light yawning through trees and melting the frost. They felt like hope. We don't have the language for it, and the lexicon we do have is too theatrical, too sycophantic. 'Friends' is a word too insubstantial. It is not good enough for the people who rush to your side and hold you up like a delicate piece of china. The people who clean your flat, stock your fridge, pour you wine, cook you dinner. The people who tell you to haul your depressed self to therapy. The people who forgive you so effortlessly for lashing out from hurt. The people who wrap themselves around you in bed so you don't have to feel the cold expanse of nothing next to you. 'Friends' is too weak, too weightless for all of that. Really, I think, this is it. This is the kind of love that makes you whole, that rebuilds you and helps you to gather all of your broken pieces and build them into something new. Something hopeful, strong. Something better. And it has been right in front of me this whole time. Maybe Matt didn't have all of those tiny pieces of me after all. Maybe, all along, my friends were keeping some safe for me.

'Don't worry, Alex,' I say. 'No matter what you decide, we will be here. Never forget that.'

Acknowledgements

Thank you to Ebury Press and Penguin Random House. To my editor, Katie Seaman, for seeing something in my work and asking me to write this book. For her thoughtful, careful, whip-smart, nail-on-the-head edits, and for telling me when I needed to tone down the swearing (regularly). For making me a better writer.

To my agent, Sarah Hornsley, for her invaluable support and guidance throughout the process.

To my home town and its people, for inspiring the home town and its people in this book. And to the over-flowing, flawed, fiery, sometimes filthy, always magical city of London, for being my home now, and the pubs of North London, for being my version of what some authors term 'writing retreats'.

To my wonderful parents, Brian and Wendy Pantony. Thank you for my love of literature. For always telling me that I 'had a book in me'. For believing in me when I forget how to believe in myself. For telling me to keep on when I forget how to keep on keeping on. For the cups of coffee, the glasses of wine, the slices of toast, the falling asleep in front of the TV, the weekend newspapers under blankets, the laughs when it's good and the mascara-sodden shoulder when it's bad. For all of this, much more, everything. Thank you.

Most importantly, the greatest *thank you* to the people who are the basis for every single chapter in this book: my group of lifelong friends. My childhood, my adulthood, my anchors. You are my greatest love affair, my daily inspiration, and by far, my proudest achievement. Without you, this book wouldn't exist. And neither would I. For that, I owe it all.

If you enjoyed

Almost Adults

we'd love to hear from you

Leave a review online
Join the conversation on social media @alipantony @
EburyPublishing #AlmostAdults
Follow Ali on Twitter and Instagram to stay up to
date with all her latest news